SING ME NO LOVE SONGS

I'LL SAY YOU NO PRAYERS

SING ME NO LOVE SONGS

I'LL SAY YOU NO PRAYERS

SELECTED STORIES BY
LEON ROOKE

THE ECCO PRESS/NEW YORK

1°/1984
Send

ACKNOWLEDGMENTS

Special thanks to the editors of the following magazines, where the stories first appeared, some in different form: *Quarry* for "The Shut-in Number"; *Descant* for "Mama Tuddi Done Over"; *Antaeus* for "In the Garden" and "The Birth Control King of the Upper Volta"; *True North/Down Under* for "Agnes and the Cobwebs"; *The Canadian Forum* for "Conversations With Ruth: The Farmer's Tale"; *Event* for "Why Agnes Left"; *Epoch* for "Sing Me No Love Songs I'll Say You No Prayers"; *Matrix* for "Some People Will Tell You . . ."; *The Malahat Review* for "Narcissus Consulted"; *Prism-International* for "Lady Godiva's Horse"; *Canadian Fiction Magazine* for "History of England."

"Friendship and Property" appeared originally in *Best Canadian Stories* 1979 and "Break and Enter" in *Vault*, Lillabulero Press. "Mama Tuddi Done Over" also appeared in *Best American Short Stories* 1980.

Eight of the stories are collected here for the first time. Others are from *Death Suite* and *The Birth Control King of the Upper Volta* (ECW Press) and *Cry Evil* (Oberon Press).

Library of Congress Cataloging in Publication Data
Rooke, Leon.
Sing me no love songs I'll say you no prayers
I. Title
PS3568.06S56   1984   813'.54   84-4064
ISBN 0-88001-036-3

For Constance and Jonathan

CONTENTS

ix

SING ME NO LOVE SONGS
I'LL SAY YOU NO PRAYERS

FRIENDSHIP AND PROPERTY

*L*eopold and the lawyer Sparks were approaching the familiar door of the Wild Boar Tavern when they saw Rodin passing on the other side of the street. The lawyer raised an arm in greeting, but Leopold quickly pulled it down. "It's been a good day," he said, "why spoil it now?"

Rodin went on, perhaps not seeing them, his head down like a man fighting a strong gale.

"Look at that suit," the lawyer suggested, "you think he slept in it?"

"Oh, he's finished now," remarked Leopold, "no question about it."

The lawyer asked how long it had been since Aimée's death, and Leopold, whose spirits seemed uncharacteristically high, replied that he didn't keep track of that sort of thing but about four months, four or five, he guessed.

Sparks confessed that he hadn't made it to the funeral and asked Leopold whether he had.

"Wouldn't have missed it for the world. Nothing like a

good funeral for concluding deals." Leopold dabbled in a great many things, including insurance, and in fact had sold a big policy at Aimée's funeral.

They watched as Rodin turned at the corner and was gone.

As if inspired by the sight of his dejected figure, they wheeled hurriedly inside the Boar, thirsty for the day's first drink.

"Shocking, his wife's death," the lawyer volunteered, once seated. "She looked the picture of health."

Leopold said that he disagreed, that Aimée had always seemed to him to have been a bit pale around the gills.

"Not pale enough to keep you from going after her," winked the lawyer. "What did she die of anyway?"

"Too much Rodin," said Leopold, and gave a long, hard laugh.

The lawyer drew a solemn face. He thought of himself as a man of superior moral fiber and felt there was something wrong with this flippant attitude his companion was taking. All the same, a few seconds later he too laughed. "I guess I know what you mean," he said.

The two men signaled to the waiter to hurry their drinks along.

"Funny," observed Sparks, "I thought you and Rodin were as thick as thieves."

Leopold grimaced, tugging at his collar, which was one of his few nervous habits. "Rodin had his uses," he said, "but he was always so joyless, you know, it was a real grind being with him."

"I wouldn't go that far."

"Morbid," continued Leopold. "I would say that his true character is emerging now that Aimée's kicked off. No backbone."

The lawyer looked uncertain, although a trifle amused. "If you're saying she was the better half of the team I wouldn't argue with you. She had sparkle, that woman did."

"Bit of a phony though," offered Leopold.

"What do you mean?"

"All that enthusiasm. All that good will. You can't tell me much of it wasn't put on."

The lawyer's lips tightened, as if he meant to reserve any final opinion. He thought of himself in something of the same terms and wondered whether Leopold was not baiting him.

"No," said Leopold, "she wasn't the angel everyone thought she was. I saw her more than once when she took the mask off."

"I guess you did," muttered Sparks hesitantly. He had in truth admired Aimée and couldn't see why Leopold was choosing to malign her now. But that's the way Leopold is, he thought, you've got to take him or leave him.

In most instances Sparks, like most people, preferred to leave him.

Leopold snapped his fingers at the waiter who was going by just then with drinks for another table. The waiter ignored him.

Sparks was shaking his head. "Beautiful woman," he reflected. "You're the first person I've ever heard say a word against her."

Leopold brought his face up close to the lawyer, who blinked and tried to lean away from him. "It burns me up," hissed Leopold, "all this talk about Aimée's saintliness. Christ, not even the Pope is spoken of with such reverence. In my book she was just another woman." He settled back in his chair, still glaring, but his voice when he spoke again was altogether reasonable. "You can't deny she called the tune in that household. She kept Rodin's head in a noose."

"Sure," laughed the lawyer, "but I guess he liked it."

"Lapped it up! In his eyes even her excrement was sacred. That's what I can't forgive him for, the way he was mush whenever she was around. Twelve years of marriage and the guy still flushed when she touched him!"

"Yes," murmured the lawyer, "everyone could see they were in love."

Leopold hooted. His arms thumped down on the table, his shoulders rocked, his laughter continued until the lawyer too was willing to concede that his interpretation had been silly.

Their laughter eventually subsided and Leopold querulously asked why they were wasting their time talking about that guy, that Rodin was a loser and worse than a loser because he was a quitter, he had no backbone and what was worse than that, no sense of humor.

Sparks acquiesced in most of these remarks, but felt called upon to observe that with his wife fresh in the ground, you could hardly expect the man to go around laughing his head off.

"Says you," countered Leopold. "If Alice kicked off you wouldn't catch me dragging my tail. Tell the truth now, wouldn't you feel something like relief if your old lady kicked the bucket?"

"Of course not," objected the lawyer, suddenly quite angry. "You should be ashamed, talking that way."

Leopold grinned. "Don't try to snow me, I bet you would."

"I wouldn't," snapped the lawyer.

Leopold stretched out his legs, speaking nonchalantly. "I've got a double-indemnity provision on old Alice. If an axe murderer hacked her to pieces tomorrow I'd be on Easy Street."

Sparks thought he could read a man's character pretty well but he was unable to decide whether Leopold was serious. That was Leopold's fascination. One simply could not accept that he was the scoundrel he seemed.

"You could always hire someone to do the job," Sparks told Leopold coldly, hoping his manner would curtail any further discussion.

"Don't think I haven't thought about it." His voice

dropped. "Anyway," he added apologetically, "I don't have the contacts just now. And as for that, old Alice knows what's what, she's been toeing the mark pretty well."

"Good God!" muttered the lawyer. "If you ever find yourself charged, I want no part of it, this conversation never happened, I haven't heard a word you've said."

Leopold laughed, waving Sparks back into his chair. Then he got up himself and went in pursuit of the bartender. At Leopold's approach the man turned his back and began polishing a glass.

The lawyer, agitated, awaited Leopold's return. He was concerned that Leopold understand that his marriage was one of mutual harmony.

Leopold returned, balancing two martinis. He sipped from each glass before surrendering one to the lawyer.

"It seems to me," began Sparks, "that you've got a few hang-ups on the marital question. I've heard that you've had your ups and downs with Alice, and God knows your first marriage was rocky enough. But they're not all like that. Mine, for instance, is perfect."

Leopold raised an eyebrow.

"Yes, I'd say that, I'd say we were the perfect couple. Not so lovey-dovey as was the case with Rodin and Aimée, but we get along, I'm thoughtful of her and she's thoughtful of me."

Leopold cradled his chin in his hand, staring at Sparks with one eye open.

"I wanted to make that clear. I love my wife. I don't know what I'd do without her."

Leopold sat up. "I do. You would bring that woman in your office out of the closet and have an open affair with her. No more lies. Think of the relief you'd feel."

Sparks' face showed actual terror. He'd been carrying on this affair for three years and had convinced himself that no one knew.

Leopold patted his arm. "Oh, don't worry, you know your

little secret is safe with me. More power to you. By the way, when do we go to court?"

Leopold was referring to a suit he had brought against a man who had brought him home one night from a party drunk. The car had rammed into a lamppost and Leopold was claiming physical, social and mental injuries. Sparks was working without fee but would keep one-half of all he could collect. His usual cut was one-third but, as he had told Leopold, this case had to be built up out of nothing.

The lawyer groaned.

"How is it you came to know about Bonny and me?"

Leopold shrugged.

"I want an answer. How do you know?"

Leopold sipped at his martini, played with the olive for a while, then said: "I was banging Bonny a long time before you came on the scene."

The lawyer swore. She had told him he was the first.

"Don't feel bad about it," taunted Leopold. "There isn't much Bonny does that I don't know about it." He smiled lasciviously: "She's a fine young girl."

By God, I loved that woman, gave her everything, now I find out she's been hooked up with this weasel. "Are you still seeing her?" he asked. "I'll kill the bitch."

"Not me," consoled Leopold. "I'd sooner come between a mother and her baby."

The lawyer left the table. When he returned a few minutes later he found Leopold had ordered two more drinks.

"I put them on your tab. Knew you wouldn't mind."

The lawyer didn't blink. He was familiar with Leopold's habit of cadging drinks; he would put these drinks on Leopold's expense account, in any case—that is, if anything was won by the suit.

He told Leopold he didn't blame him for the Bonny business but that he was going to give her a piece of his mind.

"Sure," said Leopold. "Knock her teeth out."

Sparks wrapped both hands around his martini and snuggled up to it. Leopold was beginning to tire him out. You could never relax with the man, you always had to remain on the alert for fear he'd cut off your head. "God, but you're a violent bastard," he observed. "It's a wonder someone didn't put you in a wheelchair long ago."

"Don't think they haven't tried. But my philosophy is strike first and ask questions later. That's what galls me about Rodin, he's still such a thumbsucker, an old lady could knock him over with her fan."

"I wouldn't bet on it. I figure he's tougher than you think."

A young woman entered, shielding her eyes against the dim light, and both men turned to look her over. She wore a black scarf tied around her neck and a black floppy hat and a black coat which went all the way to her heels. Her face was also black. She sat down at a nearby table, dug into her black purse for a cigarette, and watched the door.

Leopold and the lawyer continued to examine her until the woman at last rewarded them with a curious stare.

"If you would be so kind," she said, her voice quite level.

The bartender apparently knew her for he placed a small glass filled with an amber liquid in front of her, then went behind her and slid the coat free of her shoulders. She wore a silk blouse, scarlet, and numerous gold chains shimmered against the skin of her open neck.

Leopold removed his feet from their resting place on the edge of her chair. He and Sparks watched the bartender light up her cigarette and say something to her which they could not hear but which won a smile from the woman.

"What do you think?" asked Leopold.

The lawyer placed both hands over his crotch and rolled his eyes. Leopold laughed. He might easily have done the same himself.

"I could set you up with her if you're interested."

"Christ," whispered Sparks, "are you pimping now? Do you know her?"

"No, but I know women."

"God, you're disgusting," declared the lawyer. "How do you live with yourself?" He was about to say more, but saw something in Leopold's expression that made him quickly throw up his arms in a gesture meant to convey that he had only been kidding.

"I'm no worse than you, Sparks, and everybody else. It's just that I act exactly the way I feel, I don't wear my heart on my sleeve and I don't pussyfoot around with supposed good intentions."

The lawyer said he saw the sense in that and no doubt it was one way of avoiding a lot of difficulty. "Me," he said, "I'm always in hot water because I tend to let a lot of people take advantage of my good nature."

"Nonsense," said Leopold. "You're a snake if ever I saw one."

Both men smiled as if they had just arranged a permanent peace between nations.

"About that accident you were involved in," said the lawyer. "What happened after the car hit the lamppost? Did you smash the guy's head against the windshield and pull him over to the driver's side before the cops came?" He paused. "Don't answer that, I don't want to know."

"That's right," replied Leopold, his glass raised in a toast, "you keep a clear head. To wealth!" The two men drank. The bartender returned to the woman's table with a bowl of cheddar cheese crackers shaped like tiny goldfish. "How about us?" asked Leopold, who had a special fondness for these. The bartender ignored them. The black woman also seemed unaware of their existence.

Leopold told Sparks that he was going to get that jerk of a waiter in a dark alley one night and saw off his legs. He picked up the ashtray from the table's center and calmly dumped its contents on the floor. "I hate these joints that can't keep their ashtrays clean," he said. The black woman's mouth was open and he gave her a big wink. He turned back to Sparks. "You interested in horses?"

This seemed to the lawyer a strange topic for his companion to be introducing. "Sure," he said. "Do I play them? What do you mean?"

Leopold casually announced that he'd picked up a thoroughbred down south some months back.

The lawyer grabbed at his arm. "You're kidding! You own a racehorse?"

"Sure do."

"Well, I'll be a blue Jesus," sighed the lawyer, sinking down into his chair. "How about that! I've always dreamed of owning one myself." He sat back up excitedly, thrust out an arm and shook Leopold's hand in vigorous congratulation. "How much she set you back?"

"The fact is I rather overextended myself."

Sparks instantly became wary. "If you're thinking of putting the bite on me you're barking up the wrong tree, I ain't giving nobody no loans. My own sister came to me the other day, she's left her old man and has got hungry mouths to feed, but I said no deal. I say the same to you."

"It isn't that," said Leopold, unruffled, "though I am open to a partnership. I might let the right man have a small share."

"Not interested," the lawyer declared.

"She's a terrific piece of horseflesh. Runs under the name Two Flags, well known on the East Coast and especially on the Florida tracks. I thought you might have heard of her."

"Uh-huh. Well, I haven't."

"I could maybe skin off ten percent, no more."

The lawyer repeated that he wasn't interested. They had been signaling to the bartender for another round and now at last he brought them. For a time the two men were content to sip their martinis and eye the black woman and say no more about Leopold's racehorse. A tall man of middle age, with very pale skin and wearing a blue wool suit, came through the door and went directly to the black woman's table. He smiled warmly, kissed the top of her head, then bent and nudged his face up against her neck. She smiled dreamily past Leopold's shoulder. Then the newcomer's lips grazed her ear, he sat down, and the two held hands on the table.

"Look at that diamond he's wearing," whispered Sparks. "Choke a horse."

"Fake," said Leopold, who was still made uneasy by the sight of a white and black couple. Not, he might have remembered, that he hadn't bought himself that same privilege on more than one occasion.

"Do you mind?" said the woman. She looked down at Leopold's shoes which were once more propped against her chair. Leopold let several seconds go by before dropping his feet to the floor. The woman said "Thank you" and, standing, brushed his shoe's imprint from her hip. The pale-looking man stared sleepily at Leopold as if this was a routine he'd been through many times before. The woman's hand settled on his thigh and this time it was her face which nestled against his shoulder.

"Regular lovebirds," muttered Leopold. "Makes you sick to the stomach, doesn't it?" He had in mind his wife Alice who was always after him to show her a little public affection. She could stand it, she maintained, that he never did so in private, but that the world knew that he cared nothing at all for her was almost more than she could bear.

In an undertone the lawyer stated that he couldn't care less if they rolled on the floor. "No," he told Leopold, "you won't find me talking down the blacks. Though personally I think they've got the morals of an alley cat, they bring me a lot of business."

Leopold again brought up the subject of his horse.

"She's a beauty, is she?" said Sparks, repeating his friend's comment.

"I'll say so. She picked up $20,000 in purse money this past year and that was an off season for her. Next time around I expect her winnings will double."

"Funny," said Sparks, "I didn't hear any mention of her in the Derby."

Leopold poked at his cigarette package, peered inside, and finally gave it a twist before dropping it on the floor. He had been trying to stop smoking, liked to think he was succeeding, but could remember buying this package after breakfast this morning. He looked irritably at Sparks. Sparks didn't smoke. Too cheap, in Leopold's opinion. Then something white was shoved under his nose and he became aware of the blue-suited man standing beside him.

"Always glad to help out a stranger," the man said, and thumped a cigarette farther out of his package. Leopold, without thanks, accepted the smoke. "Take two," the man suggested. Leopold took another. Then he shifted awkwardly, sucking on the cigarette as the man put a butane lighter to the tip.

"My pleasure," he said, and stepping back, took the woman's arm for it appeared they were leaving.

Leopold had the vague notion that he had just been insulted.

The man threw up a hand, the woman smiled pleasantly at Leopold, and the two disappeared outside. Leopold said, "Go stuff yourselves" under his breath, and turned his attention back to Sparks. He didn't yet count Sparks out. He prided himself on knowing his man. He was certain that Sparks was arrogant enough and greedy enough and snobbish enough—and stupid enough as well—for part ownership of a thoroughbred to appeal to him. But he wanted money in his pocket and it displeased him greatly that the lawyer had not already put it there.

"No," he said now, "I didn't say she was in the Derby, she's not quite ready for that league. But you'd be surprised at the money there is in these small local turfs." He reached into his breast pocket. "Tell you what, I'll show you her picture, like to know what you think. If she isn't the most beautiful piece you ever saw, I'll buy the next round."

Sparks contended that he had to be getting home, that his wife would shoot him. All the same he made no move to leave, and seemed pleased to examine the photographs. He grunted several times, not yes, not no, before passing the picture back to Leopold. "Seattle Slew she ain't," he then concluded.

Leopold hastily returned the photo to his pocket, a little rattled. The lawyer had correctly identified the horse in the picture.

"You'd have to show me a lot more than a brushed-up glossy," Sparks added. "I'd have to see her pedigree, her record, and I'd have to know what kind of money we're really talking about. Fact is, I'd have to rub noses with the animal myself." He tugged at his trousers, which had pulled up in tight wrinkles about his thighs. "Anyway, I don't buy into anything I can't own 51 percent of."

Leopold whistled to show that he was impressed, though secretly he thought what a smug SOB Sparks was. "I doubt you could afford a piece of cake that size," Leopold told him.

"Don't worry about that," said the lawyer, patting his hip pocket. He opened his mouth to continue, intending to ask Leopold where the horse was stabled, but an expression of such malevolence passed over Leopold's face that he was startled into silence.

Leopold was indeed contemplating his companion with hatred. It had crossed his mind that Bonny had tossed him over for this high-waisted shyster and probably for no other reason than that Sparks was willing to spend money on her. He had a lifelong, deeply ingrained rancor for anyone better off than himself. Even as a kid he had used his fists and when that didn't work, his wits, to get nickels and dimes off other kids in his neighborhood. He had conveniently forgotten now the merry chase he had led Bonny, who had not known he was already married, and who had been misled by his promises into fully expecting one day to be his wife. (Leopold had been driven almost to distraction in that relationship by Bonny's habit of referring to him as her "one and only.") She had finally found out about the existence of Alice—from Leopold, who by that time had decided to dump her—and had responded to the lawyer's advances on the rebound. None of this, however, went through Leopold's mind. His major fault as a promoter and con man was that he was frequently subject to such self-deceptions; on the other hand, it was his great strength, as many who had been stuck by him could testify, because it enabled him to conduct his deals without the usual inhibitions of a human conscience.

"You can't see her," Leopold now said, his aplomb regained, "unless you want to fly to Florida."

The lawyer scowled, not immediately replying. If Leopold thought he was going to pay out good money for a nag he'd never seen, he was off his cracker. "How old is she?" he asked.

"Two years."

"Good breeding?"

"The daughter of champions."

"You must think I'm naïve. How many wins did she really have last year?"

"Two."

"She was entered in seven?"

"That's right. She got a late start."

"She place?"

"What?"

"Did she place in the other races?"

Leopold chuckled. "I tell you she's money in the bank." He pulled out a sheaf of papers from his breast pocket and slapped them down beside Sparks' martini. "Mama and Papa," he said. From another pocket he extracted a rumpled typewritten sheet which he said listed the races she'd been entered in during her running, her performance in each, and the amount of money she'd brought home.

"It says here," said the lawyer after a time, "that she was in the winner's circle only once."

Leopold consulted the sheet. "Oh yeah," he said, "I forgot that one in Jersey where she was edged out by a nose."

Sparks ran his finger down a column of figures reputed to be Two Flags' earnings. He stopped at the bottom. "It says here $3,000. I thought you told me she won over twenty grand last year."

"That's net," said Leopold.

Sparks threw down the sheet in disgust. "Chicken feed," he said.

Leopold surprised the lawyer by smiling. "Inefficiency," he said. "It's a different story since I took over. I fired the guy who had been her trainer and got me another guy—beautiful credentials, a pensioner—at one-third the wages. I moved her to another stable, better and cheaper. And I got a jockey who owes me a favor. Next season I expect to bust $30,000. Net. Call that chicken feed if you want to."

The lawyer dusted imaginary lint from his knees. "Funny. I had the feeling you were only a broker on this deal. Tell the truth now, how much of the nag do you own?"

"One hundred percent. Well, there is another guy owns ten percent but I plan to buy up that."

Sparks' eyes lit up. "Whoa," he said. "You're planning on buying this guy's ten percent while at the same time you're offering to sell me ten percent?" He scrunched up his face, began sniffing about and slapping at the air. "Woo!" he exclaimed, "I smell a stench in here."

"I offered you nothing," Leopold said. "I'm sitting here talking to you in a friendly way about this horse I own because

I know you play the track and I thought you might be interested. The fact is, this guy sitting on the ten percent has his back to the wall and can be got at cheap."

"In other words, you need my money so you can buy the jerk out."

"I said I was open to some kind of partnership if the right kind of guy came up with the right kind of money. That's all I said."

"Who's the creep with ten?" asked the lawyer, who now stood up and pulled the knot tighter in his tie.

"You wouldn't know him. Anyway, if I told you we'd wind up bidding against each other."

"Me? I got better things to invest in than horses."

Leopold finished his drink and slammed the glass down on the table, disgusted. The deal had gone sour somewhere and he wanted to blame Sparks.

At that moment the two men heard a distant roar from outside, the dim overhead lights did a jiggle and the floor shook.

"What the hell!" said Sparks.

Leopold sprang to his feet and both men marched quickly to the window, pulled the drapes back and peered outside. The sky had darkened, everything outside had darkened, and they had to press their faces close to the glass to see at all. Wind was whipping trash down the street. Another explosion sounded, more distant this time, and lightning streaked across the sky like cracked glass.

Sparks drew back. "Wouldn't you know it. Now I'll get drenched going home."

"Go to Bonny's," Leopold advised, "she lives closer."

Rain began slashing down. Two men rushed into the bar, wet, shaking themselves and looking up with excited faces as if all the world should have been there to greet them. Leopold and Sparks didn't know them, and went to stand by the fireplace where the wood was laid but had not yet been ignited. Sparks laughed nervously, despondently. "For a while there," he admitted to Leopold, "it crossed my mind that you were trying to blackmail me over this Bonny thing."

"Did it now?"

"Not seriously," laughed Sparks. "Just a flicker of suspicion."

"Do tell."

Sparks became more nervous because Leopold was refusing to take it in the joking way he had intended.

"Now don't get on your high horse, you can't blame me. You know the kind of talk that goes on about you behind your back."

Leopold bristled. "Who?" he demanded. "No one would dare. Rodin, I suppose. Has that stuck pig been squealing?"

"Aw, come on," said Sparks, whose hands had begun to sweat, "you must know you're not the most popular man in the world." He decided then and there that if Leopold hit him he would go immediately to the cops and sign an assault charge against him that would pack him away for six months. Be doing everyone a favor, he thought.

But the remark seemed to please Leopold. His features relaxed and he threw a brotherly arm around the lawyer. "That kind of gossip doesn't worry me. Any man who doesn't roll over and play dead will be subjected to it. It's jealousy. People are a nasty bunch of back-stabbers. Look at the sort of thing you hear said about any powerful individual who refuses to take any crap. Look at . . ." He paused, momentarily at a loss. ". . . Jimmy Connors or Idi Amin."

"You're right, of course. Some people, my own colleagues even, try to pull me down."

"So I've heard."

Sparks was eager to learn what Leopold had heard about him and asked a few pointed questions, but these Leopold adroitly evaded.

In a softened voice he announced that the previous day he had been talking to Yaplovich.

"You're kidding," said Sparks, astonished. "You talked to Yaplovich?"

"He was after me to buy a piece of Two Flags. What do you think?"

Sparks was even more surprised. Yaplovich knew nothing whatever about horses and moreover was strictly opposed to all forms of gambling and taunted Sparks at every turn for the money he dropped at the track. Furthermore, he despised Leopold. By the same token, he was rolling in money and could easily afford to buy ten or twenty such horses.

It didn't occur to the lawyer that Leopold had fabricated this meeting.

"What do you think?" asked Leopold.

"Yaplovich is not to be trusted. You need someone you can get along with. Bad management can kill a good horse quicker than a lame jockey."

"My view exactly."

"Now the two of us could get along."

"That's true. You have my respect and I hope I have yours."

For reasons not entirely clear to Sparks he found himself shaking Leopold's hand as if they had just met.

"Naturally," said Leopold, "you would want to confer with your wife before buying anything so extravagant as a race-horse."

"I don't see why. I make my own decisions."

"Oh, I see. I was assuming that you might even want to buy into Two Flags as a present for Phoebe. To take her mind off this Bonny mess you've got into. I mean, it's hard to keep an affair like that quiet and it's possible she's got wind of it. You know how women are. If she knew for sure you'd been carrying on with trash like Bonny she might decide to leave you and take you for everything you have."

The lawyer had gone stiff. "Only three people know," he said. "You, me, and Bonny."

"Well, you can't trust women any more than you can trust Yaplovich."

Yaplovich was Sparks' law partner.

"Bonny wouldn't tell."

"She told me."

Sparks fell silent.

"As far as that goes, you could buy into Two Flags and give it to Bonny as a gift. You know how she likes presents, and that, I feel sure, would assure her silence."

Sparks thought he was beginning to get Leopold's drift. One way or another he was going to have to buy a piece of the goddamned horse. Not to pacify his wife or to shut Bonny's mouth, but to keep Leopold himself from running to Phoebe as fast as he could. Blackmail, he thought. I was right all along.

He knew there was nothing for him to do except take the plunge.

"How much?" he asked.

Leopold was in no hurry. He made a trip to the bar, bummed a cigarette off a stranger, and returned in a minute or two with two dripping martinis. With a certain jubilance he began ticking off the various things that could go wrong with Sparks' life if Phoebe found out about Bonny. "I suppose you know," he said, "that she's a vindictive woman." Phoebe, his children, his Lincoln Continental, a good portion of his stocks and bonds portfolio, the acreage on the lake where he was planning on building, not to mention the respect of his colleagues and the fellowship of friends who would inevitably side with the woman—he would lose all these.

He began to have very sentimental feelings toward poor Phoebe who would probably leave him, would probably try to strip him of everything he owned, but would be sure to take him through hell first. She would cry and threaten suicide. She would say he had never loved her, that he was no good as a man or as a lover or as a lawyer, that there was nothing he respected or cared for, least of all her and their marriage and their three children and the new one who was on the way.

Because while he had been out chasing after Bonny, Phoebe had turned up mysteriously pregnant. "Well, I can't help it," she had said, "if you're going to keep on poking and jabbing at me."

He was moved to tenderness for the unborn child as well, thinking, *the poor bugger, he would have to grow up without a father.*

Sparks determined that he wouldn't lose her, that he would just have to see this through and take his medicine like the good sport he was, and bide his time until he could stick a sharp one through Leopold's ribs.

He got out his pen, sipped at his martini, and on a Wild Boar napkin drafted this contract:

> KNOW ALL MEN BY THESE PRESENTS: *that the undersigned* _____ hereby agrees to purchase ____ shares interest in the thoroughbred racehorse known as Two Flags and stabled at _____ subject to the following understanding, namely that the animal be in sound health and as elsewhere stated in this agreement including that the aforesaid property be free and clear of all liens, attachments, liabilities and other encumbrances—

He slid over another napkin and continued his scratchings:

> —except those specifically set forth here from _____ (seller) as rightful and legal owner of the aforesaid property at the price of _____

"You're going to have to come up with a reasonable figure," he stopped to tell Leopold, who was following all this with considerable interest—

of lawful money of Canada, payable by cheque/cash as a deposit to be credited on account of purchase money on closing, and the Purchaser _____ agrees to pay the balance of _____ as follows, to wit: that pedigree papers on the property be sworn to and certified by a notary public together with all other documents purporting to relate to the property's health, mental condition, lodging, etc.

He then shoved those napkins aside and quickly composed another contract which spelled out the terms of their partnership as Two Flags' owners and guaranteed him a voice in her management in proportion to the final percentage owned by himself.

The agreements were next to meaningless, but as an attorney he felt it only proper that he make a stab at protecting his interests. He then pulled out a $100 bill—that, he believed, would keep Leopold silent for a week—and slapped the money down in front of Leopold.

Leopold did not like the many stipulations in the contracts. He would prefer, he said, a verbal agreement between gentlemen.

He and Sparks then got down to the real bargaining.

Throughout these sticky negotiations Sparks was both burdened and gratified by the image of Phoebe at home waiting for him with a dinner that had gone cold and his children littered in front of the TV, of Phoebe with her stomach now rounded like an inflated pear, her face hardening as he came through the front door, of Phoebe advancing over the new Armstrong carpet with her complaints of swollen ankles and migraine headaches and stubbornly insisting on her right to know where he had been.

"Buying you a racehorse," he would say—and when she finally was made to understand that he had done just that, tears would flood her eyes and she would hurl her arms around him and they would at last be united in another of their quiet perfect evenings at home.

The lawyer put much store on the family maintenance of a united front, and periodically felt something close to gratitude to Leopold for this inspired present which would make it possible.

"He's kicking now," Phoebe would say of the unborn child, stretched out on their king-size bed; and she would guide his hand gently over her stomach, her face curious and expectant and radiant, for Phoebe was never so beautiful as when she was pregnant.

Of course, to cover all bets, he would have to send Bonny a gift as well. A case of rye, he decided, would fit the bill there.

A little while later, after the lawyer had gone home, Rodin showed up. That he looked terrible everyone agreed, and more than a few made vain attempts to get him over by the fire where at least he could dry off. "Look at you," they said, "you're wringing wet, if you don't watch out you'll catch a bitch of a cold." Others, less concerned but still warmhearted and made even more so by their various stages of inebriation, did their best to lure him to their tables. "Come on, Rodin, join us, a stiff belt will put you on your feet, make you forget your troubles." For they agreed that Rodin had his troubles and was taking them hard.

Rodin barely noticed. Any other time—any other time before Aimée's death, that is—he would have been moved almost to tears by such displays of human warmth whether aimed at himself or any other lucky individual—but tonight he was too despondent, too worn out. He had been drinking all that day. He had started that morning with a short nip before breakfast (intending to let it stop there), he had continued it through the morning while drooped in a chair in his study staring at a photograph of Aimée, and he had kept it up through the afternoon—with a flask of Jamieson's Irish—while seated half-recumbent and sometimes dozing in the stale darkness of a second-run movie house which he had come across without design or intention and which he had entered only because it would increase his sadness. He had never cared for movies, but Aimée had liked attending them. As nearly as he could determine, the movie was about an amazingly innocent young couple in love, one of whom had contacted a deadly virus just as he was completing his law degree, and the picture had closed with the girl bringing flowers to his grave along with a favorite book on contract law, and determining to live, prosper and be happy because this is what he would want her to do and because this was a test God was giving her and one which she must pass. Although Rodin had been crying much of the time and rooting for this ludicrous couple when he could focus upon their terrible ordeal, he laughed at that point (the girl had kissed the law book, squared it over the dead boy's chest and covered it with sand), knowing full well that the pretty survivor would herself soon be dead from an overdose or from pitching herself out of a high window or by throwing herself into the sea. It had occurred to him, stumbling back into sunshine a few minutes later, that Aimée would hate him now—not for his despair or for his blasphemy or for drinking his way through yet another day, but for his cynicism, the one great equalizer which had thus far served to keep him from such desirable ends.

He could not remember how he had got from the movie house to the bar down the street where he had finished the afternoon, any more than he could think now, hours later, how or why he had come to be at the Wild Boar Tavern, a place which filled him with dread and the anticipation of a hundred misgivings, since it was a place he had frequently come to with Aimée. He pushed past the arms that reached out to guide or embrace him, muttered distractedly, even impolitely, to those who expressed concern, and somehow without falling down or tipping over anyone's glass made it to the empty stool in the shadows at the end of the bar, the refuge he had been aiming for since the moment he first entered. He slumped down on the stool and allowed his head a brief rest on the black marble counter. Then, with an effort, he sat erect, blinking at the bartender who was speaking to him, apparently to inform him of the availability of a back room where he could lie down. He had forgotten to take off his hat, and rainwater dripped onto his shoulders from the brim and onto the counter where, as rapidly as it fell, the bartender wiped with a white towel.

"You ought to go home, Rodin," the bartender was saying, "would you like me to get someone to take you home?"

"Not going home," Rodin muttered. "Why should I go home? Don't have a home."

The bartender nodded and smiled and lifted Rodin's hat from his head, shook it and stored it out of sight under the counter. Then he brought forth a fresh towel and suggested to Rodin in a gentle way that he might want to dry his face.

"Don't have a home," said Rodin. "I had one, but not any more."

The bartender patted Rodin's face dry, and someone else, seeing what he was up to, came up behind Rodin and draped a coat over his shoulders.

Then a shocked expression hit the faces of both these men because they clearly heard Rodin ask, "Where's Aimée, has either of you seen Aimée in here this evening?"—a remark which upset both of them because Rodin's voice was suddenly not in the least slurred, he spoke distinctly, and for an instant looked cold sober. They next saw Rodin's own face reflect surprise, his eyes misted over, and a moment before his head sagged to the counter they heard him say, "I'm sorry, forgive me, I must be terribly drunk, I don't know why I said that."

The bartender and the other man hoisted Rodin between them and walked him into one of the Boar's private rooms.

Leopold, quite drunk himself by this hour, watched all this transpire with bleary disinterest in Rodin's condition, but with secret and venomous rage that Rodin's drunkenness tonight stood in the way of the scheme he had been devising since the lawyer Sparks' departure. He repeated to himself and to anyone else who would listen that he hated and despised and mistrusted any man who could not hold his whisky and who had no more pride than to make a public nuisance of himself and who ought furthermore to be locked up in the drunk tank with all the other crow-bait losers and misfits, and not fussed over by those bums like he was a baby left on the doorstep. Rodin, he argued, was a grown man and ought to take life's little miseries in style and show the same backbone any man who was a man would. "My ass is fried in oil every day," he told his table, "but when have you heard me complaining?"

One or two of those there ventured to suggest many such times, but Leopold shouted them down.

"Anyone who has anything to say against me," he cried, "let him stand up now and say it to my face!"

No one insisted, Leopold's wrath abated, and over the next half-hour he proceeded to intimidate, vex, or bore them with a considerable amount of nonsense about racehorses, on which subject he said he could speak as one of the world's few authorities. He drank and got drunker, though he rarely forgot his secret objective and was on the whole content to entertain, as he thought of them, this table of scorpions.

He was waiting for Rodin's recovery. He had been waiting for Rodin since the lawyer had gone. He had to see and talk to Rodin because until he did so his pockets would remain empty and Sparks' ridiculous scraps of paper would have no value. A month or so before Aimée's death she had come to him with the demand that he pay back every cent of money her husband had lent him or which Leopold had beat out of him. She had come armed with enough information to ruin him, to see him, she said, locked up forever, and she had convinced him that she would have no hesitation in doing it. He in turn had convinced her he had no money. "You can rot in jail then," she had said, "and the air around here will be very much cleaner."

To stave off that, he had agreed to transfer ownership of the horse in partial payment of a debt which startled even him by its enormity.

That was just like Rodin, he later concluded, to let a woman go fighting his battles.

"There's just one thing," he had told Aimée. "I gave Alice ten percent one time when she was going to leave me. I guess you'll want that too."

She had treated him with contempt, but he had salvaged at least that much, for underneath it all Aimée was as mush-hearted as her old man and she had been unwilling to take anything from Alice whom she pitied.

So that was how matters now stood.

With Aimée now dead and Rodin a wreck, Leopold foresaw no problem in retrieving his property, although a few questions were yet to be decided. Should he take a hard or soft line with Rodin? Sparks was right in that Rodin was not precisely a fool. There was nothing to be got from him by twisting his arm or browbeating him. And it was unlikely that he would fall for another sob story since his own life now was so much one. No, to get to Rodin he would have to get him where he hurt. He would have to get at him through Aimée.

When your wife came to me that time, he would say, *I could see she was dying. All of us who knew her knew she was dying, and we couldn't understand, Rodin, why you couldn't see it or why you refused to do anything about it. I did, I said to her "Aimée, you're in a bad way, we've got to get you into* a hospital, we've got to get medical help for you if you're to last out the week," and she admitted it, she said she knew she was dying but that she didn't want to be a burden to you, if she had only a week left, then she wanted to spend that week with you rather than be locked up in a hospital room. That's what she said, Rodin, but the truth is that she was in a deeply depressed state, so much so that even Alice noticed, Alice said to me that she was afraid Aimée would commit suicide, that's how depressed she was, and the day she came to me, well I suppose you thought it was about those little debts I owed you but the truth is that Aimée was so sick she was on the verge of killing herself just so she could have a little peace; thank God I was there, Rodin, or she might have done it that very day, I've never seen a woman so ready to slash her own wrist. Anyway I comforted her the best I could, I talked to her, I told her how much we all liked and respected her, she said that wasn't true, that no one cared for her, least of all you or you would have noticed how bad off she was. Come to think of it, that's why I gave up possession of my horse, just a gesture to cheer her up, to get her mind off death and suffering and all the unhappiness she was going through. Of course, it was to be a loan only, you understand, a temporary exchange of owner-ship, our understanding was that I'd get the horse back eventually, which is why I'm approaching you now, to see if you'll honor the private agreement Aimée and I had, I know you've been through a period of grief, old Aimée is gone and will never come back but there's no point in crying in the towel day in and day out, you've got to stand on your own two feet and face up to your responsibilities to your fellow man, get in a good day's work, mind you I respect a man's grief and didn't want to come to you with anything about money or debts or to ask if I could have my horse back now, though I'm sure Aimée would tell you if she could that I've been very patient and that the horse rightfully belongs to me, not that

*I have to say any of this because I know you won't want to
smear and dishonor her memory by refusing to turn her over,
what do you say . . . ?*

Something like that, salt in the wounds, appeal on moral
grounds, that would turn the trick, Rodin would do anything
once he was convinced it was the moral, honorable thing to
do, the jerk.

THE SHUT-IN NUMBER

*M*r. Charles collected his first child on a cold, cloudy day in the dead of winter. He wanted to get down to it before spring came, figuring the child would be less active. The abduction went well. He lured the child off the street and into his car with no difficulty, and simply shot hell away, around the corner on squealing tires before anyone knew he'd struck.

In subsequent years, encouraged by admiring friends, he was fond of reflecting on this early adventure.

"Well, I was stupid, you see, like most young men of that age, but I like to think I was different. I had ambition. Back in those days what I thought I would do, the career I planned for myself, was pro football. If that didn't work out, then I planned something equally extraordinary. A sideline I could fall back on. So I had this one child staked out from about the time I was in grade nine. I kept my distance, but I knew he was the one I wanted. Fact is, I practically gave up the idea of football. It didn't have the same attraction, the same ex-

citement, once I delved into this other idea. Football seemed
to be kind of *stupid*, if you know what I mean. Suppose I got
hurt? Suppose I just couldn't cut it? I was only an average
player, nothing spectacular. My coach, to tell the truth, hardly
noticed me. Still, pro football was a distinct possibility; I didn't
altogether rule it out. What I told myself was, well, if you
get into a game and you lose it, say you fumble the ball on the
goalpost line, then everyone knows who to blame. But if you
collect this kid and do it right, well, who's going to blame
you? No one. So far as anyone knows, you had nothing to do
with it. That was the great advantage of this back-up plan. It
made the idea very attractive. So one cold, blustery day in the
dead of winter, figuring the child would be less active than in
spring, I went out and did it. I stole him."

Mr. Charles' friends, when he tells them this, when he
reflects on his thinking at the time and describes the plan's
skillful execution, find themselves vastly amused. They can't
help wanting to know the details.

"You *kidnapped* this boy, then, did you?"

"Kidnapped? Oh heck no. Some people might call it that,
but it's not a word I would use. I *took* him. I *collected* him.
But kidnapping, I'd say, would be going too far. Wrong over-
tones. By that time, you see, I'd already decided there was no
point in making the *making* of money the point of my life.
I wasn't interested, per se, in any ransoming scheme. And
even at that time I had an income. Not much, but nice and
steady, certainly enough to get by on. I was a long shot from
being the kind of social deadwood that Rex Humbard talks
about. How there's nothing *wrong* with making money. How
if you don't make it, then you become part of the problem.
No, I was self-sufficient. I had enough for more than a few
people in my household, assuming I skimped a bit and didn't
get to thinking about skylights and pile carpets, *dish*washers,
that kind of thing. And, of course, I figured—correctly, it

turned out—my income would go up as the years went by. So I'm all right on the financial end, without draining too much from these children's parents."

"What would Oral Roberts say?" his friends ask.

"This doesn't concern Oral. Oral's wonderful. He's a fine singer. I get a big kick out of him."

"Dr. Schuller? Ernest Angley?"

"Dr. Robert Schuller has the finest face I ever saw on a human being. He's got sincerity on his side, and a whole lot more. I'd be happy to throw in with Schuller *or* Angley. Angley, as you can see, is more my physical type. God used the same hand on us, I mean. But, look, I don't want to talk about that. The second child I stole was in August, the year following my first heist, just before I joined the Young Conservative Party and the YRA. That time it was entirely impulsive—a creative act. I was cruising along the boulevard, I saw this chap, I pulled ahead, stopped the car, opened the door. When he drew abreast I asked him where Ninth Street was, something like that, and when he poked his head in I rapped him over the head with a piece of stove wood. Not a peep out of him. Not a soul anywhere knew I'd struck again."

"That's amazing, Mr. Charles," say his friends. "You certainly seem to have the knack. But how do you reconcile these activities with your religious views?"

"No difficulty. None whatsoever. My conscience is clear on all fronts. Really, it all comes out of the same bag. Now look here. One, there's belief in the holy scripture. That's paramount. The holy word has come down to us through His caring, and we have it, and by God what else could we want? Two, there's prayer. Prayer is a powerful thing. It *works*. I *know* it works. I've used prayer all my life—all my life, that is, since I was born again—and it's helped me out a thousand times. Three, there's salvation and life eternal, if only you will *accept*. Accept Jesus in your life and take him as your personal savior. No, I don't have any problem reconciling my activities with my religious views. There's no conflict."

"Do you use prayer in *this* work? Did you pray, for instance, that your second—or third or fourth—victim would come along and everything would go well?"

"Not for any of the *detailed* stuff. I do ask for His *guidance*. My life wouldn't be complete if I didn't. That's where the 700 Club is so helpful. That they are there to help you on a daily basis. It's like the man says: you can put your hand up to the TV screen and right away feel the holy spirit flooding through your bones. And you pick up a lot of useful information. Heartfelt stuff that offers considerable relief from the ordinary facts of life that we have to live with, like deficit spending, military cutbacks, abortion-on-demand, no more prayers in the schools, and the like. Did you know Adam and Eve were six thousand years in the garden? I only learned that last week, with my hand up to the tube. It's all authenticated. How they do it is they look at the rock strata and check out fossils, sea-wash, etc. composing the different strata. Stratum? Something. Biblical scholarship is a very progressive field. I've often thought, if my income ever petered out, that I might give it a whirl. Yes, six thousand years Adam and Eve were in the garden. Then the Devil said, your land is my land, give me my land and I will give you all the pleasure you want. Eve gave in, and it's been history ever since. See what I mean? See how fascinating it all is? That's where heterosexual sex got its start. It's that simple. It's amazing, isn't it?"

"We understand, Mr. Charles, that not too long ago you made your biggest haul."

"You heard about that? Yes, three years ago I stole sixteen people all in one go. I leased this mini-bus from Greyhound. It took some doing because they kept insisting their driver be part of the deal. Finally, I went along. Actually, including him, the total came to seventeen. It cost me bucks, but I went whole-hog on that caper. What I did was, up where it normally tells you where a bus is going I had a sign saying FREE HOT DOGS. And circus music, you know. There wasn't much more to it. Easy as pie. Of course, some of that group I let go. It was easy to see they weren't going to work out."

"Those you've kept, are they of mixed sex?"

"I've got one girl. She says she's about fourteen, but I don't believe it. She was a mistake. Her hair was short, she had a cap on, and she was wearing boots and these Western britches. So, one, yes, I've got one, and God help me I wish I didn't. Females, generally, I see as troublemakers. They distract my boys, they sow discord, they simply are not harmonious human beings. Still, she's good with a broom, this one I got. And the boys like her. They're glad I picked her up."

"So you give your—victims? is that word too harsh?—a say in what goes on?"

"Not much. Very little, in fact. But I try to leave them with the *impression* that they're contributing to the day-by-day management. Keeps them docile. They don't complain so much."

"How difficult has it been for them, leaving the family hearth and such?"

"They've made the adjustment quite nicely. A few even say they *prefer* it here with me, which is a comforting thought. Naturally, they have their hang-ups, their growing pangs, as all children do. They want spending money, toys, video games, and the like, and it really puts them in a foul mood sometimes that they can't go outside and play, go to movies, knock about on the streets, that kind of thing. Mostly, though, they're a contented bunch. They show as much life, I guess, as most kids."

Mr. Charles' friends usually find themselves quite moved by these reports. They look at him with a new respect, and wonder, the insecure ones, whether their own lives are being put to such good purpose. They can see the pride he takes in his chosen field, the pride of knowing his is a job well done. Plain to see he's not hurt that the pro football career never materialized. His sense of self, the esteem with which he regards himself, is perfectly obvious.

"That's right," he says. "My life is in order. When you put God first, everything else sort of takes care of itself. You don't get upset by life's little imponderables. You hear of millions of people starving in the third world and elsewhere and of thousands being assassinated in this or that yippie republic and you sort of shake your head, but mostly you think, well, that's God's plan. You figure TV evangelism will eventually take care of that. He planned a good life for me and I'm grateful. I never forget to mention it in my prayers and those I've got here under my roof I try to impress upon them the importance of thanking God for their blessings. The Catholics, I've found, are very easy to please on that score. But, well, with them it's a little bit like starting over from scratch. In point of fact, everyone here is saved. They are standing up for God, and I wouldn't have it any other way. We have back-sliding of course, but that goes with the territory."

"How many young folks do you actually have—retained?—retained here now?"

"Twenty-two, at the moment. Twenty-two that are *healthy*. I have one or two others on the sick roster—bruises, sprains, that sort of thing—and another two or three who are on *report* for infraction of the rules. Misuse of the telephone, that kind of thing."

"Your plans, then, are to continue on pretty much the way you're going?"

"I'd like to step it up, actually. Grab a few more really *young* boys off the street. Broad daylight raids, real avant-garde stuff, if you follow me. And I want to branch out. Try to figure out some daring, revolutionary way to get at the shut-ins. I've always had a soft spot in my heart for shut-ins. I want to figure out a risk-free way of getting at these people. Something that will truly shake up old Rex, old Oral, old Jerry, Dr. Bob, and that crowd. Let them know I'm here and on the scene, you know. *Witnessing*. Getting in my two-cents worth. Getting the Lord's work done."

Mr. Charles' friends love these talks. His enthusiasm, his flair, they find inspiring. They hate to leave, but are already looking forward to the next visit.

"Could we *see* one of your—guests?—one of your boys, Mr. Charles? It would mean so much to us."

Mr. Charles ponders this request. He's a bit put off by it.

"Just to *see* him?" he asks. "Or talk to him?"

"Well . . . both, if possible."

Mr. Charles closes his Bible, rises from his easy chair by the fire, and walks over to the wall where a velvet cord hangs below a bronze study of Jesus on the cross. "It's unusual," he says, still pondering. "I don't know that I ought to allow it."

"Surely it can't hurt, sir."

"Hurt? No, it can't hurt. Not normally. But I put my boys through a pretty rough weekend. I'm not sure they are at their best today. Still, I . . . well, you want to see one of my *typical* boys, is that right?"

"Right! That would do wonderfully."

Mr. Charles gives a slow nod. He pulls on the cord. Apparently a speaker system is installed in the wall as well, for they hear Mr. Charles saying in a clear voice: "Send up Samson." He then turns to his friends, casting out his arms as if to embrace them. "I owe it to you," he says. "Your support has meant all the world to me, and I don't know if I would have been able to carry on without your help. I've had a few mishaps, you know. Not your usual aborted missions, but a few that were truly dirty. Narrow escapes. Once, down in the dreary part of town, across the tracks, so to speak, a child no more than five years old kicked me in the face when I tried grabbing him. It messed up my nose a little. Another time a mother came at me with her umbrella. I hadn't even seen her. Truly outlandish behavior. One time a police car chased me. I thought my goose was cooked, until I found an obscure alley. I sweated all night, thinking they might have got my license-plate number. No, looking at me, you'd think I was on Easy Street. There are hidden terrors, that's all I'm saying."

A few of Mr. Charles' friends patted him on the back. They shook their heads and murmured sympathetic noises. A Mrs. Diamond, whose leg was crooked, gave him a big bear hug.

A timid knock sounded at the door; Mr. Charles, extricating himself, responded to it. A round-faced boy dressed in a green bathrobe stood looking at the floor. He was sniveling a little, and trembling. His left eye was swollen and discolored. His cheek was bruised.

"This is Samson," said Mr. Charles. "My very latest acquisition. I snapped him off the playground just last Sunday. I'm very proud of Samson. He's an upper-income child, with excellent table manners. Samson, say hello to these nice people."

The boy mumbled something. He remained cringing by the door, his shoulders drawn up tight, trembling even more. He tilted his head, gazing up at them with one wet, entreating eye. His little hands churned. He mumbled again.

"What is he saying, Mr. Charles?" one of the friends asked.

Mr. Charles struck a prideful pose.

"He is saying he hopes to become a good Christian."

Mrs. Diamond, with the lame leg, swooped forward and picked the boy up in her arms. "He's so *adorable!*" she gushed. "I *love* him! I wish I could have him!" She kissed the limp, sobbing boy numerous times on his face and neck.

"I'm afraid that's out of the question," said Mr. Charles. "I demand that you stop kissing him this instant."

Chagrined, Mrs. Diamond replaced the boy on the floor.

"After the meek," observed one of Mr. Charles' friends, "children were our Lord's favorites."

Mr. Charles draped an arm around Samson and led him—somewhat roughly, to tell the truth—to the door. "Shoulders back," he said. "Let's see some spirit in you."

The boy went whimpering away.

Mr. Charles and his friends shook hands. He began ushering them out. "Now *that!*" they said, "was a genuinely moving experience! It was a darn uplifting encounter!"

Mr. Charles thanked his friends for coming. He reminded them there was a silver bowl by the door, should they want to drop into it any little contribution they cared to make. He let Mrs. Diamond peck his cheek.

"Keep up the good work, Mr. Charles!" his departing friends said. "You know you've got us behind you one hundred percent."

"Blessings to you all," Mr. Charles called.

With his friends gone, Mr. Charles took off his shoes and sat for some minutes in the easy chair, his feet up to the fire. Then he slipped out of his tie and suit coat and took a dressing gown from his closet and put that on. He poured himself a drink and again returned to his chair by the fire . . . where he sat on, sipping, nodding to this and that thought, contentedly staring into the flames.

Finally he pulled on the wall cord and spoke into the intercom: "Send up that girl," he said. "Send up Samson. Send up both immediately."

The box squawked back an obedient reply.

Mr. Charles freshened his drink, poked the fire, and waited.

BREAK AND ENTER

*G*ore the Critick, who owns this house, has gone abroad. Where to exactly? His correspondence, strewn about his desk, strewn over the floor, in bands and packages that overflow, does not say. But there is every sign of intention to return. Drapes open, the icebox plugged. His car in the open garage. Water running drip-drip in the sink and lights burning in the upper floor. His mail still arrives. He is reminded of his speech to the Wilderness Club and a fee is enclosed. My husband vows he will take the Critick's place—moreover, no one will ever know. Who could spot a Critick's face in these times? My husband is stern, he wants his way: what right have I to refuse? Yet I do not favor his taking another identity on. Even for one day. That was not our purpose in moving here. Nor was it our wish to make use of Gore's new General Motors car, or his pantry tins, his wash that was left hanging on the basement line. We have always paid our way, seeking out livelihoods that inspire.

Something is happening to us. We are not so carefree, so unburdened as we were. That is what my husband said.

Already he was packing away potted weeds, my pots and pans, my herbs. Taking off his shirt, rolling it up, throwing that in. Scooping up silverware. Getting the move under way before I had yet said a word, or yet asked where.

"What are you doing!" I cried, "dinner is ready, I was just now about to set the table."

"Throw a lid on it," he said, "tonight we'll dine at Gore's."

Thus our first night here we had cold stew, cold garlic bread, and lettuce salad that should have made us gag.

"Now that we are settled," said my husband, wiping clean his plate and pushing back his chair, "we must leave Gore's things as they are. We must respect the man in his absence, and take no steps to repulse the hidden flow of his life here."

We slept on cold clean sheets in a strange high bed in his master room, leaving Gore's soiled linen in a pile by the door. Where yet it is. For something has come over me: I have not the energy to renew all things nor even to unpack us here, though my husband takes no mind, seeming to need only the clothes he wears, the change of garments that he finds.

&⅌ &⅌ &⅌

I am thinking of Jessie about whom word reached us the other day. She had been taken to the hospital, placed under Intensive Care. Though a thousand miles separated us, though I love her better than myself, I dared not move. I dared not call. I scarcely dared to think "Jessie's sick, she needs her friends now." I would not ask "How sick?" or what her chances are. The slightest act of mine might tip the balance either way. So I hung about this house, subdued as the very dust, cold inside my bones, waiting—waiting for the next word.

Henry called.

"She's dead."

"Dead?"

"During the night. Her heart quit pumping, they could not activate."

Nor could I. The slightest petal dropped on the surface can alter the course of streams. Yet one finger in the dike can prevail over the force of a hundred waves. One never knows which route to take. I take a deeper limbo now. Would that have served her while she lived? A visit, coming at the proper time, might have served her too. Who knows?

"Her friends are of the opinion you have let her down."

Henry is tactful: he believes the same.

"They are all there?"

"All."

Where are you?

My mind shoots off into a dozen directions as I move. It is the same, whether seated in Gore's easy chair. His hip-print molds my flesh. Perhaps it is just this sort of desuetude he was fleeing from.

Hello, Jessie. I say that to the vacant dark, and the darkness appears to thin before my stare. Yet no one is there. It is my own hand clutching my breast.

"We will send out for dinner tonight," my husband suggests. "You're in no mood."

The fact is he recognizes precisely the mood I'm in. A Chinese dinner cannot circumvent the thing.

"You've been doodling," he says. "Let me see."

I pass him the doodle, which he praises for its likeness to a cloverleaf. Transcendental intersections in my skull.

Lips crack open under the strain. "It's Gore's house," I say. "It's this wretched way we live!" My husband folds the paper, tucks it away. He saves scraps, my husband does—a man who can make good news out of any bad-news day.

"Oil and water," he says, "oil and water. Why consider it an intrusion? Look at it this way: we are here to tend these rooms. Gore is a man of the world! Surely he would understand!"

"I want to write him a letter," I say. "I want to let him know that I can be a Critick too." Yet, what's the use? Even as I speak, his reply is ringing in my head. *Personally, I am incensed,* Gore is saying. *Personally, I consider your commandeering of my ancestral home an immoral, desecratory act without the least redeeming societal virtue and one which furthermore is consistent with our recent vulgar betrothals on the one hand and dark descents on the other and all engendered, no doubt, by that obedience to the slothful contemptible strain our culture so persistently romances with and which has now become part and parcel of the very air we breathe, as witness rampant nudism on our beaches, the pilgrimage of elders, a decline in the salutary purveyorship of war, uprooting of disease, etc., child reform, bold hirsutes strutting our streets, etc., etc.*

"Oh, now!" remarks my husband, "that's not Gore! Gore's a prince, you know that!"

Dear Gore:

Your home overpowers us. Different furniture in every room —desk, rug, and drape—yet each room projects the same conquering air. An unidentified mosaic creeping over the house. And I sense it was here before we came. Is this the reason you left? Perhaps it is only his ghostprint on every space; I open closets expecting dissected bones to fall out. I superimpose my own flesh over them and stuff them back. *Yet my husband and I take a certain pride in being here. We mirror you. Your last published volume* Work for This Age *we have pored over through many a desperate day and night. Consider our delight, upon arriving, in finding one entire wall of our (your) study papered with jackets of this book in all its various editions. I am happy to know the Japanese, the Germans—even the Sudanese—are into your work. The ironic double thrust of your life assails us each time we pass . . .*

I put the letter aside. A Critick does not require such spelling out. What I have not said he will read into me.

My husband worries. Stands, rocking in Gore's slippers, beholding the swollen rooms. "How I envy this man!" My husband knows that, for myself, I envy him. I would consume my selfsame space but for his affection which storms all barricades.

Pastoral Scenes, Private Lives

We walk a pine trail, needless to say, one of many. Past meadows set with clover and dandelion, past dozing trees and chirping birds. We jump clay-bottom streams. Were Jessie with me we might sit for a spell, constructing clay castles, letting the clay squish between our toes. At the least we would pause to wet our feet, holding our skirts high. Laughing, splashing each other and ourselves.

"If my students saw me like this," she'd say, "how pleased they'd be. They'd not have to listen to me anymore."

"They love you."

"I fascinate them, yes."

Jessie: who is without grace but whose dignity was such that she needed none. I listen for a chorus, *Jessie is dead*, but it is only my own shallow breathing and the sway of trees.

My husband hurries. He has much to do. He is intent on pacing off the land—he would know how many acres we have here, what curious number of feet the Critick's land spreads south, east, north and west. Where and what the boundaries are. I pace along after him, stepping over brush, over fallen limbs, up hill and down hill, through thickets too tight for him. I mark saplings, dead trunks, trees my arms cannot gird, with yellow cloth. He does not rest and I drive behind or away from him, trying not to distract his single-mindedness by breathing hard.

I see no sense to this but cannot deny him the pleasure he has found.

It does not occur to him that I may tire.

"The Black Hills," he says, "—over there." I follow his uplifted arm to contemplate pale gray rims unmolested by the closing sky. "And over there." Obscured, they rise again. The Black Hills encircle us. "See that fence? In the Newgate style, named after an early Virginia settler." Gray poles between gray prongs. When I jostle them the poles crumble where they touch earth. The mulch bugs run about, perplexed. "The boundary lies along here. That trunk—see the wire cut deep into it! Growing long after it was presumed dead—that trunk marks the boundary turn. Of course, it was a healthy living tree when the line was first walked off."

I nod in a convincing way, vaguely comprehending what he means. He laughs at me but is undeterred. "What a piece of property this is! Yet I can't find where the south side ends. It seems to stretch on past that grove of poplars we saw."

"The stream," I say, to show I am listening, to cloak my boredom that is beginning to perplex him "—was that the eastern boundary?"

"No," he says, "you're turned around. The *east* boundary was about a mile back that way. Along that ravine you couldn't climb. Remember?"

"Yes, of course, I do now."

Water—springs of clear water icy to my fingertips— abounds. I scoop palmfuls up and munch at them with my lips like a cow chewing grass.

"And the thing you called a stream is in actual fact the river you crossed in getting here."

I don't believe him. I know sometimes he lies, injects deliberate tests to determine where I draw the line between the fanciful and the true. That river was a hundred yards wide and could be found on any map.

We have brought lunch and eat under the trees.

The wooden fences that have fallen down seem mystic in my view. The land goes where it goes. But my husband is computing figures, scoring timber stands, diagraming the lay

of the land with a sweeping elemental hand, even as he chews
this ham and drinks this lemonade. Men are different, that is
all. They must know these things before they can be content.
Before he can touch my arm and say it is beautiful here.

Squirrels squawk at us, leaping limb to limb.

"What do they want?" I ask him.

"Pizza," he replies. "A cold beer."

I do not ask if he wants—would prefer—these things himself. It is enough to concede that I would prefer them too. We
are together, my husband and I. We want whatever the other
does not know he has.

Afterwards, we lie back on the grass, cushioning our heads
with our hands, and I do not mind that I have ruined my
shoes. And my dress. That my legs burn as though a switch has
been taken to them. That ants crawl over my still hand.

"He's kept the land in primitive state, the Critick has," my
husband says, "I'll say that much for him."

"It is not to his credit," I argue, "since that is how it came."

"He found it—which is the same as pointing out that it was
here."

"It takes no special courage to do this."

"True," he says. But we go on arguing anyhow.

We find our way back along devious routes that dead-end,
no openings in the sky save through trees whose high leaves
spin like a child's whirling top. He waits up for me, takes my
arm.

"Your friend Jessie," he says, "would have liked it here."

I say nothing.

ે◆ ે◆ ે◆

I am thinking of the time some far-time back when Jessie
and I were walking the Great Trail, by which I mean the
Appalachian one.

"Great as this is," Jessie said, "I feel the need for a detour."
Five hours before, we had passed another party, hiking south-

west to our northeast. Their appearance had gladdened—and
saddened—us, but after a parliamentary exchange of warnings
and good will the sadness had won. We ventured off the trail
and eventually, as had been our expectation, accepted that
now we were lost, without any idea of how to find our way
again.

"But we have food, and water is no problem and for shelter
we can use this moss, these limbs. Effect lean-tos, perhaps
grow old here."

We had wandered into a rain forest. We passed the night
on dry moss and dry moss sheltered us from the wind. And
though we shivered, though we would sleep but with spurts
startling in their brevity—all the same we regretted nothing.
Intermittent through the night Jessie alerting herself, iden-
tifying sound:

"What is that? Do you hear it?"

"Croakers. The nights-are-for-lovemaking kind."

Yet when the rain came that was the one sound she could
not identify—a faint rustling whir, a hum—and then over us
like a sleeve, the green drowning fall of it. And we stumbled
on, wet as elves, drenched as the leaves. Heroic times! Two
women alone, with resources the equal of any males'.

"If we had to we could! Think of Pioneering Wife! We can
pull the plow, turn the earth. If we had to. We can damn well
tread this rain forest by ourselves."

"She would have liked it here."

I study his face for irony; can find just loyalty there.

Night-time Practices, Every-day Ordeals

FRAGMENT 1, DREAM 1:
I am seated on a couch.
I am being interviewed.
The doctor tells me

I may smoke if I wish.
   Yes? Go ahead, please.
I am downtown.
I am in a hotel window,
very high up. The twelfth floor,
I believe.
Yes, the twelfth floor.
I am prepared to jump.
I think of something Jung said:
When you go, take your left breast with you.
Not Jung. No,
it was Theodor Reik.
Giving advice to a ballerina.
Someone entered, cleared his throat. We are tearing down
   this entire area, he said.
   Tear it down?
You will have to move to another place, he said.
   Move?
This building is condemned, he said.
   Yes. Go ahead.
We will help you, if you wish. We will relocate you, if you
   wish. If you will enter your name on our files. We promise
   nothing, of course: but we try.

I have these dreams. How do I interpret them? Dreams? The
trick is to let them interpret you. I must go back and approach
my life from that point of view.

*Serene. How tranquil here. The grandeur! How I will hate it—
hate my husband, myself, this place!—when Gore returns.*

My husband enters, bearing lemonade in a silver jug. He
hesitates. Smiles. Remarks that I look cool here in the window
in my sheer black negligee, with the wind on my shoulders
and my feet propped on the sill.

11/1/46   I am at home. I am a child. My eyes are huge with all they see. Nothing I see has any end to it. We cover flower beds, my mother and I. My father shaves. The flowers grow. We haul away dead trees, my mother and I. They are everywhere. Where did the flowers go? My mother's Zen friend is here. Shake the trunk, he tells us, and let the branches go. My mother shakes the trunk. My father shaves. Ten thousand apples fall. Make a pie, my mother says. I gather apples. I pick them from the ground. They continue to fall. Her own apron fills. The huge pie bakes in an oven larger than this space I hold. We eat, Tom* and I.** The plate*** never empties. I cry out: *please! please! please!*

The apples fall.

Yes, I do feel cool. The lemonade is very dear.

My husband stands behind me, bent at the waist, peering forth. "This window has no elevation," he says. "A man hidden in those bushes could see everything in this room. We're sitting ducks for a voyeur's broom."

I nod; he goes. Of all, the suicide is least alone. Space commands, space is compelling: Occupy *me!*

I went to Chapel Hill, pursuing a Ph.D. Following Dobbleman from Tulane after the attempt there to murder everyone. From Oaxaca came a postcard from my husband, then enjoying his status as distant friend. Not at that time my husband, I mean. A photograph with rounded edges of two people on the back of a single horse in some central plaza there. The horse rearing on his hind legs out of which the pedestal grew. A terse caption typewritten on the rear: ZAPATA AND FRIEND. I looked more closely. The forward figure was

---

    * A fictitious name?
   ** Yes, and the fictitious me.
  *** But the plate, I say, is very real.

Zapata to be sure—but behind him, her arms outflung, dour-looking beneath her wide brim, Jessie rode, her heels wide as though she had that moment stung the animal with her spurs. "It's in all the shops," a later letter explained. "A companion of hers—Max—had them printed up. I would have bought more but I like to think the idea will spread."

Now Jessie rides no more. I have lost the one picture in which once she did. After many years hunting for it, have at last given it up as lost. Have lost Max too who had it done. But I won my husband who came home at summer's end, took me to an expensive restaurant, and casually suggested I marry him.

"If you can take an old man with one leg, with jaundiced skin, glass eye and glass chin. A *mal hombre* with no ideas in his head."

"So long as you go on giving me presents like the last. So long as you promise to sleep with me, *venir de malas*, each evening of the year."

"Good," he said, "it's settled then. I reckoned you were a sucker for a fancy restaurant."

I went with him home and eventually we did sleep.

"I guess you had heard I was a good lay."

"Promiscuous," he said. "Marriage will change all that."

It had seemed romantic then.

And what had I reckoned or what have I reckoned since? That he is better than previous men in my life had given me any reason to expect? We are both agreed on that.

Predictions and Guarantees

"Pardon me, I noticed someone had moved in." The lamp-shaded ghost of J. Edgar is at the door. Speaking in official voice: "You're friends of Gore?" Octoroon trousers milk her heavy rear, a gardener's tunic squares her breasts. Her jowls mix like apple pie but her eyes have a dangerous glint. She removes the enormous sun hat and dust motes dance above her thinning scalp. "Friends of Gore?" she barks.

"Like long-lost brothers," my husband replies.

"Said nothing to me about guests." A brusque, efficient style: one tutored to wreak havoc wherever she goes.

"A last minute affair," replies my husband to her piqued, vengeful face. "No time to call reporters in."

"Said nothing to me."

Held to the open doorway, barred at every turn, she stood finally on tiptoe to look about. Had we disturbed anything? Were there others too? She distrusted us, that much she made clear.

"Nice bonnet," my husband said, "you have there."

It was beneath her to consider this. Still, a gleam was manifest where glint had been: the early-aggressive, the late-cautious kind.

"Celebrated?"

My husband looked to me but what help am I?

"Pardon me?"

"Pardon me," she said, giving the words a nasty turn "—I suppose you're celebrated too!"

"Like Gore, you mean? Or perhaps you're . . ."

Famous too, he was about to say. But her lips folded over, she spat saliva, we saw her coated tongue. "Live down the road," she said, as if that summed her up, was sufficient to convey her threat.

"Oh, where?" he asked, and stepped outside to have the place pointed out. She strode past him, walked in. Counted Gore's furniture, his knickknacks, at close range.

"Relatives, you say?"

My husband returned, placed an arm around my waist, turned on his smile. The charm of a cornered man. "Like brother and sister. From the day we were born until the day we die. That Gore! A fantastic man, don't you think?"

"Not her," she said, measuring me. Studying first my face and then my figure which obviously disgusted her. "Not his eyes!" Her own eyes needed attention. Needed draining. Coagulating liquid, dark as nicotine. She saw me staring and placed her bonnet on.

"All the same," she said.

"Yes?"

"Said nothing to me about the premises being occupied. Empty, he said. Wanted it that way."

"Sit down, sit down," my husband said, relenting, shouldering her to the privileged chair. "You've got troubles, I can see that." Forced a pillow at her back. And winking at me, strolled to the Critick's desk, there whipping out the supposed address of Gore in Rome.

"Write him, you'll see. We have nothing to hide."

She sat uncomfortable, too deep within the chair, palms upturned on her lap. "Said nothing to me about Rome."

"Ah! He wanted to confide but a Critick can't be too careful, you know that! Young guns out to shoot him down, old guns out to blow him up. Mercenaries everywhere! A sniper in every tree! With a man of Gore's stature Caesar's story is told every day. Where can he go? To Rome. On the Q.T."

"Same mouth," she said.

"What?"

"Got his mouth. Hadn't seen that before. Got his way of standing too. What else you got?" She wrenched the pillow free, set it on the floor. Placed her feet on it. And stroked her thighs. The bonnet hid all but the tip of her nose and a drooling chin.

"What I got? If I got it it's more than I had. What did you have in mind?"

"Five dollars," she said, "unless you got more."

"This settles it," I said, and promptly left the room. Was in weeping on Gore's spongy bed when my husband entered to search his trousers for change, to get the Kennedy half-dollars if he could. "She's bad wash," I said, "I can't take her anymore. I wonder if she leaks at the bottom too."

"Check the carpets," he said. "You'll warm to her, you'll see."

"I see five dollars we can't spare."

"You sound like Gore," he said, intending to be severe. "Gore dismissing everything he doesn't understand and mis-understanding everything he supports. Get on with you."

I bit my lips and tested for blood. Blood there was but not where he could see. He whacked my backside, his diplomatic touch, and went.

To feed her biscuits, to ply her with buttermilk. To give her pickings from the garden and a round of butter claimed as homemade.

"Tastes like mine," she said.

"Ah, but I bet yours is homemade too."

She wouldn't commit herself. He elevated her fat ankles to the brocaded velvet stool while she looked on content, accepting this as well. "Swollen, I see. Perhaps you're pregnant, dear." Her laughter had the snarl of a wounded dog. "I can see why," he said, and the snarls were unleashed again.

In the end he had her house pointed out to him—though it was not where anyone could see, or likely would care to find.

"You and the faint-headed one come calling," she told him. "Down the road a piece."

I was up to meet him as he came in. "What's happened to you?" I asked.

"Gore's house," he said. "It's mine, you see."

It isn't yours, he means. Your youth is finished but old times continue closing in.

FRAGMENT 2, DREAM 1: I sit on a wall saying this wretched me. A woman walks by. It is Jessie and I follow her home. We never arrive though the house we stop at has four walls without a floor. When morning comes she is still knocking at a door that has been open all the while. I am at the window saying "Jessie, is this the one you would jump from?"

"*Venir de malas*," I say, "do you remember that?"

He spreads butter, spreads marmalade, slices my bread. Circles the table and sets it in front of me. Circles and butters his own. Though he's sitting now the circles go on.

"*De malas* indeed," he says. "Evil intentions pursue each trail. But I wouldn't call it sickness, would you?"

"When was it that you last slept with me?"

"Last night," he says. "This morning too. And once during the night when you kicked the covers free."

"What does that mean?"

"It means I slept with you all the time you were there."

"Perhaps you could get me a glass of cold buttermilk," I say, "I've got fat ankles too."

His face reflects concern. He reaches across the table and touches my hand. "Bad dreams?" he asks. I shake my head. Or is it my head shaking me? "Jessie, then?" I shake it again, pushing the toast aside. He gives me his wedding hand. "I'll help you if I can. I'll replace your Kennedy coins if that will give you your gladness back."

"That doesn't matter," I say. Though it was Jessie who gave them to me. She had said: It's Kennedy all right. But still the same old bread.

"*Venir de malas*," I say, though I don't mean for him to hear.

"How's that again?" He has pushed his own toast aside now. Sits slumped, fingering his coffee spoon. He loves coffee but this morning has yet to taste it once.

"What did you mean," I ask, "that time from Oaxaca when you said you hoped the idea would spread?"

"I don't know. From Oaxaca? That was a long time back."

I am not cut out for riding. My thighs are rubbed raw, my rear end aches. My neck is stiff with sitting high. ZA-PA-TAAAZA-PA-TAAA! It is Jessie screaming his name. He sweeps her up at dead run, swings her behind him. On the rim of a gray hill the stallion neighs. My own slow donkey grazes mud.

&❧ &❧ &❧

My husband enters the house at noon. He is grimy and sweaty and empties soil from his shoes at the door. He has been working at a garden the Critick's hired men no longer tend. Two rings of dirt circle his neck, and his nails which turn into my arms are black. I press myself to him and pray that he will press back.

"Weird morning," I say, "the wrong side of the bed."

"Say no more," he says, and leaves me when I let him to look into the pot.

"It's homemade," I say, and he smiles back.

"Probably tastes it, too."

FRAGMENT 3, DREAM 1: The subject is peas.

"I can never eat without remembering my childhood when they made me eat peas. They would cram my mouth full and clamp their hands over my jaws."

"The one thing," he says, "they didn't want to save for the starving children in China. Reminds me of Gore's *Work for This Age*."

I admit to him that I had not quite viewed it that way.

We have dessert in the Critick's study with the jacket-lined wall.

My husband turns formal, which is sometimes his way.

"I've been hesitating to mention this," he says, "but the choices have all scattered now." His look is doleful and I don't know what to say. He spoons his strawberries and tells me again they are good. Whipped the cream yourself?

I tell him I did.

"I hate funerals," he sighs. "I know you can accept that. I sat through every minute of Kennedy's and King's and then again Robert's too. Did you? Well, you know what it's like. After a while it got so the box seemed to be on but no one was there—everyone was out looking for the grief that the rage wouldn't have. Showing, I guess, that the bottom of grief and the top of the world occupy the same geographic shelf— from such levels you don't see anything anymore. Anyway, it's put me off funerals for a while. I don't want to think there will ever be another one I can't miss." He pauses, closes his lips over a spoonful of pure cream. He doesn't swallow so much as allow it to trickle down. It's thick cream and takes some time. "Reminds me of the good old days," he claims. "Got your milk and your cream in the same jug." He leans over, lays a small puff of cream on my nose.

"I got a long tongue," I say, "but it never was that long." My voice is high and I am aware of a cool sweating under my arms. He reaches again, takes the cream on his finger and puts the finger in his mouth. I close my eyes, fearing a magician's stunt: when he removes his hand the finger will be gone.

"If I could do that at a funeral," he says, "I'd be the first one there."

I can feel the shifts in my chair. I know it is the chair moving me. "What is this getting at?" I ask. "I know Jessie died well over a week ago."

"No," he says. "—No." And, rising, goes to the window as if he believes I will accept it is the sight of clouds or the sway of trees that draws him there. "No, that's by Gore's time, not ours. It hardly seems worthwhile to mention that she died this or that day or even that she ever did. But I do know the funeral is today."

Berry juice colors the cream, which is thinning now. Berries emerge in the dish like small pink bodies shorn of their limbs and heads.

"I should go but you can't? Is that what you're saying?"

"Given the choice," he says. "Given the choice, if that's ever what the choice is, I'd opt to admire swollen ankles or to massage the fat feet of that woman down the road a piece. But that's not my choice today. I've got my address at the Wilderness Club to give."

"You've prepared a speech?"

"Let's just say I'm prepared."

ও ও ও

8/1/73   It is Henry's hand now on my arm. I am dressed in black though not everyone is.

"We were hoping you would come. We were up late last night waiting for you to get in."

The sun is hot, the air is yellowish and splits as we move. Here in Chapel Hill it is the worst of the day.

"I've been thinking of her," I find myself saying, "I guess you know that." I look about for Henry but they are all waiting by the cars and I am alone at her grave.

ও ও ও

He has never asked What was she to you? Has never mentioned that we all acquired her from him. Nor yet demanded Whose friendship served her best.

The truck mutters through the night. My thoughts are of Max and he is silent at the wheel, driving me to the first direct connection where agents have promised yes they have a bus that will take me where I am going. And though Max is gallant and kind, though he was her good friend and once was mine, where I am going is where I would be. The truck has an out-spoken shimmy, there is a nagging *whump* in one of the tires. Headlamps are crookedly set, illuminating less the highway and more the red-dirt shoulder which we rattle onto now and again. For Max claims the front wheels suffer strange align-ment as well, and as for that, we have not had the courage, since it occurred to us, to determine whether our plates are valid for the trip.

So we mutter on through the night, the truck, Max and I, each of us primed here, purloined for the hour, entrusted to Jessie's care as if she could receive us now. It is or was her truck and this is the transportation we would have.

"I don't intend to pry," says Max tentatively, "but is it Gore, or your husband, that's at Gore's place now?"

I turn to look and catch his eye and we are both surprised. I see his hands tighten on the wheel, fighting the road.

"You remembering," I ask, "how I was, or how I wasn't?"

"It would be more to the point," he replies, "to say I'm trying to determine how you are."

I say, "Max, I'm fine, how are you?"

And he slows down and thinks about it for a mile or two and then replies that so far as he knows he's doing better than he was. "Now," he adds, "that there's no more catching up to do."

After an hour or more we arrive at my terminal and Max pulls into a taxi zone. "Since that's what we have here." He yanks on the emergency and it comes free in his hand. He passes it to me for a souvenir. "Twenty years ago," he says, "Jessie and I drove this same truck west. Speaking for myself, I started off young but by the time I set eyes on the Pacific I was a full-grown man. It wasn't so much what we saw as what saw us."

"Here's seeing you, then."

We shook hands and he saw me to the bus.

Work for This Age

An old man in a wagon picks me up as I am walking along the side of the road. He has no eyes for me, nor yet a how-do-you-do, but as he waits for me to climb aboard and root a place out among his bags of manure, he maintains a steady scrutiny of the emergency handle, as though to suggest he'd find a use for that somehow.

"Been traveling long? On foot, I mean."

"Since the bus turned left," I say, "back there a spell."

"Far piece for a girl with iron in her hand."

As we take the turn down Gore's lane we have to wait for another wagon to pass out.

"Brisk business this morning, eh, Tom?"

"Had me a fella," the second driver said. "Talked off my ears. What you got there?"

"Mine's quiet as a kitten but she's got iron in her hand. I wouldn't want to cross her none."

I leave them talking out of pause that threatens to claim all speech, standing with legs spread wide and stiff, a light hand on the reins of their beasts inching this way and that, their wagons perched at enduring angles, abreast, on the narrow lane. "Yes sir," I hear mine say, "had iron in her hand. Come to the crossing to the low ground in shoes I reckon she can see through now."

True, the shoes are ruined but I am happy to be rid of them. *I am happy—I am?* . . . the phrase turns upon itself, would take an accounting now. But I am tired and want to sleep and I slide in bed beside my husband who himself slides the way his arms hold me best.

FRAGMENT 4, DREAM 1: One by one the apples fall. So slowly I can sketch their red skins as they come down. A man with a butterfly net is in a green field collecting them. The net

fills and he empties it into the apron I hold for him. The tree
—all the trees—disappear.

I wake alone in bed. What time is it? I go to the window and
can see by the sun that it is afternoon but not whether it is
early or late. Though I can tell it is cool and private here and
there are real apples on the trees. I am about to go find Harry
when I see him clearly some distance down, spread-eagled on
the grass. And now on his knees moving fast. Into the ring of
laurel that serves as last fortress for this house. He wheels
about—spots me here. His hand chops at and flattens the air.
He mouths a message for me: *Get down, get down!* I hasten
to drop down. When next I look up he is on his stomach,
using his elbows to squirm towards another obstruction he
has found. And now he's up, running hard for this room.

"What's up?" I whisper. "Who is here?"

He speaks with such hoarseness it startles even him. "Gore:
He's back. Pawing around out there to find . . . I don't know
what. He's had binoculars on us since I waked."

Original Sin

Gore is back though he isn't here. Though it's still his wash—
graying now—on the basement line. He looked and waited—
perhaps walked his boundary lines—but never came to the
door. Never came in. Never claimed his car or sent men to
chock up its wheels. He lives in the city—has taken and fur-
nished an apartment there. They say he's writing a new
treatise, sequel to his *Work* . . . but we wouldn't know: we
never hear from him.

MAMA TUDDI
DONE OVER

*Y*ou have heard about Mama Tuddi. If you got eyes and ears or a brain in your head then you know that Mama Tuddi is a big celebrity, that she have her own show. The Mama Tuddi Show on TV and radio where she sell soft drinks by the bottle and the crate, especially on TV where everyone know what she look like and how much she enjoy her work. On this day I am talking about, Mama Tuddi arrives at the doorstep of the house where Reno Brown have lived his life and said goodbye to it and there she pause and take a deep breath and think a final time about what it is she have to do. It is not right, that is what she think, but it is too late now to talk anybody out of it. Her sponsor have told her it is the right thing to do, she owe it to the public, that it is maybe in bad taste, a little on the obscene side, but it is good public relations all the same.

So she knocks on the door and waits. Somebody will come soon for sure because everybody must know it is Mama Tuddi at the door and she don't have all day, she got more important business elsewhere and she only have a little time to devote to the public service the Brown family and relatives and friends have ask for and apparently expect.

She is thirsty, Mama Tuddi is, waiting in the sun, and she wish she have swallowed down a soda pop or two before she start out on this job. Also it happen this afternoon that her teeth ache. She have time for this nonsense, but no, she have no time for her health, no one care if she ever find a minute to go to Dr. Pome and get her bad tooth knocked out. That is what Mama Tuddi think as she fidget at the door, how selfish everybody is. So this put her in a worse mood and she stand there beating on the door, grumbling to herself that it ain't right, all the time impatient for someone to come roll out the red carpet, give her the official greeting she expect.

But they don't come, it is like everybody inside—not just Reno—is dead.

Finally she say to herself *I be damned if I'm going to wait out here all day in the boiling sunshine,* and kick open the door and stride right in.

"Yoo-hoo!" she call, "Mama Tuddi have come!" But the room is empty, not a sound anywhere.

But she knows she have the right address. Looking around, the first thing Mama Tuddi notice is that all the mirrors are turn to the walls, all the pictures on the walls and tables have a black cloth draped over them, all except the face of Jesus who is looking at her. She don't mind the look, it seem to her natural that Jesus is going to look over anyone who walk into the room and that he especially will want to take a long hard look at someone famous as Mama Tuddi. She even give him a little nod and a smile. It occur to her for her next show that maybe she can have a big picture of Jesus at The Last Supper and the sponsor can hire a man to paint in a picture of Double Ola in front of all the apostles at the table. That way, it seem to her, her work is done before she speak a single word. So the look of Jesus give pleasure to Mama Tuddi, it seem to her he have the same idea.

However, the black cloth hanging everywhere and the mirrors turn to the wall, that is another story. They send a shiver up Mama Tuddi's spine. It seem to her a tacky thing to do, what you'd expect from ignorant folks but not from anyone in the Mama Tuddi Fan Club. Not from anyone who like the Mama Tuddi Show. She hate it, that is what Mama Tuddi think to herself. She have a good mind to sail on out the door and never come back.

Still no one come and Mama Tuddi don't know what to do with herself.

It remind her of her early days in the Green Room when she was waiting to go on after the weatherman, a long time ago before she make a name for herself.

"Tooth, be quiet," she say to her tooth, but it go right on aching.

Mama Tuddi opens up her purse and takes out the aspirin bottle and she pick out a pill and put the top back on and goes to one of the mirrors on the wall which she take off the hook and turn around so she can see herself. Then she puts the mirror back up on the hook again. She hold her face real close so she can see inside her mouth. It is hard to tell which tooth hurt, so she does the best she can. She push the tablet down beside the most guilty-looking tooth, then she close her mouth to see what kind of bump the tablet make in her jaw.

"It look all right," she say to herself, "nobody notice a thing."

"I be as good as new," she say, "soon as that pill dissolve."

Already she can feel the medicine flowing round her gum. It is on the sour side, but Mama Tuddi don't mind pills, she think it taste pretty good. She puts the aspirin bottle back in her purse and gets out the lipstick tube. Again she hold her face up close to the mirror, she scrunch up her nose and shape her mouth and paint on the red paint and licks her lips and backs up to look at herself. By now she is feeling pretty good, Reno Brown is the last thing on her mind. Her only regret is

that in the rush to get here, the Double Ola man pushing and
pulling her every which way she turn, she have not had time to
black out her two front teeth which is how she always look on
the Mama Tuddi Show and which is what her public have
come to expect. She always feel much better when she know
she have done all she can to please her public, when she spare
not one iota of herself. It is proof to her mind of the kind of
world we are living in and how bad things have got that the
station people and the Double Ola man have not give her time
to black out her front teeth, a Mama Tuddi trademark known
far and wide. Be just as bad, she thinks, if she show up at the
studio without her special Double Ola shoes or if she forget to
put on her hat or get out her checkbook when she talk about
the money a family save when they buy Double Ola by the
case.

A smell was bothering Mama Tuddi, something in the air.
She had got a whiff of it first coming in, but now it was heavier
and if Mama Tuddi had a spray she would use it right here,
she thought, her house or not. She liked a house where folks
were not stingy on the spray, and she was beginning to have
some second thoughts about these Brown folks and whether
they were the right kind of people, the kind to appreciate a
personal appearance from Mama Tuddi and know how much
she was putting herself out for them, never mind their ignor-
ance of how to run a clean, happy home.

Things were dusted, she could say that much for them.

And arranged nice, if you was to shove this studio couch
back against the wall.

Mama Tuddi pulled the black cloth off a pair of bronze
baby shoes resting atop a pile of maple leaves also in bronze.
She poked her finger inside one and brought out a shriveled
up spider which she flung with a gasp to the floor. Beside the
shoes, under another cloth, was a picture of a boy with a flat
nose and curls of tight black hair growing low over his forehead. He was spruced up smart in a Ben Blue short pants suit

and to Mama Tuddi's mind he would have been a real heart-
breaker but for his smart-alecky expression, which his mama
ought to have smacked off his face before she let him step up
to the camera. He had broomstick legs too and his socks was
bunched up at his heels, what part hadn't been eat up by his
shoes.

She wondered if this was the Reno Brown who had loved
her so much.

She heard a giggle behind her and turned in time to see the
same face jumped out of the picture frame to poke itself out
at her from the doorway across the room. Mama Tuddi waved
the picture at him, about to say "Well, your nose have improve!" but before she could get it out the boy's teeth flashed
white and he have vaporized.

A minute later the whole back part of the house seem to
blow up and people, men mostly, men in blue seersucker suits
and men in nice sport jackets all yellows and blues, in stripes
and in pinwheels like targets to be shooting at, were springing
at Mama Tuddi from every side, their faces plastered with the
biggest grins, running around her like a pack of dogs let loose
suddenly from whatever was fencing them in, shouting out
their welcomes to her, reaching for and shaking and then
letting another of these creatures take her hand. Before Mama
Tuddi know it she have been shove back against the wall, her
breath all sucked out of her from so many faces to say "How
you do?" to the way a lady would, with the dignity an enter-
tainer of her standing have to maintain—but still they are
coming, more men folks thrusting out their hands, beaming
down on her, saying what an honor it is, while the few women
who crowd in, as dowdy uninteresting females as Mama Tuddi
have ever seen together under one roof, mill around the edge
casting glances back and forth and smiling quick polite smiles
when Mama Tuddi let her eyes light on them.

"Now listen here," Mama Tuddi find herself saying once

the gentlemen have done pawing at her, "what is that smell I smell?"—which someone say is cabbage, just pot luck, nothing special, only something the women folk have been cooking up for after the service. Mama Tuddi is about to inform them how a can of good spray can cut through a smell like sand stifling a fire when it strikes her that a man is standing over by the mirror she have turn around, just standing there with his mouth dropped open and a look of horror on his face. So Mama Tuddi forgets about the spray, the man with the open mouth have reminded her and she say, "Listen here, how come all these mirrors are turn and all the wall pictures except Jesus covered with this black cheesecloth double-folded over them like that, I never see the like of it to this day?" Everyone's look is blank followed by surprise, then they begin at once to jabber their response, saying, "Sho-nuff, Mama Tuddi, you pulling a laig, don't you know what they is thataway faw?" or some such variation, while all through this time the struck-dumb man is staring from the mirror to Mama Tuddi as if he think his very life or hers is in peril.

"No, I do not," Mama Tuddi say, keeping her eyes off him for she is beginning to think may be she have done something wrong judging by the few gasps she see, wishing these boisterous people would take her on in to see the dead boy so that she can get on back to the station for her evening broadcast and her TV Mama Tuddi Show which have an audience growing by leaps and bounds and which she have her duty to keep informed and entertained.

"Mama Tuddi," they say, "why Mama Tuddi, how you do be a cutup, what a rascal, here pretending you don't know why they is thataway faw!"—poking each other in the ribs and swarming around her like they have lost the little mind they have. The man with the open mouth have put the mirror face-away back on the wall, and now he is bearing down on her, his face set like he is face to face with death. "Why, don't you

know, Mama Tuddi, whoever see hisself in the glass a time
like this don't you know the devil take his soul, Mama Tuddi,
we surprised at you!"

"Hogwash," Mama Tuddi say once she find her voice.
Someone is pushing behind Mama Tuddi and a little child is
down between her legs trying to crawl through after another
one on the floor. She want to kick both of them and tell the
man behind her to get his hands off her, but before she can
someone else have take her arm while another person shove
in front and swing open the door so it seem to her finally that
they are ready to get on with what they have ask her for; in
some way-off part of the house she can hear a tin can piana
making feeble notes of reverence. Mama Tuddi have a rush of
mixed thought, not wanting to go in to see the laid-out body
of Reno Brown she presume, not wanting to look on anybody
dead, not even if he have love her like a mother, which is what
the program manager and the Double Ola man have told her
when they say she have to come here for the public service of
the thing. Mama Tuddi's hands and feet in fact have gone
cold, her legs are stiff and in fact she would not be moving at
all but for the elbow pushing her in the back. Her throat have
gone dry too for want of a soda pop or even a drink of water
now that she think of it. She lick her tongue over the two front
teeth which ought to been blacked out because that is the
Mama Tuddi trademark, though she glad these people recognize her all the same. She glad at least she have remembered
to wrap the fox tail around her neck, never that she have yet
gone a place without it. She crane her head round to catch
sight of Reno Brown or to see where the music is coming
from and what kind of creature must be propped up on the
stool playing it so bad with his bony fingers that have no
weight on the keys. She can see nothing but the sway of
shoulders and backs and ugly-women faces turning to study
her as she enter through the held-open door and move slowly
down the aisle that is being cleared for her. Now some wretch

can't control himself and he catch at her arm. Without looking Mama Tuddi smack out at his hand, she struggle to go
on, but he have arms like an octopus, he catch her again. Turn
out it is the struck-dumb man, now climbing over someone
to root his worried face up close to Mama Tuddi, his eyes lit
up like orange peel, tugging at her to get a firm hold and
spitting his saliva into her ear drum. He is screaming at Mama
Tuddi, she can't tell what because other folks are hugging the
aisle wanting Mama Tuddi to touch them, but Mama Tuddi
know it is not good news he bring. People in her walk of life,
people above the crowd, they have to put up with so much
from the unruly mob, from crazy people in the mob, that
sometime Mama Tuddi rue the day she ever start The Mama
Tuddi Show, she wish she back at home in her rocking chair
maybe dipping a little snuff, talking quiet with neighbors,
seeing the best in people. *It wear her out all this public-service
stuff*, that is what she think as she try her best to sweep on
down the aisle, it plumb tire her out and ain't worth the effort
no how.

"*Pray!*" the man is screeching, "*Pray*, Mama Tuddi, for
you have look in the mirror and Satan himself will run amuck
inside your soul!"

"Shoo!" Mama Tuddi say, "Shoo!"—fanning her arms like
she have walk into a nest of bees. One of the men beside her
says, "Shut your mouth, Rufus, what you want to be upsetting
Mama Tuddi faw?" and another one push the man called
Rufus back while a third person whispers into Mama Tuddi's
ear, "That's Rufus, he got the devil on his brain, don't you
mind Rufus, he just a stupid superstitious type." Mama Tuddi
does not know what to say to this, she hardly know what to
think. Clearly the man have religion, he wearing a nice tie
and is no lazy driftabout, all the same Mama Tuddi think they
be doing everyone a favor they lock this Rufus creature up.
Still, she don't mind, a person in her position have to learn
to take the icing with the cake or they sink back under the

mud. The pain in Mama Tuddi's bad tooth have vanish thanks to the aspirin tablet, her hands and feet are no longer cold and her limbs can function normal now, she have conquered her vexation and is as a matter of fact beginning to be glad she stoop to come, she glad to do these folks a favor, their good friendly feelings and the love they have for Mama Tuddi remind her of the time she first set foot on a naked stage, with hot lights around her and the little red light on the camera she have to look at for the zoom. It remind her of the joy she feel the first time she sit down with a Double Ola on the table and her front teeth blacked in good, and the wonderful way she have scored a big hit with the public who have tune in not even knowing in them days who she was. She got no time now, she tell herself, to be bothering about no trashy Rufus; she in no mood for ignorant superstition, folks will stay ignorant no matter how many times you tell them what's what.

It never cross Mama Tuddi's mind that a crowd this large will be on hand for the service of Reno Brown, she guess it is news of her presence which have bring them out, maybe a hundred or so with not enough chairs to go around, the windowsills full too and everyone squirming for a place to put their knees. She give these onlookers her best smile, her Double Ola smile, which keep the station phone ringing every time she do her show. These folks are all smiling too, whispering, "Dare she is, Dare Mama Tuddi, lookadare, son, Dare she is. Our own Mama Tuddi!"

Mama Tuddi keep her poise, she have a rule never to let cheers go to her head: she walk with the same regal bearing she have learn by heart at the Poise Clinic she have attended for one day, her head kind of thrown back, her chin stiff and erect, not walking like her legs made of rubber like some tarty women do. Mama Tuddi know she have sex appeal, if you got it flaunt it that is what Mama Tuddi say. Over in a side room Mama Tuddi spots where the music coming from, a piano with a dark oak frame, and playing it is the most skinny

woman Mama Tuddi have ever seen this side of a pickling
jar, though to give the music lady credit she have on a stunning
hat in black layers like a wedding cake, which Mama Tuddi
very much admire. But she got her fox collar and her jewels,
Mama Tuddi ain't worried none. Down near the front row
Mama Tuddi see a man standing, pointing out his arm at her,
shouting, "Lookadare! What I tell you? Mama Tuddi is got
tooths, I tole you she have tooths!" and the man next to him
dig in his pocket and it look to Mama Tuddi like he pass the
first man a dollar bill.

It is at this point that Mama Tuddi observe at the front a
tiny coffin stretched over two sawhorses there. "Is that Reno?"
she ask, and a figure near her nod in a somber voice, "Dat's
old Reno, bless the poor chile's heart," and Mama Tuddi
can't take her eyes off the coffin which thank the Lord have a
lid on it.

Suddenly her escorts touch her elbows, they do a little dip,
and a second later to Mama Tuddi's astonishment they have
fade away.

Suddenly the room fill up with total quiet.

Mama Tuddi licks her lips, she have a mild case of nerves,
wondering if now is the time to do her speech in praise of the
dead boy. That is all she have been told she have to do, maybe
cry a little as she read off the credits for Reno Brown and tell
how he is bound for heaven on the glory train.

Mama Tuddi feel a tug on her skirt but she have her poise
and won't look down.

The music lady play three quiet notes on a new song.

Suddenly a low groan begin in the room:

U*mmmmmmmmmmmmmmmmmm*. . . .

It stretch out on the same key and commence to grow:

U*mmmmmmmmmmmmmmm*MMMMMMMMMMMM. . . .

It hold on for the longest time, then it advance up a note
and swell, it keep on swelling, sending a shiver up Mama
Tuddi's spine.

MMMMMMMMMMMMMMMMMMMMMMMMMM . . .

The floor under Mama Tuddi shake, she got goose bumps on her arm: it the most beautiful singing Mama Tuddi have ever heard, she think for a second God himself is lifting her out of her shoes. MMMMMMMMMMMMMMMMMM. . . . Then the sound just explode out of these folks' popping jaws, it wham into Mama Tuddi most to knock her down, in the split instant before it sweep on past her like a mighty wave:

> Bringing in the sheep
> Bringing in the sheep
> We be here rejoicing
> Bringing in the sheep

Mama Tuddi unhook her fox, she close her mouth, and sit down.

Amen, murmur a soft voice next to Mama Tuddi. Amen. De Lawd is bringing in de sheep, de Lawd is taking Reno home. Then the woman whose voice it is begin to wail, she begin to wail and shriek, and Mama Tuddi hold her mouth tight, she look straight ahead over the coffin lid, correctly figuring in her head that the broken-hearted woman beside her must be the bereft mother of the child. They have give Mama Tuddi the seat of honor but although she think the world of motherhood Mama Tuddi wish they give her another chair.

A few other women join Reno's mother in the tribute to her son, their moans kind of snake around the room, but the grief does not get very far. It seem the outburst have been premature, for one thing Mama Tuddi overhear a remark that the preacher have not yet come, he held up in traffic on the freeway. This cause Mama Tuddi some concern since it have always seem to her that preaching ain't now what it was in her day, that their heads are too big, they ought to take their lesson from her and be on time, that is what she think.

A heavy hand fall on Mama Tuddi's knee, and although she give a little jump of surprise it does not go away. She look down at the man's big hand and slowly turn her head meaning to give the hand's owner a cut of her tongue, it rile her the familiar ways certain men have who are so full of themselves they think they can get away with anything. But she see the man in question have a friendly smile, he have a certain charm to him. "I'se LeRoy," he say teasing-like, fixing on her a half-wink. "You was Reno's favorite to the end." He have nice black hair all straighten-out and smooth on his head, he a handsome man, Mama Tuddi can see, with winning ways, and she hear a small voice inside her head saying *Mama Tuddi you watch out for him.*

For some reason Mama Tuddi gets it in her mind he is Reno Brown's daddy. "Pardon me," she say, "I assume you are the departed boy's father?"

LeRoy just grin. "No'm," he say, "I's the boy friend."

"The boy friend," Mama Tuddi repeat, not knowing what else she can say.

"Of Mrs. Brown," LeRoy explain, leaning forward to poke his head in the direction of Reno's mother on her other side. And Reno's mother come out of her crying spell long enough to look Mama Tuddi in the eye and present her hand, saying, "So please you could come. Me and LeRoy was worried on Reno's account, this mean all the world to him."

"He was a dear little boy, I'm sure," Mama Tuddi say.

"Old Reno," observe LeRoy, "they break the mold when they make him. They throw away the key."

Scrunched up in the seat on the other side of Mrs. Brown, with his hands covering his face and looking out at Mama Tuddi between split fingers, is a small boy. Mrs. Brown smack at his hands, saying, "This here be Reno's twin brother Las-vegas, he the man in the family now." The boy give Mama Tuddi a grin and once more hide his face. Then he wrench around and whisper something in Mrs. Brown's ear.

"He say to tell you he's older," Mrs. Brown informs Mama Tuddi. "He older by three minutes, to tell the truth. You knock me over with a feather when the doctor tells me another one knocking at the gate."

Although Mama Tuddi nod and think to say she never have a child herself and proud of it, her mind is elsewhere. LeRoy's hand have crept up her thigh, it continue to rest there, and Mama Tuddi have her hands full trying to decide what to do with it. He certainly a forward type, she think, and it strange to her that Mrs. Brown don't appear to mind. He a flashy dresser, this LeRoy, he is too young too, and plainly Mrs. Brown have snatched the cradle to get him. Mama Tuddi puzzle to herself how Mrs. Brown have manage to bring this off. She is not an overly smart-looking woman, sorry to say, with not much meat on her bones and none of the *savoir-faire* a man appreciate. She is over the hill, Mama Tuddi would say. And in the wardrobe category she is running a pretty bad race. The black mourning dress is all right, but it have a three-inch hem of fancy lace, which have no place at a funeral. Not to mention black net stockings. At the moment Mrs. Brown have one leg crossed over her knee and she is swinging it pretty good. Also she have something flashing there. Mama Tuddi reach down to scratch her own ankle, wondering what it is. Turn out it is a gold anklet Mrs. Brown have on, with a big moon disc which have inscribed on it the word MINE.

Pretty tacky stuff, Mama Tuddi theorize.

"LeRoy give it to me," the woman now say, leaning close. "He a cutup from the word Go." Then she hook up her dress and show Mama Tuddi her other ankle, which have the word HIS.

Although Mama Tuddi is interested and she nod, she have her mind elsewhere. LeRoy have lifted his hand from her leg and now either a fly landed on her neck or that Romeo have put his hand there. She hope it is his hand. Mama Tuddi have a fear of little fly feet walking all over her neck, getting his dirt and disease everywhere. Now the little feet are walking around, it tickle and tingle until it drive Mama Tuddi almost to distraction. She clamp her knees together and hold her body straight, wondering where it going to walk next. She hears the little boy whine, "Mama, I wants a drink," and "Mama, I wants to go to the bafroom," and "Mama, I'se hongry," and Mama Tuddi wish Mrs. Brown would tell him to hush up. The piano lady starts up another tune, and another woman pass in front of Mama Tuddi, saying back to someone that she think she best go stir up the runnin beans. Mama Tuddi wish all these people would hush up so she could give her attention to the thing on her neck. She no longer think it is LeRoy's hand on her neck because he have both his hands down in front of him looking for "The Old Rugged Cross," which is the song the piano lady is playing. Although the fly have now stopped walking it have not gone away, and Mama Tuddi think standing still is worse than moving because she cannot bear the thought of what the fly might do next. She think to herself that if they kept this place clean they wouldn't have so many flies around here, and it seem to her that was the least they could do since they knew she was coming. Reno Brown may have love her like everybody say, he may have believe the sun and moon rose and set on Mama Tuddi, but there is a limit to what she will put up with, whether from him or somebody else.

The fact is Mama Tuddi have sunk so deep in thought she have failed to observe that the audience is now getting up and filing by the box which hold the remains of Reno Brown, the lid lifted and held up by a red broomstick, the folks who have already had their last look at the boy now crowding around Mrs. Brown to tell her what their last look at Reno have meant to them, telling her that he look so peaceful you would swear he was only sleeping, telling her they never seen him looking so good, he the prettiest child they ever set eyes on, he is safe at rest in the arms of the Lord—hugging her and

patting her hands and sort of being swept along until they
come to Mama Tuddi where they bend their knees and take a
close look at her fox tail with the head of the fox still on it
and at her two front teeth, which they know now is real, and
at her dyed-orange hair and even at her shiny black purse
which have the words Double Ola in big letters on the flap—
then to slouch on by and return to their seats or their standing
place and join in on another verse of "The Old Rugged
Cross," which is the cross Jesus and Reno and everyone in this
room have to wear until they exchange it for a crown.

The song goes on and everybody files by to pay Reno their
last respects. Then the music lady half-lifts from her stool,
she fix a look on Mama Tuddi who is slapping at her neck, she
lets her eyes go bong-bong and roll around in her head, then
she shrug to show her confusion and sit down again to play
"The Old Rugged Cross" all over again in the hope that
Mama Tuddi will stand up and do what's right, that being the
same hope others have, which is why they are beginning to
whisper and shuffle about and wonder aloud why Mama Tuddi
will not pay her last respects to Reno, wondering if maybe she
have something up her sleeve.

Mrs. Brown in the meantime know nothing of this, she is
up by the coffin sobbing and moaning, crying for her dead
child, now and then letting fly a big shriek which go through
the room like a fast curveball which send others down on their
knees weaving and moaning and shrieking back. Mrs. Brown
is telling Reno that Mama Tuddi have come, that old LeRoy
have come, that Lasvegas is standing by, that Reno be happy
to learn all his close friends and loved ones are here paying
their last respects, that the preacher will be here to say a few
kind words soon as his car gets off the freeway jam, that they
are all praying for his soul and never forget him till their dying
day. She is looking up through the ceiling and flailing her arms
to get her message through to heaven, reminding the Lord to
look after His humble servant Reno, her poor beloved son

Reno, to place a chair for Reno close-by to God's own chair,
to watch over his growth the way a mama would because she
know in her heart Reno would have make something of hisself
if he had the chance, a nice bright boy like Reno who didn't
have a hurtful bone in his body, a believer who commit his
heart to Jesus on the very day he was born, who turn a helping
hand to his mama anytime she ask and who love his daddy
and treat him with respect even if his daddy was a sorry worth-
less no-count snake who never walk God's road a day in his
life, that worm who also gone to his reward praise be to God,
taken away by the Grim Reaper and none too soon if God
want to know the sorry truth of the case. His daddy burning
in hell where he ought to be, Mrs. Brown cry out, but her
precious lamb Reno he will walk right out of the valley of
death into the stretched-out arms of Jesus, GLORY GLORY, to
ride around heaven in the golden chariot God have carved out
of ebony bone for all the innocent children of the world.
"GLORY GLORY!" she say, "LIVE AGAIN!"

"Thine the glory!" come the chorus behind Mrs. Brown;
"Hallelujah Amen!" the chorus shout, now drumming their
feet on the floor in a quick rhythm that makes the whole
building shake, that cause the sawhorses on which Reno's
coffin repose to quiver and bounce as if old Reno himself want
to climb out and show these folks how grateful he is, to show
them the power of God's love, that His power have no end,
that God Himself climbed down on Jacob's ladder from
heaven to show He approve, to show the poor people's welfare
is ever close to His heart. Mrs. Brown now have a grip on the
coffin, her head momentarily disappear as she stoop down to
give her boy one final kiss on his sorrowful closed eyes, now
emerging with tears streaming down her ravaged face, her
body twisting about, her mouth opening and closing though
silence have the day, her feet lifting and lifting as if she have
set them down in a bed of burning coal, while her friends in
the audience look on with half-envy, with their hearts caught

up in their throats, for it plain to them that Mrs. Brown is
now in the rapture of God's strong embrace, that God Himself
have taken hold of her tongue, that He have come to claim
this hour for His own. And they is proud in fact that this have
happen, for in no other way can it be explain why this
innocent boy have been plucked away in his tender years, poor
Reno who have never done no harm to no one, as nice a boy
as you ever hope to see, with always a kind word for the old
and the lame and the sick, who give his last dime to any
stranger ask it of him. This is why they have come in the first
place, it is why they are thumping their feet so hard against
this floor, and clapping their hands, and twisting about themselves, and aiding Mrs. Brown with their shouts as best they
can—all to urge God on, to argue Him into showing His face
or showing His presence with a sign like He have give to
Moses with the burning bush, or to them with their tents
pitched by the Red Sea. If you love God He will not let you
down, that is what they think and know and believe, and they
have not doubted He will show up today because God have
plucked out of a mother's arms an innocent child and even
God would not do this without some good excuse, He have a
reason for it just as He have a reason for the sun and moon
and for resting on the seventh day. God's power is awesome,
it is both a terrible and beautiful thing, it take the breath
away, all the same He will not take an innocent child less He
have to, and it is clear this time He have been force to for
how else can He remind them they are a sorry bunch and evil
live in their hearts, the eyes they see with are blind as whale
bone, the mouth they talk with is bitter as a snake's tooth,
their soul is slick as marble, they come to Truth slow as a
wheelbarrow. They are sinners all. Only by plucking away poor
Reno have God been able to make them face up to the error
of their ways, only by this pilgrimage through a mother's grief
can He guide their footsteps after His into the everlasting
Hereafter. "Gone!" Mrs. Brown cry out. "My baby gone, first

he here and then he gone, out of my arms he stolen like a
thief in the night, my poor baby gone on High, gone on
ahead to Gloryland!"

Throughout this Mama Tuddi sits high in her seat, her
backbone straight as a barber pole, even so her breath quicken-
ing as if hurried along by the drumming of feet. Except for
sheer willpower and reminding herself who she is her own feet
would be beating against the floor. But she have her dignity to
uphold so she hold herself steady and oppose the tide that
sweep the rabble along. She blink her eyes and hold on tight
to her fox, fearing for her personal mortal safety as this untidy
crowd invoke the Lord and exalt this doomed child Reno
above any station she expect he might have truly achieve. It
do no harm she guess, but still to her mind it is a tacky show,
it hardly the sort of performance to go down well on TV. All
the same it have a point, she kind of like it to tell the truth, it
have the hocus-pocus that keep her on the edge of her seat,
some of it have hit like something from a slingshot, she too
have felt a stirring in her breast. Now she see Mrs. Brown
pulling at the red stick which hold up the coffin lid, yanking
it away with fire in her eyes, slamming the lid down with a
loud crack while she shout over Mama Tuddi's head and
everyone else's loud enough to cause anyone walking by in the
street to stop and think: *"Gone! Gone! My sweet baby gone!"*
—and she sink down in a puddle, which LeRoy leap up and
bring back to its seat.

"Mama Tuddi," someone calls, "Mama Tuddi, for shame!"

And Mama Tuddi cannot believe her ears, it have been ages
since she hear anyone speak her name in vain. She rise in her
seat and glare around, she search these faces looking at her
with accusation and reproof, these looks that say *Mama Tuddi*
you have let us down. Mama Tuddi is in a dither close to outrage as she look perplexed at a man standing in the rear who
jab out his finger and keep on jabbing it her way, yelling, "She
in league with the Devil, pray sinners pray!" and it is the man

Mama Tuddi recognize as the man who have said Mama Tuddi in her vanity and pride have looked at herself in the mirror, thereby prompting Satan to enter her skin, the man who have first accused her with his stinging eyes. LeRoy have Mrs. Brown back in her seat now and Mama Tuddi swing on her, she wanting Mrs. Brown to tell this man he is a fool, that Reno have wanted Mama Tuddi to come here because he love her so, which Mama Tuddi have done as a public service on her own time with no question of money in the bank, she wants Mrs. Brown to tell this buffoon that very thing.

But Mrs. Brown shrink away, it looks like she is angry too, that she too believe Mama Tuddi have not done right by her departed child. Mama Tuddi switch to LeRoy, she gets his ear and whispers to him, "What went wrong?" but LeRoy only give her a quick sad smile, he duck his head toward the close coffin and that is all he do before he go back to tending Mrs. Brown, now a weeping ghost of her former self. Suddenly it come to Mama Tuddi what she have done wrong, it hit her like a flash; she have been too high and mighty in the eyes of these people to give a last look at the remains of Reno Brown. She have remain in her seat fussing about flies and thinking of the pleasures of the flesh while others have paid tributes to his name.

Something scrunch up in the brain of Mama Tuddi, it form a tight ball and pulse there to gather strength, it seem to get down on its hind legs awaiting the perfect moment to fly forth —that is what everyone feel watching Mama Tuddi, and a sigh of relief goes up, you can see it and feel it rising dense as a cloud, the tension leave these folks for they can see now that Mama Tuddi mean to make matters right, she have only been jiving them, she have something up her sleeve sure as night be night and day be day and dream be something in between. They see Mama Tuddi square her shoulders back, they see the way her tongue is licking over her front teeth like she intend to black them out, they see the blood swelling in her face.

They hold their breath as she stride around Reno's coffin, as she position herself behind it on her spread-out legs, her both hands gripping the fox tail and pulling at each end like she mean to tear it in two. They fall silent, waiting in a hush for what it is Mama Tuddi will say to them.

Indeed Mama Tuddi have at last got into the spirit of the thing. She glaring out at these folks, she is letting them see she have poise and dignity and above all she have nerve. She letting them know she don't like it that they have even for a minute give up on her. She stroke the coffin slowly as she stare them down, she sweeps her body over the lid and both her hands now move over it like she is washing this body of Reno Brown, bathing Reno with her own hands for this holy trip. LeRoy comes out of his spell, he the first one to sense what Mama Tuddi require, and he leap up to retrieve the stick which have propped up the lid, he is all business as he pass it to Mama Tuddi who reward him with a stern nod of her head.

Mama Tuddi props up the lid though she don't yet look down. She is looking out into this sea of faces, compelling them to admit the personal wrong they have done to a celebrity of her importance. Now she lick her lips, she take a breath way down so folks know that when she speak she is someone to be listen to. The cords thicken in her neck, she let out a big groan sweeping up both her arms. *"Now let me see,"* thunders Mama Tuddi's TV voice—*"Let me see this heah Reno Brown!"* Her eyes rake on past everyone, they roll over the ceiling, then drop and settle peacefully on Reno Brown.

"Praise the Lawd," someone murmur nearby. "Praise the Lawd." And the spirit pass around, it multiplies as Mama Tuddi study the face of Reno Brown, her own face softening as she study his tender remains. Mama Tuddi is in fact quite a bit surprised that Reno is as he seem: so young, so composed, yet so small, so tiny, so shrunken almost to nothing in the Ben Blue suit which lie flat on his bones. For a second she let her eyes dart over the space in that box, space which to her seem horrible, more than a person can understand or cope with and which she hates to believe—a terrible thing, that is what Mama Tuddi sees. It is like doom stretching all around, defeating not just this shriveled child; not something simply lying in wait for Mama Tuddi and everyone else sharing this globe, but just bigger, bigger, so big one almost want to hang the head, condemn God, cuss Him out, say "It ain't right, God, this little space You let us have, how can we live it well when death loom so large?" But Mama Tuddi falter only for a second, no one in fact realize she falters at all; quite the other story for in fact everyone is amazed. Mama Tuddi bends right down, her orange hair descend inside the coffin with Reno Brown. Then she straighten up and suddenly both are there, Mama Tuddi with her arms around Reno, Reno with his head stiff against her breast.

In that position she look down on him, she stroke his hair. Her voice when she speak is quiet as a lamppost at first dark, it have the soft lick of a single flame under glass. *"This heah be Reno Brown,"* she intone. *"This heah be Reno Brown who adore his mama and his poppa and who love LeRoy and all you folks. He dead now but Mama Tuddi say he not dead, he live forever in the Book and in The Mama Tuddi Show. I now rename this child. I rename him Calvary, for Mama Tuddi can do what she please and it please me to name him that. Now I say adios to Reno Brown renamed Calvary from this moment on. I say to you that this boy Calvary alias Reno have withstood the birth, he have withstood the pain, he have stood off the infidels and let his light shine wherever he go. Now he gone like his mama say. She right insofar as she know but she don't know yet Mama Tuddi going to speed him safe and sound on his way."*

That is all Mama Tuddi say. She grip the boy's shoulders firm in each hand. It seem a marvel to everyone that Reno's head don't fall back but indeed it stay there flat and indeed it seem to some that Reno lifts his head to meet Mama Tuddi as she come down to put a kiss on his mouth.

"*Glory!*" some folks cry, "*now he riding fast!*"

"*Lickety-split! Look out Lawd, here he come!*"

Mama Tuddi complete that kiss pretty soon, she give a smart look all around and stand a minute patting her foot. It seem she still have more to do. She suck in her breath through her nose, she unwrap her fox fur and stretch it out full-length over Reno. Then she give it one last look goodbye and close the lid.

The man in the back row who have accuse Mama Tuddi can only shake his head and try to drop down out of sight. Everybody else too stunned with happiness to do anything but sit and look. It a long minute before they collect themselves and give Mama Tuddi her earned applause. Then you can see them exchanging smiled-at remarks, saying as how Mama Tuddi have sure speed him up to heaven with her kiss —laughing at the thought of old Reno—old Calvary—streaking from star to star like a fox. "From now on," one of them suggest, "I reckon it will be the swish of his tail making them blink and swing." "If he don't make it to heaven," LeRoy tell Mrs. Brown, "at least we know he have made it to the Milky Way."

ह॰ ह॰ ह॰

After that it seem the people have enough and they breaks up, though milling around, still waiting for the preacher to come. For good as Mama Tuddi have done—and she have done more than they bargain for—it take the preacher to make Reno's passage complete. Folks pass on to the kitchen to get their food, they pass on through and eat in the yard, after first seeing to it that Mama Tuddi have started in on hers. She is the guest of honor and they don't eat nothing Mama Tuddi haven't tasted of first. She eats the ham biscuits and she eats the corn, she eats the mashed potatoes and pokes at the succotash. She eats the cornbread and the yams and she have a bite or two of the greens, she eats the chicken livers. She pass up for some reason, maybe not seeing them or because her plate is limber and won't hold no more, the runnin beans. Everybody else have no choice but to pass them up too, which riles somewhat the woman who have cooked them up. But she is a forgiving sort and is the first to let Mama Tuddi know she don't hold no grudge.

It is out in the yard by the honeysuckle vines that Mama Tuddi learn the story of Reno Brown and what have happen to him; there too that she learn what LeRoy have done when the boy's daddy out of spite and meanness thought to put the killing stick to him. It is hard telling some of this to Mama Tuddi because, much as they regret it and hope the misfortune here will end, the plain truth of it is Reno's death have a bearing on her. So they mostly leave that part out, that part about Reno looking in the mirror at the burying for his daddy that took place. His daddy had been whupped fair in a knife fight with LeRoy, which nobody could blame LeRoy for doing since it was a case of doing it or having it done to him. Reno's daddy was no good, the wonder of it was it hadn't been done to him long before. He like his drink that man did and whenever he had it he lit up real good and nobody could do a thing with him, he as soon light into a person as look at him. Usually who he lit into was Reno or Lasvegas or their mama because she wouldn't give in, she'd stand between him and them daring that drunk fool to raise his hand to her own flesh and blood. She had any sense she would of run, but she never did. So he'd pour it on, or try to, even if he couldn't stand up. You never saw a man so keen on beating the daylights out of what was closest to him. Everybody have seen the licks that poor woman receive fighting him off her boys. Nor did they blame her for taking up with LeRoy. LeRoy was young and high of blood, but he was dependable where it count. He wasn't about to let nobody walk over him. Or over those what were dear to him. Mrs. Brown was older but she know her own mind and LeRoy make it plain that he like a woman who is mature in her views. And she have a warm way with him, she know how to please a man who return her love. That is all she was looking for, that and a man who is soft with her boys. She don't mind taking a stick to them herself when they do something low-down and deserve it, but she don't like it when her husband just take up a stick to them for no good reason.

So yes she is with LeRoy one night trying to have a good time and forget for a minute her bad homelife when her husband catch up with her. He calls that woman names no one here will repeat, for no need to offend Mama Tuddi with name-calling she no doubt have heard herself, being a woman who have got around and not one who hide her head under a stone. He calls her names and starts beating up on her and on Reno who it happens is tagging along. He pulls out a knife he have obviously brought with him intending to do bodily harm and he start swinging it around.

LeRoy is not going to stand for that. He lays into him and somebody throws him a tool just to even it up. Her husband don't even have the excuse of drinking this time, he's just mean. He just want to carve on someone, it don't matter who. LeRoy he don't mean for it to happen most likely, he just want the man to come to his senses and stop but he don't so after LeRoy take a nick or two on the wrist and have that blade switching over his throat when he is down, after that he gets down to business, throwing Brown off. They tumble in the grass, they roll in the bushes, folks looking on hold their breath—in a minute it's LeRoy who crawl out. He's looking for Mrs. Brown, who is standing over under a shed hiding Reno under her dress so he can't see, and LeRoy get them and take them on home. I guess he stayed on after that.

Some folks claim the law ought to be called, but anyone with eyes could see it happened too fast. LeRoy was scratched up bad, he must of lost a gallon of blood. Brown he was dead, nothing anybody could do to change that. He got what was coming to him, what he been asking for. The truth is everybody breathes a little easier around here with him gone. Nobody like him. Everybody know he worse than dirt. We glad to be rid of him.

Anyway, it ain't right that a man, bad as he is, be left to rot so we have a notion to give him a decent turn in the ground. We hold the service right here, after all she is his wife. We try to think of something good to say about him. We hedge a little on his virtues is what I mean. Some of the women say he was a right good-looking man, for he was that. And sometimes he would work, though naturally he throw it all away. No need grieving, that's just how some folks are. He was one of them: plain no good.

He stupid, that what the trouble was.

❧ ❧ ❧

So that part they tell Mama Tuddi and glad to get it off their chest. The part that more directly concern Reno is the part they attempt to skate around. How he raise the black cloth which he knew better than to touch and which he been told a dozen times to keep away from. Reno was a good boy, but nobody ever deny he have a hard head. Stubborn as the day is long. A service for the dead no time to be primping, he told that time and time again. Still he look. He in one of his know-everything jackass moods and he do it anyway. He took sick pretty soon after. Nothing anybody can do, he have done it to himself. He hung on for five days, wasting away, wasting down to skin and bones. No use to call in a doctor, but they call in one for lack of any better idea and the doctor all he can do is throw up his hands. He bring LeRoy and Lasvegas and Mrs. Brown into the kitchen and he says, "I throw up my hands." He say this boy have been looking into mirrors, and the family have to agree. "All I can do," the doctor say, "is give him something to stop his foaming at the mouth. If the devil have walked in you will be seeing a lot of that." Mrs. Brown cry, what other relief she have? Lasvegas cry, LeRoy cry too I guess. Mrs. Brown blame herself, thinking she have not parade the danger enough across Reno's brain. That don't do no good. LeRoy blame the husband, he gets to feeling low just when he was bouncing back from what he have to do to him. LeRoy ain't killed nobody before. Mrs. Brown she comforts him. LeRoy he comforts her. Lasvegas he a little short when the brains passed out, he don't much seem to know what is going on. He just a nice fella, he do the best he can. LeRoy and Mrs. Brown they get their heads together, they agree they doing nobody no good, so they figure out what they can do to help Reno pass the time in his final days. They pools their money and come up with enough to buy Reno a little twelve-inch TV set. That is how Mama Tuddi come into the picture. Reno never have no TV of his own to watch before. Still nothing cheer him up, he don't care a hoot about no wagon train or shootumup cops nor none of that soapy doctor stuff.

Then one night Lasvegas have turn in and LeRoy and Mrs. Brown are drinking tea in the kitchen when they hear a shriek from Reno. They run in fearing he is dying on the spot, but what they see is Reno rolling on the floor, giggling and wheezing himself blue in the face, getting up to point at Mama Tuddi on the screen then rolling on the floor again. Old solemn-faced Reno who is on his sick bed, at death's door, yet they have never seen him having so much fun before.

"I going to marry her," Reno say. "She going to be my bride. What her name?"

"Why shore," Mrs. Brown answer him. "You know her! That's Mama Tuddi. Everybody know Mama Tuddi."

Reno drag himself up to the tiny screen, he get close enough to look Mama Tuddi in the eyes and trace out her face with his finger on the glass. "She don't have no tooths," he say, "that woman have no tooths," and he laughs hard and kicks his thin legs into the air with a loud whoop that wake Lasvegas in a yonder room.

"You never seen Mama Tuddi before?" his mother ask. "Land sakes alive, Mama Tuddi is a household name."

"No tooths," Reno repeat, and he clutch his sides laughing all the more.

"Yes, she is," LeRoy say, "she got tooths all right, they just blacked out because that her trademark."

"No she ain't. If she had um I could see um, you trickin me."

"You watch," his mother say, "we prove it to you."

Mama Tuddi is talking about her sponsor Double Ola, a bottle in her hand with the other hand pointing to it while she tell them how good it is. The camera come in full-face on her, she opens her mouth wide and recline her head and put the bottle between her lips. The liquid go chug-chug in the narrow bottle neck, Mama Tuddi hold it there a long time, her eyes growing bigger with every swallow she take. They count fifteen swallows and Mama Tuddi bring the bottle down, she say "АНННННННННННННН!" and with the backside of her hand wipe the spittle from her mouth. Then she tilt the bottle back between her lips, she swallow fifteen times more and then she say "АНННННННННННН!" and hold the bottle straight out in her hand and study it awhile, her head shaking as if she cannot believe her luck. Then she hold her head way back and hold the bottle upside down, the liquid go chug-chug down the neck, and when she have finish the last of it Mama Tuddi again cries "АННННННННННННННН!", smacking her lips and rubbing her belly and standing with her shaking head and winking eyes so that everybody watching The Mama Tuddi Show will know that Mama Tuddi love Double Ola and they will too the first chance they have to go out and get some.

"Now look here," Reno's mother say.

For right there the camera come in on Mama Tuddi's mouth alone—wide open, smiling, inviting anyone who want to have a look—and Reno lets out a shout, "SEE! SEE! I TOLE YOU, SHE GOT NO TOOTHS," Mrs. Brown and LeRoy at the same time screaming, "SEE! SEE! SHE HAVE!", Lasvegas also yelling from his part of the house for them to hush their mouths, he sleepin—while in the meantime it seem the camera have gone right on through Mama Tuddi's mouth to come out on the other side where it turn so that Mama Tuddi's hind-side can be seen as she throw her fox fur over her shoulder and maybe pin a small hat on her head and pick up her Double Ola shopping bag, on her way out now to get some more.

The screen fade to black and that is all of Mama Tuddi for this hour.

"I loves Mama Tuddi," Reno say. "I going to marry her."

There is no other way around it either, that boy have fallen head over heels. He keep the TV set running 128 hours straight, he will let no one turn off the thing for fear he miss a minute of her show. Even when later in the week he can't hardly walk or crawl or see his own hand in front of him he have somehow drag himself in front the box and laugh for joy as he trace out her picture on the screen.

"I saving up my money," Reno say. "Her hand gone be mine one sweet day."

Then he die.

Mama Tuddi, hearing this tale told, is sure it is the saddest tale she have heard since her own daddy's mule have run away with him and broken three legs. "Hush up now," she say to Mrs. Brown, "you have my heart clanging and twisting like someone have taken a meat cleaver to it. You have me wanting to go back in there and lift the lid and give that sweet boy these very shoes I have on, my best walking pair. I wants to take off these jewels from my neck and string them around his."

"They nice jewels," Reno's mother agree. A sorrowful look reclaim her face, and she add: "He was a sweet thing. No one ever take his place."

They with some others are now sitting out in the yard, enjoying a leisurely chat while the debris—white paper plates and Dixie Cups—is being cleaned away. Plates and cups blow about the yard and dogs chase after them, pouncing with their front legs to lick at them.

Everybody getting a little drowsy after this fine feed. From time to time a family will step up to shake Mama Tuddi's hand and give Mrs. Brown a good hug, to say what they have to say while they have the chance.

LeRoy is over by the rosebushes kicking a tin can with Lasvegas who now seem a kind of dreamy child.

"I hopes you don't mind him," Mrs. Brown confide, meaning LeRoy. "His hand on your leg, he don't mean a thing, it just his way of showing he like you."

"I hardly notice," Mama Tuddi reply. Her heart have been moved today, but now the juice have gone out of her and she is beginning to wonder how she is ever going to get out of here.

"Well, maybe not, but I see lots of women slap his face. First month I know LeRoy he walk around with my hand print on his face six or seven times a day. I say to him, Listen LeRoy if you see something you like if you like it enough it is worth waiting for. Finally he ask me if I see anything I like, and it was his saying that that baked the cake. It don't pay to argue with LeRoy."

Mama Tuddi have a watch on a dog's wagging rear-end. She feel somehow she is slowing down, getting tired—"Losing my zip," that is what go through her mind. She feel a mite woozy in the sun and come close to asking if there is a place she can use for lying down. But her pride save her in time. One person is already here lying down and that to her way of thinking is enough. It occur to her that some prankster have put a spike in her tea. The top layer of her head seem to be floating away from the rest of her.

She is aware of the peculiar way Mrs. Brown is looking at

her. Of how she keep leaning forward to ask, "Is something wrong, is something troubling you?" To be sure, something is. Mama Tuddi have a notion that the air have thicken between them. She can hear a bluejay prattling in a tree, she can even see the limb the bird is sitting on, but it seem to her the bird's song come from another place.

"I was just thinking," Mrs. Brown confess, "I like you better off the air than on. It seem to me you have more poise." More "paws," she say.

Mama Tuddi nod. She try to focus on one part of the woman's face the way she have to learn to look at the red button on the camera box.

"Your dignity come through."

"That my trademark in life," Mama Tuddi agree. She turn her head to look out over the yard and down to a leaning shed which LeRoy with Lasvegas is standing beside. It appear the two are trying to plant a tree. The tree to her eyes is nothing, maybe three feet tall, a couple of scraggly limbs which the foliage have drop away from or it never have.

"That a fruit tree," Mrs. Brown explain. "Apple, could be. Reno was partial to apples. He had it in his head that one day he like to plant a orchard full."

"I like trees," Mama Tuddi say to keep her end of the conversation going. Her voice sound strange to her, like it have entered her ear from some distance far away. She switch her head back to notice Mrs. Brown have her leg crossed over one knee, swinging that free leg hard. The gold anklet catch a glitter from the sun and Mama Tuddi see she have on her face a wayward smile.

Mrs. Brown catch Mama Tuddi looking and laughs out loud. "My motor running," she say. "It a disgraceful thing to be feeling in this time and place with my Reno not yet in the ground, but it have a way of coming over me when I looks at that man." She hitch her head off LeRoy's way, wanting herself plainly understood.

Mama Tuddi give a little push and her head wag slowly up and down. "He have any other women?" she ask.

"Could be he do but they don't have him."

"You lucky, I guess."

"I guess. I have my cross to bear but cross ain't all."

Mama Tuddi at a loss to understand what have come over her. It been ages—since way before she embark on a career—since she have sat rocking in a chair out in the yard talking to another person like she have all day. She observe Mrs. Brown and think to herself she could like this woman, she could be friends with her. She is part trash, maybe more trash than she let on, but Mama Tuddi find herself admiring her. It sadden her, now that she think of it, to realize she never have any woman friends, never have the time, always from the minute her alarm clock ring it is a case of GET UP AND GO. Get up and go because if you don't whatever you are after won't be there.

Yet now she surprise herself by wondering what it all come to. She wonder if maybe she ought not to gone into politics, since she get along so well with people. She wonder what the Double Ola people say if she march in and tell them, "You can get yourself another Mama Tuddi, this one's retiring."

The roof, she is sure, would cave right in, they would have a fit.

She wonder if she can chalk the fox fur up to her expense account.

A chill suddenly steal through Mama Tuddi. The sun is shining bright on Mrs. Brown, the sun shine all over the yard, but it seem to her as if dark shade have suddenly envelop her chair. Her bad tooth begin to ache again, the throb spreading all through her mouth. She feel weak clear through to her bones.

Now there be fresh excitement in the yard. Folks are scurrying this way and that, relating that the preacher have come, he have escaped with his life from the freeway jam. Mama Tuddi looks off at the gate where five men are turning through single file like they are playing a CHOO-CHOO game. The one in front she take to be the preacher since he have a Bible in his hand. She spots right away he have back trouble because of his stiff legs with the feet pointing off opposite each other and the way his shoulders are slung back like they can't quite catch up with the rest of him. He have a pointy head, Mama Tuddi can tell even though he have a hat on.

The train come right on up to her chair. The man behind the preacher step out from the line, coughing a few times while Mama Tuddi scramble to get her shoes on. Then he grin and say, "Mama Tuddi, this heah be Preacher Teebone who express a pleasure to meet you."

"T-Bone?" Mama Tuddi inquire.

The preacher's eyebrows, trimmed to a boomerang shape and pomaded down, now shoot up, which make his pointy head more extreme.

"T-E-E-Bone," the preacher say, spelling it out. He have an expression of doom which never change and he stares deep into Mamma Tuddi's eyes, which is why she can't stand preachers in the first place. "I heah," Preacher Teebone say, "you have kiss the boy and give him a fur coat. My feelings is you be best off kissing the Holy Book, but I ain't against kissing in the circumstance irregardless of which wherever he go that coat ain't liable to hep him none."

Mama Tuddi stay quiet. Her experience at the station have taught her that the preachers of the world are engaged in an international conspiracy to take over every second, minute and hour of TV time. And if they doing it, she tells herself, you can bet this T-Bone is in on it.

The minister abruptly turn on his heels and him and his train wheel along inside the house.

Wouldn't you know it, everybody out in the yard having a perfectly nice time up to this point, toot along after him.

Folks would follow a toad frog, Mama Tuddi thinks, *if first you slick down its hair and put the* Good Book *into its mouth.*

After a minute or two of sober thought during which time
Mama Tuddi expect someone to come superintend her needs,
she gets up and follows them. The preacher is already down
at the front wiping a white handkerchief over his face. One of
his sidekicks takes away his hat while another one is setting
up a speaker's stand which have draped from it a red cloth
with a gold fringe which have stamped on it the words ONE
GOD and something like a lightning bolt shooting down the
middle. The music woman is taking her seat at the piano and
Lasvegas have been set up with a candle on a plate and told
where to stand up by the coffin. Curtains are being pulled and
it is almost dark by the time Mama Tuddi is able to claim her
front seat. LeRoy's seat is empty and for all Mama Tuddi
know he have gone for good. It gives her a funny feeling that
empty chair beside her, and a second chill come over her when
she is surrounded on both sides by empty chairs because Mrs.
Brown is now being led up to the coffin also, she and her boy
now standing with lit candles at both ends like a pair of watch-
dogs. That is Mama Tuddi's view of the matter and it is all
tacky tacky tacky, that is the only word she have for it.
Preacher Teebone himself lights up a row of candles on the
coffin lid.

The whole room then plunge into darkness except for the
light up there. Preacher Teebone, standing behind the coffin,
stretches out his arms and his hands fall square on top the
heads of Mrs. Brown and her living son. His face have a yellow
glow, his ears stand out from his head like he would flap right
on up to heaven unless he have this duty to hold him down.
He have not yet spoken a word but the sweat is already pouring off him, and Mama Tuddi is beside herself thinking *tacky
tacky tacky, I could do better with my hands tied behind me
and my feet in a bucket of concrete.*

"LAWD GOD IN HEAVEN," rings out the preacher's voice,
"PROP THESE HEAH TWO PEOPLE UP ON THEIR WEAK AND

LEANEST SIDES IN THEIR HOUR OF SACRIFICE FOR THEY ARE BUT
THE CHILDREN OF YOUR HANDIWORK." Mama Tuddi almost
falls out of her chair since it comes to her such a big surprise
that this pointy-headed man with his bad back have got so
much thunder up his sleeve.

"Prop um up!" replies a few in the back. "Preach on,
Reverend."

The preacher withdraws into the darkness and the music
lady does a roll on her piano. When next he appears, behind
the rostrum, his suit is washed in shiny magenta and he have
his head thrown back so that all Mama Tuddi can see of his
face is mouth. *"Friends,"* he begins . . .

Something crawls over Mama Tuddi's skin, first up her legs
and over her knees then wrapping her thighs and hips and
finally settling like a feathery waked-up thing that thinks to
play possum in her lap.

And suddenly the preacher's voice have leaped out at her,
forcing Mama Tuddi's spine straight back against her chair:
FRIENDS WHEN YOU GO TO SHECAGO YOU KNOW WHAT TIME YO
BUS DEPART AND WHEN YOU GOT YO TICKET TO BATON ROUGE
OR FOWT WAYNE OR IF YOU GOING TO NU YAWK OR MONTRAWL
OR WHETHER YOU GOING TO DEETROIT OR THE YUKON
TERRITORY YOU KNOW WHAT TIME THE BUS LEAVE AND WHAT
TIME SHE GET THERE AND SO YOU GOT YO BAGS PACKED AND
YOU GOT YO SKIVVIES IN ORDER AND YOU WOMEN'S GOT YO
FACE MADE AND YO HAIR CURLED AND YOU ALL SET CAUSE YOU
KNOW—
—CAUSE YOU KNOW THE HOUR AND THE MINUTE AND THE
DAY YO BUS GON GO CAUSE YOU DONE SEEN THE TIMETABLE OR
YOU DONE ASK OVER THE TELEPHONE AND THE VOICE DONE
TOLE YOU THAT BUS LEAVE AT NINE FAWTY FIVE OR TWELVE P.M.
OR ON THE BUTTON AT SIX O'CLOCK AND YOU IS HAD TIME
FRIENDS—

Tacky tacky, Mama Tuddi think. Yet even as she say this to herself the thing in her lap darts up its head, listening to her, and Mama Tuddi's scalp tightens as once more it begin to crawl.

—YOU IS HAD TIME FRIENDS TO MAKE YO PREPARATION COMPLETE!

"*Amen!*" someone cried.

"*My baby gone,*" moan Mrs. Brown, "*he gone.*"

"*Gone!*" everybody sing.

BUT BROTHERS AND SISTERS WHEN YOU TAKE THE TRIP THAT RENO BROWN TAKE WHICH IS ONE THE QUICKEST RIDES YOU GON EVER HAVE—WHEN YOU TAKE THE GLORY RIDE YOU AIN'T GOT NO TIME TO PUT THE CURL IN YO HAIR—

"No, you ain't!"

OR TO SLICK IT DOWN—

"No, you ain't!"

OR TO POLISH UP YO SHOES OR PAINT UP YO LIPS—

"No, you ain't!"

CAUSE THERE AIN'T NO TIMETABLE OF THE LAWD'S PLAN AND THERE AIN'T TELEPHONE POLE OR FREEWAY TO THAT FAR KINGDOM—

"No, you ain't!"

AND SO MY FRIENDS UNLESS YOU CAREFUL AND GOT YO FINGERS CROSSED YOU GONNA HAVE TO MAKE THAT TRIP WHAT RUN BY NO SKADULE YOU LIKELY TO UNDERSTAND—

"Praise the Lawd!"

YOU GONE BE CAUGHT WITH THE WINE IN YO MOUTH AND YO FOOT IN THE TRAP! YO BED OF PLEASURE GONE BE YO BED OF PAIN, YO PATH OF SIN GONE BE YO PATH OF WOE, THE DEVIL HIMSELF GON COME AND SWEEP YOU UP LIKE A MONKEY WITH A BROOM, YES MY FRIENDS THE HIGH AND THE LOW!

"The high and the low!"

The room is aquiver with this preacher's work, in the din Mama Tuddi cannot hear herself think. Teebone's eyes are boring in on her from his face gone shiny-slick, she can see the

flash of his gold teeth and the sweep of his arms as he grab the
red banner and flaps it hard and fast, like he mean to shake
out the words ONE GOD and hurl them around her neck. Mrs.
Brown and her boy are down on their knees, bent over like
two melted piles. Candle flames jump off their wicks and spin
through the black air, clearing a path for Reno's spirit to
follow. His spirit is climbing out of the box. Mama Tuddi
sees it clear as day passing on up through the lifted lid, walking
barefoot through the throbbing air. Mama Tuddi sucks in her
breath, she grind her teeth together and sucks again. She press
her hands tight between her legs, whining all the time,
whining despite all her desire to maintain her dignity and
poise, for the crawly thing have twisted down over her stomach
and is hissing out its tongue and she can feel its rough nose
pushing cold and wet under her hands, aiming to slide up
through her woman's trough to lodge inside of her. "*How
many*?" Teebone asks . . .

The snake thing slides in.

HOW MANY OF YOU FOLKS BEEN TO THE RIVER?

"We been there, preacher!"

HOW MANY OF YOU POOR SINNERS HAVE BEEN TO THE RIVER?

"The river, amen!"

I SEE SOME OF YOU FOLKS HAVE BEEN TO THE RIVER AND I
KNOW YOU HAVE BEEN THERE AND JUMPED RIGHT IN—

"Right in!"

—WHILE OTHERS OF YOU HAVE STOOD ON THE SHORE AND
WAITED FOR THE WATER TO DIVIDE SO YOU COULD WALK A DRY
BOTTOM RIGHT INTO GLORY LAND NOW AIN'T THAT THE TRUTH?

"It's the truth!"

YOU HAVE STOOD ON THE SHORE BIDING YO TIME AND WHILE
YOU HAVE BEEN BIDING YO TIME THE DEVIL HAVE CUT THROUGH
THE WATER LIKE A SILVER FISH AND HE HAVE COME RIGHT ON UP
INSIDE. YOU HAVE STOOD ON THE SHORE WATCHING YO FACE IN
THE WATER AND LIKING WHAT YOU SEE AND THINKING YOU ARE

GOD'S PLAN AND THE DEVIL'S HUNGRY FISH HAVE JUMPED OUT OF THE WATER AND DROVE HIMSELF SMACK-DAB INSIDE YO EVIL HEART.

"Save us, preacher!"

I SAY TO YOU THE SAME AS I HAVE SAID TO THAT BOY IN THE BOX I SAY BROTHERS AND SISTERS IF YOU WENT TO THE RIVER WHY WERE YOU NOT BAPTIZED? I SAY TO YOU IF YOU WENT TO THE RIVER WHY DID YOU NOT JUMP RIGHT IN AND SWIM CLEAN ON HOME?

"Show us how, preacher!"

"You bring us home!"

MAYBE YOU THINK YO FUR COAT OR YO TV GON GET YOU THERE—

"No, we don't!"

MAYBE YOU THINK YO DEEP FREEZE OR YO POCKETBOOK OR YO LOOSE WAYS GON GET YOU THERE—

"No, we don't!"

MAYBE YOU THINK YO SODA POP GON SWING IT WITH JESUS MAYBE YOU THINK YOU CAN GIT OUT ON THE FREEWAY AND THAT GON TAKE YOU THERE OR MAYBE YOU THINK THIS BOY GON GO ON AHEAD AND PUT IN A GOOD WORD AND THAT GON GET YOU THERE BUT I SAY TO YOU THE SAME AS I WOULD SAY TO A MAN BLIND IN ONE EYE AND UNABLE TO SEE OUT OF THE OTHER FRIENDS I SAY THERE IS BUT ONE GOD ONE HEAVEN AND ONE WAY OF GETTING THERE WHILE THE WAY OF THE DEVIL IS LEGION AND HE CAN CLIMB INTO YO HEART AND TAKE CHARGE WITH NO MORE SECOND THOUGHT THAN A VAIN WOMAN HAVE WHEN SHE APPROACH THE LOOKING GLASS!

"Amen!"

"Thine the glory!"

Preacher Teebone speaks on. The music woman's fingers roll over the keys like someone stripping bark from a living tree; the voices in the room shake the roof with their song and one by one the long line form to head down to Teebone, who have a bucket of water to sprinkle from, saying "Sister, I baptize thee."

Going home, we going home, the song goes.

But Mama Tuddi can see through her heart and she like what she see. She like what she feel. The thing inside her is warm and quiet, he have come inside and curled up and it seem to her he have brought her peace. He have taken her a long way from these people, she hardly aware of them. She have her hands full just thinking how good she feel.

The thing inside her is sleeping now. He satisfied now. But she have a notion he is going to wake up the minute she tell him to. She going to have new strength for her show; this thing going to lead her out of this backwoods town into the bright lights of bigger places and more important work: pretty soon all the world going to know Mama Tuddi's name and bow down to her esteem.

THE MAN IN THE GREEN BATHROBE

On the Thursday after Memorial Day Ronald Binks met Johnny Ballantyne on Porter Street down where the fire hydrant in summer is always gushing. Having just left the arms of a lady, Binks was feeling chipper and quite handsome, perhaps even a trifle giddy. He had a white silk scarf looped around his throat and wore white shoes with no mud on them. The women passing Binks on the street, in his private estimation, were giving him close, whimsical, dreamy looks—which he savored. He'd never known it to fail: every time you leave the arms of one woman, other women, seeing you, can't help where their imaginations take them. They scent *woman*, they scent *female*, and their nostrils quiver. Puts them in a fever. Happens every time. I better watch it or I'll get myself molested.

He wished it would happen sometimes when he was needy.

Some of this Binks was telling to Johnny Ballantyne, an old acquaintance. Johnny was feeling fairly chipper himself. He'd had a good morning, by his own reckoning. Johnny was down on his luck at the moment, but he wasn't about to toss in the towel. "Daylight," he told Binks. "I definitely see daylight. Heads up, feet pointed straight, that's my motto."

"Oh yeah," said Binks. "That'll take you far. Same here."

Johnny was employed. That in itself was a stroke of good luck, and much beyond his usual fortunes. Old Solomon paid him four dollars a day to keep the sidewalk and gutter outside his shop free of litter. This was no easy job, given the prevailing winds, and given that none of the other proprietors on Porter Street cared a damn.

"Some days," said Johnny, " I pick up four or five barrelfuls. With this stick. See this stick? See that icepick taped to the end? I don't even have to stoop over. This was my own idea. Solomon said it was a beauty. But he said it made the job too easy. He wanted to cut my salary to three a day. I said, 'No way. Get yourself another boy.' That's what I said. You ought to seen old Solomon go blue in the face. He was the proprietor, he said. I was just his stooge. I ought not to talk to him that way. But what I say is I got to look out for myself. You know that's the truth. I got my own self to look out for. Johnny Ballantyne first, that's how I see it."

Binks laughed. He'd always got a big kick out of Johnny Ballantyne, although in his private opinion Johnny Ballantyne was the stupidist moron this side of a Hong Kong sunset. The guy didn't know whether he was coming or going. But Binks, feeling chipper today, was today willing to give him the benefit of the doubt.

"You can laugh if you want to," said Johnny, "but most of the time this is a sit-down job. You see that chair over there against the storefront? That's Solomon's chair. I got it out of his back room. 'No chair, no work,' I told him. Once I get the gutter and sidewalk cleared I can sit down in that chair, lean back, and enjoy the show. The people on this street, pedestrians, I mean, are crazy as hell. Now and then someone will drop a coin in my lap. Sometimes a whole dollar. They're generous, I mean. It doesn't even occur to them that Johnny

Ballantyne don't beg. But what they think to wear is the
amazing thing. You'll see women coming along wearing practically nothing. Lots of silk shirts, mainly, silk's big these days
—you can see right through them. I've seen some of the
prettiest little titties in the world from that chair. And thighs.
I mean, the whole show. With some of them I can even count
the pubic hairs. *Public* hairs, I'm thinking of calling it. But
mostly theirs is a happy lot. The smiles I get. You'd think
most people didn't have a care in the world. You'd swear
there was no economy crunch. I see people coming out of
Solomon's waving a fifty-sixty-dollar dry-cleaning bill. They
don't even blink. I do in fact manage to pick up a lot of extra
cash. There's one guy parks here every day, in his big car.
Cadillac, black with wire wheels. A beauty. He'll pay me five
dollars to see nobody steals it, nobody puts a scratch on it. I
can even sit inside if I want to, under the wheel. V'room,
v'room!—quite the auto. Real leather seats. But I was telling
you of these people coming by. One guy comes along every
day, blacker than aces. *Black*, I mean. He wears this dingy
green bathrobe down to his ankles, and those green, sort of
angel-hair shoes. What they call mules. Yet he's got rings on
every finger. Genuine diamonds. And he's got this gold chain
looped around his neck, with a big black glass eye on a swivel.
What he says is if someone ever looks into the center of that
eye then that someone will be his servant forever. Swear to
God. What he wants is my chair. He wants to sit there swivel-
ing this big glass eye. Say some flashy woman comes by, he'll
grab her arm, swoop her down, and try to make her stare into
this black eye on his chest. '*Look into my eye*,' he'll say. '*You're
growing drowsy. Your lids are getting heavy. Look, look into
the eye. You're drowsy, yes. You will do as the eye commands.
You will be my slave forever.*' No kidding. Sometimes these
women will haul back and knock holy hell out of him. Or
they'll scramble away before he can start his hex number. It's

weird, but really he's a likable guy. But *grungy*, you know? Yesterday I noticed he'd worked his big toe clean through one of his shoes. Biggest, ugliest toenail you ever saw. Cracked, all cater-corner, and black. I asked him had a piano fell on it. I asked him if he didn't think maybe he could use a new pair of shoes. I told him about this shoemaker down the street, maybe could fix him up. What he does is he grabs my shoulder, he says, *'Look into my eye. Look deep into my eye. You are growing drowsy. Sleep, sleep. Look into my eye. Your lids are closing. Sleep, sleep. You are sleeping now. You are my slave. You are my slave forever.'*

"Spooky. I mean, he had me going. Christ, another minute and I would have been snoring. The guy has some power, no denying it. If he didn't wear those ladies' mules, if his bathrobe was a little less grungy, there's no telling where he'd be. *'Look into my eye!'*—I swear he can't help it. It's as if *he's* looked into the eye and *he's* the slave. And he's only one of the many funny people walking this street. What I'm saying is this is the most rewarding job I ever had. It's making me believe in myself and in other people. At night on my bed I just lie there chuckling. That's how good it makes me feel. Of course, I don't tell Solomon that. Solomon would say, Well if this job makes you so happy suppose in future you do it for nothing. That's exactly what he'd say. I'm having my hands full with him, tell you the truth. The guy don't *live*. Stays hunched over his steam press back there in his shop, no lights on. Breathing that *ether*, is what it smells like. I swear, you smell it and you want to reach for your scalpel, start operating. Solomon *hates* this black guy in the dingy robe. He turns *livid* when he sees this guy sitting in my chair. He comes running out with his broom to chase him off. But the guy don't buckle. *'Look, look into my eye!'* he says. It kills me. The guy's plain terrific. I love him. I don't even care if he leaves this angel-hair all over the sidewalk. That, and cigarette butts, for he smokes like a fish. '*Look—puff puff—into my eye—puff puff,*' that's how he does it."

Binks, at this time, was himself sitting in the chair. He was listening with one ear to Johnny Ballantyne go on with this crap, though mostly he was watching the women. That much of what Johnny said was true: it was amazing what some women would choose to wear. No doubt about it, silk was hot stuff this year. And you could see right through it. Christ-almighty, you had to admit it: the number of beautiful creatures in this world was staggering. And, boy, did they flaunt it!

What Binks wanted to do was go right back to the apartment he'd just come from. Grab another armful of his lady. Because while she was not as beautiful as some of these, and while she had not *exactly* let him sleep with her, she was plenty the hot ticket. And she'd be pleased if he did come back, no doubt about that, because probably what she was thinking right this minute—what most thought once Ronald Binks left their company—was that she'd never see him again. "Yep, he's gone, he got what he wanted. I'll never see that honey again." Not that he had got *quite* what he wanted. Not quite.

But Binks wasn't any too convinced he was able. It would be embarrassing to go back there, talking big, and then to find he couldn't perform. Not that he *couldn't,* just that he wasn't sure how much heart he could put into it. Also, she'd been claiming exhaustion. *Claiming* disinterest. *Claiming* Ronald Binks left her cold. *Saying* he meant nothing to her. "Nothing, do you hear? Zero! Totally zilch!" *Swearing* that she didn't like him, couldn't stand him, that she wished he didn't exist! *Screaming*: "Stop calling me your lady! Stop it! It makes me sick!" *Claiming* he was driving her crazy. "Stop hanging around!" she'd said. "Get lost! Drop dead! Go bother some-one else! Where did you come from? Who are you? How did you get into my life? You're bad news, Binks! You're nothing! You're vapid! You're hollow! You got no more substance than my big toe!"

Pretty extraordinary behavior, now that he thought of it. A real joker. *Plenty* theatrical. And what a temper! If he hadn't known her better—hadn't remembered how at the start of the evening, at Boar's Head Tavern, she'd fawned all over him— he might have been convinced she meant it.

So maybe it would be best to give her a little rest. Take a little break from the action. Maybe give this bruise on his leg, from where she'd kicked him, time to heal.

A nice cooling-off period.

Some of this he was telling Johnny Ballantyne. "Yep. I been having this lovers' spat with my lady. Must be that time of the month, I guess. Nothing much to it. Another few hours and I'll be right back on target. I figure I got her wrapped around my little finger."

Johnny Ballantyne was out with his stick stabbing at a paper bag the wind had blown into the gutter. "They come in all sizes and shapes," he said. "More power to'm."

Binks was watching a bunch of kids frolicking around the gushing fire hydrant at the street corner. They were hooting it up, a shrill bunch, laughing and chasing each other through the powerful spray of water, rushing up to the hydrant mouth and being knocked back to land screaming on their rumps. Some six or seven kids, none much older than that, naked as jaybirds and having themselves a terrific time. Funny little buttocks no thicker than a tin can. Kids, thought Binks, what I wouldn't give to be a kid again. Taking life easy, not a care in the world. Yep, thought Binks, I had me no worries when I was a kid. I was *loose*, then. I was a real humdinger.

He mentioned this to Johnny Ballantyne.

Ballantyne laughed. "I remember you as a kid," he said. "We used to wonder if you had all your marbles." He hawked up, facing the wind, and broke suddenly into a happy grin.

"Looky there," he said. "Here he comes. The old reliable. The Green Hornet."

Binks wasn't listening. He was diddling with his scarf end, now stooping to erase a minuscule scuff mark from one of his shoes. He wished he had something to nibble on, like a candy bar. Maybe even a carrot. What he figured he'd maybe do, once he left here, was go over to his mother's. See if he couldn't mooch a nice warm meal, maybe sweet-talk her into hitting his palm with a twenty. Little something to tide him over till his pay-truck came in.

Binks became aware after a time that the sun was no longer on him. A long dark shadow stretched up from the sidewalk over the entire length of his body. "What the heck—!" he started to say—but found, staring back, level with his own gaze, perfectly still, placid as a saint, a huge black eye in which his own features were mirrored. *"Look into my eye,"* he heard someone say. *"Look deep into my eye. You are drowsy. You want to sleep. Sleep, sleep, soon you will sleep. Look into my eye."* The voice was melodious, soft and caressing, and Binks was unaware that a rapt, somewhat imbecilic expression already had settled over his face. *"The eye is deep, the eye is all-seeing. Look into my all-seeing eye. Your lids are closing. Sleep, sleep, now you are sleeping. You are my slave. You are my slave forever. Give me my shoes."*

Binks gave the eye his shoes.

"Give me your silk scarf."

Binks handed up his silk scarf. The man in the green bathrobe put these on.

"Sleep, sleep," he said. *"Look into my eye. You are my slave. Put on these mules. Rise, slave, and follow me."*

Binks slid his feet into the mules. He stood up.

"Follow me. Follow the eye. The eye commands it. Come, slave."

The man in the green bathrobe, with his white shoes and white silk scarf and with his great black eye, passed slowly along Porter Street, on past the fire hydrant which was gushing, and where no children now played, and on around the corner to wherever he was going. Binks, in the flopping angelhair mules, tracked docilely behind him.

Johnny Ballantyne stood out in the clean gutter, scratching his chin, mutely observing their departure. By God, he thought, he did it! It works. I never would have believed it.

Solomon appeared in his doorway, studying the length of pavement down from his shop with a tranquil, stupefied air. "Who was that?" he asked.

"The bathrobe man?"

"No. The other one."

"Ronald Binks, you mean?"

"Ronald Binks? I'll be damned. Just like his father. Hasn't changed a bit in twenty years." He stooped down, brushing up a couple of cigarettes off the sidewalk into his palm. "You missed these," he said. "What am I paying you for?"

Johnny Ballantyne laughed. Sometimes he got a big kick out of Solomon.

THE WOMAN WHO TALKED TO HORSES

"T hat's right," she said, "I talk to them. They will talk to me when they will talk to no one else."

"But they *can* talk," I said.

"Oh, sure."

"To each other?"

"All the time."

I looked over at the horses. They were in their stalls, eating hay, their rumps and hind legs about all I could see of them. They looked the same as they always had. I didn't believe they talked. I certainly didn't believe they would talk to her.

"What's your fee?" I asked.

She looked off at the horses, too, then glanced at me, then worked one toe into the ground and looked at that. She was wearing blue cloth shoes with thick white shoelaces—all very clean. Too clean. She looked clean all over. I didn't think she knew snot about horseflesh or about anything ese. I figured she was a straight-out phony.

"Your fee," I said.

She had a little itch behind one ear. She scratched there.

"Before we go into my fee structure," she said, "we need to have a quiet discussion."

Fee structures? Holy Christ.

I had a good mind to turn and walk away.

"You won't tell me your fee?"

She pawed the ground again and the hand again went up to get at that itch. I stared at that hand. She had long, slender fingers and white immaculate skin with hardly any fuzz on it, and wrists no thicker than my thumb. All very feminine. She wasn't wearing a ring; I noticed that. I had her figured by this time. She was another one of those frail, inhibited, emaciated females who knew nothing about the real world but like to think they could tell you about horses. One of those grim, pitiful creatures who was forever saying to themselves and to each other, *I can relate to horses.*

I'd had my share of that lot back when I had been boarding.

"I can't tell you my fee," she said, "until I know what you want of me and why you want it."

I nearly laughed in her face. The whole business was stupid. I didn't know why I'd let myself get talked into calling her. I wished now that she'd just get in her car and go away, so I could go into the house and tell Sarah, "Well, Sarah, you got any more of your dumb ideas? Let's hear them, Sarah." Something like that. And watch her shrivel up. Watch her mew and sob and burn and hide away.

Christ, the time I was wasting. *All* the time I had wasted, listening to Sarah. Trying to take her seriously. Giving in when I knew it would prove a waste of time, all to keep a little peace in the house. To keep poor Sarah upright and not shriveling.

I stared up at the house. Wondering if Sarah was watching. If she wasn't up there gritting her teeth, gnawing the woodwork, the broom in one hand, shoving hair out of her eyes with another, as she pressed her scared little face against a secret window. That was Sarah. Ever spying. The one way she had—so she'd tell it—of keeping her guard up.

"Mr. Gaddis?" the woman said.

"Yes, what is it?"

"All I need to know is what trouble it is you are having. With your horses. Then we can talk price."

"How about we talk *method*," I said. "*Then* price. You going to go up and whisper sweet nothings in these horses' ears? Is that what I'm paying you for?"

The woman eyed me peculiarly. Her head tilted, her mouth a shade open. It wasn't dislike so much—though I knew she did. Nor was she making judgments. I didn't know what it was. A quiet distance. A watching.

Disapproval, too: that was there.

"I don't know what the trouble is," I said. "That's why I called you. I want to know what's going on. All I know is they've been acting funny lately."

"Funny how?"

"It's hard to say. Standoffish, maybe."

"Horses are like that. Can't horses have moods, Mr. Gaddis?"

"Not on my time," I said. "They're not producing. You'd think the bastards had gone on vacation. Zombies, the lot of them."

"I see," the woman said.

Bull. She saw nothing.

I stared at her open throat. She had on this soft cottony blouse, tinted like old rose, with a wide, folded collar, and at her throat a gold necklace no thicker than a fish line.

She had on these black britches.

Up at the house Sarah had all the doors and windows shut up tight and outside not a hint of wind was stirring. Even the grass wasn't growing. It seemed to me all the life had gone out of that house. It looked dumb and impenetrable and cold.

"Sure they can have moods," I said. "And they do. All the time. But this time it's different. This time it's affecting me."

She closed the blouse and held the hand at her throat.

"How do you mean?"

"I'm losing. I haven't had a horse in the running all year."

"That could be bad luck. It could be that the other horses are better."

"Could be but it isn't," I said. "These are good horses."

She glanced up at the house. Then she went on to the roofline and from there up to the hills behind it. She wanted me to know she'd heard that story a thousand times before. Every owner thought he had good horses.

I thought to tell her I had a fortune tied up in these horses. That they were top dollar. Then I thought I had better not. You didn't talk fortune and top dollar when some nut was trying to get it from you. Especially a nut who imagined she could talk to horses.

"About fees," she said. "Naturally, if your horses that now are losing begin winning after I've had my chat with them, then my fee will be higher."

"A chat!" I said. "You're going to have a chat with them?"

"A serious discussion. Do you like that better?"

"I don't like any of it," I said. "You wouldn't be here if—" I stopped. I didn't see any point in raking up the family history.

"I didn't invite myself, Mr. Gaddis. You invited me."

She didn't say that with any anger. She was playing it very cool.

We both heard a door slam, and turned. Over at the back door of the house my wife stood, splashing out water from a white enamel pot. Then she swayed a little, standing there with her head bowed. Something must have told her we were looking. She glared our way, then flung her pot into the yard, and strutted back inside.

The woman beside me laughed.

I was pretty surprised myself. Sarah is prone to the odd explosion now and then—for reasons totally incomprehensible —but she'd never done anything like this before, not when someone else was around. Meek and long-suffering: that was the word for Sarah.

"I gather your wife dislikes that pot," the woman said. She laughed again, a velvety, softly arching laugh. I wanted to tell her it was none of her business.

"Forget Sarah," I said. "A minute ago you were saying something about your fee structure and my hypothetical winnings."

"Was I?"

For no reason at all this woman suddenly squatted down on her legs and began rooting through the thin grass with her long fingers. I couldn't make it out. I couldn't tell whether she was searching for rock or flower or clover, or for nothing at all. Maybe she had dropped a nickel. I had no idea what the hell she was doing. I moved a little closer. I was tempted to step on her hand. Her blouse ballooned out and I could see down her neckline to her breasts. She wasn't wearing any brassiere.

Maybe that's why she was kneeling there.

She began speaking without lifting her head. "Yes," she said, "I think that's fair. Obviously much more is involved, more work for me, if I am to talk to your horses, root out their troubles, and get them winning. On the other hand, if you simply want me to walk over to the stalls and ask how they're doing today—'How you making it, kid,' that sort of thing— and then come back here and simply repeat to you what they said, well in that case my fee would be minimum. Thirty dollars, let's say. Is that what you want?"

My wife was standing at the back door again. She had this fixed, zombielike expression which altered even as I watched. The skin reddened, her lips twitched, and in a moment she was twitching all over.

Then she pitched a pillow out into the yard. One of our big bed-pillows with the green slipcover still on it. Then she retreated.

The horse lady, down on the grass, hadn't noticed.

I had got around so that my back was to the door. "I was looking for something more solid," I told her. "Something tangible that I could act on. *Useful*, you know. Useful information. I *have heard* that you get good results."

She stood up. She turned and silently regarded the pillow in the yard.

"But you want my services for free, is that it, Mr. Gaddis?"

This made me mad. It was clear to me that this woman carried some sort of chip around on her shoulder. That she had no use for men. One of *those*, I thought.

"Now listen," I said. "George Gaddis pays for goods and services properly rendered, and he always has. He pays top dollar. But it's crazy for me to fork over hundreds of dollars just to watch you go over there for an hour or two and whisper into the ears of my horses."

She stopped studying the pillow and looked across at the door. No one was at the door. Sarah had closed the screen door, then she'd closed the cedar door behind it. It was quiet as a tomb in there.

"I don't often whisper, Mr. Gaddis," she said. "I speak distinctly and usually with some force, and if you'll allow me, most horses do the same."

Haughty and reproving. She seemed to think I deserved this.

"Their powers of articulation are quite well-developed, Mr. Gaddis. Perhaps more so than our own."

"They *do* talk?"

She bristled. "*Yes, they talk!*"

She struck off, moving down towards the fence at a determined pace. She truly disliked me. There, she stood leaning up against the fence with her hands in her pockets. She had narrow shoulders and narrow bony hips that would fit in a cigar box. She was a woman all right, but she was too mean and skimpy for me.

"That filly I got from Quebec," I said, "she'd be speaking French, I suppose? *J'ai la mort dans mon â, J'ai la mort dans mon â, mon coeur se tend comme un lourd fardeau.*"

She spun and stared directly at me, her face burning. Mercy, one of the horses, plodded up to the fence and nuzzled her neck and shoulders. I wasn't impressed. Mercy was a dreamer. She liked people.

The woman strolled back, calm once more.

"We are getting nowhere," she said, "and my time is valuable. I did not drive out here to give you a free estimate, or to illustrate my capabilities, or to listen to your troubles. No, Mr. Gaddis, the horses do not *talk* as such, not as we are talking, but they do think and develop their thoughts logically, except in dire cases. I am able, in a word, to read their minds."

"ESP, you mean?"

"Something like that." She fluttered a vague hand.

"You can guarantee this?"

"I do not give guarantees. I can swear to you that I shall talk to your horses, but the effectiveness with which you utilize the information I glean is clearly out of my hands."

"All right," I said. "Suppose I employ you and make good use of your information, and my horses begin winning. What's your standard contract? How much do you get?"

"Normally, ten percent."

"Good God! As much as that?"

"Yes. But in this instance I shall demand twenty-five."

She shot that out. She wasn't negotiating any more.

"You're out of your mind," I told her. "You got a screw loose."

"You are a difficult person to talk to," she said. "You are a distrusting person, a bullying one, and I should imagine your horses have picked up these traits or are responding to them. It will make my job that much more difficult."

"Twenty-five *percent!*" I laughed. I still couldn't believe it. "Hell, lady, you'd be costing me more than my trainer does!"

"Then let your trainer talk to your horses."

It was my turn to walk down to the fence. Mercy saw me coming, and plodded away.

"I'll have to think about this," I said. "I don't know if any of it makes any sense."

"You have my literature, sir," she said. "You have my testimonials. Call or not call, as you wish."

She started over to her car, a low convertible, red and shining and new, which stood in my driveway with the top down. Very expensive. Just as she was.

"I'd much prefer you *didn't* call," she said, stopping. "I don't believe I like you. Your situation does not attract my interest."

I waited until she got in the car.

"I don't suppose you like my horses *either*," I said. "I suppose you find *them* dull, too. I suppose you're one of those sanctified, scrubbed-out bitches who puts the dollar sign first. I don't suppose you care one crap about my horses' well-being."

Go for the throat, I thought. Get them in the old jugular.

She wasn't offended. Her expression was placid, composed, even a little amused. I knew that look. It was the look Sarah had when she found me in something foolish. The look would last about two minutes, then she'd begin slamming doors.

She started the engine.

I stayed by the fence, close to laughter, waiting to see if this was a woman who knew how to drive a car.

She cut the engine. She stared a long time over at my house, her hands still up on the wheel, that same benign, watchful, untroubled look in her face. Then she turned in her seat and looked down at my fences and barn. All four horses had come out. Mercy had her nose between the lowest boards, trying to get at grass, but the other three had their necks out over the fence, looking at the woman in the car.

Something funny happened in the woman's eyes and in her whole face. She went soft. You could see it soaking through her, warming her flesh.

"Go on," I said. "Get out of here."

She wasn't listening to me. She seemed, for the moment, unaware of my presence. She was attuned to something else. Her jaw dropped open—not prettily . . . she *was* a pretty woman—her brows went up, she grinned, and a second later her face broke out into a full-fledged smile. Then a good solid laugh.

She had a nice laugh. It was the only time since her arrival that I had liked her.

"What is it?" I asked.

"Your stallion," she said. "Egorinski, is that his name? He was telling me a joke. Not very flattering to you."

Her eyes sparkled. She was genuinely enjoying herself. I looked over at Egor. The damned beast had his rear end turned to me. His head, too. He seemed to be laughing.

She got her car started again and slapped it up into first gear. "I shall send you a bill for my time," she said. "Good-bye, Mr. Gaddis."

As she drove out, down the narrow, circling lane, throwing up dust behind her and over the white fence, I could still hear her laughing. I imagined I heard her—sportive now, cackling, giving full rein to her pleasure—even as she turned her spiffy car out onto the highway.

Sarah was at the yard pump. She'd picked up the enamel pot and was filling it with water. She was wearing her print work-dress, but for some reason she'd put back on the high heels she'd been wearing last night. She'd put on her lipstick. The little scratch on her forehead was still there. It had swollen some.

She'd brought out a blanket and dumped that out in the yard beside the pillow.

As I approached, she glanced up, severe and meaning business.

"Stay away," she said. "Don't touch me. Go on with whatever you were doing."

I could see now wasn't the time. That the time hadn't come. That maybe it would be a long time before it did.

I went on down to the barn, scooted up the ladder, and sat on a bale of hay at the loft door. I looked out over the stables, over the fields, over the workout track and the further pasture and out over all of the long valley. I looked at the gray ring of hills. I wondered what had gone wrong with my life. How I had become this bad person.

IN THE GARDEN

*T*he woman—the one who stands here at her apartment windows in her blue stockings and blue shoes and a blue raincoat that hangs to her heels—the woman up here behind her windows high over the city's wayward slopes (Oh snow, oh hoary winter's drool!) and over the murky green waters (Needs stirring, I'll say) of Fisherman's Bay . . . is thinking: *What next? What to do with myself today that can be half the fun yesterday was?*

"Life *calls!*" she suddenly trumpets, surprised herself by the sound of her voice and by all the joy that, like a grinning lunatic, has leapt inside her. (I'm happy as a tick, one might conclude I've been drinkin'.)

She carefully puts down her glass.

"Eleven a.m.," she gloats, "all's well."

She steps out on her narrow balcony, shivering (Merciless winter, oh sweetjesus will spring never come?), bending low and dangerously over the railing to peer inside the recessed sliding doors of the apartment below.

Feet, feet, she thinks, that's all I've ever seen. Shine your shoes, Mister-Man-Down-There.

No feet today, however. The glass needs cleaning and he ought to throw out those two dying ferns.

"I'll call Estelle," she says. "My good friend Estelle."

Do *do* call Estelle, give the little lady a fine thrill.

But Estelle, it turns out (Dear me, I've split my britches), is not home. (Not in? At this hour? What *is* that elfin horror trying to prove?)

So Rebecca—woman by the window—goes back to the window and again looks out over the close-rippling water (Ten years in this place and I've yet to see a fisherman there, only boats and more boats, teensy putt-putts, you'd think civilized people would have better things to do)—looks out over the city slopes to the high, snowy mountains beyond (Oh fold upon fold upon fold, tedious and exhausting, but rather exquisite; yes, I *do* like it, this is such a friendly part of the world).

Oh, she thinks, what *can* I have been thinking of!

Of course.

She goes into her bedroom and takes her time selecting a nice scarf from her dresser drawer, something in a fetching complimentary blue—

"Yes, this one I think."

and ties the silk loosely about her throat.

"Now I'm so pretty," she remarks aloud, "I am pretty enough to *sing sing sing!* And why not, while I'm at it, telephone Estelle?"

Estelle's phone—can you believe it?—rings and rings.

But Rebecca—following a crow's black flight across the bay (Oh look at him swerve and dive, if only I could fly like that!)—is not fooled. Oh, she's *home*, she thinks. Certainly she's home. Where else could she be but at home!

In one of her moods, possibly.

Mustn't discount her elfish moods.

One of her I-don't-want-to-see-anyone days. Doubtlessly nursing old grudges by the ton. Got the brush-off from Harold, could be. Oh, the poor little downtrodden bird.

"None of your business," Rebecca tells herself. "Honey, you stay out of this."

She laughs. Estelle is so funny when she's in her moods. No, one can't help laughing.

A fruitcake, that's what Estelle is on her rainy-day days.

"No way out of it," Rebecca says. "I'd better shoot right over."

A swarm of gnats—fruit flies, she supposes (Genus *drosophila*, dipteria, transparent of mind and wing, oh go away, gnats!)—hangs in the air just short of Estelle's door, which swam Rebecca steers straight through, thinking surely they will scatter. But they come right along with her, a net of floating black dots. They swirl about, an inch up, an inch down, untouched, as she swats. "Shoo, shoo!" she says, "oh, scat!" Finally she wades through, knocks on Estelle's bright red door.

All the curtains drawn, house sealed up tight. Estelle, honey, is it as bad as all that?

"Yoo-hoo! It's me!"

She can hear music playing over the stereo—or radio—something classical. Harpsichordish, may be. Old Worldish anyway.

Estelle being *grand*.

Grim *church* music to aid and abet the foul downspin.

"Let me in *at once*, darling!"

The door opens an inch and no more. The chain remains in place.

"Why have you kept me waiting here for so long?" Rebecca says. "You should do something about this plague of wild gnats."

All she can see of her friend Estelle is one eye in the crack. She appears to have a bandage of some sort half-covering it.

"Go *away*," whispers Estelle.

"But I've walked miles," replies Rebecca, not worried in the least by such rudeness. Ooo-la-la, that's Estelle. "My feet hurt. It isn't easy in these high heels. I've probably got a blister, if you want to know. Anyway, I've got to talk to you. It's imperative. You *are* my best friend."

The door quietly closes.

Uncanny. Oh Estelle, why are you treating me this way?

She can hear Estelle's footsteps across the floor, something clattering down (Temper, temper, oh what a temper she has!) —then the music coming on again, bit louder this time, some kind of silly piano piece, like four birds chirping from a high fence.

Rebecca swatted at the gnats. "Shoo!" she said. "Shoo! Oh, rats! . . ." She walked slowly out to the street, her head down. At the curb she turned and regarded Estelle's house most pensively (Drab, Estelle, very drab. Most shoddy). The house was indeed drab, small and low-slung, like a Crackerjacks box down on its side, and ridiculous with its red door.

Rebecca patted one foot against the pavement. She knotted the scarf tighter against her throat.

Poor Estelle, she thought, how *can* I cheer her up?

She wondered if any of the other people in their houses along the street were watching her. I certainly should be, she thought. I would *continue the investigation* until I knew precisely what was going on. Who *is* that woman? I'd ask myself. What can she *possibly* want? Or, if I were another woman watching me, I'd think: where could she have *found* that beautiful blue coat!

I'd smoke, that's what I'd do. I'd light up a lovely blue cigarette, oh I'd have a killing-good taste of the weed.

I will anyway.

No, no, children might be watching.

An old man, four houses down, was out in his driveway washing his car. Rebecca studied him. Wouldn't it be pleasant, and a nice thing to do, to go and talk to him?

". . . I was dropping in on my friend up the street," she said, speaking from a distance of several dozen yards, "but she does not appear to be receiving."

The man, less old than she had presumed, was down on his knees sudsing a hubcap; he did not look up.

"Her name is E. Beverly Sims," Rebecca went on, drawing closer. "She lives in that flat house with the scrawny box hedge by the front porch. I'm sure you must know her well. Estelle is the very outgoing type, and she has a splendid figure. In a nice friendly neighborhood such as this one is everyone must know everyone."

The man, she now observed, stepping up beside him, had a pokey face and practically no hair. He was chewing on the nub of a cigar while squinting up at her. She admired his way of sitting on his heels.

"Where I live it is not the least like that. I live in a small but very efficient apartment down by the Bay. A condominium. You wouldn't believe what it cost. I'm way up on the twelfth floor, and can see for miles. Do you know that huge ships pass my window at night? Far out, of course. But I have a large telescope mounted on a nice tripod. I am continuing my investigation of these ships. It's easily the most interesting hobby I ever had."

"I'm washing this car," the man grumbled.

Rebecca realized that the remark was somehow meant to put her in her place. She laughed.

"I can *see* that. It must have been extremely dirty."

This comment clearly interested him. He rose up off his haunches, backed up a few paces, lit his cigar, and stared appreciatively at the automobile.

"It *was* filthy," he said. "My son had let this car go to the dogs." He spat, very close to his feet, and backed up a bit more. "They tell me young boys like nothing better than sharp cars to show off with the girls, but I give this car to my son and he has not yet got behind the wheel once."

"Oh my," said Rebecca. "That is curious behavior indeed."

Soap suds all along the car side were drying in the sun. But the man seemed more interested in the hubcap. He stooped beside it, buffing up the chrome with his sleeve. "Of course, he doesn't have his license yet. I give this car to him for his sixteenth birthday, but he has some months to go." He peered up at Rebecca. "Do you know Harold?"

"Your son? No, I—"

"You wouldn't like him. He is the most stuck-up boy I ever saw. Something of a sissy, too, you want to know the truth. Bet you can't guess why."

"Hormones, I bet," said Rebecca. "I bet his hormones got sent straight up a tree."

"Not hormones," he said. "His mother. His mother has pampered the little rat since the day he was born." He paused, flipping his cigar in the dirt. Then he walked over and ground at it with his heel. "He is out now at Symphony School. Harold. He plays the oboe." He picked up the cigar, examining its mangled leaves between his fingers. "This cigar," he said, "it's real Havana. I got a pal sends them to me from Canada. Real cold up there. I got maybe twenty, twenty-five these rascals left." He spread the tobacco out in his palm and poked at it with a finger. "Real beauties, these cigars. I bet they cost my buddy a mint. But he owes me. He owes me a fortune, tell you the truth. You know why?"

Rebecca batted her eyes. "Why?" she asked. It had struck her that this man was somewhat *odd*.

"Because I stole his wife. I stole her right out from under his nose. One day there he was, married to the prettiest woman you ever saw, and the next day she wasn't there anymore. She liked me best, you see. I had the real goods but Ralph—old Ralph—well, old Ralph didn't have *nothing* and the next thing he knew he was out in the cold. Yep, between the two of us we really put it to him."

Rebecca considered this. She wasn't sure she liked it.

"Happy?" the man said. "You never saw two people so happy as the wife and me. Regular lovebirds." He shot a hasty look at Rebecca. "Then we had Harold. Beginning of the end."

Rebecca laughed. That phrase had always been one of her favorites.

"You probably know what I mean," he said. "Kids! Look at Job. He had a house full of kids, but what good did they ever do him? Only more misery."

Rebecca felt that she had been silent far too long. She thought it only right that she should point out *there was another side.*

"You would not think that," she told him lightly, "if you were in India, or in Greece, or even in Japan. Suppose you were in China and believed as you do? At the minimum, you'd be ostracized, and probably you'd be shot."

"Fine by me," he replied. "If I had to live in those places I'd *want* to be shot."

Rebecca walked over to the concrete steps leading up to the front door and sat down, crossing her legs prettily. She lit up a cigarette with her gold lighter and closed her eyes, holding her head back, blowing out the first draw of smoke in a long, measured stream.

"Nobody told you to sit there," the man reproached her. "This is private property." He seemed suddenly very angry.

". . . But sit there if you want to. What the hell, who ever listens to me?"

"I'm sure you've a very strong character," said Rebecca. "I'm sure you must dominate any circle you enter."

He puzzled over this a moment, then, shrugging, dropped down on his ankles again and began scrubbing the rear hub-cap, his back to Rebecca. She noticed for the first time the baseball cap stuffed into his pocket. She found this intriguing, a strongly personal touch. She wondered what kind of hat he would have stuffed there had he been born in India. She found it charming, where men put their hats. He looked so round and full, stooped like that, a complete little world, total to the point even of where he put his hat. She smiled. She liked the way he bobbed up and down on his ankles, how his heels lifted up out of his shoes; his little grunts, too, were very charming. She could see an expanse of pink skin and now his underpants—swatch of black polka dots—rode up over his hips. She wondered if he would be interested in hearing what she had read about Babe Ruth—not so long ago that she had forgotten—in *The New Columbia Encyclopedia*. Sixty homers, imagine that. And born of people so rag-tail poor he had to be sent away to a training school, made to sweep floors for his daily bread. A pitcher, too. Eighty-seven wins in five years, now that was true pitching, that was real horseshoes.

She became aware after a while that the man was watching her out of the corners of his eyes.

She took off one shoe and held it above her head, shaking it as if to dislodge pebbles. But secretly she watched him.

He dropped his sponge into the sudsy bucket, spinning on his heels. His jacket was wet up to the elbows. "Harold's brother now," he announced sullenly, "he's another case. Been begging me for a car for years, but I wouldn't give him the time of day, not even if he got down on bended knee."

Rebecca nodded. "He must have done something extremely reprehensible," she said.

The man gave her a blank look, then shook his head. "Not *my* son," he explained darkly. "No, Norman's the *wife's* son. I keep telling him he ought to go off live with his *real* father, but he just whines '*Aw, Dad.*' Can't even wipe his nose." He picked up his bucket and went around to suds up the grille.

"Estelle is like that, too," Rebecca said.

The man hiked up his pants. He looked off at the closed windows of his house and over at a stunted, leafless tree at the edge of his yard. "That friend of yours," he said gruffly, ". . . that Estelle, she's moved out, you know. That place is *empty* now. No, you'll waste your time knocking on *that* door."

Rebecca decided to let this pass, and the man dropped back down to his bucket. "I wouldn't give ten cents," he grumbled, "to know anybody on this block. Including your long-gone friend."

Rebecca ignored all this. "Beverly was her maiden name," she told him. "She married a man named Sims when she was twenty-eight, and although that union lasted only a short time she and Mr. Sims remain good friends to this day." She smiled mischievously. "Nowadays Estelle has other interests, I understand. She's in love."

"Spit," he said.

"Actually, she's feverish about this particular gentleman, but I have reason to believe the relationship is undergoing its difficult moments."

"Pa-tooey," the man said.

"I'm sure you must have seen him. He drives an orange Toyota."

At this the man perked up. He wheeled about, pointing to a spot on the street vaguely in front of Estelle's house. "Orange?" he said. Rebecca took this to mean that he had seen the car in question parked out in front of Estelle's house through nights too numerous to mention.

"They may be good cars," he said gruffly, "but only a traitor would buy one." He smacked a flat, wet hand against the top of his own automobile. "I've seen him," he said. "He wears a hat."

This news tantalized Rebecca. She had never seen Estelle's lover wearing a chapeau of any sort. She stood up now. She had smoked her cigarette and had her visit and was now ready to leave.

"Where you going?" the man asked her.

She smiled, surprised. "Why, I don't know," she said. "I haven't thought about it."

He strode past her to the side of the house, beckoning. "Come inside," he grumbled. "Something to show you. I bought my son a .22 for his birthday. I've got it on a gun rack in the den. I don't suppose you shoot, being a woman —my wife *hates* it—but what I say is if Harold doesn't go out and shoot something with it the very minute he turns sixteen I'm going to throw him out of the house." He shoved his hands deep into his jacket pockets, scowling back at Rebecca who was lingering. "It beats me," he said, "why women don't like hunting. And fishing. There is not anything more fun than that. Character-building, too. My old man had me out on the marsh with a rifle in my arms before I was two years old. Women! I'll tell you about women. Women have got themselves into this trouble out of their own choosing. They deserve everything they get. Bunch of fools, if you ask me. Silliest thing on two feet. Look at you, for instance. All sky-baby-blue in that silly raincoat and those silly shoes. Well, it's *feminine* all right, but that's all I can say for it."

Rebecca laughed, a low breasty chuckle that brightened her face. She loved insults. She wished he'd say something else— perhaps about her hair or her nice scarf or her blue pocketbook. She wished he'd put on his funny little cap.

"Come on," he ordered. "Want to show you that gun."

Rebecca was tempted. Few things pleased her more than seeing how other people lived. She could imagine herself inside browsing through his cupboards, checking out cereal boxes, opening the refrigerator door to read out the brand names on frozen foods. But she'd been looking at Estelle's house; she was certain she'd seen the front curtain move. "No thank you," she said. "Perhaps another time. I'm often in the neighborhood."

"Buzz off then," he said. "Who asked you? I got better things to do."

The gnats had moved on from Estelle's door. They were now up around the telephone wire where it entered the house, a larger body now, black patch silently lifting and falling, swaying, against the clear blue sky.

"It's me again," Rebecca called, knocking.

The house was silent. Four or five rolled newspapers were on the ground beneath the hedge, soiled and wet, further indication to Rebecca that Estelle's love life had reached the cut-throat stage.

"I've brought you your reading matter!" she shouted, bent at the keyhole, thinking she detected shadowy movement inside.

"I'll huff and I'll puff!" she called. "Stand back!"

Estelle didn't respond.

A tomb.

The back of the house was deserted, too. Curtains were drawn over the windows, and a beautiful spider web had been spun over the upper portion of the door. Crumpled newspaper filled a hole down in the corner of one cracked window. Under the roof line stretched a series of old hornets' nests, or dirt-daubers' sturdy quarters. The garbage can was overturned, but empty. A rusty barbecue stand was down on its side in the tall grass. Numerous tin cans and milk cartons lay about; a huge cardboard box had been flattened by the rain.

Rebecca took her time contemplating the debris, seated in a white metal chair out near where a composting fixture once had stood. She smoked, and pitched her head back to catch the sunshine. She would have been happy if only she had a drink to sip on.

Gloves, she thought. Why haven't I bought myself a pair of nice blue gloves?

The silence of the place fascinated her. She realized she was genuinely enjoying this.

A large fluffy cat, golden in color, hopped up on the picnic table in the neighboring yard. It took turns idly scrutinizing her and, just as idly, licking its fur.

"Gin," said Rebecca. "Gin and tonic, I think."

And she stayed on another ten minutes or so, enjoying the invisible drink.

Someone not far away was calling. A woman's fragile, unhurried voice repeating: *"Oro! . . . Oro! . . . Come home, Oro."*

Very musical, Rebecca thought.

A breeze played gently across her face, further subduing her mood, and she let herself drift along in a sweet, dreamy doze, seeing the world before her as though through a haze in which all things moved in tranquil, harmonic order, pleasant and kind.

The sun dropped down rays thick as a lattice fence, golden and alluring.

What splendor, she thought. I could be in someone's enchanted garden.

Afterwards, drawing the blue collar up against her neck, feeling somewhat chilled, she stepped again up to Estelle's rear window. She rapped on the glass, looking for a peephole through the curtains.

"Estelle? Estelle, darling, please open the door."

She heard a quick catch of breath within and could feel Estelle's presence on the other side of the wall.

"It's lovely out here, it truly is. You should come out and talk to me. He hasn't hurt you, has he?" She heard a whisper of footsteps, the creak of floorboards, and beat her knuckles sharply against the window. "Oh don't be unhappy!" she pleaded. "Please let me in. He isn't worth this pining, Estelle..."

The floor creaked again.

A cat squawked somewhere in the neighborhood, much as if someone were repeatedly pulling its tail.

Rebecca stiffened; she shivered. She whipped her head around, certain that someone had stolen up and was about to hit her on the head.

No...

A very old man with an enormous stomach, wearing a checkered shirt and carrying his shoes in his hands, was out on the steps next door, watching her. He leaned against the door frame, putting on one shoe. Then he leaned the opposite way and put on the other.

"I think she's left that place," he said. "I think she moved out four, five days ago."

Rebecca smiled at him.

The man backed up, slowly withdrawing into the house.

Nearby, someone was singing, or perhaps it was a radio.

Rebecca stared a moment at the dusty, faded newspaper stuffed into the window crack. "I've got my troubles too, Estelle," she said. "My phone rings every night. It's that man I told you about. He refuses to let up. Every night I think, 'Well, tonight he's going to threaten me' . . . but he never quite does. He's extremely cunning. What do I do, Estelle?"

When Estelle didn't answer, Rebecca went up on tiptoe and tugged the stiff paper free. Then she went up again on tiptoe, straightening her arm, and poked her hand into the small opening. She worked her hand past the jagged glass and past the curtain edge and thrust her arm deeper into the room. It felt cold, very cold, in there.

Something brushed or cut or struck against her flesh and with a faint cry of pain, of fear, she snatched back her arm.

Shards of glass tinkled down, her heel twisted in the uneven dirt, and she stumbled back, holding in her breath; she staggered, banged one knee against dirt, then lost her balance totally and landed gracelessly on one hip.

Dizzily, she got to her feet. Her coat sleeve was torn, scar in the blue fabric scarcely larger than a dime; a straight line of blood was popping up in droplets across the back of her hand. It stung.

"You've cut me, Estelle," she said, her voice calm, amazed.

She had a clear vision of Estelle inside the cold room, pressed against the wall, eyes slitted, knife poised, waiting for her again to poke her arm through.

But she wasn't sure. It could have been the glass.

She licked the line clean, hastily pulled free her scarf, and wrapped it around her hand.

"That was uncalled-for, Estelle. That was very mean."

She drew back, watching the window.

"But I forgive you."

At the corner of the house she turned, calling again.

"I know you're not yourself today. I really wish you'd let me help you."

She went once more to the front of the house and sat down on Estelle's stoop, brooding on this turn of events.

No, the fault wasn't Estelle's. The fault was Arnold's.

She unfolded one of the newspapers. The moisture had soaked through and the sheet had to be peeled apart. Displayed across the front page was a photograph of Nureyev leaping, his legs flung wide, bare buttocks to the camera, arrow pointing to where his tights had ripped. DANCER SHOWS TRUE FORM, the caption read. But Rebecca shivered at the black headlines. Shivered, and let her head swoop down against the page. 58 DIE IN BLOODBATH ... OIL RIG GOES DOWN OFF NEWFOUNDLAND, NO SURVIVORS ... WARSAW ERUPTS.

Yes, she thought, and my mother is dead, my husband has left me, I have no children, hardly any life, and no one knows anything at all—or cares!—about poor Rebecca.

But when her head came up she was ruefully smiling.

Yes, all true, she thought, but we shall continue the investigation.

She turned, peering through Estelle's keyhole.

"Peace Promised for One Zillion Years!" she shouted. "Happiness Lays Golden Egg! . . . Man Steps in Pothole, Breaks Leg!"

·She removed the scarf from her hand and closely observed the wound. "Nineteen Stitches Required!" she called. "Noted Plastic Surgeon Called In! . . . Lady Recovers from Heartless Attack!"

The tear in the coat bothered her more. She wondered whether a good seamstress could save the day.

A boy was approaching, yet some distance down the street, slouching, his hands deep into his pockets, small black case tucked up under one arm, his face white as plaster in the sunlight.

Harold.

The man who had been washing the car was no longer in the yard, nor was the car. A woman now stood out in front of the house, arms crossed over her chest. She was looking past Rebecca at the dawdling boy. She wore a print dress, too bold for her thick figure; the hem hung unevenly and the grass cut off her legs. She called wanly to the boy:

"Harold! Harold! He hit me, Harold!"

Harold stopped. Now nearly abreast of Estelle's house, he looked not at his mother but at Rebecca coolly watching from the stoop.

"You don't live there," he said to her. "That place is deserted."

Rebecca loved this frontal approach. He was sullen, nasty even, but she wanted to reach out and hug him. He was abusive, yes, but it seemed to her that those who were most insulting were also those who most willingly offered enthusiastic praise.

"What's that under your arm?" she asked him. "Is that an oboe?"

The boy's face clouded. He kicked a shoe against the pavement, standing with his body bent like a quarter moon.

"I wish you'd play for me," Rebecca said. "I haven't heard an oboist play really well in years."

"Who are you?" he growled. "What are you doing in our neighborhood?"

"*Harold! He hit me, Harold,*" called his mother.

The boy put his case on the sidewalk and, crouching, took the instrument from it, polishing the bulbous end on his sleeve.

"I give the pitch to the whole orchestra," he said, standing, glaring at Rebecca.

He blew a strong, high note, which then seemed to falter—but the note came back stronger, more penetrating, thin, only a little plaintive, and it intensified and kept on coming.

"*Harold!*" called the mother. "*He really hit me hard.*"

His mother now stood at the edge of her yard, her hands twisting around the narrow trunk of a leafless tree.

The boy scowled at Rebecca. "Sure, I could play," he said. "But I won't. Harold only plays for money."

Rebecca nodded doubtfully, her thoughts drifting, watching the swarm of gnats at the side of the house, hovering a few feet above the scraggly grass.

"You're a very good-looking boy," Rebecca said. "I'll bet you must be every inch of six feet tall."

"*He hurt me, Harold!*"

The boy came up and sat down on the stoop beside Rebecca.

"I'm very advanced for my age," he told her. "I'm very unusual. In fact, I'm eccentric."

"Well, it is a strange neighborhood," she said.

"Not that strange. The woman who lived here—what was her name?"

"Estelle."

"Estelle was strange. I saw her one night out back of this house, practically naked—in a flowing gown, I mean—down on her knees in front of that chair she's got back there, bowing and bowing, like an Arab. *That's* strange."

Rebecca smiled. "Not if you know Estelle," she replied softly.

Across the way his mother advanced a few paces, her footsteps weighted, as if deep holes were opening in front of her. When she saw them looking at her she backed up, returning hastily to the tree.

The boy moistened the mouthpiece, allowed his head to settle deep between his shoulders, then played several quick, rather piercing, notes. "Listen to this," he said.

He closed his eyes.

He played.

When the last lingering note faded, Rebecca, only now opening her eyes, clapped enthusiastically. "Oh God," she sighed, genuinely moved. "You're going to be immortal."

The boy stretched out one hand, palm upwards.

"*I'm bleeding, Harold!*" his mother called.

Rebecca opened her purse. She looked thoughtfully at her bills, then unsnapped her change purse, and dropped two quarters into his hand.

The boy stared glumly at the coins. "What can this buy?" he asked.

"Happiness," Rebecca said. And she smiled in a bewitched way, as if indeed it had.

The boy walked away, pointing with his instrument to the swarm of gnats.

"Those gnats are mating," he said.

At his yard he turned and went on past his mother without

a word and entered the house and a few seconds later she left the tree and scooted in after him.

Rebecca leaned back against Estelle's door. "The music was lovely, wasn't it?" she said. "I wonder where such genius comes from."

It seemed to her that from inside the house there came a whispery, half-strangled *yes!*

Rebecca stayed on, pursuing stray thoughts as they popped into her head. Harold's music, unquestionably very beautiful, had put the Garden of Eden into her mind. A kind of dreamy, springtime garden. Yet now several hundred men, no larger than bees, were erecting a barbed-wire fence around the place.

She laughed. How silly.

"A blight has hit the garden," she said.

Men with rifles were up sniping from their towers. *Plunk plunk plunk!* Bullets stirred up soft puffs of dust in the arid soil.

Off in the corner, darkened, the Tree of Knowledge hunkered down, like a rat gone fat from too much wine and cheese. The bullets went on plunking.

Plunk plunk plunk!

Rebecca giggled. It's absurd, she thought, but what can be done about it?

"*Aim over their heads,*" a voice said. "*We don't want to harm anyone.*"

Rebecca's heart caught. She recognized that voice.

"*Well, one or two,*" God said, "*as an example.*"

Two or three hundred of the small bee people began to fall. They rolled down into the grass, kicked and lay still, or they screamed and went limp, snagged on the wire.

Plunk plunk plunk!

Rebecca leaped up, throwing her hands over her eyes. "Estelle," she said, "I've just had the most awful vision!" She knocked again on Estelle's door, and kicked at it, and put her eye against the keyhole, and for a moment believed she saw another eye looking back—but then decided this was nonsense, since Estelle lacked any such curiosity. No, Estelle, after such a busy day, would be spread out on her bed, damp cloth across her brow, claiming headaches, claiming troubles, agony too painful to mention.

I too was once like that, Rebecca thought. I believed I didn't have a friend in the world.

Like something shoved over the edge . . . and still falling.

But she had learned better long ago. People valued her. Friends were ever eager to see her. They let her know without any guile or trickery—without any reservations whatsoever—that their doors were always open.

"*Any time, Rebecca. For you we are always home.*"

She brushed off the seat of her raincoat, fluffed her hair, and started towards the street. "I'm going now!" she called. ". . . Take care of yourself! . . . Enjoyed visiting! . . . See you tomorrow!"

Maybe. Maybe she would see her tomorrow.

At any moment she expected to see Estelle yanking open the door, flinging herself down the path, embracing and pulling her back.

"Chin up, darling! . . . Accept no wooden nickels!"

But the red door remained firmly shut.

She wondered what Harold would be doing. Where Arnold would be in his orange Toyota.

What next? Who to see?

She'd go home first, laze around a bit. Have a quiet smoke, perhaps a nice gin and tonic. Watch the big, distant ships hulking ever so silently by on Fisherman's Bay. Watch the fog—watch darkness—descend slowly over the water.

Think this matter through.

Think about it tomorrow.

AGNES AND THE COBWEBS

*W*ould Mrs. Forshumund compare with Agnes?

That is what Herman was wondering as he padded down Queensquay to his rendezvous. Would she have Agnes' easy temperament, her fine way of seeing things? Let's hope so, he thought, passing the windows of the Donkey restaurant. If not, I may well wish I had never made this trip.

Donkey? What a curious name for an eating spot. Almost as if the owner *wants* to fail.

Herman backed up, wondering about that.

Lo and bedamned! The place was packed to the rafters. A long line of smartly dressed people contentedly waiting for tables.

The place *smelled* of money.

Curious. Really curious, Herman thought. These days— well, these days you never knew what people might go for.

"Why don't they call it The Muck Heap?" he said to a passerby, "and really rake in the gravy."

The man he'd spoken to actually did a little jig, hastening on.

Is there ketchup on my tie? Herman asked himself. Spittle on my chin?

He, too, performed a little jig—winning a grin or two from those entering the dining place.

Herman put his nose up to the window glass. Some kind of open-grill arrangement in the rear, big orange flames flapping about.

Looks dangerous, he thought. A regular firetrap. If you got caught in there, in that mob, you'd really be screaming for mercy.

Ought to be a law, he thought.

Still, if he had an extra dollar or two, he might give it a whirl. Nothing ventured, nothing gained: that was his attitude. And it had served him pretty well, that way of seeing things. He'd got by all on his own, no help from anyone.

Well . . . excluding Agnes.

Had to count her in.

But no, you wouldn't find him, Herman Hotchkiss, holding his hand out for scraps. There was such a thing as pride. Dignity.

Pride and dignity, he reflected—that is what most people lack.

Bunch of animals, if you wanted to know the truth.

"Okay," he said, "make a date for the Donkey. Once my ship comes in. Once the insurance company pays off."

He padded on, wondering again what Mrs. Florence Forshumund would be like. Whether she'd compare favorably with Agnes.

Not that many could. Agnes was tops. Well, she *had been* tops. In her prime—he might as well come right out and say it—when in her prime, *no one* had held a candle to Agnes.

My one-and-only, he thought. Yep, an angel, that was Agnes.

*   *   *

The traffic at Queensquay and Orbit held him up. He decided to sit and rest his feet a bit on the bus bench at the corner. Early yet. Time to kill. No point in arriving early. Punctuality, he imagined, to someone like Mrs. Florence Forshumund was everything.

"Punctuality counts, Mr. Hotchkiss!"

Yep, he could practically hear her saying those very words.

Agnes had been the same. Be late for a meeting with Agnes and she'd scream bloody murder. Scratch your eyes out.

No, you couldn't put much past old Agnes.

Herman studied his watch face. Was kind of fun, watching that little second hand go bumping around. No tick-tock either. A very good watch.

He wondered where he had got it.

Nice band, too.

Fifteen minutes more before he was due at Mrs. Forshumund's residence. He certainly hoped Mrs. Florence Forshumund would not prove to be a washout. He didn't *think* she would be. In court she'd certainly shown some moxie. A lot of class.

Presence, that's what it was—she'd had presence.

"Just like Agnes," Herman said aloud. "I thought to myself at the time, *Now there's one that can give Agnes a run for her money.*"

Cute, too, though a touch overripe, a touch *hefty.*

But not *too* hefty, God knows.

Ample, that was the word.

Mrs. Florence Forshumund was *ample.*

She had what it took and knew where she kept it, that was Mrs. FF. And what moxie. She hadn't batted an eye when he'd stared straight at her. She'd stared straight back, unflinching, as if to say, "Well, I can see, Mr. Hotchkiss, that *you* are something special. I only hope that you can see I am, too."

He'd seen it, yes sir.

The WALK and WAIT signs interested Herman. That was a good touch, having the different colors, green for WALK and red for WAIT A COTTON-PICKIN' MINUTE. Just the sort of idea he might have come up with himself.

Works, too, he observed. Otherwise, probably fifty people a day would get their butts run over. Blood and guts all over the place.

What pandemonium. A guy like me would never get across the street. I'd probably still be sitting here when the Last Judgment came down.

Matters such as this *light* business—on a day such as this—was one of the things Herman found so fascinating about life. So many people doing—or thinking about doing—exactly the same thing he was doing.

Inventing *signals*, for God's sake.

Really blows the mind.

WALK.

WAIT.

WALK.

WAIT.

Christ, it made you feel warm all over, just watching the little bastard do its job. And knowing there was a human brain behind it, no different from his own.

The common bond, Herman thought, that's what it is.

No, it didn't pay to stomp down on people, to see them as washouts. They were always up to something, *busy-busy*, so busy sometimes they'd make your head spin. And most of it worthwhile, obviously. I mean, thought Herman, take those people back there at the Donkey place. You'd swear—Agnes would have—they were just there to swill wine and fill their gullets . . . to while away a sappy lunch hour. But, in fact, an hour from now, their hunger satisfied, they'll be back at their jobs—back home or wherever it is they go. Getting things done, whipping away at important work.

Knocking shit out of all the old cobwebs.

Precisely the kind of stuff old Agnes never had understood. *Button your lip,* she'd say. *What do you know about it, muscle-mouth?*

Too keyed up, that had been Agnes' trouble. Quick to tear everything down. Zest, yes, vigor, yes—but no true, deep, abiding spirit. No respect for how things worked. And *awfully* bossy. Like that time they had been eating peanuts.

Chew them, Herman, she'd said. *Watch me. You'll soon get the hang of it.*

Yep. Might be time to apply a little of the *revisionist's* theory to old Agnes.

Herman fumbled out a cigarette and stared at it. Did he really want to smoke? Did he really want this cigarette? Couldn't he just chew on a mint instead?

Agnes would have said, "Smoke if you want. It can't kill all of us."

And naturally she'd have one going herself. A regular chimney, Agnes was.

"And have a drink while you're at it. Put your feet up. Relax, Herman. It isn't the end of the world."

Funny thing, though: with Agnes pacing and exclaiming— having a fit about this and that—you certainly *felt* it was.

Put out the dog, Herman.

Put out the lights, Herman.

Roll over, Herman.

Yep, she'd had a bossy streak, no question about that. It hadn't been all peaches and honey. She'd been a tough cookie. Hard as nails. No point in wasting sentiment on Agnes. In trying to rub up to her good side.

Like that time he'd showed up with a red bathtub.

Take it back, Herman. I told you and told you I wanted blue. Or white. Blue or white, Herman. I told you red was my absolute last choice.

Or how flamboyant she got if he came in sporting a new bow tie or had got himself a sharp haircut or had gone looking for a girl friend.

Oh God. Oh God God God, Herman, you look hideous! Practically inhuman! A girl friend? You? Have ALL your screws come loose?

Yes, the future was looking brighter, minute by minute, for Mrs. Florence Forshumund.

It's the back seat for Agnes, thought Herman.

He wondered what Mrs. F. truly thought about him. Did she say to herself, "Well, he's innocent, that's perfectly clear. Herman is in no way guilty of this crime." Or did she say, "Well, I have *some* doubt. The evidence is all circumstantial. His previous character is without blemish. No, I cannot bring myself to convict a man on the basis of what I've heard here." Or did she say, "Nonsense. It's an open-and-shut case. He's guilty as can be." But did she then look into his face and say, "I have looked into his face and what I see when I look there is that there must have been extenuating circumstances. He must have had good reason for what he did. That Agnes person, for instance; I'm not sure but what she didn't drive him to it. Therefore, I am voting not guilty. I say let Herman go scot-free."

Could be. Could be she had reasoned any of these ways. Could be she had stood by him from the start. Could have said, "He's innocent, and I don't want to hear any more about it. The case is perfectly absurd. It is an outrage that a man of his caliber was ever brought to trial in the first place."

But one thing he knew with dead certainty she hadn't done was conclude he was *non compos mentis. Fanatico*, unhinged, shatterpated, crackbrained, demented, etc.

Not even Agnes, who got carried away now and then, had ever gone that far. "Oh, you're a nut," she'd say. "But you're harmless. You're disordered, but that's about all. Nothing to get hysterics over."

"Just like your father," she'd add.

Oh, Agnes did know how to stick the knife in. How to break the blade off inside.

Mrs. F., if he knew anything about human nature—and he did—wouldn't be like that. She might be *flawed*, but she wouldn't be bringing his *father* into every conversation.

Or kicking up a fuss about girls.

It *was* interesting, Herman found—delightful, really—trying to figure out how Mrs. Forshumund and the other jurors had seen him. And what the judge thought, for that matter, although try as he may he had been totally incapable of entering the judge's head. No, the judge was an enigma. The judge had not struck a cord in him anywhere. There was something downright dishonest—and presumptuous—about a judge's position in the first place.

Be a lot better, Herman thought, if they'd simply abolish that whole idea. Altogether dump that judge part.

Maybe put up a little flashing sign where the judge sat:

STAND.

SIT.

SPEAK.

GO.

STOP.

—that kind of thing.

GUILTY.

NOT GUILTY.

Maybe something more complicated for the really difficult cases.

PART-WAY GUILTY. Maybe that. Or: GUILTY BUT NOT HIS FAULT. After all, this was a modern age, not everything was so open-and-shut. Or: TEMPORARY IN-SANITY. That was a good one, no harm there. It still left you with your dignity intact. After all, it was human nature to lose control now and then. Kind of came with being human.

"Yeah, me too," everyone could say. "I can relate to that. I've gone off the deep end a time or two myself. Know what it's like."

Sure. Something electronic. Be a lot better than having a judge. Judges, now, what did they know except what somebody told them? But a sign—say, even a fancy computer—would be able to sort it out a lot better.

Of course, a computer would need maintenance, for Christsake. Be good for the economy, come to think of it. Jobs. Software.

Bet those Japanese are working on it this very minute. Getting ready to flood the market.

Set jurisprudence ahead a hundred years.

Those little rascals! No, you had to get up awfully early to get the jump on them.

Oh well, *time*, thought Herman. Time to shake a leg and get over to Mrs. Florence Forshumund's. See what's cooking in that corner. Maybe take up this whole business with her, see what she thinks. Let her know that Herman Hotchkiss is a man with ideas. That she didn't have him pegged wrong.

Man-on-the-move, thought Herman—that's probably how she sees me. Hell, we might even get together. Get a place of our own. *Share the same bed!* Woo! Now how about that? Is that an idea!

I am really hitting on all cylinders today, thought Herman. Yep, the old brain is really going clickity-clack today. Agnes would be gaga. *In the same bed*: that would make Agnes roll over. Would make her shiver and shake.

Wooeee!

"The right side or the left side?" he'd say. "Which side do you like best, Mrs. Forshumund?"

Not that there were any two ways about it: he'd take the left side, because he always had. Agnes had seen to that.

"*Don't hog the middle. Herman, you stay right where I put you. And no turning over unless I do.*"

Set in her ways, was Agnes.

Of course, what Agnes would say to that charge was: "Herman, you are looking at a person who knows her own mind. And if you don't like it, buddy-boy, you know what you can do."

Know where you can get off.

If Agnes had said that getting-off line once she'd said it a thousand times.

She wouldn't say it any more, however. No, he'd seen to that.

And Mrs. Forshumund and the other jurors had backed him up. They'd said, "We're on *your* side, Herman. You have done no wrong in *our* eyes."

Bully for you, is what they'd said.

Funny thing was, and something else they ought to think about, they'd not trooped by to shake his hand once it was all over. They'd not even acknowledged it *was* over, except for Mrs. Forshumund.

Needed more *ceremony*, that's what the proceedings needed. Maybe a little after-hours celebration down at the Donkey restaurant.

Thank God for Mrs. Forshumund—was how he felt.

Herman looked at his watch. Still another minute or two to go.

Mrs. F., waiting, would probably have ants in her pants. Yep. Pins and needles, he guessed.

Funny thing about this watch. How the face was upside-down on his arm, all the numbers backwards. You really had to twist your head about to read it.

Hadn't been that way yesterday, near as he recalled.

Still, it hadn't buffaloed him. He was going to be right on time.

He gave a great whack to Mrs. Forshumund's door. Might as well let her know from the start what kind of man she was dealing with, he figured.

Not one that would take any crap off *anybody*! Including Agnes, bless her heart.

Mothering isn't easy, Herman, she'd always said. *You ought to try it sometime.*

Then she'd pull the covers up to her neck—and if he touched her when she wasn't in the mood, *look out!*

That touching business now, that had been a hundred percent of the problem.

Not NOW! she'd say.

Just like your father! she'd say.

All you men think of!

Then, with him dead asleep, there she'd come:

NOW, Herman!

Roll over, Herman!

Tell me how sweet I am, Herman!

This old bed has seen some good times, Herman!

A real headache, Agnes was. Left you hardly knowing *what* to think. And old age hadn't helped her any.

Made her *worse*, if the truth were known.

Yep, it was time for a little of the revisionist's work on Agnes. She was a long way from being *ideal.*

Like, for instance, all that head-smacking he'd got as a kid because of his inability to tie his shoelaces.

Smack! Take that, Herman, you clod! You sniveler. How you come to be of my own flesh and blood is beyond me.

So Mrs. Florence Forshumund had better watch out. She'd better mind her P's and Q's. He wasn't going to put up with any more behavior like *that.*

* * *

He could hear her footsteps approaching. *Thump, thump, thump*—she had a pretty heavy foottread, Mrs. F. did. Not at all light on her toes like Agnes.

Well, you couldn't have everything.

Nice little peephole in the walnut door. Get a good bead on me, Mrs. F., he thought. Take a good long gander at the man who is going to change your life.

Herman adjusted his tie. Smiled.

Time to turn on the charm, he thought. Give her a good eyeful.

Mrs. Forshumund stood in the doorway regarding him closely, something indecisive in her face. Then her features softened.

"Mr. Hotchkiss?" she said. "Herman?"

"Son?" she said.

Herman felt a thrill of apprehension as he looked her over. As he thought about taking his first step across her threshold. He wondered if maybe he shouldn't have left warning notes scattered about the city. Scattered along his trail. *Gone to F's. Inform authorities, should circumstances warrant. Should Herman Hotchkiss never be seen again.*

Mrs. Forshumund was beckoning, however. Coaxing. A black, motherly shawl swung half across her face. Her eyelids fluttering.

Yep. A bit of the flirt here, thought Herman. Bit of the same cut as Agnes. But a whole lot classier, somehow.

He could hear a bird—nasty parrot, it sounded like—shrieking from the hidden depths of the house. *Odious* noise. That bird would have to go.

Herman squared back his shoulders, and entered. Taking her hand. Taking the plunge.

CONVERSATIONS WITH RUTH: THE FARMER'S TALE

"The farmer appeared at our door today," she told me. "Something about him," she said, her voice wan, "that compelled me to invite him inside."

I didn't reply to this. I went directly to the liquor cabinet and had a good snort.

"I wish you would use a glass," she said. "It's asking so little."

"Did he use a glass?" I said. I sat in the easy chair and put up my feet and closed my eyes. "Did he have his overalls on? His hat? His longjohns? Did he have dirt under his nails?" I raised the bottle, had a second pull. It swirled down my pipes, landed splash in my gut; raised a little fire, then settled down. "Pleasant?" I asked. "Did you and your farmer have a pleasant time?"

She let out the smallest moan. I looked at her. My wife's eyes are luminous; they are quick and green; her eyes, at times, are all that one may see of her. Made that way, I would guess, out of fear and stubborn hope, and because she knows she has lost something she never knew she'd found.

"I'll take it in the glass now," I said. "Up to the brim and mind it doesn't splash out."

Groan. She has a heart and organs and limbs and a human head, but all that has anything to do with me is to be found within her luminous, watery eyes.

She seated herself on the edge of a velvet-black chair. Two inches, that's all she needs. Knees together now, chin up, eyes forward, speak:

"He was here for most of one hour," she said. "I brought him into this room but I sensed he was uneasy so I took him back into the kitchen."

She smiled sadly—such a charmer—and obliged me by pouring two fingers from the bottle.

"Ice? Ice?"

"No ice," I said.

I removed my shoes and stared at my big lumpy feet. My big ugly feet.

"He tracked up the carpet, even so."

"Did he? Did he, now? It seems to have come up all right. No harm done, wouldn't you say?"

Poor wife, she sat with her head bowed. Working her thumbs.

Agitated? Are you agitated, dear?

I took the two fingers and swallowed all of it at once and then gave the glass back to her.

It's empty, my darling. No comfort in an empty glass.

Her hand as she took it was cold. Her hands always are. Only her eyes are warm. Her deep, warm, watery, luminous eyes. See how she sits. Portrait of Wife. Once a lovely butterfly, now back again to her mothlike stage.

"Another?" she said. "You want another?"

By all means. By all means, another. Make that two. Make it ten. Keep it coming, my honey.

She turned on the table lamp, a devious route. A cunning trail. Oh, he drinks too much, he'll fall one day in a heap. It was already darkening outside. A big, dark, ugly, brutal world.

I laughed. I was giving myself the creeps.

I heard her sigh. Heard the tinkle of glass.

I studied the lamp. It cast a soft light, a gentle glow. It cast light from ceiling to the floor, a funnel built for pouring at either end. Oh, farmer-in-the-dell, I thought. High-ho the Merry O. I dislike this hour of the evening, this moment when the first lamp is lit. Another day stalking you to the death. I dislike winter in this part of the world. The lamp's illumination is pathetic, it is light of a desperate kind. Foul glow, making us only more aware of the world's solitude. Of my own and hers. Of these houses, of the great empty fields and the bigger-than-life tree groves of once-upon-a-time. Of all it is that winter kills.

Open your pockets, winter. Let's see what you have in there.

"Another, yes, by all means. Why not have one yourself? Tie one on. Live dangerously. Scout the razor's edge. Bring me over a big troughful."

"You're so morbid," she said. "So morbid when you get like this."

"Right. I'm hardly human when I get like this. . . . What happened today?"

"Nothing happened. The farmer called. That's all that happened today."

Groan, groan. She stood about nine feet away, inching towards the front door. Dressed for travel. The long coat came to her heels.

"Going out? Got errands to run? Chores? Got fences to mend?"

Her eyes blinked. They almost never do. Her eyes are swollen, luminous; when they are closed we both disappear.

"Sorry," she said. A whisper. She stood by the liquor cabinet now, wringing her hands. "Yes. Yes. I think I was. I believe I should."

"Ah. You won't be treated this way."

"Yes. No. I won't."

"Good. Good for you."

She dropped her head. Searched for patterns on the floor. Look, there's one. There's another. There is where the farmer stood.

"Nice?" I asked. "Is he nice? Your farmer? A bit taciturn, no doubt. Tracked up the carpets, did he? Let's shoot him. Did he give a favorable weather report? Cloudy? Rain, wind, more snow on the way? That sort of thing."

She took her coat off, draped it over a chair. Over the black chair. "These," she said. She pointed to a large bag down in the corner. Tugged it out. Gunny sack. Loosely knotted at the top. Oh, I know those bags. Seen them on women, seen them on clotheslines. Seen them flapping away. Bring back the good times. Bring back Farmer-in-the-Dell. "He brought these. Spuds, he called them. A gift. Spuds. 'What are neighbors for?' That is what he said. 'Spuds. We ought to get to know each other. All is forgiven.'"

"Forgiven?" I said. "You don't forgive farmers. What is he thinking about? I'd sooner shoot myself."

She retreated several paces. Lowered her head. Wrung her hands. "I try so hard," she said. "You don't try. He's a nice man." Fear keeps my wife pressed back against walls. That, or hope, keeps her inching towards the door. But don't be deceived. I am not what she fears. The farmer, that poor skunk: he is.

"More? Please? Do you mind? Before you go?"

She brought the bottle over. Old Bushmills. It had gone down some. Old Bushmills is the only whisky I ever touch. One can never become an alcoholic so long as one sticks to a single quality label and never keeps more than one case in the pantry. One in the pantry, another under the belt.

"Home ten minutes and already pie-eyed."

She poured my glass full. Pie-eyed, yes. Bent like that, pouring, her collar high around the proud head, her shoulders round, she looked more than ever like some good stolid beast rerouted from its plodding labor in the fields. Beautiful luminous eyes no more than a hand's length from my own. Aroma, too. Visiting someone? Beautiful, yes. And in that one-lamp glow mysterious, like the smoky-snowy sodden grays of our mountain peaks before dawn. So beautiful and so cold too, that you'd swear something other than blood flowed in her timid veins. Liquid earth. Chilling somehow, like the Juan de Fuca Strait which hems us in. Like what was left over long ago after the cold waters of these seas got tired.

"We have only to ask," she said.

Her voice startled me. She was down on all fours, black coat dragging the floor, built suddenly like a bear. Rooting into the spud bag.

"Only to ask," she repeated. "Should we want more."

"Move over," I said. "Let's see how the crop was this year."

I peered with her into the dark sack. It held a few potatoes, no doubt of that. Musky odor. Old earth. We crawled head and shoulders into the bag. Sniffed. Musky indeed. Black as the pits. "He's got something going here," I said. "Farmer or potato, one or the other, it knew what it was doing."

"I'm a city girl," her voice said. "I don't understand any of this."

Oh, so black in there. Her aroma, her warm skin. Not an eye anywhere. I buzzed her ear, snuggled in to her neck, put my mouth wet where I thought hers was.

"Not in here," she said. "Hardly the place." She backed up. I let the sack flop down. New Spanish reds with the dirt still clinging to them, the flesh nicked with hoe stabs. Moist earth. I rouged my face with the black soil.

"Want some?"

"No thanks."

She watched. I peeled off a spot of black earth, brought it up to my tongue. "I could eat this," I said. "Eat it, eat you. I could get my heart's worth full."

"Do," she said.

The swallowing wasn't hard.

"More?"

"More," she said. "Eat it up to the brim. No spills."

I slurped another taste of cold earth. Swallowed it down.

"Now me," she said.

My wife. City slicker, mother-of-pearl. Mother of Jesus, wife of Joseph, bride of the shorn lamb. You there, sweetheart, with your timeless, luminous, beatific eyes.

"No speeches," she said. "No haunting love songs. Dig in."

And, bless me, I did.

"You farmers," she said after a while. "Enough of this. Get on with the job."

And honey that is honey, oh honey, we did.

Now the summing up. Now the sinking down, the putting-matters-to-rest.

She arranged a pillow behind my head. Arranged music on the wheel: *Etude: Psalm of the Somnolent Eves.*

"What gave adventure," she said, "to Shakespeare."

I closed my eyes.

"There," she said. "What all the farming is for. Sit. Sit. Don't move a muscle from there."

I sat as commanded, remembering, however, a detail from my early and sordid childhood. The old pellagra days. A boy crawling under the house to hide from all the terrors familiar to him. Crouching in that pit the dogs had channeled there. Cool hole for hot days, a hole safe from prying eyes. Move over, dog. Move over, old pal of mine.

Keeping a steady bead on the swept yard, on the earth packed even too tight for wild grass. On the weathered fences, the chicken coops and barns. Clicking lids at the haze of distant fields. Waiting for bones.

"I'll get your dinner," my wife said. "Then we can talk. We need to settle this."

The door closed and I was alone.

Me and Bluenose, the recalcitrant dog. Blackie the terrier, and Tick the distempered hound.

At the side window, gaudy bubble cut at considerable expense into the red brick wall, I looked out over my own narrow yard. Our own pitiless estate, mine and hers. We go green into winter. Our trees sculpted. The hedge like gargoyles. What are we doing here? One could shoot billiards on this grass. Green into winter, black into the new year. Our little Pan, even during snowfalls, continues to urinate into his mossy pool. Frogs hoot, the heated goldfish gape. No rusted plow to stand as our mailbox. I looked out over the neighbor's wide acreage. Historical man, last farmer on the block. Looked past his weathered chicken coops, his fences and barns. Looked into the haze of distant fields. Lifted the bottle in a muddled toast to him:

"Here's to you, farmer!" I cried. "Here's to another bumper crop next year!"

For how many years now have I heard the wind rattling his dried-up corn? Seen him on his knees at the first sign of frost, stretching white muslin over rumpled ground? Solitary dooms-day figure following his bull tongue plow. Throwing down seed. Hoeing crabgrass out.

I hear my mother calling to us. The potatoes boil. Parsley is chopped. The table is set.

Don't forget to wash your faces.

Butter melts over the beautiful shapes.

I sit with my brothers and sisters on the rough board, elbows on the table, chin flying low—primed for that moment when the prayer amens.

Amen. Dig in.

I spear a potato and it divides on my plate. My mother ladles thick gravy on.

How you boys eat so much, she says, *is beyond me.*

Me, too. It is way beyond me. I stare down the table. Stare into my mother's luminous, all-forgiving eyes. "Once a farmer, always a farmer," she says. "None of you children shall ever leave this place."

THE BIRTH CONTROL KING OF THE UPPER VOLTA

*T*he most extraordinary thing happened to me today. I woke up and discovered that I had lost yesterday. Amazing! Not a slither, parcel or dot of it remained. Yes! The sun was dazzling bright, my entire room was lit up like a storefront. I stretched, I yawned, I kicked off my sheets: oh lovely, perfect lovely!—is what I said.

Absolutely. That's how innocent I was.

And here I am forty-seven years old. You'd think I would have had a hint.

Dogs outside my window were having a romp. Squealing, yowling—how I had slept through their hubbub was more than I could imagine. Yet I felt wonderfully excited. Renewed, you might say. "What a dreamy day!" That's exactly what I said to myself—and right away set about performing my exercises. A somersault. Another one. Nothing broke, thank goodness. My room is so small I have to do these flip-flops on a pinhead. But the exhilaration!—I truly felt superb, even while lifting my barbells. Twenty, thirty, this is too easy, I told myself—add more weight! Add a ton. I slid on the ton.

Ten, twenty, thirty—no trouble at all. I could have gone on all day pressing these feathers, with barely a pause for breath.

"Oh you're fit," I said laughing, addressing my form in the mirror. "You're in peak condition, Adlai!" I pulled on my pants, scooped back my hair. Washed my face and neck in the little sink, eager to run down to my breakfast. "Eat a horse, Adlai," I said, "yes you could. What an appetite you've worked up! Hurry up, now!"

Ah, what a babe. What an innocent. For it was then, hustling through the door, that I made the discovery. The beautiful calendar hanging by the nail drew my eye. And why not, for pictured there was my sweetheart, Greta Gustafsson. I always notice her, entering or leaving. Sultry woman, she'd mope—she'd scratch out my eyes—if I didn't. Everyone needs noticing is what Greta would say. "What a beauty you are," I said, rubbing my cheek against this image. Kissing her bare shoulders. Greta moaned. I moaned also. "Good morning, my darling," I said. "Sleep well, my beauty?" She lowered her eyes. This morning she seemed preoccupied—seemed distant. My heart ached. Greta deserved better than I could give her. She deserved, in the least, a silver frame, a wall with a good view. Yet as it is there is hardly room for myself. For my footlocker and narrow bed. The walls!—stretch out your arms and there you have it. And so ugly! Uneven and fly-specked— filthy!—with immense zigzags cracking all about.

"No, the door," I said, smoothing down her hair, "the door is best for you, beautiful Greta. Don't complain. Don't scold. Things will be looking up for us once I get that job with the Pole. Give me a smile, darling. What would you like for breakfast, my honey? Say the word and I shall get it." I kissed her eyes. Greta likes that. She purred. Oh Greta adores eye-kissing. My perfect Greta.

But wait, for here's the news. Drawing back, I happened to glance at the date. Mercy! "What's this?" I asked myself. Impossible. But yes, there it was. Yesterday had disappeared.

Had become, I mean, today. What *do* I mean? I mean at that very second I discovered there had been no August ten in my life. The bold red type was clearly announcing itself: August eleven—anniversary of Blondin's crossing of Niagara Falls on a tightrope wire, so the little historical note informed me. *"God help me!"* I cried, *"I've lost yesterday! What happened to the tenth?"* Greta giggled. Then she saw my stricken face and fell quiet.

Gone, I thought. One whole day! Jesus God!

I stumbled out into the hall. Voices floated up from the dining room, jibber-jabber, everyone talking at once, the way they always do. Slurp-slurp—you'd think I slept above a hog pen. Jibber-jabber, slurp-slurp—what imps!

"I say," I called, "what's the date down there?"

Silence. Not a word. You'd think I had dropped a giant brickbat on their heads. And out of the stillness came Mergentoire's sprightly reply: "Wednesday! It's Wednesday, you ape!"

Ape? Ape? What had got into sweet Mergentoire?

"Idiot!" I screeched. "Get control of yourself, woman. The *date*, what's the *date*?"

More silence. Utter stealth, you'd have thought. One would have sworn the entire table had fallen asleep. Then Mergentoire's voice again, laughing this time, shrill as a rat: "The eleventh, you rogue! Wednesday the eleventh. The day Blondin went over Niagara on a tightrope!"

Then the clatter of dishes once more, and everyone else shouting up the hideous message too. Chomping away on pancakes, scraping back in their chairs—where's the butter, who's got the milk jug, *oops!*—that sort of thing. All the confusion and turmoil, the belching and bellyaching you get when twenty hardhat laborers are trying to gulp down their protein before rushing off to their jobs. No shilly-shallying, I mean, quick-quick, sorry old mate, got to run!

What a waste of man and woman's best hour. My old mam

and I, we would sit for hours about the breakfast table, munching carrot sticks, dipping our bread into tea, perusing the journals and up-to-date magazines, rattling the tabloids.

—"Ah, son, here's another one."

—"Another one, my mam?"

—"Guinea-Bissau, this one's called. How many does that make, son?"

—"I don't know, my mam. What's your guess?"

—"I count forty-one, son. Forty-one since your old Daddy went into the field."

—"That's a lot of emerging nations, my mam! That's a whole hodgepodge full! Oh, they are really carving it up. What do you think old Daddy would say, my mam?"

—"He'd say 'Roll me over, dear. Role me over in my grave and throw another white right on top of me.' "

—"Tell me about it, my mam."

—"It was the Upper Volta that broke your old Dad's heart. Oh, son, when they let the Upper Volta go they as much as put a dagger through his chest."

—"Cold-blooded murder, my mam?"

—"That's right, son. It was a mean, depraved act and who's to reap the whirlwind now?"

—"Us, my mam?"

—"That's the bite of it, son. But eat your carrots, Adlai, they don't grow on trees and a boy needs to hoard up his strength."

I went back into my room, thinking about poor old mam and all the black African hordes yet to sweep down. Crossing the water on rafts and matchstick canoes, beaming their great white teeth and kicking their great black legs, all to gobble up our jobs and steal our women and make a garbage hole of our neighborhoods. "Not yet, my mam," I wanted to tell her. "Adlai is holding on. Old Adlai's got the biceps and the brawn, he's got the willpower; you won't find him kissing no woolly hair."

I could see old mam nodding her approval even as I stared with remorse and disbelief at my calendar's lost date. Where was yesterday? Old mam would say the blacks had got it, just as they'd take away anything else I'd be foolish enough to leave lying about.

—"That's right, son, they got it. They'll take the shoes off your feet if you don't tie them up tight!"

Greta Gustafsson gave me her alluring smile. I swayed in close, putting the kiss of sin into her smoldering eyes.

"*I vunt to be alone,*" she whispered, turning away.

My heart skipped; it always puts me in a torture, seeing Greta in her moods.

"But Greta!" I whined.

"*Yoo lust a day,*" she murmured, resentful and hurt. "*They are my days too und I hold yoo responsible.*"

I dropped down on my narrow bed. Scrunching up my toes, for there was not enough room for my feet between it and the wall. Something fishy going on here is what I thought. Adlai, you've got to use your wits if you intend to figure this one out.

Days, I thought—as you would have yourself—just don't disappear.

I consulted my diary, lying open on the footlocker table. Lying open to August ten. To the day that had never been.

7:00—Wake up, lazybones! Exercise. Wash. 7:30—Pancakes with the gang, mmmmm! 8–6:00 p.m.—Job, uggg (but don't complain!). 7:00 p.m.—Talk to the Pole. 8:00—Home. Dust room. Wipe sink. Exercise. Bedtime snack. Shuteye. (And no messing about with Greta.)

"Oh there's monkey business afoot here, Adlai," I said— for it looked to me as if I'd had a very busy day. And why not?—a thousand irons in the fire, things to get done, people to see! Life to *live*! My old mam, looking at my diary, would have patted my head. She would have said, "That's dreamy, son. That's top marks. How you get it all done is beyond me. Oh yes, you're a chop off the old block."

So.

So I'd say myself.

Yet I was blotto. I had not even the fumes, not even the ashes, of my past day. Zero.

Greta was sulking, giving me first one cold shoulder and then the next. Drop dead, is what Greta was saying. What a disappointment you are. What a rathead. "You expect too much of me, Greta," I told her. "I do the best I can." But she flounced her hair and thrust out her chin and drew the cloak of gloom over herself.

A *hard* woman. A *tough* woman. Just, I thought, like old mam.

So I forgave her. I decided she was right to be mad. I had let her down. I had promised her she would be safe with me. That I had what it took to keep a good woman happy.

A newshawker was shouting his headlines out on the street, and I rushed to the window. "You!" I yelled, "what's the date?"

His startled black face sought to find mine.

"August 11, boss," he said.

The dogs were still fighting in the dirt, squealing and yowling and spinning in a fury.

"Are those mongrels yours, boy?" I asked.

"Not mine, boss."

The dogs momentarily ceased their yowling to blink up at me. Then they went back to it with renewed ferocity.

"Well then," I asked the boy, "what's the news today?" And he held up his grim headlines to me:

SUMMIT TALKS COLLAPSE

+

AUTO-MAKERS LAY OFF ANOTHER 30,000

+

INFLATION HITS NEW HIGH

My world, I thought, and still there.

"That all, boss?" asked the black face.

And when I didn't answer immediately, he did a little soft-shoe.

It seemed to me I'd seen him before—him or his twin—standing in the lineup to receive his dole, wearing butter-yellow shoes, a red eye patch, a watch chain long as his arm—and streaming off in his big Rolls-Royce with three boisterous women white as white eggs and laughing like mud flaps.

But was this true or was it my old Daddy sending his vision across the licking water?

"Listen, kid," I called, "did I buy a paper off you yesterday?"

His black face grinned up at me over his watermelon. "Not off me, boss. I'm fresh brand-new in the country, first day on the job." He danced a swift jig along the pavement, playing a mean tune with his harmonica comb. "I aims to make my fortune, boss," he chirped. "Me and my fourteen brothers looking no way but up. We got a toe-hole on progress. Gonna git our relatives in. From here on out de sky is de limit!"

I slammed my window down on this strapping young grinner, and proceeded to do one hundred push-ups—a few headstands—to work the vitriol out of my system. It had been the vitriol that had slammed down my old Daddy and made his gums bleed. That had turned him boots up.

—"What killed him, my mam?"

—"Vitriol, son. When the blacks painted up their bodies and screamed their heebie-jeebies he was filled up with vitriol and flung himself into the first river."

—"What was he doing there, my mam, in the distant Upper Volta?"

—"Selling birth control to the Roman Catholics, son. No easy job."

Greta was breathing hard. Clenching her fists as she strode

this way and that. Hissing. Stopping me cold with her hot fury. I knew what was on her mind. She wanted me stepping up in the world. Wanted me out of my red suspenders and into top hats. She wanted me to call up the Pole, find out about that job. I stole a look at her, wondering. Trying to figure out what it is about women. Why they drive their men so hard. Why they can't be satisfied. It crossed my mind that I wasn't cut out for a go-getter like Greta. That I'd be better off with some redhead lounging back in a bikini on a leopard-skin rug, selling fertilizer to farmers. With someone all bosom and legs who would say, "I'm for my man, right or wrong. My man is a macho-doctor, good for what ails me." But I didn't think this long. Greta was my heart's need, my solace, my joy. Without her I'd be swinging on vines.

So I stepped out into the hall to make my call.

Mergentoire, I noticed, had put up a new sign: DON'T HOG THE PHONE. This was tacked up beside another one that said NO CALLS AFTER 8 P.M. And another one, dripping blood, that said THIS MEANS YOU.

"The Pole here," the Pole's voice shrieked in my ear. "Speak up!"

But there was thunder overhead. Then the thunder was rumbling down from the third floor, down the stairs, driving towards me. "Out of my way, fat man!" came the nasty cry. Wong, the slant-eye. I shrunk back, hugging the wall. His yellow face whirled past, bumping me—hurling himself off to his job. Late again. This Chinaman, one more of the number-less hordes. "Fat men!" he screeched. "Always fat men! Never looking where they're going! Always hogging the phone!" He clattered on down, flinging back more abuse.

A big country like that, you'd think they'd stay in their rice fields.

The Pole was shouting, too. "Who is it? Speak up! I haven't got all day!"

I gave him my name.

"Oh," he said. "Oh, it's you! The nincompoop! What's on your mind, nincompoop? Why are you bothering me?"

Hold on here, I said to myself. Why is the Pole addressing me in this unseemly fashion? What gives? It had been my impression that the Pole, more than most, held me in high regard. Respected my talents. Why otherwise would he have been trying to give me a job?

"If it's about that job," he now was saying, "you can blow it out of your stovepipe. I told you yesterday. I've hired someone else. I got some foreign bird at half the pay. Strong! Eight feet tall! Can't speak a word of English. But I'll work the stink off him, don't worry about that!"

And before I could get my wits raked clean the rascal had hung up.

Poles, I thought: what can you say about Poles?

I thought: what a relief! Changing jobs, what a nuisance that would have been! I mopped my brow, thinking: what a close call!

Anyway, I told myself, I like the job I've got. I'm happy, Greta's happy, what's the worry?

I slouched back into my room, feeling pretty good.

"It's the Pole's bad luck," I told Greta. "He missed a good bet. Hiring me was his golden opportunity."

Greta wasn't talking to me. She had put on one of her hats, the one with feathers. Plumed like a cavalier. Scooped low, the brim shading one eye. String of pearls at her throat, as if she intended going someplace.

Well, I didn't mind. I liked to see Greta all dressed up.

But she had fire in her eyes—a torrid spitball.

"*Rats!*" she hissed—or something like that.

Her shoulders arched back as she paced, pivoting her hips. I watched those hips, those eyes, stole glances at her flat chest. She looked so luscious, so mysterious—so magnificent and sure of herself.

I wanted to hug and hold her, to weep in her thighs.

But I put the brave face on. "That Pole," I said, "he must have been out of his mind to think I wanted his soft job. Me, at a desk! What a laugh. None of that white-collar malarkey for me. I like being outside breathing in the fresh air. Hauling those rocks. Working in rain, wind, snow. Working up a good sweat in the hard freeze. A man's work, that's what I'm cut out for."

Greta's cruel veil of derision fluttered down.

—"It keeps a body fit, my mam. In tune with nature. It's nice being out there where only the fittest survive. It's educational, old mam. Not a day goes by I don't tip my hat to old Darwin the theorizer."

I could swear my old mam had walked right into the room. She stood not a foot away, shaking a finger.

—"So long as you don't get the heebie-jeebies, son. That's what done in your Daddy. That and the vitriol."

—"I've heard it said he was a drinker too, my mam."

—"Envy, son. The envy and malice of small minds. It was the envy of him that spread that story."

—"And womanizing, my mam? Was he a womanizer, as I've heard?"

She sat down on my bed, spreading her hands palms-up on her lap. She had a spot of soot on her chin, and watery eyes. I reached over and brushed away the soot. Her hair had a singed odor, as if she'd fallen head first into a smoker's flame.

—"Womanizing won't kill a person, son. There are some as would say it's what keeps a body going. But your Daddy wasn't like that. And if he had been, it isn't likely he would ever have touched black. Now listen to me, Adlai. You listen good. Three thousand nautical miles separated your Daddy in the Upper Volta from us where we were, not to mention umpteen years—but your Daddy's eyes were always looking back home. He kept his heart and his eyes dead set on us. On me and you.

He put love first, but he knew he had that. Had our love and our trust. But he was a committed man. An obsessed man. I've told you a thousand times: your Daddy had a mission to protect us, and others like us. Our very way of life. And he went with my blessings. I remember the very day he left I said to him, 'Go and do it, Humpter, and do it well, and always know you have me here thumping my feet for every success you have.' Humpter, that was my secret pet name for him. Every time I would call him Humpter he would blush. Yes, and I would too, for we were just newlyweds, you see. We still had the rice in our hair. But I knew my duty. And he knew his. So he pecked his mouth to my cheek and said to me, 'You're the one woman every man dreams of! You know a man's duty comes first!'—and then he shook my shoulder, and left. It was so beautiful, so beautiful the way he said it that I broke down and cried."

—"Did I cry too, my mam?" I asked. But old mam was gazing off into the blue, as if she were back there with him, and didn't answer me straight out.

—"What's that, son? What did you say?"

She had a clump of mud down on her knee, and I brushed this off. Her old skin was leathery and brown and there seemed to be mites running in her hair. This, or some trickery in the air.

She was giving my walls and the room the hard-eye.

—"Is this the best you can do, son? Why, this room is hardly bigger than a burying hole. And look there! You've tracked dirt all over the floor. Don't you every clean up?"

—"Down on my knees, mam, every evening. Down with soap and rag, just like you."

For old mam always had; she'd liked a place clean.

—"Not *last* evening, son."

—"No, old mam. Something must have come up."

—"Excuses won't get you into paradise, Adlai. I'm only glad your Daddy isn't here to see it. And that!" she said, pointing—"Who is that? That smoky-looking temptress up on your door?"

I made way to introduce my sweetheart Greta, but old mam was having none of it. "*Shame, baby, shame!*" she was saying. She stretched back groaning on the bed, letting her feet flop over the edge. She still wore the same ankle-high work boots that had mesmerized me in my childhood. They had the rot of thirty years messing about with turnips and spuds, a lifetime of kicking at grass and dandelion. The laces were covered with mold. The socks on her thin bones were both shoved down.

Old mam closed her eyes.

—"Are you going to take a nap, my mam?"

Greta was hissing at me to get that woman—"that *voh-mahn*"—out of here.

—"I never shut my eyes in the daytime," mam sadly replied. "No, nor sleep in the nighttime either, if you want to know the truth."

—"Why not, my mam?"

She reached up—as though dreaming—and with a small sob stroked bent fingers across my cheek.

—"From worrying about you, son, the way I never had to worry about your Daddy, though I'm pained to say it."

—"Why's that, my mam?"

I crouched down, my face only inches from her bird-tracked skin. I was pained, too, and jumping with nerves. My mam looked a thousand years old, all helpless and withery and done in. I wanted to fling myself down across her bosom, and moan. To say, *Old mam, what's happened to us?* For I had lost a day and my life was going nowhere—but where had hers gone? She smelled musty and—well, moldy—as if she'd been put away in some high cupboard and left there a long time, and now had come down all wizened and crusty.

But I stayed still. I couldn't bring myself to hurt or confuse or embarrass old mam.

—"There are moments, son, when I think you don't care about your old mam. Moments when I wonder if you don't think I brought you up wrong. Times when I think you are holding me responsible for so much that goes on in this mean world."

—"I'd never think that," I said, half-horrified.

—"Or that you don't revere your Daddy, that you don't uphold his cause."

—"No, mam!" I cried, "how could you think that?"

She was gripping my hand tightly, her mouth twitching. Her eyes boring up into mine. Yet she looked so ancient, so feeble, so ahead of or behind her times. Her brow as wrinkled as a scrub board. The flesh so speckled it was as though a flock of perky chickens had got loose to scratch at her skin, which sagged down over her bones—but all so thin it was practically translucent.

—"Oh don't look at my face!" she suddenly cried out. "Don't stare at me like that! I know what you're thinking! Know how you've turned against me! How you've come to hate your own flesh and blood!"

This speech utterly amazed me.

—"*Me?*" I said. "*Me*, my mam!"

For I'd always thought of us as close. As tight, I'd thought, as nectar and honey.

Mam sobbed. She rolled over, burying her head in the pillow. I eased down on my footlocker, shivering for her. Slowly stroking my hand up and down her backside. Saying, There, there, mam. There, there, good lady.

A fine little weave of bones was about all I could feel.

Her body felt cold. Cold and *icy*. And moist, too. And there arose again that smell, all earthy and wormy, as if she'd washed up from some foul pit or tomb, some ill and dank un-resting place.

—"Don't worry," I soothed her. "Don't trouble yourself,

old mam. It was us together through thick and thin for all of those years. For *so many* years. And I tell you the truth, I never knew one from the other, never knew thick *from* thin, that was how much I knew I could count on your love. True, old mam. And it's how much you can count on mine now."

—"Do you mean it, Adlai?"

—"I do, mam. I sure-as-shooting do."

She clawed at my hand. Grappled my fingers up to her lips, and kissed them. "My man," she sobbed. "My little man. My comfort in this sick old age."

We had us a good cry.

And I think old mam might have dozed, for I saw her breath slacken, felt her bones soften and smooth out underneath my stroking hand. I might have dozed or daydreamed myself—dappled off on beams of sunlight—for at any rate when I next blinked my eyes back to it the aura in the room seemed to have changed. It seemed as if not just minutes but hours, days, whole weeks had tumbled by.

The dogs were setting up a din outside my window, snarling and yowling.

I could hear Mergentoire at the foot of the stairs, shouting up at me. Get off the pot! Quit slacking! Get a move on! Saying she wasn't holding breakfast all day. Not for the likes of me. Then growling at her son Hedgepolt. Telling him too to shake a leg.

Women. You'd think they were shot from the womb to ferret out wrongdoers and hobnail them to a pristine trail.

What a nag.

Greta was in a huff, down on her knees on the floor, going at the dry mud tracks with a scrunched-up hat. At *my* mud tracks, or so it appeared. For they had my hoofprint. But who? How come? Greta throwing up insults at me: *ape* this and *ape* that. She is such a puzzle, Greta is. Aloof much of the time, yet now ready to scratch out my eyes because I had let my own sweet mam walk in and take a moment's rest on my unmade bed.

Isn't Greta funny? I thought. Oh how I wish I knew what makes Greta tick!

But my stomach was growling; I needed my pancakes fast.

—"Mam? You feeling okay?"

Mam sat up, wiping her wet cheeks with the back of one frail hand.

—"Oh," she said with a brave smile, "it was just like in the old days, us having that good cry. It has done my heart good."

—"Mine too, my mam."

She patted my head—"That's a good lamb!"—then hopped up spry as a cat with four legs to catch herself and knowing she would. "Time's a battlefield, son," she gaily observed, "but thems that's got the backbone will whack through it to the other side."

—"I'm whacking, mam," I said. "I'm whacking hard."

Her eyes lit up; the old color came back to her cheeks. "Yes, you got the backbone, the same as your Daddy did. I only hope you got his grit. That you're willing to stand up for what's what."

—"I will, mam. You can count on me."

She came in for a big hug, and I could swear she lifted me right off the floor.

—"Don't get me wrong, son, what I was saying earlier. I'm not renouncing any of the ways you were raised. I don't apologize for swat. Right is right, and a mother has got to stick to that. No, it was just your Daddy's ghost preying on my mind. Me feeling low, wishing I could be with him. They broke the mold, you know, when they made him."

—"He stood tall, that he did."

She stared off, all misty-eyed. Her hands up to her temples, looking back to those days. "Poor man, it was the birth control that sapped him. Think of the pressure he lived under. Imagine the Upper Volta as it was the day he set foot there. Two hundred thousand Roman Catholics reproducing all over the place. They're like dogs, where two drop down ten more will pop up. So that was the RC's. And that's not to mention three million Mossis with the soles of their feet white as yours or mine and every bit as busy. Or half a million Lobis, another half-million Bobis, plus the thousands of itchy Gurunsis. Not one ever having heard of birth control until he came. And everyone black, black, black! The brightest sunshine makes no difference to a continent like that. Daytime or nighttime, you'd never know it. That's what so many blacks can do to a country. Your Daddy had to walk about with a good Everready just to tell one black hole from another, and hope he didn't fall in. A woman wanting a baby she'd fall down in a ditch and let the men poke at her. That's all there was to it, so your Daddy said. It makes you sick, don't it? Just thinking about it. It does me. But your Daddy was no crybaby. He was not the man to tuck tail under his britches and run. No, he kept plugging. Kept singing the glories of birth control. He knew it was *us*, our very way of life, our very freedoms, that he was defending. He knew all about their matchstick canoes; knew they'd soon be finding their way across the water. That they'd take our jobs, gut our neighborhoods, throw down and have their mean pleasure with our women!"

She stood trembling, radiant with his memory, yet sickened by the reality of that other vision.

—"I know it, my mam. I take my hat off to him the same as I take it off to you."

—"So I thumped my foot and said, 'Go to it, Humpter. It's your job and you do it well.' "

—"He did it too, mam. He sure did."

Mam vacantly nodded, still trapped back there in time with

him. I saw her little foot tapping; saw the worship flare in her eyes.

—"You were tops too, mam," I said. "You kept the home fires burning."

Mam smiled, in a drowsy, far-off way. Her voice went all wispy:

—"Now and then I'd get a sweet letter from him. 'Chalk up another one,' he'd say—and I'd know he'd saved another white child his rightful spot in the world. Another white boy his freedom. His job, his sweetheart, his neighborhood. And I'd go down on my knees, saying, 'Bless him, bless him, bless Humpter, for that spot he's saved could be my Adlai's!' "

—"He did it too, my mam! He saved my spot! Except for him I bet this very minute some black man would be standing right here where I'm standing. That bed would be his, and the footlocker would be his, my barbells, and probably he'd even have Greta!"

But old mam had switched off. She was beginning to have that tuckered-out look again. She seemed to be fading.

—"It was always my hope," she said wanly, "that one day you'd take up your Daddy's mighty cudgel."

My head sagged down. I looked dumbly at my shoes.

—"I did, Adlai."

I had been dreading this remark since first she entered. I looked miserably at my dirty thumbnails. Whimpering:

—"I'm sorry, my mam."

Mam stared right through me. Her tongue slashed like a lizard's:

—"As it is, you haven't even married. You don't even have children."

I saw Greta suck in her breath. Saw her face go scarlet.

—"Nary a one," continued mam. "No, you've let your spot, and your children's spots, go to some gang of unruly, howling blacks! You've let the blacks take charge!"

Old mam, I knew, did not mean to hurt. She was only ex-pressing her disappointment in me. Telling me how my Daddy would hang his head.

—"But remember I'm whacking, mam! I'm whacking away. I've got Greta! I've got that Pole I was telling you about!"

But mam wasn't listening. She was simply smiling her sad understanding at me. Smiling her sad, abandoned hope; letting me see how her dreams and my Daddy's dreams had got splattered by the whirlwind. She laughed, trying to lighten both our loads. "Thick and thin," she said, "it doesn't rain but it pours."

—"I'll shape up," I moaned. "I'll shape up yet!"

Mam was slowly buttoning up her coat. Her fingers were gnarled and spotted. The color of oatmeal. Nothing but bones. Somehow the soot had got back on her nose. Her hair was like wires. Even as I looked, her fingernails seemed to be growing. Her cheeks were sunken. She had on her favorite coat. The coat was faded and tatty and hung unevenly at her heels. I remembered that coat. She'd got it off some hook at the bingo parlor. She had the little gold locket around her neck. Heart-shaped. My Daddy's image would be on one side; I would be on the other. If, unbeknownst to us, some black face hadn't jumped in.

She backed, groaning, out into the hall. Her finger beckoned to me. "Our kind is no more than a spit in the bucket," she said. "You remember that. It's all one big tub out there and what part isn't filled with blacks is stacked up to the brim with Chinese. It's overflowing with Poles and A-rabs and Indians and even Huguenots. That's another bunch your Daddy didn't like, them Huguenots. And the whirlwind's coming. But that don't mean we toss in the towel, does it, son?"

—"You bet!" I said. "You bet, my wonderful old mam!"

She was already vanishing. Holding up her old Victory fist.

—"One more thing, son. Get that tarty woman off your door."

Folding back into the wall, becoming the wall. Stumbling once or twice and then . . . gone. Yes, gone.

Yet I hung in the doorway, hoping for one final glimpse.

—"Mam?" I whispered. "Mam, are you still there?"

I ran over and kissed the wall. Put my cheek where her visage had been.

—"Mam?" I said. "Will I see you again?"

But she *was* gone. Wall or world, it had swallowed her up. And I stood trembling, pining for a sweet farewell. Longing for one unsullied word of love. Wanting total forgiveness—full recognition—from her.

Afraid—shivering with fear!—that my Daddy next would walk in.

Sighing. Unable to admit that what I wanted most was what I never could have. This: that *both* would leave me alone.

And Christ, which way *now* could I turn? For I wasn't out of these woods yet. I made out Mergentoire at the foot of the stairs, stomping the floor, shaking a spoon.

"I've told you!" she shouted. "Told you and told you! Breakfast this minute or you go hungry!" And spun off.

Hedgepolt, hidden away, was banging on pots and pans.

The dogs were nipping and yowling.

Inside my room Greta was heaping up rage. Barking out her scorn. Quite furious.

"*Kooom* here!" she ordered.

Defiant, sullen, raving Greta. My angry beloved. She'd come down out of her calendar to wipe up mud and listen to the prattle of old mam. To stride the cramped room, to whirl contemptuously about and with guttural, raking voice—dramatic as a blizzard—declare that she had never been so insulted, so humiliated. So violated and abused. "*Like dirt I am treated! Yes? No?"* To ask what kind of flea or toad was I, what creature, what sniveling worm, what formless, horrible, gamboling idiot? *Yes? No?* To ask how *"dot voh-mahn"* could dare invade our privacy, rumple our sheets, question the way we conducted our lives. *"Who is dot death-hag to tell me I shood marry, I shood haf children! How dare she? Und did yoo see dot coat? Dose shoes? It's lunacy, sheer lunacy, und I, Greta Gustofsson, I moost put up with theece!"* To rail at the callousness, the bigotry, the inanity, the perversity—at the dim-witted nature of mankind in its totality and my blood-line in its particulars.

"Vy do I stay vith yoo?" she shouted. "Vy do I make myself preet-tee? Vy did I ev-vair koom to theece half mahn, to theece child, theece mental deficient! Vot a place your room izz! Vot a stinkhole! I haf seen shoeboxes big-gair. Me, Greta, who has lived in palaces, who kood haf kings vith the krook of my fing-gair!"

"Oh!" she cried, galloping about, thumping her fists against my head, wrenching up and down. "O-O-O-Oh! De an-sair is only one. *Une!* Me, I am craze-eee too! Greta is bird-brain!"

This Stockholm beauty, what a flamethrower! What acid! And how beautiful. How divine. How my heart soared to see her in this mood. Sultry. Passionate. Maddeningly dramatic. I had seen her a hundred times this way on the shimmering screen: breathing this fierce energy, this mystery, this power. A dynamo of unrelenting love. Yielding only *to* love, no matter how fatal. Love came first, above her very life. Her every performance insisting that love *was* life. That every risk was worth the taking. *Mata Hari. Camille. Ninotchka. Wild Orchids. The Blue Sea. The Yellow Bed. Anna Karenina.* —Garbo. My very own Garbo. The great Greta Lovisa Gustafsson. Yet never so in my little room. Always the cold shoulder, the blank stare, the senseless smoldering—elusive, self-absorbed, afraid of her shadow! *Above* life.

"*Liar!*" she now screeched. "*Yoo haf not loved me enough! I haf not vunted your idolization! I haf vunted to be loved as I am! As you haf loved your lunatic old mam! Greta does not vunt to be alone! She does not vunt alvays to be on de vall. Hold me, darling!*"

Oh Greta, Greta, Greta. This much I now knew of Greta, as I was coming to know it of myself: every encounter, including those only imagined, is an affair of the soul. Is cut-throat war. The soul is at vigil; it is in last-ditch battle. It is in armed conflict against the grinning dark, the waiting terror, the foul abyss. It holds off the stinking Hereafter. The soul would defend and preserve our tenuous and fleeting bones. This pitiful, slime-sinking body. Soul is heroic! It goes on warring despite impossible odds of stone and brickbat and the immense conflagration, the high flames that ever sweep around it.

This I find remarkable.

Nothing else in life is so beautiful.

And Greta now accepted this, too. Greta was willing. "*Any-zing!*" she now wept. "*I vill do any-zing to hold your love! Even theece ugliest of rooms, theece fleabox, theece hole, theece dot! Let it be ours! Hold me, Adlai. Hold and kiss and save your demented Greta!*"

Oh, what a speech! My flesh tingled. Bells clanged in a thousand towers. For we were saving ourselves. We were discovering again that one body alone cannot hold back, cannot assuage, bend, or diffuse the wicked dark. The vile, thunderous, rampaging dark. One's frame falls apart, bones scatter, flesh flies apart like birds over water, but true love, true life, charges on. The bones explode, they mix with air and water, with air and flower, and when they come down they come down rearranged. Love, dreadful love, slouches in.

And so her lips plunged down on mine. The famous Garbo mouth burned, burned and parted. Our tongues slithered and slid like a hundred snakes uncoiling in a single wet hole. A wet, luscious, heavenly bog. We moaned—exultant! What a picnic! What a dreamy, wondrous, spine-tingling dark! What ecstasy! For mouth was nice, but mouth wasn't all. We locked limbs, we licked and scratched, we yowled and bit and spun. Howl, spit, and claw. What a whimpering, roaring, blood-boiling feast love is! The floor scraped at our elbows. Knees cooked. But our singing flesh went on multiplying. Steel replaced backbone. Fire replaced lips. Hands tugged and stroked, tongues slurped, our hips hummed. *Hmmmmmmmmmmm!* Our hearts clanged like a Cyclops' thunderbolts. We crashed against the footlocker, kicked against the wall, and came grappling—breathless!—up over it. We slithered as one onto the crumbling bed. The mattress sizzled. Smoke shot from my ears. The roof lifted right out of my skull. And still our tongues went on working. For mouth was nice but mouth wasn't all. Matters got deadly. The hum quickened. *EEEEE-EEEEEEE!!!*

"I want you, Garbo!" I thundered.

"Dun't talk, idiot!"

We romped past passion, past love's fury, and settled in for holy worship of piquant—exquisite—lust. And I thought, as I have always thought: What a treasure woman is! What a world! What a dreamtime! Oh, wow, Adlai, how lucky you are!

The first time.

The first time ever.

My baptism.

Soul's immersion.

Thus when it was over I still couldn't believe it. Impossible. Greta had wanted *me*? Pitiful me? I studied her sleeping body, amazed. Her little feet! What extraordinary toes!—like the curved white petals of a flower. Her bent knees and the fingers so softly folded. How fragile she seemed. The chin tucked so

childishly into her bosom. Her breath so faint, so sweet, so . . .
not there . . . that I wanted to convey it into heaven on a
quivering rainbow.

This dream had wanted me? Uncanny. No, it was beyond
truth. Reality couldn't touch this.

But I touched her—one finger along the ribs—and knew
that it had.

"*All the news you want!*" shouted the black vendor. "*Get it
here, boss!*"

I went at last down to breakfast.

Mergentoire and her son Hedgepolt sat at the massive table,
alone but for each other and a sea of soiled dishes. The steaming atmosphere of daily exhaustion and a mother's eternal,
despairing vigilance. What wreckage! Oh the appetite, the
furnace-stoking, gut-storming wizardry of twenty hardhat
laborers at their meal! Reaching, sweating, chomping—packing in the fuel. My brusque, unroped companions from the
mines, the factories, from field, ditch, and stable: our century's
dogly warriors. Our last heroes.

Mergentoire was slumped low, brooding in half-doze, raking
a hand idly up and down Hedgepolt's spine. The boy didn't
hear me enter; he stayed limp as a rag. Mergentoire's eyes
shifted grievously to me. "Here he is," she moaned. "The man
who doesn't know what day it is. Who doesn't know today
from tomorrow or yesterday from a mile of cotton candy." She
looked away dreamily, scratching away at some itch under
her bra strap. "How was the funeral?" she asked softly.

My eyebrows went up.

I sat down.

Mergentoire's mood underwent another subtle shifting. She
glowered, hoisting a heavy arm in the direction of my room.
"I could shoot you," she said, "for what you do up there."

I grinned sheepishly into my lap. My body was still

humming; the hum was silent, but I yet had it. *Ummmmmm.*
Like ripples on a lake when the sky is becalmed.

Mergentoire sighed heavily. "Well," she said, "if there's
anything left, feel free to gobble it up."

The bread dish was empty. The fruit dish was too. No eggs,
no porridge. The coffee pot had six drops left in it.

I didn't mind. My stomach was motorboating away but my
head was off in dreamland. My thighs still had the quiver.

Mergentoire's voice softened again. "The old lady," she
said, "I hope she went happy. I hope she'd made her peace
with God."

I was studying Hedgepolt, who had a fly trapped in his
hand. He opened his fingers slowly, but the fly remained as
found—in his palm's center, faintly buzzing, mindlessly
grooming its ugly head.

Mergentoire and I stared at the fly. We stared at Hedgepolt
as well, though it was the fly we kept returning to.

Hedgepolt poked a finger at the fly. The fly flipped over and
lay on its back, unmoving.

"The old lady," murmured Mergentoire. "How did it go?"

But I hardly heard her. What about that? I was thinking:
Hedgepolt has a pet fly.

"The funeral, you ape!" growled Mergentoire. "How did it
go?"

The fly lifted, banking away.

"Did anyone come? Did she have flowers?"

Whoa, I thought. *Whoa,* Mergentoire. What gives here?
For I knew not at all what she was talking about.

Yet, as I blinked at her my confusion, something tapped
at my eyelids. A dim, gray shadow lifted on the previous day.
The littered table gave way to rain-soaked ground.

Leaning headstones.

A black, snarling sky.

Rain thundering down.

My shoes sloshing through muck.

176 &▶ LEON ROOKE

Wind whistling past my ears like shrieks from a shut-up thing.

Hedgepolt's sticky hand in mine.

Mergentoire saw something too. And looked to see if she could find evidence of it in my trembling hand. In my besotted eyes.

Whoa, I thought. *Whoa*, Mergentoire. Let's not go too fast.

"I was up all night cleaning his shoes," she said. "Lucky for you he didn't catch cold." She eyed me shrewdly, raking a coil of hair back behind one ear. Tugging her housecoat up to her throat. "Well, I'm not the one to say it, and God forgive me, but what I say is you can count your blessings she's gone."

Whoa, Mergentoire.

"I mean, she was *old*. I mean, she's out of her misery now."

Hedgepolt, I noticed, was now studying me. His mouth opened a little wider. His eyes too. Drool coagulated around his chin.

"Hello, Hedgepolt," I said.

He closed up his hand. The fly had returned.

I can't understand Hedgepolt and here's why: he looks to be every bit of thirty, yet he's still in grammar school. Still wears his trousers rolled to his knees, still has a runny nose. Can usually be found sucking on a filthy dishrag. I call it so; Mergentoire calls it his security cloth.

This morning he didn't have the cloth. His great head was slung out over the table like an ironing board. Studying me, when he should have been training his fly.

"Say good morning, Hedgepolt," Mergentoire told him.

Hedgepolt blinked. His tongue slipped out. Slowly he dipped his head and began licking at a clear spot on the table.

I laughed, though his behavior made me uneasy. This was regressive conditioning, it was backsliding. It went against the pact I had with him. Even so, I went on laughing. "Hey, Hedgepolt," I said, "who's your mam?"

His eyes jiggled, he straightened rigidly in his seat—then his arm flopped up to point directly at me.

"Good old Hedgepolt," I warmly murmured. Touched, as I always was, by this odd familial display. Such a good-hearted, agreeable lad, I thought. I leaned over and roughed his hair.

Mergentoire glared.

I ignored her crossness. We all have such days.

"It won't work," she snapped. "It's time you faced up to things. The old lady—"

But I cut her off. "The boy needs a haircut," I said. "He needs to give more attention to his appearance. One of these days old Hedgepolt is going to start thinking of girls."

Mergentoire's face went red. She caught her breath. Her fists bunched up and her close little eyes stared angrily into mine. "Not under my roof he won't," she said heatedly. "Not while I live and breathe!"

Hedgepolt was nodding excitedly, a grand smile on his face.

We had had talks, him and me. I'd set him straight on the birds and the bees.

"Look at him," I said. "He's ready right now. You do want a girl friend, don't you, Hedgepolt?"

He was nodding as Mergentoire's fist slammed down. She was genuinely fed up now. "Stop saying that!" she cried. "Stop dreaming dreams for my Hedgepolt! Quit giving him expectations!"

I thought: *Ah, that Mergentoire, what a case!* I thought: *Dream the dreams, Hedgepolt. Dare to be God!*

And Mergentoire's face drained. She rose up, clutching a fork, clutching the folds of her loose gown—fit to be tied. You'd think she had stepped right into my head. "So it's God now, is it?" she raged. "It's God you want him to be? When he can't even go to the bathroom by himself!"

I thought: *Small stuff, Mergentoire.* Thought: *Poor Mergentoire.*

For Mergentoire disliked the interest I took in her boy.

Hated the care I had taken in grooming this boy for a normal life. It alarmed her, our walks in the moonlight, our talking of birds and bees. The way he hung onto my every word. Nor could she admit to herself the long way he'd come, under my wing. A *sea of expectations,* I thought. A *sea for everyone.*

"God!" she shouted. "When he can't even tie his shoes? When he doesn't even know what shoes are for?"

Hedgepolt was crying. His wide thick shoulders shook and actual tears were splashing down. One quivering hand reached for the tablecloth. He tried stuffing that into his mouth. Terrible. Oh, what sounds. I knew he was suffering. I knew the hurt he felt. I ached with him. But a mere six months before this he'd been docile as a turnip patch. Empty. A vacuum. His face had never revealed the faintest expression, beyond a stony watching. He had never cried.

It hurt. But this was progress.

Mergentoire whimpered, embracing him, tugging his head to her bosom. "Don't cry," she whispered, sobbing herself. "Oh, don't cry. Mam's sorry. Mam got out on the wrong side of the bed this morning. Mam's sorry she raised her voice. Forgive your mam? Forgive me, Hedgepolt? Mam would never hurt her Hedgepolt. Mam loves Hedgepolt."

Beautiful. I loved Mergentoire at her mothering.

"Let's see your fly again. Let mam and Adlai see your nice fly."

They went on blubbering. And, yes, I did too. For I was remembering my own old mam. I was back there with her, my head on her bosom. Sobbing. Getting charley horses in my gut from all the ache I was carrying.

—"There, there," she'd say. "You're thinking of him, aren't you, son? Of the good Daddy you've never seen? But don't cry. Don't blubber. You know your Daddy has got his work to do. Just as one day you'll have yours."

—"Will I, mam?"

—"Sure you will. Your spot is saved. It's waiting for you."

—"Mam? My mam? Did he ever try it out on you?"

—"Try what, my boy?"

—"His birth control."

—"Oh gracious. Goodness gracious. Of course he did. I was the first."

—"But mam!"

—"It didn't take, son. Otherwise, would I have had you?"

—"I'm here, am I not, my mam? I'm *real*?"

—"Oh you're real, son."

—"Are you sorry, my mam? That I'm here?"

—"Now, son, don't cry! Don't blubber. Hold those shoulders back. Don't you want your Daddy to be proud of you?"

—"Will he be? Will I grow up to fill his fine shoes?"

—"Oh I doubt that. There can be only one of him. And there's this to think about: long before you've come of age the black tide will have swept over all of us."

—"But my *spot*, my mam!"

—"I've upset you, haven't I? There, there. Mam's sorry. Give a kiss to your potty, unthinking old mam. Mam got up on the wrong side of the bed today. That's it—give a smile to your old mam."

Dear wonderful mam. Dear comforting mam. She was aged then herself, and her back stiff from weeding spuds. From keeping together house and home. Between my Daddy and the bingo I was all she lived for.

—"Is that true, mam? Am I your pudding and pie?"

—"You're it, Adlai. The apple of my eye."

—"I wasn't dropped off on your doorstep? By some man on a black horse?"

Mam would get cross when I'd ask that. She'd get out what she said was my Daddy's old walking stick and switch my behind.

—"Who's been telling you them stories? Putting these tales in your head."

For it was a fact I'd been hearing things. There was talk that mam wasn't all she said she was. That mam had never wed, for one, and that I'd come down the chimney like a chimney-black.

—"Lies! Lies! Don't listen to them!"

But I'd been wondering. Not all I'd heard was going out of both ears.

—"They hint that I'm tarbrushed, old mam. That there's a tarbrush somewhere! That there's not smoke without fire!"

—"Hush! Hush! Don't even whisper it, child. Your Daddy is away yonder in the Upper Volta doing his work. You're making his ears burn."

But I'd find myself looking and wondering. For something else was occurring. Putting the heebie-jeebies on *me*. I'd look at mam's elbows and her knees. I'd look at her hands and feet. I'd examine her skin. I'd catch her with her housecoat undone and I'd think: *that's* strange. For it seemed to me mam's skin was changing. That her flesh was darkening with every day that went by.

—"What's happening, my mam?" I'd say. "What's happening to you?"

And mam would cover up her face, she'd shiver and shake.

—"It's old age!" she'd moan. "It's my . . . my Change! It . . . it's from thinking all the dark thoughts of a lifetime! It's . . . from having you!"

And I'd laugh. Old mam, what a joker.

But later I'd be looking in mirrors. In bed at night I'd be feeling my hair. A bit *stiff*, I'd think. A bit *wiry*. A bit on the black side.

And next day I'd nag at old mam. I'd say, Mam, don't you have a photo of my Daddy? Don't you have *one* picture of him?

Mam would thump her chest. "In here," she'd say. "In my heart, that's where your Daddy's photo is. And in yours, too, if you had any decency left."

Sweet, dear old mam. Her stick was hard on the behind, but she was ever straight with me.

The dog's yowling, and not Hedgepolt's weeping, broke up my reverie. They'd come yowling three times around the house and twice up the nettle tree, and now had parked under the dining room window to kick up dust and yowl all the harder. It was blood-curdling murder out there, with maybe a cat or two mixed in.

I nibbled on a toast scrap from the neighboring plate. I licked on bacon rind found under the chair.

It didn't matter. Appetite was the last thing I had.

I was remembering a letter I'd received. *Dear Son. My spot's about used up. I'm slipping. Not long left now. Will you come? Can you do that for me?*

And I hadn't gone. No, I'd let her dot fade right out.

August 11: anniversary of Blondin's crossing Niagara on a tightrope wire. And mam stretched out in a box on the rain-soaked ground.

"Do you love me, Hedgepolt?" Mergentoire was asking. "Do you love Mergentoire most in the world?" She had his head on her shoulder, was stroking his hair. Her voice soothing, even to me. "Your mam loves *you*," she said. "Adlai loves you too. We are all one big family." Her foot nudged mine under the table. "Tell him, Adlai. Tell him how happy we are."

For Hedgepolt's sake I managed a smile. A nice little nod of the head. "You bet," I said. "She's said a mouthful, son."

Hedgepolt's robe-chewing slackened. His eyes widened. His look swam from her to me. "Brace up, Hedgepolt," I said. "Life has its little monkey wrenches, but you can follow my example."

And I sat erect, my shoulders back, my expression firm. Pretending I was looking intelligence at him. Happiness, too.

We sat a long time that way.

Strangely, his face shook loose of its idiocy until at last it became one radiant angel's smile.

"*Dad-dee*," he said.

Our jaws dropped. Hedgepolt had never been known to speak before.

"*Dad-dee*," he said again. And his arm flopped towards me. Then with more grace than I could believe he swung it around to point at Mergentoire. "*Mam-mee!*" He patted her head.

Mergentoire's lips quivered. Her eyes glazed over, then moistened. With a deep moan, half-sob, half-joy, she swooped her arms around him. But Hedgepolt's own arm kept on rising. His face was flushed, his heart pounding; I could see he was getting the hang of speech. "*Gret-ta*," he said. "*Gret-ta Gus-TAFS-son!*" He wheeled about, beaming. Dashing to the window. "*Dogs!*" he cried. "*Brutish, snarling dogs!*"

Mergentoire bolted up. We were both dazed. For a moment we shared an uncomprehending look. Then bliss streamed out of her pores. "*You're cured!*" shouted Mergentoire. "*Oh, Adlai, he's cured! My son is cured!*" She embraced him, lifted him off his feet, swirled him around. "*My baby! My baby's no baby no more!*" And she—and both of them— broke off into riotous laughter. They danced and hugged and jumped on the floor. But Hedgepolt was still wanting to talk. He was stammering in excitement, wanting to get it all out:

"*Shoes!*" he crowed. "*Adlai and Hedgepolt get shoes wet? Walk in muck? See old Mother? Throw flower in grave? Kiss old Mother goodbye? Walk home in rain? Adlai hold Hedgepolt's hand? . . .*"

He spoke on, radiant. And joy, pure joy, in that moment seemed to serenade my bones. It seemed to seep up through my chair and to surge through me like light through a door. And it went on blazing. It went on rising. It shot up through the long table, rattling the dishes; it pulsed over our heads, and spun; it crashed up into the ceiling and went on rising; it crashed through our very walls and went on splashing and tumbling, whirling like a fireball through the atmosphere. Even the dogs, vicious that second before, fell silent. Joy rolled on, flooding the universe. And even then it swept on, shining and beautiful.

We were all in rapture.

"*Adlai happy!*" screeched Hedgepolt. "*Adlai happy for his old mother? He happy for Hedgepolt? He happy with world?*"

Hold on, I thought. Adlai, hold on.

For it wasn't mam I saw, or Hedgepolt's glee, or the two of us reeling over mam's sorrowful grave, or mud on our shoes. These were but a flick at the eyelids. Joy, purest joy, was shunting these aside. What I was seeing was deep water and over the mammoth face of that water legion upon legion of matchstick canoes and in those canoes a thousand black faces and those faces whooping delight at me the same as I was whooping it back at them. And nothing poor mam could do about it. One by one they were crying out, *I'm coming, I'm coming, make way for me! I'm going no place but UP UP UP! Oh look at the Devil running!* Flags I saw waving by the hundreds. There were the Upper Volta colors and beside it little Benin and Guinea-Bissau. Over there were Gabon and Cameroon, Ghana and the Ivory Coast. Here came Somalia and Djibouti and Botswana, Nigeria and Malawi and Kenya. And a great chorus was riding the waves: *We coming! We are coming, brother!*

Hold on, I thought. Hold on.

For I could hear myself shouting back, as if from a planet a breath's space removed: *Come on, you polecats! There are spots for all of us!* The Upper Volta ears picked up. Their eyes did a double take. *Is that you, boss?* they asked. *Is that you? Is that the king?* And I gave them my biggest wave: *Come on! Come on! Git the lead out!* At this, the Mossis, the Lobis, even the itchy Gurunsis, scooped their hands into the water, rode the crests of waves, and came crashing forward. *We coming, boss!*

Crashing on past me as I sat rocking in my chair—in my chair or wherever my spot was—delirious in the face of this vision, wondering which was vision and which was real life and finally where it, or they, or even myself, had gone.

Something wet was licking my hand.

My scalp felt tingly.

This day, too, I thought, was slipping away from me. The light seemed eerie. Had I slipped forward into some future year? Adlai, where are you? Adlai is on his tightrope out over the swirling water, balanced between rope and sky, wavering and floundering with his balancing pole. Adlai steering for the river's other shore. Adlai saying Mam, are you there? Mam, will you forgive me? Adlai falling. Adlai crying. Then only the quivering rope and the crashing water there.

"You've done it, Adlai! Hooray for you!"

What's this? I thought. What's happening now? For Mergentoire was hugging me. Hedgepolt was hugging me. And I was hugging myself, too. I was trembling inside a rapture totally new and strange. What a mystery! Sweat dripped from my nose. Is this happiness? I asked.

I could hear Greta upstairs gaily chirping. Calling to me. "Adlai, come draw my bath. Come up and scrub my back and sit with me."

Mergentoire and Hedgepolt were silent. Their eyes rapt.

The dogs beneath the window were silent. Or gone. I thought I could see them racing as a pack down the long street to another place. Soon, perhaps, to splay off into green countryside.

I closed my eyes.

Peace.

Soul's ascension.

And mam's watchful eye splayed off, too. It went whirling away into the dark.

"Adlai, are you coming?" Greta called.

I had the strangest desire. I wanted to say to Greta, "Go

home, honey. There are people at home who have need of you."

But I said nothing. I stayed on. Stayed, I say, as if bolted to my chair, as Hedgepolt's head lay warmly in my lap, and Mergentoire leaned against my knees, emptied of her joyful weeping. I sat on, thinking: So many people in the world depend on you. So many. Even if you're nothing—even if you're no one and you don't know which way to turn or whether turning is a thing you're capable of—even then they do.

Oh, mam, they do.

WHY AGNES LEFT

*T*he woman with no hair has gone home. The body stocking woman has gone home. Agnes has gone. Everyone has gone home and so should I.

You should go home, my hostess Sulvie tells me. What are you waiting for? Everyone left hours ago, and Zephyr and I would like to get some sleep.

Zephyr adds her two cents.

The place is all cleaned up, no one would ever guess that a few short hours ago twenty-seven women were here talking, laughing, having a gay old time.

The place *looks* empty. Its emptiness has permeated my bones, brought me close to tears. It reminds me of a play on closing night when all the beautiful walls come down. Vanishing life. There and then gone.

Zephyr's two cents amount to this:

You should go home, Mr. Banks. We don't know you all this well and in any event Sulvie and I don't allow men to stay overnight.

It isn't that so much, says Sulvie. We have no place to put

you. The sofa isn't at all comfortable. You'd catch a cold sleeping on the floor.

Yes, says Zephyr. You'll have to go. Please leave.

It's true, I really must. I have no right to inflict my presence on these two no-nonsense, straightforward women.

Zephyr stands with my overcoat held high to receive my arms. Sulvie extends my hat. I slip my arms into the coat and button up. I put on the hat. A moment later, however—I can't explain it—I am again sitting down.

One more cigarette, I say. Let me finish this and I promise I'll get out of your hair.

Zephyr explodes. *God!*—and stalks off to slam a door.

Sulvie, too, is no longer content to reason with me. *Get out!* she all but screams. My patience is exhausted! Get out this minute!

I drag on the cigarette. They have removed all the ash trays and I have to thump my ashes into the palm of my hand.

It was a lovely party, I tell her. One of the best I've been to in years.

She smolders.

I'm amazed that you two could so quickly clean up the place. What a lot of mess!

She mushes a pillow into a chair. I'm not talking to you, Mr. Banks. We have asked you nicely to leave. You refuse. You don't frighten us, if that's what you're thinking. Not at all. You have about five seconds, then Zephyr and I are going to physically throw you out.

No need for that, I say. Just let me have this last cigarette.

You said that an hour ago.

Was it really that long?

Her nostrils flare. Her face has changed color, gone a deep red.

Zephyr reenters, drawing the cord on a long blue velvet robe. She has very pretty feet, I notice.

I've called the police, she announces. If you want to avoid

spending the night in jail you'd best pack yourself off this minute.

Sulvie has decided to cry. Zephyr tells her to stop sniveling, there is absolutely nothing to warrant tears. I am an oaf, she tells her, but I will be gone soon.

She's only tired, I say. She will feel better in a minute.

They glare at me. Both women have spent all day preparing for the party, no doubt, and they are obviously exhausted.

I am, too, for that matter. I must be. Otherwise, I would not find myself in this awkward situation.

My palm is quite full of ashes. I look about for a place to put them. The two women watch. Zephyr taps her foot. They are quite certain my ashes shall at any second despoil their vacuumed sky-blue carpet.

I slide the ashes into my side pocket. I pinch out the cigarette and drop it inside as well.

You're finished, Zephyr says. She opens the door and stands beside it.

Just let me wipe my hands, I say. I stand. Would it trouble you too much, I ask, if I had a glass of water?

Sulvie screams. Zephyr rushes over to comfort her.

I go in and draw a glass of water from the kitchen tap. Dishes are piled up on the drainboard. The counter and the twin sinks have been wiped clean. The entire kitchen sparkles.

Suddenly Zephyr is behind me, asking what I think I am doing.

Oh, I thought I'd help out, I say. Put away a few dishes, the two of you have worked so hard. It was a lovely dinner you served, by the way. Don't know if I mentioned it before.

Zephyr snatches a golden serving tray from my hand. *Out!* she yells. *Get out of here!* The dish clatters down.

Sorry, I say. Didn't mean to offend.

I thump out another cigarette, heading out into the living room in front of her.

Sulvie, on the sofa, has her head buried under several pillows. I flop down into the nearest chair.

Won't be a second, I say. Just let me finish this.

Sulvie looks up, is horrified, then again buries her head. Zephyr leans against the sofa back, snarling to herself.

Go on with whatever it is you have to do, I suggest. Don't mind me.

Neither replies.

I make a stab explaining this business of the cigarette. When I was very young, I tell them, I made a vow to myself never to smoke on the streets. A lot of people do, I think. At home, driving, at a restaurant, at these places okay, but never on the street. It's one way of controlling the habit, you see.

Sulvie, without looking at me, got up and left the room. A few seconds later I heard water running in the bath.

Zephyr approached, stopping directly in front of me. If you don't leave, she said, her teeth clenched, I'm going to kill you. I swear I will, I am not joking.

I could see she wasn't.

She held the robe collar clenched under her neck. Her eyes were hard and blazing. Her skin was very white, all the make-up scrubbed off. Her hair needed brushing.

Who the hell do you think you are? she asked. We hardly know you. Know nothing about you. We didn't invite you. You practically ruined the party for everyone. You're a truly contemptible human being, do you know that?

I'm sorry you feel that way, I said. As far as the party-crashing goes, you know I came with a friend. My friend assured me you wouldn't mind, that the two of you were very open-minded about that sort of thing.

Yes, she said, her fists balled up at her side, but your friend had the good grace to leave at a proper hour. We didn't have to kick her out. As far as that goes, we hardly know her either.

This surprised me. It had been my impression that Agnes

was on the closest of terms with these two women. That was all I had been hearing for months: what an amazing pair this Zephyr and Sulvie were.

She's almost a total stranger, Zephyr went on.

Don't talk to me about Agnes, I said. That woman can drop dead for all I care.

Zephyr was about to say something more when Sulvie appeared, going from the bedroom to the bath, a chocolate-colored beach towel wrapped around her.

If that man isn't out of here by the time I finish my bath, she said, I am going to kill him.

Zephyr rushed over to her. I could hear them whispering. Zephyr was asking Sulvie not to leave her alone with me. She was frightened, she said. There was no telling what I might do.

It puzzled me that she should say this. I had not raised my voice to anyone all evening, had not got in anyone's way; since the party ended I had done little more than sit and smoke and say to them over and over not to worry on my behalf, that I'd be leaving soon.

The two women approached together and sat down on the sofa facing me. They stared. For a long time the three of us maintained a strained silence. My ash dropped on the carpet, but I scooped it up so carefully it left no mark. Then Zephyr bounced up, shot at me, and began shaking my shoulders.

What is it you want? she demanded. Is it sex? Do you imagine we will let you sleep with us if you stay long enough?

Sulvie snorted. Fat chance! she said.

You're sick, Zephyr went on, now yelling, slapping at me. You're a cockroach.

He's a bore, Sulvie said.

I wish you wouldn't abuse me like that, I told them. I assure you I mean neither of you any harm. I find you both attractive, to speak frankly, but I certainly have no intention to make advances.

Then what do you want? both shouted at once. Why won't you leave?

I raised my cigarette, nodding at it, by way of impressing on them my firm intention to leave once this last one was smoked down.

Zephyr stopped shaking me. She sucked on a broken nail.

We were all startled when the phone rang. Zephyr snatched it up. She listened a moment, caught Sulvie's eye, then said:

Yes, he's still here. He absolutely refuses to leave.

I moved to take the phone, thinking it was Agnes checking up on me.

Zephyr jumped back. *Don't touch me!* she screamed. Sulvie leapt to her side, both looking panic-stricken. *You leave her alone!* Sulvie hissed.

I sank back down.

No! No! No! Zephyr yelled into the phone. We can handle it! We are quite up to handling this ourselves, thank you! She slammed the receiver down.

The two young women returned to the sofa. They sat close together, Zephyr's hand gripping Sulvie's knee, Sulvie with an arm slung around Zephyr's neck.

I was steaming inside my overcoat. My hatband had tightened, giving me a bad headache. I had no more cigarettes.

I had stayed too long simply to get up now and casually walk out. I'd have to exert myself, do my best to win the friendship of these two. I couldn't have them thinking Agnes would waste her time on the contemptible creature they took me to be.

My mouth tasted sour. It seemed to me that if I didn't brush my teeth that very minute I would gag.

May I use your washroom? I asked. That final favor and then I promise you I shall be going.

The women said nothing. They were like lifeless dummies staring back at me.

In their washroom feminine scent abounded. Sulvie's un-used bath water had been drawn extremely deep, its steam dampening the blue tiles and mirror. The water was colored blue. On a white stool beside the tub were folded two thick yellow towels. Their toothbrushes were an identical white. The bristles of the one I chose were hard and cut my gums. I spat out blood, rinsed the toothbrush under a quiet trickle of water, and returned it to its holder.

I looked out. They had not moved from the sofa, although their heads had come together. Their backs were to me; I could not hear what they were saying.

The bathroom was amazingly warm. My face was soaked with sweat. I felt almost too dizzy to stand.

A skylight occupied one entire half of the ceiling. A clever arrangement of shelves extended up to it and on these shelves rested scores of African violets all in bloom and thriving.

Agnes, too, had lately been collecting these dwarfish, un-communicative plants.

I am a shower person. It has been years since my body has known the luxury of a long hot bath. I slid in, and kept on sliding. The water rose up my chest, my neck, stopping at last just short of my mouth. I sighed back with closed eyes, half-afloat now, very much at peace with myself, wishing only for a book, soft music, or a cigarette.

For Agnes too, possibly. Have to think about that.

SING ME NO LOVE SONGS I'LL SAY YOU NO PRAYERS

Bingo Duncan and the Clothesline

Now Bingo Duncan started out in the logging business first as a choker-setter working the dog chains behind a five-ton Cat and graduated from this to second loading, which is easier on the lungs and limbs as it is more stationary, but all of this was in his carefree youth, those good wild days before he ever set eyes or anything else on little Judy (one hundred and sixteen sweet pounds and every inch sugar to his tongue, when eventually the wild days came to that). By the time he got to Northern Cal and the Sundown Company job he was a full-fledged sawman who could trolley the big blade with the best of them, and Judy, bless her heart, weighed a good deal more than the one hundred sixteen pounds he had bargained for. But as she liked to say, he was not much of a bargain himself. Only kidding, you know. On arriving in Cal he got a job sawing for Arcadia Lumber at their plant up in the Wichapec range, and kept it until one day the floodwater carried their plant out to sea (and me with it, Bingo was fond of telling, had I not been hanging on to Judy at the time. Them flash floods rooted up redwoods and hauled bears out of treetops but my Judy never budged a mite. Glad I had been feeding her so good). Month after month after this, Bingo haunted the Eureka employment office and watched some drab spit of a man write in whitewash on the window the jobs available thereabouts. Nothing decent, nothing permanent, nothing that might bring solace or sunshine to his pounding, urgent heart.

"Just *toe* work," Bingo told Judy. "Bottle washers and gas pumpers, clerks and manure stompers, seems that's all the world has need of nowadays. How I wish—"

"Wish, wash this dish!" Judy would say. "Wish, take this garbage out, and while you're at it bring in my clothes off the clothesline."

Bingo and Judy and How Pride Precedes the Fall

"If you weren't so high-and-mighty, Bingo Duncan, you'd go south and pick the fields. The wetbacks do it, why can't you?"

"I am your Logger Lover, not no wetback who roots for two bucks a day."

"You and monkeys, scratching's all some monkeys know."

"Rub it in, Judy. Hit a man while he's down."

"He's down, but is he prone? Then here I come with my spreaded knees."

Big Judy, Past, Present, and Future

She was born, she said it herself, to take what a man had to give and to give it back to him in the way nature liked best, in the form of a darling child. One or two to start with, then four or five, five or ten. More's less the worry, or so I've heard. I was made to bear offspring the way a hen's good for laying eggs. And I am plumb fed up with them ramrod women who hate the sight of a friendly child's face, with them who think the sunshine stops after birth of the first. Me, I'd as soon have a whole houseful.

Periodically over the years she stopped strangers in the supermarket aisles, touched their shoulders on the street, saying, "I swear all that man of mine has to do is look at me and I'm pregnant again. It takes a big, solid woman to stand up to a gift like that."

Blows a Melody from the Past, Some Discord in the Wings

Out here, west to the sea, falcon and cormorant riding the breeze—out here Bingo said a man could breathe. He could fill up his chest, fill up his eyes and ears, and feel something of the sky's sway—something of God's power—in his own mean little mind and soul.

"I swear it," he'd say. "I been a different person since I come out here."

Out here a man could roll back his sleeves and work up an honest sweat. He could rely on his biceps and his brains. Work was easy on the troubled mind, fine medicine for the tumble-down heart.

"Look at Judy," he'd say. "She ain't stopped smiling since we came."

But what now? Where's work now, now that Arcadia got washed out to sea? I'll tell you, there's a cruel wind blowing nobody no good. And what's my Judy gone and done? What has that woman let happen to herself? A year ago I could lift her off the floor with one hand. Now look. It grieves me to see all my wild oats come to this. Lord help me, yes.

For in the meantime she had given birth to the first bleeding youngan and the second was pressing at the gates.

"He's pressing, Bingo. I can hear his little nose going rat-a-tat-tat."

All as Bingo cursed the employment man for his HELP WANTEDS and the Wichapec range for its floods and the earth for not bowing when a good sawman stood. Meanwhile, Judy took a job at the All-Nite Highway Cafe down on 101. "What's it matter," she'd say, "if a mother-to-be has to plod and plod."

My pride, Bingo would think, watching her go, ain't what it was.

The Sundown Company: Bringing You Up to Date

I could have told you, Judy told Bingo. I could have told you from the start.

Where's the start? asked Bingo. Where's the end? I been told and told, since the day I first stepped from the womb.

Well, you stopped listening somewhere. You got your ear to your own hurts and that's all you hear now.

Sundown, a wildcat gypo outfit, was on its last leg the first day it opened for work. Hit and run. That's the kind of seedy outfit it was and what Judy would have told him. Sundown had taken over and whipped into almost working shape a deserted mill far up Wichapec Road, 57 miles from the nearest town. And that barely what you would call a town. Bingo heard about the job opening at six o'clock one morning, standing outside the employment office window blowing on his hands, stomping his boots to keep warm. Fit to be tied. Wondering why he bothered.

Pzzzzt.

Yeah?

A driver who hauled timber on his own truck, patron of the All-Nite Highway Cafe, sidled up to him, saying, "It's a lot of much, ain't it, we ought to gone into politics."

So?

Bingo didn't like him. He didn't like drivers in general, and especially those who owned their own trucks. It made him sick, just the way they got in and out of their cabs.

Listen, the man said. I had a talk with the little lady.

Who?

Your old woman. Sweetest face I ever saw. When *that* woman blows in your ear I bet you listen. I know *I* would.

Yeah?

Things rough, huh? Having a rough patch? That's what the little woman said.

It's rough all right. Not a pot to piss in and it's been that way since the flood. Manure stompers, that's all the world has need of nowadays.

I got news, said the driver. You interested in news? You bring your lunch pail?

I got it right here.

He lifted up his lunch box and they looked inside. A roast beef sandwich, an apple, and three cookies wrapped in the tinfoil of a Camel package.

Up on the Wichapec, the driver said, this here sawman fell off his sawyer's seat into the belt run. Carried him all the way up to the waste chute to the scrap pit. Nearly fried his ass. They was still working on him when I come down with my load.

There's a job? You saying they need a new man?

They find wine, nothing but wine, in his Thermos jug. One drunk skunk. They give him the boot while I'm standing there.

What is the company?

It ain't much, let me tell you. A gypo outfit, they call themselves the Sundown Company. Bunch of scabs. Union wouldn't touch it. But they say they paying ten, twelve bucks the hour for a steady man.

That's it. I'm their man. Hell, I'd work for nothing.

But when Bingo arrived up Wichapec he found the Sundown was only working part time, hardly enough to keep the machinery from rusting any more than it already had. They could not get enough logs to work full time, he was told, and the equipment kept breaking down, too—mysteriously.

Mysteriously? How you mean?

We don't know. There ain't nobody can figure it out. It's like the whole damn operation is jinxed.

They did not pay good wages either. The sawyer's pay was eight dollars the hour, take it or leave it. Nor had the former sawman simply fallen off his work seat from too much to drink. The boss man and four or five others had given the matter a close look-see. And they didn't like what they had found.

What you mean?

Well, the bolts holding up the seat was right rusty. Could'a been the bolts just gave way. It happens. I mean, the machinery is old and tired. But I don't know. Sort'a looks like somebody might'a taken a hacksaw to them.

Christ!

Anyway, the seat give way and the sawman tumbled down onto the pulley. Poor bastard was lucky, he might'a been sawed up into a two-by-four. But he only broke his leg.

His leg?

That's right. The belt carried him to the scrap pit, then the chains caught him and carried him up the waste chute. Poor bastard was about to drop off into the cone burner. He decided to jump instead.

You don't say.

I ain't saying nothing. Nothing about no hacksaw, anyway. But that's what I hear.

I'll be damned.

You're one of us, then. Glad to have you aboard.

Late that evening Bingo slung a jacket over the baby and drove in his pickup to the cafe where Judy stood, she'd told him, ten hours a day on her feet, with no rest for the weary. He found her sitting in the corner booth, lapping up a hamburger steak and a big pile of mashed potatoes. First thing she did was reach over and wipe the child's nose.

He's awfully runny, she said. I hope he ain't coming down with nothing.

Then she fed him a spoonful of potatoes.

Did you get the job?

Bet your sweet ass, Bingo said. Although take my word for it, it ain't much.

What's it like up there?

So Bingo borrowed her pencil and drew Judy Duncan a map of what had happened and how it looked from a bird's eye.

The Map

What's mysterious about rust? said Judy. That child's sleepy. You best take the little honey on home.

Me with it, I guess, said Bingo. I got to git up before the cock crows if I am to hold this job.

Bingo and How Hard Times Hardly Got Better

On good days, with no breakdowns, Sundown might cut 50,000 feet of lumber, which was good enough, God knows, Bingo said, but those days together with the bad did not hardly pay enough to pay the rent or the grocery bills for Judy back in the Eureka outskirts where each morning he left her. The days got leaner and leaner, but not Judy still at her job, and each time Bingo dipped the big blade into a log and sliced it along easy as cucumbers he thought with some distaste how it took a lot of money to upkeep a big woman like her, who wouldn't slice at all.

Worse luck yet, he found he missed her.

What my wild oats have come down to, he would say to himself, is nostalgia. What I have got a bad case of is sexual longing.

On one of the leanest days of all he met Crow Kay G.

Crow Kay G.

At the time Bingo met Crow Kay G. both were working the Sundown job but Crow Kay G. didn't have any Judy. He had nobody. All he had was himself and he meant to hold on to that.

"So buzz off," he told Bingo. "I already met all the people on this earth I ever want to meet."

The Working Day and Crow Kay G.

It took a lot of money and horsepower to upkeep a big woman like Judy but there was one thing saving his hide, Bingo figured, and that was that on the good days no less than the bad the equipment broke down and when this happened it always happened right after they'd started up for the day or when they were about to close down for the night—or in the afternoon just when things were humming—and as the breakdown hardly ever lasted for more than twenty minutes or half an hour the company had no choice but to pay the men simply for standing around. There was a lot of talk about how the equipment managed to break down so conveniently for the men and it was more and more that Bingo Duncan began paying attention to Crow Kay G., a nondescript little bastard with red hair whose personality took on the weirdest change when something in the mill broke down, like some ratty little thing that had come up out of a mud puddle, smiling. He had the wickedest secret smile about his lips, with his eyebrows shrugged down over his nose, and all but about to wet his pants from excitement—so much so that Bingo eventually concluded that maybe Crow Kay G. was going out of his way to bring about these breakdowns.

There was more to this redhead than met the eye.

The little snot was a saboteur.

Maybe. You wouldn't want to say a thing like that out loud.

And if he was, then Bingo and every other man on the place was indebted to the squirt for much of their earnings.

Commuting

Bingo daily had been driving up and down the twisty curves of the Wichapec in order to be with Judy and the kid and to see when and if the baby would come.

"This here drive is breaking my back," he told Judy one night. "I can hardly live on the three or four hours sleep I'm getting."

"Well, shoot," said Judy, "why don't you see if there's a place up there we can live? I've worn out my shoe leather and need to slow down some myself."

The One-Room Shack

This morning as usual Bingo got up at four o'clock, with the whole world dark as a witch's bottom, and he drove up the high Wichapec to be there at seven, but this morning he had Judy and the youngan with him and because of that and Judy wanting to brush her teeth and wrap the child up tight and because the pickup was groaning from so much extra weight, this morning he arrived late. And every man waiting, for what could a mill do with no one in the sawyer's chair? So he hopped right out of the cab and went running.

"But what about me?" cried Judy.

Bingo flung out both arms, shouting, "The shack! The shack! Go to the shack."

More On That

Earlier in the week Bingo had come to the boss man with his problems.

"I got me a woman due," he'd said.

"Do what?" the boss man replied. And when this matter had been cleared up the boss man had looked Bingo over, skeptically observing that he had not taken him to be a family man.

Why not?

Well, you seemed to me to be just another guy sowing his wild oats, footloose and fancy free. Now I see better. I see you got those scowl lines down your jaws and the worried eyes of a man looking at a lot of responsibility. Still, I don't see what Sundown can do for you.

I heard something about some cabins.

Cabins? Those old shacks, you mean? Why, they don't have no heat. They don't have no water. No furnishings. All they've got is rats and vermin and God-all. They're not fit to live in.

I heard tell that redhead was living in one.

You heard wrong. Where that redhead is living is in a big house off in the woods that some crazy Indians built. Anyway, he don't care where he lives. For all I know he is part Indian himself.

I reckon me and Judy are out of the same boot. We'd like one of them shacks.

Suit yourself. They're free for the taking.

The Upshot of It All

"What do you think?" Bingo asked Judy some time later.

"That thing! The roof's broke. The windows are all cracked. There ain't no front door. It's *small!* Where will I put my washing machine?"

"It's roomy—for one room. It's got walls. It's got a floor. I could rig up a stove out of one of them big drums out in the woods."

Bingo asked the youngan what he thought. But the child

had broken out in an ugly rash all over his body and could think of nothing but scratching himself.

"I guess it will do until something better comes along," sighed Judy.

"It's free," said Bingo. "It will be different with a woman's touch. Let's see what we can do."

An Uplifting Encounter

That day while Judy had been waiting in the truck, feeling mortified on account of how Bingo had left her, the boss man stuck his head in at her window.

"Hear you're about due, ma'm," he said pleasantly to her.

Judy's face lit up. "Yes, it's like all Bingo Duncan has to do is look at me and I'm that way again. I never saw a man with such a natural gift."

"And what's that there little towhead's name?"

"That there is Bingo Two. He's my pride and joy."

"He's a humdinger, that I can see."

"Say hello to the nice man," Judy told the child.

But Bingo Two only buried his face in his mama's bosom and would not come up for air or say hello no matter how hard Judy yanked at him.

"He sure is a humdinger," said the boss man. "Well, best of the day to you, ma'm."

And the boss man trundled back to his chores.

This exchange uplifted Judy considerably.

What Bingo and Judy Could Do

What they could do was not much. Bingo built the stove out of the drum and put in windowpanes and slapped together a door out of scrap lumber and burned a great heap of rubbish in a cleared space out back. He got the snakes out and most of the rats and he knocked in a new beam to prop up the roof.

Judy put up curtains of a kind and hung a few calendars on the walls and wore out several brooms. She put a flowering bush out in a coffee can on the log step.

"Looks real neat," said Bingo. "A proper little home."

"I best sit down," said Judy. "I am all worn out."

Time Floats On

Time floated on and Judy had her baby without mishap and the mill kept breaking down mysteriously. Bingo got his proof that Crow Kay G. was sabotaging the works one day when the green chain developed a busted cog in its flywheel just, as it turned out, in that vicinity where the redhead had been working the previous day. The mill shut down for one hour and no one could figure where the damage was, until the redhead came up from beneath the green chain table, saying, "A-ha, the trouble is down here in this gash in the cogwheel." The boss man slapped him on the back, saying, "Good work, Crow," and brought the millwright over to put another one on quickly, but it was clear to Bingo, from the crafty satisfaction on the redhead's face, that the bugger was the culprit.

Bingo said nothing to Judy or anyone else of his thoughts on the subject but it began to bother him some, this question of the right and wrong. What Crow was doing was cheating the mill owners, that was clear; but he was putting money in the workers' pockets and no one could deny that was a true blessing, especially for a family man.

Bingo did bring the issue before Judy, in its general terms.

If a man does wrong, he said to Judy—that is, if he commits *criminal acts*—but those acts serve to put money in deserving pockets—that is, it puts food on the table of the poor—then is that act wrong? Is what that man's doing morally reprehensible, is what I mean, and is it morally reprehensible for that otherwise innocent party to take it?

"Good god," said Judy, "you are talking with a mouth full of mush. I am worried about your condition, Bingo. I can't make out a word you are saying."

It is a difficult issue, thought Bingo, who tried to think about it no longer, because it was giving him a headache, with Judy's attitude only making matters worse.

"I wish you would make that baby stop squawling," he told Judy. "There is never a minute's peace around here."

She told him he could go take a walk in the woods. He could go take a flying leap, she told him.

The Seven-Room House

A couple of Indians had built it. One morning, out hunting deer, they had followed a creek trail down to the lower Wichapec.

Quiet, one told the other. I hear something.

They crept up to a knoll and peered through the brush.

Not deer, the other said. What is it?

A white man was down by the creek bed, very busy.

What is he doing? the first Indian asked.

He is digging a hole, the second replied.

It is a very big hole. It is too big to be an animal trap. Shall we tell him?

Sure. Let's tell him.

But the Indians were smarter than that, and remained hidden.

He is taking earth from one place and putting it in another, the first Indian observed.

Yes. As you say, he is digging a hole.

The Indians returned to their own area on the High Wichapec and dug themselves a similar hole. A few weeks later they again found themselves watching from the same thicket.

He has finished the hole, one said.

Yes, and the hole has filled with water. Perhaps he intends to go swimming.

Then why does he not swim in the creek?

The Indians did not care to dwell further on this.

Why is he notching those logs and stacking them one upon the other?

I believe he is building a wall.

He appears to be building several.

Yes. He intends to erect a square box in which to catch the animals.

It will not work.

Who knows? I have seen stranger things.

The Indians were impressed by what they had seen and went back to their own area on the Wichapec and duplicated the man's labor. Some time afterwards, they again came down to the creek floor.

Very impressive, the first Indian conceded.

Yes, said the second. He has divided the box into seven different spaces. He has slapped mud between the log walls, and now seems to be putting a cover over it.

It seems very snug, said the first.

Yes, replied the second. It is too bad, isn't it? Someone should have told him.

Yes. Shall we?

But the Indians were too smart for this and went away again and completed their own house, exactly as the man had made his.

Then the winter rains came and the creek swelled and rushed about mightily, and the next time they came down the Wichapec no sign remained of the white man's house, not even the hole.

But the Indians were content with their own great structure high on the Wichapec, and lived in it for many years, with their wives and children and others who thought being so enclosed was not out of keeping.

This was the seven-room house inherited by Crow Kay G.

A Bellyacheful

Things got worse and worse and no one knew which way to turn in the one-room shack where Judy and Bingo lived, with the new little baby squawling twenty-four hours a day and the other youngan acting like a juvenile delinquent, though not yet two years old, and Bingo knew that at worst he was going to kill Judy or she him, or that at best they'd leave each other or blow out their own brains or go hog-crazy if something wasn't done soon, for they hardly had room enough to breathe and they were plain sick of each other.

"I've had it up to here!" Bingo would shout, and Judy, she'd shout the same.

More and more, Bingo brooded on the green-chain man with the red hair and the big seven-room house all to his lonesome. He got to thinking, too, and reminding Judy, of how when he married her she'd weighed in at a sweet 116 pounds—"and look at you now!" he'd say. "God, you're big as a moose and about as pretty!" Until these days came along, Bingo had never really noticed or paid any attention or much minded her size. If anything, he'd liked it, and if he'd ever heard anyone joking about Judy's size he would have been inclined to say, "That's right, she's a good handful, but that's how I like it." But now that attitude and loving was ancient history. Now he'd say, "You're big as the moon! God knows what it's taking out of my paycheck to feed you!"

And Judy would mope or she'd yank up a child under each arm and stride off into the woods, or she'd go at him with her broom or her pots and pans.

"I am not a dog," she would say, "that you can talk to me

of how much it costs to feed me." And she would feel helpless and sick with fury, hatred would spin before her eyes like a ragged ball, and weight that had always felt good and smooth and prideful on her bones now felt like a leaded sinker, felt like something with claws was raking inside her, and mere sight of Bingo would set her to shaking.

"Eat-eat-eat!" he'd say, and she would think, *Surely I will kill him. I am going to stomp on him and smush him like the rat he is.*

One night Bingo went to the seven-room house and stood outside in the dark staring at it, hating and cursing the redhead, Crow Kay G., till the bones in his throat ached.

I have got a real bellyacheful, he said.

Next morning he took the boss aside and asked him how come that nasty green-chain puller had this big roomy house up the Wichapec when all he and his had was that one-room shack full of squawling youngans.

"Work it out with him," the boss said. "Some Indians built that house and it don't belong to Sundown. But I wouldn't reckon on much. When heart was passed out that Crow kid was off chopping wood."

An Overture

"How's about it, kid?" asked Bingo.

"Buzz off," said the redhead. "Your old brain's gone goat-hair."

Time Off Without Pay

After being told to buzz off, Bingo got so mad at the redhead and at himself and the world in general that he ripped through every log in the yard and through the next truckful that was brought in and in no time at all there wasn't a stump left to be sawed. And it was only two o'clock.

"That's it for the day," said the boss, "everybody gets the afternoon off without pay." Then he came up to Bingo and slapped his shoulder, saying, "That was some sawing. Gee-sus!"

The men grumbled at their lost wages and cast malevolent looks at Bingo, and when he passed Crow Kay G. the redhead whispered, "You're asking for it, saw-dog."

Bingo said to hell with it and he went home and was sweet to Judy and they hauled up the brats and went flying down the Wichapec to the Lumberjack Bar.

"Keep'm coming," he told the barkeep.

And for all that they had a roaring good time.

Judy's Perceptive Nature

"All I could see," Bingo told Judy, "while I was sawing them logs was his red eyebrows. I kept thinking of the right and wrong of it and how I had been wronged—how *we* had been wronged—and each time I went zipping through another log I thought, 'Well, Crow, you S.O.B., here's another buck out of your pocket.' "

"What's his house like?" asked Judy. She was feeding beer to her babies to keep them quiet.

"It's just what you'd expect a couple of Indians to build. But it's been standing for over a hundred years, so I reckon it's solid. But Crow don't need it. He lives in one corner off in the kitchen. He don't have a stick of furniture in the place."

The jukebox had been going, Mervis Pearl singing "Wreck on the Highway." The baby had crawled out on the dance floor. Judy told the other child to go dance with her. The boy protested:

"She can't dance. She can't hardly crawl. She barely can sit up."

"Do what I tell you," Judy said, and gave him a smack on

the bottom. The boy went out, took the baby's hand, and started circling around her.

"Look at that pair," said Judy. "Cotton candy wouldn't melt in their mouths."

Bingo, too, was all smiles. "They are a pretty sight," he concurred. "I can't hardly remember the time I was ever innocent and pretty as them."

Judy slapped playfully at his arm. "Shoot," she laughed, "you still are."

Mervis went on singing.

> *I saw the wreck on the highway,*
> *but I didn't hear nobody pray . . .*

Two or three of the lumberjacks were kicking their heels. Lots of others were yelling encouragement. Everyone was getting high.

"Maybe we should invite that Crow fellow over for a meal," said Judy. "Maybe he's lonesome. Maybe when you get to know him he's just as nice as the next guy."

"Over my grave," said Bingo.

Judy wriggled out of the booth and coaxed Bingo to dance with her. Bingo put his head on her shoulder. They rocked slowly, off in a corner by themselves, with the youngan tugging at her skirt.

"You are still my sweet one-sixteen," murmured Bingo at one point. "You got my number."

Judy liked that. She let her head sink down, too.

A woman with blonde hair swept high on her head came out of the Ladies and put her arms around them. They embraced her in return and together made several graceless circles of the floor, laughing, for the woman kept losing her balance and toppling against them. She had a tiny red mouth and a green bow up over one ear.

"You two give me hope," the woman said at the end. "I got hope in my heart so long as I know there's one loving couple left in the world." Then she smiled sadly and fluttered her fingers, ta-taing along.

On the drive back up the Wichapec, with the children asleep in her lap, it was determined that (1) Judy would have to do the inviting; (2) it must be a regular dinner, nothing special; (3) they must on no account beg or plead with the redhead to swap houses or offer to pay him a lot of money; (4) she would have to do all the talking.

"I ought to get a new dress," mused Judy. "If I had hair like that blonde woman's I'd be sitting pretty." She punched Bingo softly in the ribs. "Now don't deny it. I could see you liked her."

Big Judy and Crow Kay G.

Early the next morning soon after sunrise Judy crossed through the woods to Crow's big house and knocked on the door. He was a long time answering and when the door was finally opened all he did was look at her. He looked a good long time, until Judy began to get fidgety, and she recognized that he did not know how to talk to strangers.

He did not know how to talk to women.

She saw that.

He looked at her with a bottomless, fathomless look that made Judy not know where to look herself. His look set loose all sorts of fast and loose parts inside herself and she did not know what to think. She felt like maybe she was down to 116 pounds again and she scrunched up her toes inside her toes and swayed a time or two, trying to get hold of herself.

She looked up at the treetops and over to the side of the house where there was a big rock, and when she looked back again at him he was still looking.

My, my, she thought—and had the feeling that with wings she could fly right up to the roof or the treetops or clean out of the world.

"Bingo and I was thinking," she said in a light voice, "we were thinking how you must get terrible lonesome in this big house all alone, and we were wondering if you'd like to come over to our place tonight for potluck supper."

The redhead didn't reply to this. He had the reddest hair Judy had ever seen and she must have caught him shaving because one side of his face still had the lather.

He had only one boot on, and that half-laced.

"Supper tonight," she said. "You coming?"

She saw he did not know how to say "no" either, or any other word; he seemed straight-out entranced.

"Judy," she said, extending her hand. "Judy and Bingo . . . the sawyer . . . I'm his other half."

He blinked at that. But he took her hand and for a minute she thought he was going to kiss it.

She backed down the steps.

"About six," she said. "After I've had time to get the shack tidy."

The redhead kept on looking.

Heading back through the woods, Judy thought, *My, my, he sure can LOOK!* She thought, *If I die tomorrow I know I can go to my grave knowing I have been LOOKED AT once in my life. He has stripped my dress clean off me and seen everything I have.*

Thrilled, is how Judy felt. *Good Lord,* she thought, *and me a married woman. And me with my hair hardly even combed.*

Supper at the Shack

Waiting for the meal to get to the table, Bingo saw how Crow Kay G. and Judy kept looking at each other. He saw how .

Judy was acting flighty and tipsy and how she kept blushing. He saw how the redhead kept staring at her ankles.

But he didn't mind Crow's looking. How he felt about it was that it was a free country. Despite her size, Judy was a good-looking woman. She was a real eyeful.

It was high time she got a little attention.

He just hoped the spaghetti didn't boil over.

Supper at the Shack—Another Angle

Crow Kay G., waiting for the meal, saw how, moving about, the saw man and Judy kept bumping into one another and even into him; he saw how the little boy was always at your elbow as he played, and how the baby's squawls were right in your ear, and how the only space she could crawl was down under the table and between your feet and around the chairs; he saw how the bed had been jammed in and how pallets had to be made for the kids, and how, once the spaghetti was cooked and then lobbed out into plates, there was no room on the table for your elbows or for dish or glass, and no way you could scrape your chair back and how you couldn't move without thinking you'd step on the baby, and how when Judy had to change a diaper she had to do it right there in plain sight, and how you had to hold your nose; and how, although it was plenty cold outside, the heat from the cooking on the open barrel made the room so stifling hot you had to take off your jacket, and then no place to put it, and how, even so, a draft came up through the floorboards and froze your ankles, and how pots and pans and all their belongings were stacked all over the room—and how, despite all this, Judy kept the sparkle in her eyes and lit up the place with her sunshine, without one word of complaint.

He frankly couldn't see how human beings could live like this.

I'd die, he thought. I'd sure-as-shooting kill myself.

Midway through the meal the oldest youngan cut his knee from a nail protruding from the wall, and there was much squawling about that.

Then the baby squawled because it wanted to nurse, and the next course never did come. But Crow didn't mind, for the saw man had got out his jug.

Crow, from time to time, kept trying to get a bead on the saw-dog—on how a woman like Judy could be hooked up with a snake like that—but he couldn't get anywhere. He couldn't figure it out. This Bingo character, it seemed to him, was a born Nothing. Real low-life.

"I hear tell," said Bingo of a sudden, "that big house of yours was built by Indians."

Crow cautiously nodded.

"Must be hard for you," said Bingo, "keeping up a big house like that. The heat bill alone must keep your pocket-book empty."

"I manage," said the redhead. He thought it best not to tell the saw-dog that he had shut off the rooms and now lived entirely in the kitchen.

"Now if you'd want to trade abodes," Bingo trailed on, "I wouldn't mind—Judy and me wouldn't—sweetening the pot. To make it worth your while."

Crow remained silent. He was watching Judy burp the baby. Then he watched her button up her blouse. He watched her laugh and spin her hands as if she were chasing away flies.

"I declare," she said, "all Bingo Duncan has to do is look at me and I'm pregnant again."

Bingo let out a sound, half-groan and half-surprise. He gazed searchingly at Judy. He clearly was wondering whether she was telling him a third child was in the oven.

Shortly after this, Crow Kay G. departed. He left with mixed feelings, not quite wanting to go but thinking he'd best move fast, for in truth he found the evening confusing. He couldn't figure out what to make of all those signals he had been getting—nor even from where they had been coming.

"That Judy," he exclaimed to the air, "now *that's* a woman."

The night wind was invigorating, however, and by the time he arrived at the house the Indians had built, he felt again half-normal. He entered the back door with grand satisfaction, and before going to bed strolled through each of the seven rooms, delighted they were all of them his.

Cleaning Up from Dinner

"Well, we blew that," said Bingo. "We can say goodbye to that idea."

"Like I said," said Judy, "it's too early to count chickens."

In Bed That Night

I feel *this* light-headed! said Judy. I feel a small breeze could blow me straight up to the treetops.

What was that about an oven? said Bingo.

Stop talking, said the youngan. How can I sleep with your yakking going on?

Put your arms around me, Bingo. Hold me tight. Or I'll float on out of here.

Where would we put another one? asked Bingo. How we going to feed another one? What's the percentage?

One little gust and I'm gone, said Judy, trembling.

Bingo put his arms, and one leg, around her. She held on tight.

The boy stayed quiet. He had the feeling something strange was going on. He didn't move a muscle.

The baby was sleeping.

When tomorrow comes, said Judy, I hope I'm back down to earth. I'm getting woozy up here.

The Cup of Coffee

Lunch time the next day when the mill shut down there were only a few logs in the yard and they all knew no more trucks were bringing in logs that day and they were uneasy; talk was circulating to the effect that the mill was going to close down for good now, Sundown was going to call it quits, and some were passing along the rumor that the company wouldn't even be able to pay them for the week already put in.

Crow Kay G. sat over on the 2 x 8 stack by the green chain, eating a tomato sandwich. The bread had gone soggy and he didn't much like it.

Bingo came over and sat down beside him. He had two or three roast beef sandwiches in his lunch pail, together with a wedge of cake, a carrot, and a red apple. He had a large Thermosful of hot coffee as well.

You think they gonna shut down? Bingo asked.

Crow shook his head, not yes, not no.

C'est la vie, he said.

Bingo ate his lunch and drank his coffee. The day was a cold one and he held his hands over the steaming cup, for warmth.

I see she looks after you real good, said Crow. I see she packs a man's lunch.

Who? asked Bingo.

Your wife. That Judith.

Reflecting On That

Just as they had figured, the mill did not start back up after lunch, though there was word more logs would be coming in in the morning. Walking back to his shack, swinging the empty lunch pail, Bingo had mind to reflect back on those minutes by the green chain. *Judith*, he thought . . . *well, I'll be damned. That IS her name. I'd plumb forgot about it. Little Judith, that is exactly what I used to call her.*

History Repeated

As Bingo walked through the door, Judy asked, "Did you?"

"Did I what?"

"Bingo Duncan, don't tell me you forgot!"

Bingo hemmed and hawed. Finally, he said, "We had a lot of other stuff to talk about. I guess it slipped my mind. Anyway, it is his turn to ask us."

But Judy would have none of that, so fast as she could she went running over to ask Crow Kay G. if he wanted to come over tonight for meat and mashed potatoes.

She shortly returned, looking downcast, explaining: He could not come. He was on his way down to the beach to cut grape stakes. He says he sells them for thirty, thirty-five cents to the grape and berry people down south. It is clear he is an up-and-go-getter. Why did you not ever think of that for making extra money?

Bingo sighed. He said he was tired. He said the one thing in the world he wanted right now was a nice easy chair to sit down in.

"If you'd thought of cutting stakes like that redhead," Judy said, "maybe we'd have one. Maybe we'd have us a seven-room house, too."

Bingo went out and sat on a stump in the cleared space out back. He was in no mood to hear any more about the world's go-getters.

"He said he'd stop by on his way home," called Judy, "if our light was on."

The Light, and Crow and the Youngan, and Judy Alone with Her Thoughts

Each time Bingo turned off the light Judy came by and turned it back on.

"One would think you were taken with this fella," said Bingo.

"Don't be silly," she said. "You may not have noticed, but your oldest child is not home."

"Good God! Where is he?"

"He is out grape-sticking with Crow. He asked if he could, and I let'm."

About midnight the child came in, very excited, with his pants legs wet.

"We cut seventy-eight stakes!" the youngan exclaimed. "That's over thirty dollars!"

"Why didn't Mr. Crow come in?" asked Judy.

"He said his ass was slinged, he had to get home to bed."

Judy asked the youngan if he was hungry. She said, "Child, you must be starved."

But the boy was already dropping down on his pallet. "Not me," he said. "We had us three cans of potted meat, down on the beach."

"I didn't think you like potted meat."

"I do now. Crow has got a whole room full. He says it's about all he eats. Do you know what else he has? He has one of those old oil drums cut open with a velvet seat halfway up, and a red canopy over the top. He says he sits in it when he wants to think about his kingdom."

Judy shook her head, marveling.

Soon the child fell asleep, and Bingo with him. For a long time after the shack had settled, Judy stood at her dark window, looking up at the stars. Alone with her thoughts.

The Jeep

For three days running, four if one counts Sunday, the Sundown mill stayed shut down, and each day the youngan went out with Crow to cut stakes.

I hope he pays you, said Bingo. Then we all can retire.

The fourth day Judy went herself to bring the boy home, for he had been sleeping over, and while at the big house she told Crow Kay G. how she had heard Bingo say that the way to cut stakes was to buy or borrow a chain saw so you could go at the really big logs and how if you did that you could cut tons more stakes than you could with an axe and chisel.

"What we need is a jeep," said Crow. "With a jeep we could zip up and down the beach without getting stuck in the sand. We could hunt out the really big logs."

"I will ask him where we can get a jeep," said Judy.

He was not coming over to dinner that night, but then he said he would.

Judy perked up.

Wonder what changed his mind? thought Judy. Wonder has he been missing me? Maybe it was my saying all Bingo had to do was look at me and I'd be pregnant again.

Maybe he's jealous.

She jumped her way home, happy as a kid, uplifted by that.

Cutting Stakes on the Beach

The next weekend, Bingo had the power saw and the jeep and they drove down to the beach and looked about for a huge, washed-up redwood and when they found one they got out and sawed it into sections eight feet long like the growers wanted, and with the axes and chisels they split these into two- to three-inch stakes and chopped the points on their tips so the growers could drive them into the ground. While the men worked, Judy and the kids zoomed up and down the beach in the jeep and sometimes Judy drove the jeep into the water where the water and sand were swirling together, and the tires kicked up a splash and spun deep into the sand and she drove the jeep very fast and snake-zithered against the waves which shot up a fine spray over the jeep and made the baby and all of them cackle with laughter.

End of the first few weeks they had collected themselves over three hundred dollars.

Popcorn

One night after splitting stakes and roasting wieners on the beach they were driving through Orick when they saw on the movie marquee that what was playing was a movie called

LADY GODIVA
& THE LONE RANGER

and when Judy saw this she said, "Whoops, just what I want, a big bag of popcorn!"

The Lumberjack Bar

Where they were going was the Lumberjack Bar, and Judy brought her popcorn with her, and they took a booth in the back near the jukebox.

I want to dance-dance-dance, said Judy, and she danced first with Bingo, then with Crow, and then she danced with the baby wiggling in her arms and the other youngan swinging on her skirt. One of her old friends from the All Nite Highway Cafe, sauntering by, said, Well, darling, I see you're still dancing, and Judy said, Yes, I thought I'd best get it out of my system while I can, for I've up and got pregnant again.

Meantime, Bingo and Crow were back in the booth drinking their beers, paying no attention to the conversation of two loggers, a skinner and a faller, seated near to them.

The Skinner: "Now here, now there. Not anywhere."

The Faller: "I ain't telling, but the bastard stole my shirt."

The Skinner: "Flipped right over the canyon, bottom side up, and when I got down to him the sonofabitch was sitting up on the frame, grinning his head off."

The Faller: "Speaking of fire, that was her to a tee. So hot she burned holes in my blankets."

Bingo wiped wet circles on the formica. "What the hell are those two bullshooters talking about?" he asked Crow.

But the redhead was not feeling talkative. Sure, he could split stakes alongside this character, and drive up and down the Wichapec with him. Sure, they were partners, but still there was something about this saw-dog that rubbed him wrong, and he didn't see why he had to sit here shooting the breeze with him.

What he wanted to do was go dance with Judy.

But it looked to him like the children had her all tied up.

"Let's have another beer," he said. "Let's tie one on."

A blonde woman with piled-up hair approached and stood grinning beside their booth. Then she slipped in beside Bingo and slung an arm around him, saying, "Hi, honey. Long time no see."

The redhead watched this with an open mouth. Sonofagun, he thought, this character has been running around on Judy. And me staying pure as the snow.

He got up and went outside and sat in the jeep, banging his fist on the steering wheel.

The Eternal Question

Was he or wasn't he, that was the eternal question plaguing Judy, once Crow Kay G. first hinted at it and then said his suspicions straight out. She took to searching his pockets for phone numbers and looking over his shirts for lipstick stains and his drawers for you-know-what.

What's the matter with you? Bingo would say.

For Judy had stopped eating, too, and any time he was out of her sight for a second she would be calling his name, and some days she would walk up to the mill just to make sure he was seated in his sawyer's chair.

"I believe he's innocent," she told Crow one day.

Another day she did find a telephone number scrawled on a sheet in his pocket, but when she asked him about it he said it was some fella he'd heard of who had a dog for sale and he was thinking of buying a dog.

"Don't lie to me, Bingo. I bet it's that blonde woman's number."

But when she called, an old rasping voice said, "Hell's fire, lady, you're the second caller I've had this week. I sold that dog more than a month ago."

Not that Judy was convinced.

Family Changes

One morning Judy went up to the seven-room house and opened all the doors, aired the rooms, swept up the dust and cobwebs, washed the windows, and that night told Bingo it was as pretty a place as she'd ever seen. It was like heaven.

"Them Indians really knew what they were doing," she said.

A few days later they rushed her down the mountain and Judy gave birth to their newest baby.

"That tears it," said Bingo. "We can't all live in that shack now."

While Bingo was down overseeing Judy's condition in the hospital, the oldest youngan had taken to staying over nights at the redhead's house. For several days Bingo hardly even saw him.

"I guess I could build another room onto the shack," Bingo told Judy. "Maybe that's one solution."

Judy objected. "You think I'm going to come home to your sawing and pounding? You think I would make our baby live like that?"

"It's all I can think of. One thing for sure, we can't all put up in that one little room."

Crow, standing out in the hospital corridor, ventured in. "She could put up with me," he said. "While you're building. Judy and the baby. I wouldn't mind having them."

The Dream

That night Bingo had one of his worst dreams. He waked up sweating. What had happened was that the saw seat had warped under him and dropped him off backwards into the log chute and he'd been carried right along the belt, tumbling over midst the bark and slivers and chunks of wood, and try as he could he couldn't get upright again. Then he'd got scrambled around between the green chain hooks and the chains carrying scrap up the waste chute to drop it off in the cone burner, and first thing he knew that was what had him. He was on his way to being burned alive. Up ahead were flames licking from the burner, and the chains kept tumbling him over, wood chunks knocking him one way and the other and his arms and legs gone all twisty. And knowing he was finished, he had done a strange thing: he had started calling for his mama. *Mama, help me!*—that's what he'd screeched out. But what part of the dream his mama might have occupied was all dark and mystery and he knew there was no help there. He could feel the heat of the burner. Could see the red flames. And he made one last effort to stand—one last claim that his life was not yet over. Up that high, his clothes already catching afire, he had a clear view of the Wichapec before him. Down there was the one-room shack with nobody in it, and up there was the redhead's place, glaring bright as a mansion, and, yes, there stood Judy waving her arms from the front door, screaming in a silent way, "*Jump! Jump! Jump!*" and the funny thing about it to his mind was how Judy had skinned down to her old weight of 116, how she looked pretty as a picture, even as—when he looked twice— his kids were climbing all over her. Kids running through her like a fast-growth vine. Funny thing to him was how beautiful she looked. How clean and simple and next to ravishing. Just the way she would look—would stay looking—if she'd never hooked up with him. The other funny thing was how Crow Kay G. was absent. How he wasn't where you'd think to find him. Not up at the house with his arms around Judy, nor down there by the sawyer's seat waving a wrench, saying, "Look what I done. Look how I fixed your goose." No, the kid was nowhere to be seen. Then he came back to Judy's voice calling, "Jump! Jump!" though now she had disappeared too . . . and the shack had, and the seven-room mansion, and his three little kids . . . because all that was around him were the roaring hot flames and the clear knowledge that he was falling.

Sea Lions

One night a few weeks after this the whole gang was down on the beach having a wiener roast after cutting up stakes. They built a fire out of driftwood and the five of them stretched out in the sand.

Bingo had the new baby wrapped in a blanket under one arm.

"How are things for you up at the big house?" he asked Judy.

Judy gave a meek smile.

A bit later she said to him, "I see the shack addition is coming along."

Bingo nodded yes it was.

Crow Kay G. got the kids assembled for a ride in the jeep. He asked Judy if she'd care to come along.

"I reckon so," she said, "as no one around here will talk to me."

Bingo threw more driftwood on. He sat poking the fire, talking this and that to the baby, as the others roared in the jeep down the beach, swerving into and out of the waves.

Tonight Crow had brought his pistol along and as he burst across the dunes he would rest his pistol wrist over his driving arm and take potshots at dark shapes as they surfaced far out in the water.

"What are you shooting at?" asked Judy.

"Sea lions," said Crow. "The ocean is packed full with them."

They drove as far as they could down the stretch of sand and when they came back, more slowly now because it seemed something had gone out of each of them, they saw dead black shapes washing up on the tide.

"What's those?" asked Judy.

"Sea lions," Crow said.

Horseman, Pass By

First the youngan came in.

Then the toddler.

Bingo, stretched out on the bed with the year-old copy of a book found between the floorboards—*Eccentric Millionaires* —watched the black entrance to see who next would come.

Judy's voice, outside in the dark, summoned him forth.

"I'm home," she said, "for anyone who can carry me over the threshold."

Thirty Years Later

"Well, tell me, Bingo," Judy would say, "was it worth it?"

"Sit down," Bingo would say. "I am going to sing you a love song."

"But will it be pretty?"

"It will be a honey."

And she would sit down, patting her feet, and he would do it.

Nine children and nineteen grandchildren, she'd think, and I don't feel a day over forty.

Then they'd go to bed where, to her mind and his, every time it was like starting over.

SOME PEOPLE WILL TELL YOU THE SITUATION AT HENNY PENNY NURSERY IS GETTING INTOLERABLE

*W*e got fifty-two (52) kids in the nursery, the Henny Penny Nursery, only one teacher, and she's retarded. They come to me, the parents of these kids do, and they say, "Sir, Mr. Beacon, excuse us, sir, for butting in like this, but some of us parents, mostly those of us you see right here, what we've noticed is that Mrs. Shorts, running your place, well, sir, to make no bones about it, she's retarded." And they look at me and blink their eyes all bashful-like— "Sorry we raised it, forgive us for noticing it," sort of like that, I mean—and, well, I blink right back because frankly I don't know what they expect me to do.

"She's *slow*," I tell them, "Mrs. Shorts is slow, she's *dim*, but what makes you think she's retarded?"

Because I was looking for evidence, you see. You can't just go around sacking somebody because you hear stories passed along by every Dick and Harry.

"Begging your pardon, sir," they say, "but here's one thing, what we think, us concerned parents here—that's what we call ourselves, the Concerned Parents of Henny Penny Nursery

227

—it's like this, you see. Mrs. Shorts, she's been on the job six months now and we think we've given her every fair chance. Fact is, at the start we *liked* her, we were really bowled over, because she's so sweet and all. But, sir, Mr. Beacon, what concerns us is that now after six months on the job she don't yet know where the kids hang up their coats or where their galoshes are kept, and worse yet, she won't let them out on the playground some of us hobby-type parents put in at our own expense, because she says they could get run over by streetcars. *Streetcars*, Mr. Beacon, and we've looked it up: there hasn't been streetcars in this town for sixty-two years. Which is another thing, Mr. Beacon, her *age!*"

"I take your point," I tell them. "I have noticed myself Mrs. Shorts is on the feeble side, and elderly, though saying she's retarded is maybe going too far."

"She *dithers*, Mr. Beacon, she *dithers* all the time, and the place under her is a madhouse, it's pandemonium in there."

"I see. So you're telling me you're dissatisfied."

"We wouldn't go that far, sir, no sir. We the Concerned Parents of Henny Penny, CPHPN, we're called, we just think the matter ought to be looked into. We're paying good money to have our little Johnnies and Susies and whatnot get the best education available, have all the best opportunities like most of us never had, and, well, we just think this matter ought to be gone over some, maybe looked into with a fine-tooth comb."

"I see," I say, picking up my pen. "You're registering a formal complaint."

"Oh no, sir! This is all off the record. We just sort of hoped if we brought it to your attention that—"

"That something would be done about it. Good idea. The Concerned Parents of Henny Penny, CPHPN, may certainly consider that indeed I shall, first chance."

"Yes, sir. We know you will. It isn't that, sir, so much

as . . . well, there is the question of the petition that other group—*our* parent group, so to speak, the Tiny Totlers Protective Parents Association, TTPPA, of which we are a spin-off—there's that list of grievances they brought in last year, you'll remember, about nails in the floorboards and the Doze Room without any cots, and all that rat business, and such. We were wondering couldn't we get some action soon on that, as four or five of the totlers had to go to the hospital on account of the ptomaine."

"Ptomaine?" I say.

"Yes sir. And the pneumonia. There don't ever seem to be any heat in the place, except in Mrs. Shorts' room."

"Imagine that!" I say.

They kept blinking their eyes at me, waiting, leaning this way and that and nodding encouragement at each other and at their speaker, so I began to get a whiff of a suspicion that this bunch meant to play tough. That they had come prepared with facts and this time meant business. A much tougher bunch, overall, than the TTPPA.

So I pulled out my upkeep file. I spread out all *my* figures on my desk, face-up, so that if they wanted to they could lean over and see them.

I pointed at my *heat* figures.

"You can see here," I said, "that Henny Penny paid out over seven hundred dollars in heat bills this last quarter alone. Now that's pretty hefty *heating*, I think you'll agree, I'm shocked to hear you saying you think Henny Penny would ever let a little tot go cold."

That silenced them right up. One or two of those up front sort of leaned over to glance at the heat file, but mostly they seemed quite willing to take my word for it. "You can rest assured," I told them, "that Henny Penny doesn't shirk on expenses. If seven hundred dollars is what it takes, then seven hundred dollars is what Henny Penny will pay."

There was some whispering in the back of the room. They went into a huddle back there and after a while I heard someone say, "Ask him about the toys. Why there ain't no toys."

"Yes sir," said the leader, "there's that too. We think it'd be nice, a real joy for the kiddies, if Henny Penny provided toys and equipment to keep the little folks busy. Seems every toy our boys and girls *bring*, well, they sort of disappear or they wind up in Mrs. Shorts' lap. Mrs. Shorts, she gets them and has *herself* a good time, but *our* kids, well, they are just left to cry out their eyes. Now that's painful for us, Mr. Beacon, it's more than most of us can bear to see these little fellas and gals weeping their hearts out because Mrs. Shorts is playing with the trucks or the dolls, what-have-you, and she won't *share*! That's what we mean by retarded. She's not all there, is what we mean."

I told them I could see their point. That I could see it and —if true—I was horrified. *Naturally* these little kids, here in their formative years, their important years, when their entire mental attitude and approach to life was being formed—here when they were at this sensitive age, their character being molded and all that, *naturally* they ought to have nice toys and equipment, *good* equipment, *safe* equipment, and all they wanted. "But look here," I said. And I tapped a finger on *that* file. "Look here. Henny Penny paid out—and I know it because I wrote the check myself—Henny Penny last month alone paid out thirteen hundred dollars for new toys and that Space-Age Ghost Rider machine! For stuffed animals, big bouncy balls, fire engines, Hootenanny Dolls, picture puzzles, color books, and games—the whole shebang! So when you tell me we don't have any toys over at that school, why I'm alarmed!"

"Mrs. Shorts broke that Ghost Rider thing," someone put in. "She hit it with a hammer, then put her foot through it!"

"I'm *alarmed*, I say, I certainly am, and I have to wonder where thirteen hundred dollars have got to. Now I know once in a while one of these sweet children in all innocence will stuff a nice new toy in its pocket and take it home, meaning of course to bring it back, but what you folks seen to be telling me is that something more organized than this is going on. Something more systematic, of the rip-off variety—something that looms as out-and-out *theft*! So you can be assured I and Mrs. Shorts will give this matter our undivided attention!"

"That hammer," someone said, "she threw it at one of the children!"

"Yes, our undivided attention! That we can guarantee. We *will* get to the bottom of it, since I think you'll agree thirteen hundred dollars ain't hayseed, and, why, we'll just have to let the chips fall where they may, and if criminal charges are to be brought we will just have to bring them, without regard for race, sex, or family background. How's that? I hope you can see you've put me in a corner on this, and *action will have to be taken*!"

A few of those in the back started pushing and shoving and raising their voices, and pretty soon they all were, and it looked to me as if the whole business was about to get out of hand.

"What about the hammer!"

"The dirt!"

"Fist fights!"

"No treats!"

"Plopped down in front of the TV!"

"Ah!" I said, "the TV! Now hold it! Hold on! You can see right here that TV cost Henny Penny nine hundred dollars. Nine hundred. Nine hundred dollars don't grow on trees. It's an example of Henny Penny always providing the best. Nothing's too good for those tykes, that's Henny Penny motto. Quality first!"

"Only one channel works," said one loudmouth. "And no sound on it!"

"Hold it!" I shouted. "Now hold on! You're all adults, all parents, so I'd like to see some resemblance of order around here. Not everybody shouting at once. We can't expect our little folks to grow up with a proper perspective if the parents don't lay down a good example. So hold on!"

"I was opposed to that TV," one loudmouth said. "TV's stoopid."

But I got a few tentative apologies. Their leader was telling everyone to hush up. "First things first," he said. "Is Mrs. Shorts retarded or isn't she?"

I rode in over them. "You know," I said, "if you don't like Henny Penny's outlook on child care and child-rearing, you can always withdraw your fine children and enroll them elsewhere. There is, for instance, that Howdy Powdy Nursery next door."

"But that's all boarded up," someone let out. "We thought that place had shut down *eons* ago."

"No," I said, "begging to correct you. Howdy Powdy is operating every day, every week of the year, seven o'clock till midnight, the same as we are. And doing quite well, by my understanding. I don't mind saying a nice word for the competition. Of course, they may be full up, I doubt you'd find a vacancy there just now, but fine by me if you want to grab your kid out of Henny Penny and throw them in Howdy Powdy."

"I've heard stories of that place," someone said. "Whippings and such."

"There used to be this nice place out on Willows Road," one said. "Any time of day you could ride by, see the kids laughing and playing, singing and such. Maybe we could put our kids there."

I could see the group getting all hepped up over that idea. I let it ferment a while. Then I jumped in: "Hold on!" I said. "Hold your horses. I remember that Willows Road place the same as you. A real lively, jumping place, full of the greatest kids in the world. But I hear tell it's been bought out. By a syndicate bunch. I hear tell it's got this tall barbed-wire fence around it now, with armed guards at the gate. Nope," I said. "Nope, it looks like for the moment there's just Howdy Powdy and us."

The leader spoke up again. She was a short, thick lady touching forty, I guessed, wearing thick eyeglasses and a gray business suit with a ceramic moose on the lapel, painted green and swirly. I'd had my eyes on that moose practically the whole time her group had been inside my office. My wife, before she ran off, had one exactly like it.

"We could start our own," she was saying. "With the fees we pay for Henny Penny we could in no time have the greatest little nursey ever hit this town. We could rent us a nice roomy house on a cheerful street, hire us three or four bright graduates from the childcare school, paint it up pretty, put in a nice playground! Why, it would be the greatest thing in the world for our little kids. They'd love it! We could make it their own little home, you know, just beautiful and clean!"

The discussion got heavy. I could see they were getting truly excited. They milled about my office, exchanging ideas, toting up figures, flashing smiles—making plans.

I raised my hand.

"Hold on," I said. "Just one dang minute. I'm not opposing your ideas in the least. It's a fine idea and I want to tell you that Henny Penny is behind you one hundred percent. We will give you all the advice and encouragement you need."

That quieted them down.

"Funny thing is," I said, "you are reminding me of my very own self, some fifty-three years ago, when I marched in here, head of a concerned parents' group just like yours. I demanded the situation improve at Henny Penny School. You won't believe it but in them times the plight of the little lads and lassies was truly sickening. A real sweatshop. Little three-year-olds making wallets. They knew nothing but misery. Whippings day in and day out. Typhoid, whooping cough, measles. A true dirt hole. But I and my then wife and some of the others, we decided to march. Get organized. We marched in here and laid down the law—to a Mr. Magruder it was then, sitting behind this desk. Kill the rats, we said. Pull down the rotted trees. Cut the grass, burn out the snakes. Haul away the litter to the junk yard. Slap on a dab of paint. Put in a stove. Buy toys. Hire a nice worker. On and on we went, a list long as my arm.

"And Mr. Magruder, he laughed. He laughed in our faces. 'Try it,' he said. 'Go ahead and try it. *You*,' he said, talking to me. '*You* take this chair. This desk. Here, take it,' he said, 'it's all yours. I give you one year. Maybe two. I give you as long as it takes you to get *your* kid out of short pants. Once your own kid has moved on, you're going to start forgetting about the rats. About the refuse. About the beatings. You're going to forget about it all. You're going to wish you could go somewhere where you could never see another little child through all of your born years. You're going to *hate* the darlin' little rascals. You're going to learn that these little brats, up to and including your own, are the ugliest, rottenest, stupidest, noisiest, most venal, selfish, hurtful, *dangerous* sonsofbitches ever put on this planet since God was himself and ape. And you're going to want to *hurt* them, to *menace* them, to *wreck* the little bastards while they're in knee pants, because you'll know that is the only chance you'll ever get. You're going to want to drive home the message once and for all that adults have lives too, that not *all* the world belong to these sniveling, bug-eyed, innocent, knock-kneed, big-eared fools.'

"That's what he told me and my wife. And we spat in his face. We said, 'Not me! We love kids. Kids are the hope of the universe and we never saw a bad kid yet.' My wife and I, we stood right on this spot, pointing the finger of accusation at him. 'So yes,' I said, 'I'll take that chair. Move your fat butt over.' And I took it. And I have been sitting here ever since. Fifty-three years I been sitting here. My wife too, at first. Then she took our little Johnny and ran off. Where to, God knows. Who cares. Now I am not going to tell you what Mr. Magruder told me. I've got more respect for you than that. I want you to know I am on your side. Start your new nursery. Paint it blue. Put up your white picket fence. Call it Andy Pandy, Starky Larky, Monkey Funky. Give it your best. No, I am not going to repeat Mr. Magruder's words. All I am going to tell you is this. Mr. Magruder told the truth. Yes, he was quoting the gospel. God help the miserable cur. For every day that knowledge has been killing me. Chiseling away my heart and soul. Paring me down. I was a Henny Penny kid myself, you see. Back in the old days when the sky was truly falling. I'm a Henny Penny graduate, member of the very first class. The last *surviving* member of that class, I'd suppose. I owe all I am today to Henny Penny. Good old Henny Penny. Three cheers for Henny Penny. God knows where I'd gone, what I'd be today, without it."

NARCISSUS CONSULTED

No one ever told Rikki Newhouse she was not beautiful. When she was small, doting parents took turns with the child on their knees, passing such remarks as:

> Rikki, you're a knockout!
> Oh, Rikki, one day you're going to break hearts!

They of course believed this.

And Rikki, for that matter, took this knowledge unto herself, cherished it, and never let go of it. As the years turned she would say to herself in various mirrors she came in front of:

> Rikki, you are beautiful!

It happened too, around the time she was fourteen, that an older boy living in her neighborhood—nineteen he was and with his own car, a Buick Skylark—fell deeply and truly in love with her, and often on their periodic drives up The

Malahat and at various scenic overlooks where they parked, he would throw a heavy arm over the girl's slender shoulder and say plainly:

You know, you knock me out!

or

You are the most beautiful thing on two legs, do you know that?

or

You make me feel like I'm about sixteen!

Rikki adored hearing such remarks. And in fact if an outing with Ed Flobert—for that was the young man's name—ended with remarks of this kind not being made, she would arrive back at her doorstep depressed and silent and in such a difficult mood that even Ed—who loved her, for there was no doubting that—would feel called upon to say:

What's bugging you, sugar?

or

You know, sometimes I just don't understand you!

—although, as I say, this eventuality rarely transpired. Almost always, and repeatedly, Ed did say:

Rikki, you are something else!

or

God, I can't help myself, you are just a Great Looker!

And Rikki would lift her innocent, radiant face up to his, smiling with the same agreeableness with which she responded to her parents' early and continuing assertions in a similar vein, and allow Ed Flobert to go on teaching her how to kiss and how not to feel bad about what they were doing.

> *Oh, Rikki!*
> *Oh, Ed!*

Oh! Oh! Oh! and on and on with passionate declarations of this type until Rikki by Ed's own admission became quite expert at kissing and much else—since both were in fact normal warm-blooded individuals wanting to find out what life was all about.

That's how matters continued until she was seventeen or so, at which point it occurred to her that Ed Flobert was in essence a rather drab, unexciting person, what some people, including her parents, might call the drippy type, and that she was only young once and there were a lot more fish in the sea than Ed Flobert.

So one rainy evening on The Malahat's highest overlook she found herself having this conversation:

> *I don't know how to say this to you, Ed.*
> *Just say it.*
> *It hurts too much. I don't want to hurt you.*
> *Oh for Godsake, Rikki. Whatever it is, get it off your chest.*
> *You're sure?*
> *I'm sure. I'm a grown man, I can take it. Just hold on until I get this blouse unbuttoned.*
> *Don't, Ed. I don't feel like it. I can't say what I have to say with you doing that.*
> *God, you're mopish tonight. So all right, what is it?*

I'm dumping you, Ed.
Oh God. Oh God no, not that.
I've made up my mind, Ed.
But what have I done?
It isn't you, Ed. It's me. I've decided I want a lot more.

Rikki Newhouse did indeed want much more. Still, it hurt her to break off so suddenly with a nice guy like Ed and she could understand, she told him, the pain she knew he was going through and it hurt her too; it caused her nothing but grief for instance to be denying him the pleasures he'd got used to and which she had got used to herself, but they would just have to live with it and in the end he'd see . . .

You'll see, Ed, that it's the best thing for both of us.
Yeah yeah yeah, you're dumping me and I'm supposed to be philosophical about it.
I want you to know I admire you and still feel something for you.
Yeah yeah yeah.
I just don't feel that way about you anymore. I mean physically I just don't physically feel that way about you anymore.
God, I can't even touch you.
We can still be friends, Ed.
Oh yeah, friends, big deal!

He drove her home that night with the car whiplashing down the steep, winding Malahat, Rikki holding on to her seat, bracing herself against dash and floorboard, filled with terror, quite certain Ed Flobert meant to kill both of them. He had become suddenly a madman, his eyes glazed, now and then shouting at her, mindless of everything now that he had at last been convinced he could no longer have her.

He slammed on the brakes in front of her house, wrenched his body past hers, and held her door shut so she couldn't get out.

> *I guess you're going to go running to some other guy.*
> *Nobody specific, Ed. I told you that. I wish you would stop acting so nasty and giving me those dirty looks.*

Poor Ed sobbed down under the wheel.

> *All right, go on. I know when I'm licked. I always knew I couldn't hold you. I'm an Average Joe. You're Something Special. I'm fully aware a girl with your looks can have anybody she wants.*

He smiled sadly, finally allowing the graceful exit.

> *So long, Ed. I'll never forget you.*

She came inside to find her parents waiting.

> *Don't cry, baby. Has that brute hurt you? Did you have a lovers' argument?*
> *I've dumped the jerk.*
> *Oh? Good for you. Your Daddy and I didn't want to say it, but we've never believed Ed Flobert was good enough for you.*
> *Not nearly,*

her Daddy added.

The following days brought keen disappointment. Rikki Newhouse found it quite remarkable that boys her own age or nearly, boys from her school or those who talked to her sometimes down at the Y where for years she had been attending a weekly ballet class—that they did not immediately knock down her door or wear out the telephone requesting dates.

For several months, however, this was the case.

> *Now don't worry, honey. A girl with your looks and personality won't go lonely for long.*
> *Mom's right, Rikki. You got beauty and brains, you got pizazz, and there is no better combination. Hang in there.*

Ed, she heard, was playing the field. From all she could gather he had not wasted a single minute.

> *My God, what a Romeo he's turned into!*
> *I'll tell you something about Ed Flobert, Rikki, all Ed Flobert has to do is snap his fingers and women come running.*

One evening when her parents had taken her to Hy's Steakhouse to celebrate something or other, Rikki and her parents alike were thunderstruck to discover themselves seated at a table just opposite one occupied by Ed Flobert and his date.

The woman—for no one in his right mind would ever have taken her to be a mere girl—was seated with her back to them. She wore a black silk gown, bare in the back, with thin straps crisscrossing.

Rikki was aware, as dinner progressed, of Ed's occasional glance at her, but it was the woman's naked back which most claimed her attention.

> *What a beautiful dress! Now if you were in that getup, honey, you would be spectacular.*
> *It is a lovely dress. I wonder where she's been to have got such a Great Tan.*

Extraordinary shoulders. Probably piggish, though, in the face. Mind you, I'm not knocking her.

Rikki did not join her parents in these observations. She reminded herself that she did not care who Ed Flobert went out with, and if he could find another beauty to go out with, well, that was his good fortune. All the same, she was subject to frequent bursts of jealousy. This emotion was altogether novel to her experience, and in fact had very little to do with Ed Flobert personally. Her envy centered solely upon the woman. It seemed to her, much against her will, that here was the most glamorous woman in creation. Her parents could go on speaking of the horrible face she would have, but Rikki was convinced of the opposite. She knew the woman would be extraordinarily beautiful.

Excuse me, Mom.
Excuse me, Dad.

Twice Rikki excused herself from the table, her path to and from the powder room taking her unnecessarily near where Ed Flobert and his companion sat. On each occasion, however, the woman's face was so angled that she was unable to get a good look at her face. Each time, that is, the woman's face was averted in such manner that Rikki found herself again seated with only an impression of loveliness encountered, of smooth skin and languid hands and hair shiny as a jeweller's counter.

Now and then she could be heard laughing, the sound charmingly melodious.

Rikki's father said:

Now that's a man for you. A few months ago he thought the sun rose and set on our Rikki. Now look at him drooling over that woman.

Towards the end Ed Flobert stood up, whispered something to his companion, and strolled happily over to the Newhouse table. He nodded with a half-smile to the parents, and after receiving their reluctant acknowledgment, gave his attention to Rikki.

You've been well, I hope.
Oh fine! Wonderful.
Good. I'm glad to hear it.
And you? Everything okay?
Perfect! Couldn't ask for better.

And momentarily he remained, hands joined behind him, tilting forward in his exquisite suit—he had never bothered to dress so impeccably while dating Rikki—smiling that half-smile, nodding contentedly as Rikki stammered out awkward assurances as to how wonderful it was that everyone was doing so well.

Nice to see you all.

Then he was gone.

To Rikki's chagrin, the woman with him had not cared enough to discover who it was had claimed his attention even to turn her head.

The waiter appeared and poured a last glass of wine at the Flobert table.

This quite rattled Rikki's parents:

They get much better service over there. This is ridiculous. I've a mind to make a big fuss.
You have my blessings. Our money is as good as theirs any day.

Rikki bristled. It seemed to her that her parents had become ugly wizened creatures with no more dignity than birds scratching in a nest.

Please be quiet. Can't we try to enjoy ourselves?

Her parents lapsed into a shamed silence. Rikki had never talked to them this way before.

A few minutes later Rikki looked up and Ed Flobert's table was empty. She could see them in the dimly lit reception area, getting their coats on, the hostess and the *maître d'* hovering at their elbows as if they were royalty. The woman turned, looking back at the dining area. Rikki, even so, could not see her face: the woman's head was concealed within a hood of lavish fur.

Rikki stiffened as the *maître d'* bowed and kissed the woman's hand.

An elderly couple at an adjacent table could be heard gushing:

What a beautiful couple!
Who are they, do you suppose!

Rikki Newhouse went home that night and cried. She had cried before, of course—as a child confronting this or that unexpected pain: skinned knees, a broken collarbone when she was eight, ear trouble when she was twelve—but until now she had not known the agony of a broken heart. Before this, certainly, it would not have occurred to her to cry because another female had been found to be more beautiful. The world's great beauties—Garbo in the old days or Catherine Deneuve today with her perfume ads—were very striking, of course, but their beauty was of a type so different from her own that she had never been compelled to make close comparisons. Without being especially vain about it, she had simply accepted her beauty as a given fact.

Now it was as if every mirror she had ever looked into had cracked and broken into a million pieces.

Her parents finally gave up on her and went to bed.

Over the following days Rikki went to considerable trouble to find out something about the woman in question, though no one seemed to know very much about her. All Rikki's friends could repeat was what they had themselves heard from one or another unreliable source. All agreed, however, that she was new in town, unmarried, extremely rich, and apparently quite nice. It was also apparent, so Rikki's friends told her, that she believed Ed Flobert to be the most exciting and terrific guy ever to come down the pike.

> *She's in love with him, you mean!*
> *That's what we hear.*
> *They're serious about each other! Is that what you're saying?*
> *That's what it looks like. But why are you asking? I thought you had decided Ed Flobert was a jerk!*

The woman remained a mystery.

Rikki in time came to think of Ed Flobert as some kind of no-good gigolo; she came to believe he had betrayed her. As she confessed to her parents more than one evening, she couldn't see how Ed Flobert could have gone on so long professing his love for her, his utter adoration of her, putting her on a pedestal and all that, and letting her wipe her feet on him if she wanted to—and then a few weeks later show up arm-in-arm with another woman and have the whole town thinking he was head-over-heels in love with her.

> *Even if she is beautiful that don't make it right!*

Her parents offered what little comfort they could. Her Mom said:

It just goes to show you, honey: all men are snakes!

While her Dad said:

You can be grateful you still have your virtue, young lady. That's one fact we can all be grateful for.

And Rikki, accustomed to doing so now at every turn, would break into tears. She could see now that she must have never meant very much to Ed Flobert. No doubt he had been lying to her, talking all that mush simply to get from her what he wanted. Using her. He had latched on to her when she was fourteen and innocent, he'd driven up The Malahat and talked a lot of nonsense until he got what he wanted, and now he didn't care hell or high water what became of her.

Oh, Rikki!

her parents would say,

You've got to get over this, got to get yourself together, little lady. Got to stop all this slumping around, going about like walking death.
He's right, honey. There's that Desmond boy next door, why don't you give him a nod?

But Desmond, and all the others she might have, to her mind now—after Ed Flobert—seemed like poor fish indeed. From time to time she would find herself remembering that last night when Ed Flobert had come speeding like a madman down The Malahat, and it seemed to her that he would have done as well if he crashed into the trees and killed her because her life was over now in any case.

She remained beautiful, she didn't doubt that—but what was the big deal? What did it matter?

One day while downtown shopping for a gift to mark her parents' 25th wedding anniversary, she was crossing the intersection at the Eaton's store and waiting for the WALK light to flash on when a long, shining Rolls-Royce crept up to and parked at the curb directly in front of her. A chauffeur in smart gray uniform was at the wheel of the purring machine. In the back, past smoky glass and surrounded by soft red leather, sat a woman with crossed knees, holding a man's hand in her lap. The WALK sign flashed on, but Rikki remained on the sidewalk, oblivious of those rushing past her, hardly aware when they brushed against her and hurried on with mumbled apology. She knew the man who had his arm in this woman's lap was Ed Flobert and that in a moment he and perhaps both of them would step out of the car, and she would suddenly find herself face to face with her competitor. She would find herself looking into the eyes of this stunning mystery creature who—as she now conceived it—had stolen Ed Flobert from her. He would step out on the arm of this woman, spot her, smile his half-smile, and because he had become so socially adept, so graceful and civilized and charming, he would murmur

What a pleasant surprise! It is Rikki Newhouse, is it not?

and move to introduce her to the woman. She was utterly convinced that this is exactly what was about to happen. And for the second time in her life Rikki knew fear. She knew that this time, if it did happen, her life would truly be over. She would find herself shamed beyond measure. She would find herself confronted with Absolute Beauty. And with this thought something wrenched inside her, a pain so abrupt and severe that she gasped and all but keeled over, throwing up both hands as if to hold and protect her stricken heart.

Yet nothing happened. A few seconds later, opening her eyes, the sleek automobile was nowhere to be seen. She searched the streets, unable to find any indication that it had even been there.

She went on into Eaton's and in the third-floor Heirloom Section bought her parents a six-inch-high, exquisitely crafted Swiss clock on a silver stand with mother-of-pearl mounting. She had to pay a considerable sum—considerably more, in fact, than she could afford without later suffering—but it was a most beautiful object and she could not resist it.

Some years later, after Rikki had married a perfectly ordinary man—a gentle soul who works hard all year and looks forward to nothing so much as their brief vacation on the islands each summer—and after giving birth to two normal, healthy, obedient children, Rikki was often to find herself recalling with difficult motive those days of her childhood when her parents would take her on their knees and pass such comments as

> By God, Rikki, you are beautiful!

or those nights on the summit of The Malahat when Ed Flobert would crush her to him, saying

> Oh, Rikki, you knock me out!

And sometimes when her husband isn't too tired or when business affairs are not pressing on his mind she will succeed in dressing him up and getting him out of the house, and on the walkway to the car or in the car or once they have got to where it is they are going he will wink at her or pat her knee, saying

Dear, you look lovely!

or

How fetching you are in that dress, my Rikki!

and at such times memory of her old assurance will sweep over her and she will grasp his hand or move to embrace him, crying

Oh, Max, we are so happy, aren't we!

It is only evenings such as this current one, slow evenings when time and wistfulness accumulate, rare moments like to-night when she's susceptible to the mood and prepared to induce her heart's torture, that Rikki Newhouse can look into her dressing mirror and there see herself in black silk with her shoulders bare, Max watching her from his place on the other side of the bed, his expression so rapt you would think him mesmerized—times such as the present, I mean to say, when Rikki's own familiar face vanishes from the glass and in its place materializes that face of Perfect Beauty, of love given and received: Ed Flobert's mystery woman staring back at her with entreating, radiant eyes, and going on past her to settle forgivingly on the waiting Max.

LADY GODIVA'S HORSE

*F*rom the beginning I did not believe, could not make myself believe, Charles wanted me. "There must be some mistake here," I'd say to him, "or am I dreaming?"

"We are hitting it off beautifully," he'd reply, "don't create trouble where none exists."

The women I work with took my position, they said, "Honey, you're heading for another nosedive, prepare yourself."

Charles was livid, he straight-armed me back against the plywood wall on Hastings Street where demolition work is going on, and said, "Rebecca, if these people make such remarks they are being thoughtless and unkind, the truth is they are not good enough for you, no doubt they are jealous of our happiness. Do yourself a favor and pay absolutely no attention to them."

This exchange took place on our lunch hour and when I got back to Vancouver Brake and Wheel the women in the office stared, they said, "Look at Rebecca June Carlyle, she must have got the bad news already."

They brought me chewing gum and a package of Scotties for me to blow my nose on and I could tell they didn't believe me when I said, "No, I didn't get the kiss-off yet, it's just that I have a headache and my stomach is upset and I know I'm going to get the kiss-off soon."

"I've got some uppers I can give you," my friend Lydia offered, "for when matters go from bad to worse, aren't men dogs?"

Charles' own friends are wonderfully supportive of him, they go out of their way to let him know that whatever happens he's their man, they want only the very best for him.

When he came over that night I said as much, I threw his flowers on the floor and turned off Hourglass which is what they call the Channel 2 evening news out here, which I don't watch anyway, and I said, "Charles, it's perfectly clear to me that your friends think the world of you, time and time again I've heard them remark that nothing is too good for Charles. So tell the truth, I really would like to know: don't they wonder why you're wasting your time chasing fluff like me? Don't bother answering, I'm sure they do, but I don't blame them because the fact is I'm just not in your league."

Charles went all fence-posty, we could have heard a tack drop.

"I know exactly what they must be telling you," I went on. "'Drop her, Charles, she's bad news, that Rebecca June Carlyle is a worn-out mop and not good enough to wipe your feet on.'"

He picked up the flowers and unwrapped them from their green paper and began arranging them in the silver vase he'd given me on Groundhog Day. "Don't be dopey," he said, "my friends admire you, they see you as the answer to my prayers."

This was so absurd I laughed out loud.

I laughed about it all through dinner and in bed that night I still laughed each time I thought about it.

Oh it hurts, but I can laugh easy as the next person.

About two in the morning he got up and put on his clothes. "If you're going to keep playing that tune," he said, "I'm going home."

This is it, I thought, the kiss-off, I'll never see this beautiful man again.

"This is not the kiss-off," he told me, "it is simply that I can't take any more of it tonight and I'm going home before I get angry."

I pleaded with him to stay, I begged and begged, I have no pride. But he reminded me we both had to go to work in the morning and needed our beauty sleep.

"Especially me," I said. Then I lost my temper and threw his shoes at him, I told him it was rotten of him to leave me when I was so upset, but that I wasn't surprised, not the least little bit, no, I had always expected it.

He told me to calm down, that I was waking people, that we'd have the law on our tails.

I told him he could take his law and stuff it, I called him a lot of loud bad names and said that even if I wasn't in his league he could at least show me a little human decency and I cried and apologized and begged him to come back to my bed.

"Get up," he said, "I can't stand to see a woman weeping at my feet," and he helped me up and brushed my hair back and dried my eyes and led me back to bed and got in with me.

It was lovely after that, I truly believe it was the most exquisite night I ever had.

I didn't see him the next night. He said he had to take the ferry over to Victoria to see a man about a business he was thinking of investing in. The girls at the office said, "Yeah, I'll bet," and mentioned any of a dozen things he was more likely doing, although that day they didn't have much time for me since my friend Lydia was having a breakdown, something about her despot husband, I forget the details.

At midnight Charles called me from what he said was The Olde English Inn. He said he always stayed at the O.E.I. when in The Flower City because he loved it and because a replica of Annie Hathaway's cottage was right on the site and he wanted to build a house just like it for me sometimes.

"Who're you with?" I asked.

"I'm with my lonesome," he said, "and missing you."

I told him I was sure he had a woman with him, but I could understand it, I certainly didn't expect faithfulness to a non-person like me.

"Don't start that again," he said.

I told him about the girl in the office, my friend Lydia, who was having a breakdown brought on by her jerk husband.

He said he was sorry.

Finally I let him hang up, it must have been about one.

I couldn't sleep and tried doping myself up with a late movie. I knew he was with someone. A man like Charles can't go ten minutes without some pretty little trick pulling on his arm. The fact is, as I told Walter Pidgeon, Charles is Vancouver's most eligible bachelor. He can have any woman in town. Before I came into the picture he had women dropping in on him from as far away as the Yukon. Right there on the cover of *Miss Chatelaine* I've seen a woman who chased him for seven years. One time at his place while he was taking a shower I had a sneak look around his bedroom and found in his closet six shoe boxes stuffed full of love letters from scores of women who promised him eternal love and anything else he wanted. He can have beautiful women and smart women and women so rich I guess their feet never touch ground.

"You can see," I'd say to him, "how that makes me feel."

"Aw, dry up," he'd say. "Even if all that is true, and I doubt it, you're the girl for me."

Walter Pidgeon went to war and got shot down and June Allyson was left with his baby and with Van Johnson who had been her boy friend before Walter moved him out.

One of the office girls said she'd stayed up to see it too and had almost puked, but most of us wondered why they didn't make movies like that anymore.

Charles showed up at lunchtime right on the button and took me to a restaurant nearby, Murphy's *Chinese*.

He asked me why I was so grouchy, had I been losing sleep?

"You know I can't sleep by myself anymore," I said.

"So what's the problem?" he asked.

"Us," I said. "We are the problem. We are mismatched."

"How so?"

"You have everything and I have nothing. Charm, brains, good looks, all that was passed out when I was off somewhere hiding. I have nothing to offer a man of your qualities."

Charles ate his noodles in silence. He gave me a brochure of Annie Hathaway's cottage to take my mind off matters.

"Let's set the date," he said.

"I can't do it, Charles," I said. "If you marry me they'll laugh you out of town."

He ordered me a second glass of wine, since I wasn't eating. But he was reluctant, however, because Charles hates to see me get high. He's right, too, because when I get high I get arch and argumentative and take offense at any harmless remark passed.

I truly am an impossible person.

"That's not true," he said. "You are more apt to get vague and dreamy and happy all around. Drink it down."

I asked him why he was stringing me along. "What's in it for you?" I asked.

"I was hoping you could get me a cut price at Vancouver Brake and Wheel," he said.

Our lunch hour was over but I just sat there vague and dreamy and not the least bit happy. "Duty calls," Charles said, and came behind me to lift my chair. I refused to leave. I told him I wasn't going back to work, not ever. Vancouver Brake and Wheel could take their chintzy mindless job and shove it, nobody there liked me, I was paid dog wages and taken advantage of in every conceivable way, and I was quitting, I had just quit, I meant to spend the rest of my life at this table in Murphy's *Chinese* looking at a plate of wiped-up noodles.

Charles whispered I was making a scene and if I didn't get up that very minute he was going to leave without me.

"I know," I said, "you're only looking for an excuse to kiss me off."

He sat down and bent over the table to talk to me in reasonable tones about personal responsibility and our debts to humanity at large and how Murphy needed our table because other people were waiting.

So I got up, that's just the kind of inconsistent, led-by-the-nose person I am.

"I know I'm a wipe-out," I told Charles out on the street, "you best walk on now and forget all about me."

We stopped to look through a peephole in the wall where the demolition work is going on on Hastings Street. Their big crane was up with this huge steel ball suspended on a chain and they were slamming this ball against a building that had been perfectly satisfactory for sixty-five years and now they were knocking it all down.

Charles gave me a kiss and hurried off because he had a bunch of very important people waiting to hear what he thought about some big project of theirs.

Soon after I got back to work Lydia's husband came in looking for Lydia who hadn't showed up that day and when none of us could help him he picked up her old adding machine off her desk and threw it against the wall, and then he tore apart her desk apparently looking for secrets he believed she kept in there, and he kept shouting these awful insults about Lydia and her secret life and how he would punch her in the snoot if he ever found her and how she was crazy if she thought she could walk out on him. "You *robots*," he shouted at us, "what do any of you know about life, you're just living and working here in your little garden world at Vancouver Brake and Wheel and you know *nothing*, you might as well all be *dead*!"

I tried calming him down but he told me I was shriveled up and stupid and ought to go live my life in a cage.

Then he left before the police could come.

"Mark my words," one of the women said, "a few days from now when Lydia gets over her embarrassment and her black eyes heal she'll come in and explain that Simon was drinking or he wouldn't have behaved that way, that she feels sorry for him, that they've worked all their problems out now and their marriage is a bed of roses."

Most of us disagreed, we figured this was the final straw.

The manager made a cute speech saying how regrettable this incident was, he was sorry it had upset us, the man was an animal and ought to be beheaded, but it was over now and he hoped the company could expect a good day's work out of us.

At five o'clock every afternoon I feel this insane love for Vancouver Brake and Wheel, it takes about three seconds for everyone to clear out, one would think we were running from a sex-starved maniac.

I went home and had a slow hot bath, it turned out I had tiny slivers of glass imbedded in the skin all along my arms and shoulders from when Simon threw Lydia's glass desk top against the filing cabinets.

Charles came hurrying over, he had the idea I was bleeding to death and should be rushed immediately to the Emergency.

He used his own key to get in and when he saw me in the bath with bloody water up to my neck he almost fainted.

I hadn't planned he'd take it so seriously and had to show him the empty bottle of red food dye I'd used before he would calm down.

Then we got under the sheets and that was exquisite.

"Are you hungry?" he asked later, and I said I was ravished, I wished aloud I could just once cook him something better than bacon and eggs but in that category too I'm a washout, I was always too lazy to learn.

"Never mind," he said, "I'll cook up something nice," so he leapt out of bed and went to it.

The TV had been wheeled up to my bedside to keep me company and I threw a shoe at it and it came on. The Hourglass people were announcing that hikers earlier in the day had come across the nude body of a young girl murdered in Stanley Park, and naturally I thought of my daughter Charise and shrieked for Charles. But then they said she'd been there for months under a bed of moss so I knew it couldn't be Charise who was safe with her father, but even so Charles had to hold me until I stopped shaking.

"God," I moaned, "there are times when I think the world is coming to an end."

"Don't dwell on bad news," Charles told me, "people fell in love today, had birthdays, brought each other flowers, life goes on."

The mysterious firebomber had struck again, this time at First Federal Savings and Loan, and I let out another shriek because First Federal is only two doors down from Vancouver Brake and Wheel.

"No, it was another branch," Charles explained, but he turned off the TV and passed me a book to read, *The Lifetime*

Adventures of Mary Worth, which he'd given me as a joke but which I have come to dearly love. It has become such a comfort to me, at every crisis I find myself asking, "What would Mary do, how would Mary cope with this?"

A few minutes later Charles brought in our dinner, bacon and eggs, all he could find in my refrigerator, and we ate off the hand-sewn patchwork quilt I've carried with me all these years.

I asked him what he thought about Lydia's situation. "Do you think she really has a secret life?"

He turned traitor, he asked me about mine. "How was it," he asked, "with you and Jake?"

I went mopish and quiet. I was married for eight horrible years to a man who refused on principle to reveal any emotions about anything that happened anywhere in the world or at home, to him, to me, to our child, or our friends.

"Ask Jake," I told Charles.

"I have. Jake's like you, he dries up, won't say a word."

I didn't believe this and said so. Jake's the most horrible person imaginable, next to me, and he wouldn't pass up any opportunity to dish out the dirt on me.

Just my luck that he was Charles' best friend.

Charles had to go out that evening, "to put out a fire," he said.

I didn't ask for explanations, I was too tired and knew I could do nothing to hold him anyway. Before going to bed I sat a long time at my dressing table, contemplating my face with the intense hatred of Medea: my complexion is too sallow, my left eyelid is droopy, my face is blotchy, my eyes are blah, my skin is so oily, my nose is too short, my jaw is too square, and I've got a neck like a lamppost.

A moustache like Hitler, I'm ugly as a rat.

No bosom to speak of.

Charles is so handsome, he's everyone's dream, when I walk into a room with him everyone goes silent, they feast on him. Often the Art Museum will hire him just to come in and walk around.

I walked in my pigeon-toed fashion to the bed and slid between the sheets with all the grace of an orange crate.

I really ought to give up.

The phone rang. It was my daughter Charise, wanting to know if she could spend the weekend with me.

"Why," I asked, "is Jake having a party?"

"No," she said, "it's only that I thought it was time I saw you."

"I'm still dangerous, you know," I said, "I might slice off your thumbs."

She told me to stop talking that way. She said I sounded distant. She said if I wasn't in the mood or had plans we could make it another time.

"How's your father?" I asked.

She said he was fine, that he had been crawling around on the floor with her on his back.

I told her she should be asleep, that tomorrow was a school day and that it was outrageous of him to allow her to stay up so late. I heard her turn away from the phone and tell her father what I had said. I couldn't hear his reply.

"Can I come?" she asked me.

I told her it was sweet of her to want to and that certainly she could.

"How's Charles?" she asked.

I said fine.

"Is he there now?"

"No, he's out."

"Are you going to marry him?" she asked. "Daddy says you ought to but that you won't because all men bore you."

I told her to hang up now and go to bed.

She did.

Charles didn't wake me when he came in. But he put his arm around my waist and I must have been dreaming because

I thought it was Jake's arm and I bolted up screaming and hitting at him.

He apologized, and both of us immediately fell asleep.

In the morning Charles rolled over, asking, "What is it now?"

I was at my dressing table, weeping. My skin had broken out in a rash. My stomach was upset too. I couldn't do anything with my hair.

Charles went into the shower.

I quickly went through his suit coat pockets and the trousers he'd neatly draped over a chair, but found nothing revelatory.

He's been extremely careful lately.

Even his shoe boxes have disappeared.

I wrote out a phone number and folded it to the size of a postage stamp and hid it inside his wallet. Later on I intended to "find" it and accuse him and see how he attempted to excuse or defend himself.

A bag of groceries was on the kitchen counter and he had filled the refrigerator. I made instant coffee and toast and had them on the table waiting for him.

He said, "Oh Christ!" and dumped out the cups and began making what he considers a proper breakfast.

"Would you like pancakes?" he asked.

I said yes.

"Or an omelet."

I said an omelet would be fine.

He asked if I wanted grapefruit.

I said yes. I told him Charise was coming over for the weekend.

"That's good," he said, and stopped in his kitchen duties to kiss me because he thinks I like feeling like a mother. "I'll stay at my place."

"That's not necessary," I said. "She knows we sleep together."

He grinned. He said she might know we sleep together but she didn't know it was exquisite.

"That's not funny," I said.

He insisted it was. "You always say it's exquisite whether it is or isn't," he observed.

It's true. I don't mean to deceive or pretend, it's just that I was born a hypocrite and have always been one.

"But I can always tell when it is," he said, "because your toes turn green."

I didn't respond to this. I was thinking about being with Jake and how that had been exquisite too, much of the time. Jake was a good lover, in bed he was another person, all warm and delicious, and he would cry when at last he had to get up and put his pants on.

Charles put the first pancake down in front of me, buttery and thin and very like a crepe, and he asked should he cut it for me, should he douse it with true maple syrup and say grace if I was so inclined.

I let him.

I *adore* being looked after. That's what finally did it with Jake, he simply got fed up with pampering me.

From the stove Charles said, "Charise is the kind of girl who will very much enjoy having two fathers."

"Why is that?"

"Jake is wonderful," he said, "and I am wonderful, and together we make up for all your alleged shortcomings."

"Then you should marry Jake."

He said no he shouldn't.

He poured my coffee and brought it over, along with milk and sugar. "Shall I stir it for you?"

I admitted I was capable.

Charles makes delicious pancakes, I could eat them for a week and put on thirty pounds and then I would look more nearly the way I feel inside.

Charles was getting edgy, he showed me his watch and said

time was moving on and we'd best shake a leg or both of us would be late to work.

"The world will not end," I told him.

Charles is one of those odd people who regards punctuality as a virtue.

"I'll have to clean the apartment," I moaned. "Charise is like her father, it's white gloves every time."

"Hire someone," Charles suggested.

I said I hated doing that, people were not made to clean up after me.

Charles sighed. He put aside the pancake batter and went to get the vacuum.

He's faster and more thorough at cleaning up than Jake ever was. He's more organized. Jake liked best cleaning up those places the people never saw, like closet interiors or door moldings.

I put my dishes in the sink. I could do that much. I was feeling very depressed. It was on account of Charise, whenever she is about to visit me I go into a nosedive. She arrives and her eyes never leave me, she measures everything I say and do and then she goes back to Jake and tells him what a cripple I am, how shabby I look, she says, "Boy, were you ever wise to get rid of that loser."

It was on account of Charise and because I hate my apartment, it's the most depressing, lonely place in the world, I loathe it with every breath I take, it is exactly like me, it has no personality and it oozes laziness and stupidity and insufferable bad taste, although it isn't the fixtures or the furniture or the decorating that explains this since the place is exactly as it was when I moved in, I haven't done a solitary thing to it, not hung a single picture or slapped on a single dab of paint, just my presence in the place makes it drab and horrible and it has been that way every place I ever lived.

"You're in a mood today," Charles said.

I said No, I wasn't.

"Yes, you are." He was standing beside my plastic fern, staring at it, holding the vacuum cleaner hose in his hands, looking like a beat-up dog.

"Anything I've done?" he asked.

I told him I wished he would shut up, there was nothing worse than being told you were in a mood when you knew perfectly well that you were not.

He shrugged, and started vacuuming.

I went to the bathroom to brush my teeth. The cap had been left off the toothpaste tube and although I remembered leaving it that way myself I shouted at Charles, accusing him. The paste wouldn't come out and finally I had to stomp on it. It shot out like a thin white lasso half the length of the floor and it shocked me so that I screamed, and Charles came running.

"What is it?" he asked, and I said, "Snake," and laughed at his face, and passed him a tissue and he dropped to his knees and wiped it up.

Jake would never put up with madness like this, he'd glare at me or take a swing and then he'd storm out of the house and I wouldn't see him for a week.

"There, that's got it," Charles said, standing, and he moved to kiss me but I wouldn't let him. "God," he said, "you are being disagreeable, what has put you in this mood?"

"I don't know."

"You can tell me."

"All right," I said, "if you really want to know. The truth is that I've been thinking this morning that I'm tired of sex and think we ought to lay off it for a while, say six months or so until I'm in the mood again. I'm sorry, that's just how I feel."

He said Okay, no problem with him.

"Are you sure you don't mind?"

He said he thought we ought to talk about it.

"We have talked about it," I said, "and that's my decision, like or leave it."

He looked uncertain and deeply hurt and I could feel it coming, the kiss-off, I knew this time I had gone too far.

"I mean it," I said.

He said he knew it, and tried out a smile. He said it would be a great personal loss to him to go without sex with me for six months but that he would be willing to go five years without it if that's what it took to give me peace of mind.

"You'll go elsewhere for it," I told him.

He said No, no, he wouldn't. Then he came up behind me and put his arms around me, watching my face in the mirror. "Even so," he murmured, "I see no reason to change our plans. Let's set the date."

I finished brushing my teeth and spat lather all over the sink and didn't answer him.

Jake had never said, "Let's set the date" or anything else to me in the area of romance. I had pursued him through a dozen cities and finally had worn him down until he was forced to say, "Yes, yes, I'll marry you for God's sake if that's what it takes to get you off my back."

Of course I was carrying Charise then and he had a vague interest in sticking around to see whether she would resemble him.

No, that's wrong, Charise came a full two years later, I've got to stop making up these stories just to dramatize myself and retain the interest of men like Charles. Why bother, since the kiss-off is coming in any case.

Charles came back in to tell me someone was hammering on my door.

"Can't you answer it," I said, "are your hands tied, can't you do anything around here?" My tone was blistering, I was in a mood to kill anyone who got in my path.

Jake would have knocked me down.

He was right, the door was shaking and Lydia was calling my name.

I opened the door and she rushed in. She looked terrible.

"Whatever it is," I told her, "I can't be bothered."

"I've got to hide," she cried. "Simon is after me, he's trying to kill me!" Then she saw Charles and instantly perked up, she went from brutalized, trampled-upon womanhood to sexy female all in one amazing second. "Hi!" she said, and batted her eyes.

Lydia is what is known as vivacious or fun-loving. She is just over five feet tall, she's sway-backed to the extreme although she uses that to her advantage, and she has jet black hair cut even with her ear lobes and whenever she's in the vicinity of a man her body is a constant wiggle, she becomes part vixen and part pixie and she flirts outrageously and her whole performance makes me sick.

I was like that myself when I first took up with Jake, but he cured me of it by locking me in a closet three times a day.

Lydia never addresses her remarks to a woman if there is a man around. She was telling Charles she hadn't been home all night. "I spent the night in the train station," she said, "I know I must look awful, I can almost feel the vermin crawling over me. A thousand men must have come on to me, it's disgraceful that in a public place people can make such lewd proposals."

Charles pretended to be interested, he's much too civil for his own good.

"I thought you had given her the kiss-off," Lydia said, hooking a thumb over her shoulder at me.

"No," Charles told her, "I'm up to my neck, but I'm in it for good."

Lydia squealed, she seemed to think that very funny.

She turned to me. "You've got to hide me out for the day,"

she said, "Simon would stick an ice pick in me if he found me.
Don't breathe a word of my whereabouts to anyone because
he has his spies everywhere."

I told her I was willing but that I didn't like it, what if
Simon got it in his head to kill me too?

"He won't. Simon likes you, he says you're a very steady and
dependable person. Sometimes I even think he has a crush on
you. Anyway he's too chicken to kill anyone except me."

Charles put his arms around me. He informed Lydia he was
going to build an Annie Hathaway cottage for me, and protect
me, and keep me smiling for the rest of my life.

I broke into tears and fled into the bedroom, unable to help
myself. It seemed to me Charles was patronizing me in front
of one of my friends, he knew Lydia gossiped like a pirate and
now everyone would know how much I was being played the
fool, because whether Charles meant it or not and whether I
wanted it or not Charles would come to his senses soon and
give me the kiss-off good and fast just the way Jake did, and I
would never know true happiness. I would never know a
normal life. I would be bound to go from man to man and
be their plaything, give them the one thing I could give, give it
until they tired of me and dumped me and went out to find a
decent woman.

Lydia rushed in to comfort me. "Don't go to pieces," she
said, "I think he means it," and somehow that made me cry
all the more, I'm such a sap, I fall into these weeping frenzies
now and then, weeping is all I can do and sometimes it will
go on for weeks.

The phone rang. "Excuse me, I can't answer as it might
be Simon," Lydia said, "and Charles is finishing up the
vacuuming."

It was Vancouver Brake and Wheel wanting to know
whether my stomach was upset again, did I mean to come in
today.

I told them Yes, I had been fighting a small fire at my place but it was under control now and I would be in shortly.

I dried my eyes and told Lydia to make herself at home. I promised I wouldn't let on to Simon where she was. Then I went out to meet Charles, all smiles again because I know he expects it of his women.

Charles' car was parked on the street and someone had left a leaflet under the wiper informing him he could get his house kinetexed at a surprisingly low cost, NEVER PAINT AGAIN and MAKE BACK YOUR KINETEX COSTS BY WHAT YOU SAVE ON FUEL FROM A PROPERLY INSULATED AND KINETEXED HOME OR BUSINESS ESTABLISHMENT.

"Anne wouldn't like it," Charles said.

We didn't talk much on the way into town. I guess Charles thought I was too upset to speak but really I was thinking about what the women at Vancouver Brake and Wheel would say when I told them where Lydia was, and I wondered whether they'd agree with me that we should telephone Simon right away and put the bee in his ear.

He pulled in at the curb and grabbed at my hand as I was getting out. "Lunch?" he asked.

I said I'd have to see.

"I'd like to shake you," he said, "why are you doing this to me?"

I told him I didn't know what he was talking about, that I had to go.

He banged his fist on the wheel and spun his tires getting away, and I knew I had had it then, the kiss-off but good.

The women were in a fever, listening to me tell of Lydia's adventures, and they began exchanging stories of what had happened to them when they had been caught for the night in a train station.

Simon said he'd roar right over to my place, this time he'd teach her a lesson she wouldn't forget.

Charles didn't show up for lunch and didn't call and when I called his office his secretary told me he'd been sent spur-of-the-moment to Calgary for an important business meeting having to do with Gulf Oil's attempted takeover of Canadian nursing homes.

She obviously believed I'd swallow any lie.

But that evening I returned from work to find twenty-one boxed Canadian Beauty roses outside my door, together with a hastily scribbled note from him.

Lydia and Simon had had it out in my bedroom, I could tell by how tidy everything was.

Charles' note said I should keep the home fires burning.

I am so tired of eggs and bacon, I think the Egg Marketing Board ought to be hung, but that's what I had for dinner. I missed Charles and I wept for him, I was lonely and went through the apartment talking aloud to myself, but it also seemed Charles had never been there, that I hadn't spent all my time with him these past weeks, I felt the way one must feel when she finds everything she has ever known and loved didn't really exist and the future of her own existence is better left to those who insist that we all turn to dust anyhow.

I called Charise and when she answered I couldn't speak, I gripped the phone and stared at the black mouthpiece but didn't know how.

"Is it *you*," Charise finally said, "or is this the breather?"

I caught at the straw and began breathing.

"Hi, Mom," she said.

God, that my own daughter can speak to me as if I'm a normal person, after knowing me all these years.

"Are you coming?" I asked.

She said sure. "Jake isn't here," she said, "did you want to talk to him?"

I said no. I couldn't bear to hang up and face my apartment alone, so I told her about Lydia's troubles with Simon and asked if I had done the right thing in telling him where she was hiding.

She didn't pause to think about it. She said in her opinion a person ought to be loyal to one's friends, but that I knew the people involved better than she did so she wasn't prepared to say.

I told her she was being cloyingly diplomatic, why didn't she say straight out that I was a devious and conniving bitch who couldn't be trusted any further than I could be seen.

"Well, you've had problems," she said. "We'll talk about it tomorrow."

"What would you like to do tomorrow?" I asked.

"Oh, Mom," she said, exasperated, "don't take me to another movie."

The last time she had visited I had taken her to see *Grease* and she had thought it stupid except for the Sandra Dee number.

She said a few sweet things to me and then hung up.

Charles' note said he adored me.

I got exhausted walking around the apartment and wringing my hands and when I climbed in bed there was another Walter Pidgeon movie on the tube. This time he had Greer Garson with him and all their nine children were so cute in their raccoon coats I turned it off and tried to sleep.

Charles' letter said his star was attached to mine and that he loved me to the moon and back, what about a June wedding in Stanley Park? *Yours Forever*, he signed it, and this made me weep, I got it out from under my pillow and put it in the shoe box along with the others so it wouldn't wrinkle and so that when I was an old woman scuffing about in my slippers at Gulf's Rest and Nursing Home I could get it out again and use it to prove to the world that I had been used and misled and humiliated and deceived at every turn by men who know only one line and that one the biggest lie on God's green earth.

Charise came early on Saturday morning. I had got up early myself to unlock the door and tape a note to it saying, CHARISE, I HAD TO STEP OUT A MINUTE, BE RIGHT BACK, YOU COME RIGHT IN.

But she marched straight into the bedroom where I was hiding and told me that Jake who had brought her was not going to leave until I came out and at least said hello to him.

I wept, said I couldn't bear to, I said if she loved me she could do this much for me, she could go out there and tell him to quit my premises immediately, that I was in no shape to see him and that if I did, anything might happen.

She went out and told him.

She came back and said he was sticking put.

I was seated on the edge of the bed, quivering, and she sat down beside me and took my hands.

"You've got to figure this out for yourselves," she said, "and stop putting me in the middle. I'm only an adolescent and the strain is too hard on my nerves."

She said a lot more, we both did, and inside a few seconds each of us was weeping.

"Go out and speak to him," she said, "he won't bite."

I told her I knew what he wanted, that he wanted to tell me that the divorce was final, maybe even that he had the papers to serve on me.

"Husbands don't serve the papers," she said, "a representative from the court does that."

"Then what does he want?"

"He only wants to see you. He wants to see for himself how you're doing."

I told her I was dying, any idiot could see that.

She couldn't do anything with me and went out to tell him I guess that I was very upset.

He came in and sat down by me in her very spot.

He didn't say anything and I couldn't. I was crying and

couldn't catch my breath and after a while he put one arm around me and patted my back.

He always used to do that, it drove me crazy.

Then he began crying too.

Charise stood in the doorway watching us. She had on a red coat and looked like Little Red Riding Hood. She said we were both sensible people and ought to have our heads examined.

I begged her to come over and sit with us and Jake asked her too, but she refused to come.

"This happens every time you see each other," she said. "I'm fed up with nursemaiding you two."

I said I'd get up and get her some ice cream.

Jake didn't leave, he spent the afternoon and the evening and then it was too late for him to bother returning to his place so he spent the night, and that was exquisite.

Charles came in on Sunday. He came in smiling and shouting my name and then he saw it was Old Home Week and sat down in a chair to hang his head and to moan over and over, "So this is it, I've had it, you're giving me the kiss-off."

The three of us tried cheering him up, we told him there were lots more fish in the pond, but nothing we could say worked and he shouted that he would kill us, all three of us, but in the end he went away quietly, although he told us it would never work, that we were too pigheaded and self-indulgent, too opinionated and stupid and ridiculous ever to find true happiness with each other.

"I hope I never get the brush-off," Charise said, "I think I'd die."

THE HISTORY OF ENGLAND, PART FOUR

*T*he King of England was out courting Anne.

"Anne?" said the King of England. "I thought I was out courting Emy Dealiath of Detroit. How'd you get here, Anne?"

Anne held a wet finger up to the wind and turned out her toes. "My Mummy put me up to it," she said. "My Mummy said I could have anything I wanted, 'cepting popsicles. Have I put my foot in it?"

The King, as time went by, was delighted. He still had an ache in his heart for Emy Dealiath, but he was so pleased he took Anne to the castle and introduced her around.

The Queen Mother: "This girl is too skinny."

The Young Prince: "No bosom."

The Court: "But King, sir, you have fallen in love with an eight-year-old girl!"

Anne charmed them and soon they relented. "I'll grow up," she said. "I'll be a package of dynamite."

"Just wait," some told Anne, "till you see the King's bedroom. It will knock out your eyes."

Anne wanted to know if it contained the latest records,

including oldies, and how good the stereo was. She wanted to know whether it was a *hot-water* bedroom or a *cold-water* bedroom and whether she was expected to do her own cooking. The King told her no, no records, but she could get on the phone and order as many and whatsoever she liked. "Goody!" said Anne. She called up her Daddy and had him air-flight in tons of the stuff, including oldies. "Oh," she said, "and I want all you can get me of the Nylons, and that guy with the tattoos, whatever you call him. Throw in an old Donovan, maybe his 'Best.' You can forget Nelson Eddy, I've gone off him. Pioneer's all right on the stereo, but remember I got to have the funny continental plug with the voltage adapter. You know what I mean."

The King one day hurt his feet coming in.

"Too much wire!" he shouted. "Get rid of this wire!"

Slaves were all over the place, snipping and snipping.

"I want Pay TV!" shouted Anne. She kept ragging the King until he relented. "We'll try it for a month," he told his court, "and see what develops. This Anne has a lot of expensive notions, but I'll not be played for a damn fool. All in all, I'm putty in her hands. Now what's this I hear about crap-shooting in the halls?"

One of his mendicants, sleazy little sniveler who had lost his shirt, informed the King that there had been numerous complaints about crap-shooting in the King's halls, and the Queen Mother was upset.

"Well, stop it," said the King. "It don't look right."

Everyone scurried. The King had spoken. So that was the end of crap-shooting in the halls. For months everyone went about with a sour face; the crap-shooting edict put a real pall over the place.

Every day, when the Prince passed the King, he would say, "How you getting along, King? How you trucking it, baby?"

The King didn't like that. He put his spies in the Prince's chamber. "What do you find?" he asked them.

"The Prince is all right," they told him. "He's a right noble fellow. He's just worried a little that you'll produce an heir. You and Anne, we mean. He's afraid he's going to be pitched out into right field."

"He's smarter than I thought," the King said. "You can let him know I'm working on it."

Anne had growed up some by this time. She was practically thirteen.

"What do you expect?" she'd tell the King. "Heck-fire, I'm hardly thirteen."

"Set your mind to it," he told her. "That's half the battle. This kingdom is hungry for an heir. They are beginning to wonder if my line hasn't got weary. When the baby comes we can roast a pig. There's nothing gives this kingdom more joy than to know the King is eating roasted pig."

"I've got bosoms," Anne said. "This blue eye shadow makes me look ten years older. Admit it, King: I'm turning into a pretty hot number."

The King admitted it. "No big surprise," he said. "I've always thought you were cute."

"Cute!" said Anne. "You can stuff that!"

Anne's Mummy came visiting. "You have done it," she said. "You have worked your way into the King's household, and into his very bedchamber. Hoorah for my daughter. But tell me this, Anne. Is he a good King? Is he giving you everything you've wanted?"

"He plays around too much," said Anne. "He likes Parcheesi far too much for my taste. And I still haven't forgiven him for outlawing crap-shooting in the halls. Though most of the blame there goes to the Queen Mother. She's an old warhorse."

"Good," said the woman. "Well, your life seems to be in order. I have done everything for you that a mother could. Now I can go home and tell your father he has no need to worry."

They kissed, and the mother departed.

One day the King came into the Queen Mother's bedroom. "Mama!" he said. The Queen Mother had grown old and many reasoned she was now on her deathbed. "Call in the Bishop," they said. But the Bishop was in France, on a secret mission, so she was saved that additional discomfort. The Queen Mother's eyes rolled. "Am I dying?" she'd say. "Am I dying? Is the realm in order?" Everyone assured her the realm was in order. But she persisted with her questions: "Am I dying? Am I dying? Is the crab tree in blossom?" The entire court tired of it and more than a few suggested the old woman was being a trifle silly.

Anne would play the King his favorite records, to sweeten his disposition. She would cuddle his head in her lap and knead his brow and recite him verses and statements learnt in her kindergarten. "Now here's a good one," she'd say. "Feast on this: 'In this King's Time such abundance of Snow fell in January, continuing till the middle of March following, that almost all Cattell'—that's plain old *cattle*, King—'that all Cattell and Fowl perished, and therewith an excessive Dearth followed.' That's from Baker's Chronicles. Be still. Here's another one: 'In the general *dearth* of admiration for the right thing, even a chance bray of applause falling in time is rather fortifying.' That's George Eliot's *Middlemarch*. That man with the tattoos uses it on his record. Wait a minute! Did you say *death*? I've been doing *dearth*! My goodness! Death: All right, here's this one: 'Of the Fruit of Knowledge if thou feed, Death, dreadful Death, shall plague thee and thy seed.' Isn't that neat?"

The King would groan and turn on the Pay TV. "Suppose it was *your* mother," he'd say. "*Then* how would you feel?"

Which would send Anne up shouting in a fit of temper. "I'm doing my best!" she'd screech. "You people expect too much of me! Heck-fire, I'm still in my teens! I'm only a little girl!"

And the King would have to mollify her as best he could.

"Draw a warm milk bath," he'd tell his underlings. "Put her in it. Send in Samson to scrub her shoulders."

"Samson, sire?"

It was known that Samson was not to be trusted among women.

"Samson," said the King. "Give her the best."

After one of these baths, the King and Anne would go to the Queen Mother's chamber. "Am I dying?" asked the Queen Mother. "Am I dying? Is my parakeet still singing his merry song?" She went on with this drivel hour after hour.

Anne sat scratching a thigh, pensively regarding the Queen Mother's bejeweled finger.

"I want that ring," said Anne.

"Am I dying?" asked the Queen Mother. "Is there flax and heather in my garden?"

"*That* one," said Anne. "That one with the gold crown and the snake entwined around it."

"For Christ sake," said the King. "You got to be divinely born to wear that ring. That's a *King's* ring. You got to be a true superpatriot. Only my rightful *heir* can wear that ring."

They continued this discussion that night in the King's bedchamber, midst a now-and-then wooing.

"I want it," said Anne.

The King said no. No, a thousand times no.

"I bet *my* Mummy would let me have it," said Anne. "I bet anything she would."

"Turn to a movie," said the King. "Turn to the cultural channel. This Pay TV is a honey."

"I want it," said Anne. "I want that ring now!"

The King went out to take counsel. "She wants it, boys," he said. "She's determined to have it. Let's put our heads together."

They did so, and a short time later the King reported back to Anne, who had Samson in with her, painting tattoos all over her body. All over her lovely body. The King told

Samson to go take a smoke. "Wing it, buddy," he said. "Get lost." Next he turned to Anne: "Now what my advisers have advised me on this ring business," said the King, "is that we have a way out of it. You are no longer to sweat it. What the council has come up with is that the ring is yours by custom, if not by law. What I mean is, that whosoever is my wife gets the Queen Mother's ring on the expectation, *vis vitae, viva voce,* you dig?—on the expectation that she will come up with a natural heir to the throne, to whom she will pass it on all in her own good time. How's that, Annie?"

"That's fine," said Anne, "but where's my ring?"

The King squirmed and hollered and let out a great fuss, but finally he had to send his men to fetch it.

"Attaboy," said Anne. "Now I know you love me. You can put your head back in my nice teen-age lap. How about the Nylons for good easy listenin'?"

Unfortunately, the King's men did not return.

"What are you?" asked Anne. "The King or some stumble-bum? Is a ring such a hot item? I don't even want it anymore. I wouldn't wear it now even if you begged."

The King sent another bunch of his minions. One came back saying that the Queen Mother said that the only way she was giving up that ring was if they hacked off her finger. She was saving it, she said, for the Prince, who was next in line for the throne, the legitimate heir who had the backing of the people, and any child produced by Anne Whatzit was not to be considered on account of Anne was a minor.

"I'll be dogged," said the King. "She's out of her sickbed, I take it?"

"That's right," said the minion, "and she means nothing but trouble."

"So hack off her finger!" said Anne. "I've never cared for her high-and-mighty attitude anyway. I remember she said I was skinny, the day I first came to this kingdom. I never was skinny. I was average height and weight for a female of my years. Hack off her finger! Let's see how tough she talks then."

This led to the first argument ever to seriously flare between Anne and the King. The King became accusatory: "Here you are talking about hacking off fingers. You sound like my generals. Here you are going on about what you *want want want!* You're as greedy as the head of my treasury. *Want want want!* I declare, you make me feel plumb disgusted."

Anne hit him, smack, three times with rotten eggs, kept in a big pile on the floor under her bed. "I'm gonna get you, King!" she said—and pelted him three times more.

The King careened down his hall bellowing, "What's happening in my kingdom? Why is everyone against me? Why why why?"

The next day, in a foul mood, he raised taxes, reduced imports, enacted the death penalty for anyone found guilty of throwing eggs, and thought seriously about waging war on France. That very day he sent five thousand men and women out on horses and ponies to collect his taxes.

Turmoil reigned.

Cries went up in streets and villages throughout the land: "Down with the King! Down with tyranny! Bring back the Stuarts! Storm the castle! An honest man can't live! Down with the monarchy! Up with the Prince! Bring back Spanish wine! Bring back decency and fair play! Freedom now! Justice forever! Bring back feudalism!" On and on it went.

The rabble were everywhere.

Anarchists all over.

Mothers had to keep their tiny tots indoors.

Blood flowed throughout city and town.

"Lord, lord," muttered the King. "What a pretty kettle of fish this is. I have really let the cat out of the bag. Who would have guessed there was so much rancor out there."

"Come listen to Bing Crosby," said Anne. "Get your mind off things."

The Queen Mother summoned the Prince to her ante-chamber. "He wanted my ring," she said. "He wanted my ring for his little strumpet. He would have sawed off my finger. Henceforth and therefore, my allegiance is severed.

"And you, my boy," she said. "You appear to have aged fifty years. I know you must have found this business most unsettling."

"No, no," said the Prince. "I've been on a long binge. I've been on a long binge on a barge in Venice. I'll be back in the shade once I've visited my barber."

The Queen Mother clapped her hands. "Tea!" she commanded. "Good English tea. Tea is the great restorative."

The Prince was pacing. "Madam," he said, "as I understand this business, we have factions at court. We have a nation divided. Wherein in all this do I, lofty born and of solid purpose, stand? What is my quickest route to the throne?"

"You see here a ring," the Queen Mother said. "Whosoever shall wear this ring shall be the King, or I am not the Queen Mother. Your path is clear. You shall go at once to the King's chamber, and if the King be absent, you are to seduce his beloved Anne. You shall bring her head to me on a platter —or a reasonable facsimile. It is this child who has led the King into madness. With her dispatched, we shall then talk about killing the King. He has betrayed me. I am not a blood-thirsty Queen Mother, but he has left me no alternative. On the day this has been accomplished, you, my Prince, shall sit in the King's chair. You shall command this fair realm."

The Prince was inspired. He said he would go at once and do it.

"With my blessings," returned the Queen Mother. "*Sic itur ad astra.*"

"*Similia similibus curantur,*" said the Prince. "Before this hour quits, I shall have seduced the prima donna with the hatching bosom."

The Prince entered Anne's chamber. She was teaching

Samson a two-step and did not see him. The Prince concealed himself behind a curtain. He was concerned about Samson's loyalties. He wondered why it was that, wherever he went, Samson had arrived there before him. He watched Samson. He couldn't figure why Samson was having such trouble learning a simple two-step. He had learned this same step himself, at age four, inside two minutes. He wondered about the music. Could it be that this was a melody by that tattoo man, about whom Anne raved? Anne, he thought, looked pretty. She was on the skinny side—too tall—but otherwise just the way he liked them. He didn't imagine he would have any trouble.

The record ended. He saw Anne give a kiss to Samson's cheek. "There!" she said. "Now that wasn't so hard!"

Samson mumbled. It seemed he wanted someone to give him a shilling. It seemed he thought it was owed him. "The King promised," Samson said. "Promised a shilling."

Anne piled money into the brute's hands. "Take it!" she said. "Take it all! It is only money!"

Samson smiled, delighted. "Money, money, money," he said. "I love money." Then he thought a bit and said, "I shall give it to my poor old mother. My poor old mother is always saying to me, 'Where is the money?' This shall make her happy. Perhaps she will not whip me. Yes, I shall give her the money. Money money money!"

Anne again kissed Samson's cheek. He was a dope, but she liked him. There were times when she thought Samson to be the only true-to-God human being, aside from herself, in the entire kingdom.

"Go with my pleasure," she told this dunce. "Go with Anne's lovingliest tidings. Show your mother the two-step. Keep her dancing. Lord God, I wish I could. Go on dancing, I mean. All this political business is keeping me up nights. It's ruining my complexion. The way the King looks at me you'd think I was a hag."

Et cetera, et cetera. For although Samson departed and the Prince remained hidden, Anne kept on railing. She was fed up, she said. She wished she'd never seen these shores. She hoped her Mummy would come soon and spirit her away.

Then she fell down on the bed, crying.

The Prince thought her a pitiful sight. He had second thoughts. Have we misjudged her? he asked. All the same, his lust was raging. He was just back from a binge, and nothing cured the after-affects-of-binge better than a fast seduction. A quick and urgent coupling.

So he let out a mighty roar and in the same split second swooped down upon her.

Meantime, the Queen Mother was having a talk-to with her dressmaker, a woman named Heloise who had nine children, which is why the Queen Mother was talking to her. "I wonder," she was saying, "if I haven't sent a boy out to do a man's job. The Prince has never been good with women. He puts up a swaggart's front, but in his bones he is meek as chitterlings. Well, I might be wrong. I wouldn't have put heavy wager on the King, but he went out and won the heart of a—how old was she, Heloise?"

"Eight, I think you said."

"Yes. Eight. He went out and won the heart of an eight-year-old child. In my experience that takes some doing. He had already won the heart of Emy Dealoach or Dealiath of Detroit and I have heard it said she was a pretty sharp cookie. So maybe I just don't know men. Maybe the Prince will be able to get the job done. I know how he is when he's just off a binge. He gets pretty randy. I hope he's that way now. I know he's never liked this child and I know he wants the throne. That is a powerful combination. Perhaps it will work for him and for the good of this kingdom. I harbor no grudge against Anne, for she is only a child and innocent, and her greed is understandable, since all children are. It is a dastardly thing I am doing, for I would not hurt children, but I must think of the kingdom. My people are like children to me in my heart and their welfare must come first. The King was an okay leader before he fell under Anne's influence. He was always weak himself, though he had the good sense to appoint wise and learned counsel, and I always had his ear. He would come to me and say, 'Mama, what do I do?' and I would tell him. You know that yourself, don't you, Heloise?"

"Yes, ma'm."

"You have nine children yourself and I know for a fact it has not been easy. Yet you have saved and skimped and cared for them and brought their lives to good fruition. Isn't that true?"

"Yes, ma'm. Well, except for one or two. Little Sam ran away from home at age four."

"Age four. A pivotal age. I wonder whether the history of this household, the history of England, would not have been different had I taken a cane to the King's britches the minute he turned four."

"I did mine," said Heloise. "I did mine, every day, every year. Sometimes several times a day. I wore out their britches. That's why little Sam run off. Sometimes I wonder whatever became of him."

"Well, Heloise, you are of the lower classes, and that's how things are done in your element. But in my set you can't whip a child every day, or even hardly ever, especially if he is a King, for the wretch would take away all your monies and lock you up in the Tower and chop your head off. It's different with us, you see, and much harder."

"Yes, ma'm."

"I suppose what it boils down to is that if a child is going to go wrong he is going to do it whether he is a King or your little Sam."

"That's about how I see it. I say amen."

"I wish I had spies in the King's bedchamber," said the Queen Mother. "I wish I knew what was going on in there."

"Yes, ma'm. I do, too."

"Well, it has been good talking to you. You have set my heart to rest on many a score. Can you have this dress ready by this evening? I hope to wear it to dinner."

"I don't know, ma'm. All that lace. All them jewels. Working with silk, one can't be too careful."

"Oh, you'll have it done. I know you will. You never fail me."

" I don't know, ma'm. My eyes are weary. These old bones just don't have the strength they once did. There was that other dress last night, and the two the day before, and there was all those lovelies I made for you in your sickbed."

"I know. And no one ever said a word. I could have been laid out in a toe-sack for all they cared. Well, you have to get to work now. Me and my prattling on. I'll have someone come in with tea and biscuits. Tea's restorative. Your fingers will be flying through this dress busy as flies. Au revoir, good woman."

The Queen Mother departed. Heloise let out a considerable howl. She'd been penned up sewing for nineteen days. She hoped someone croaked. "Old cow!" she said. "And me here having to double-stitch every seam. I'll never see daylight. My family, such as is left, probably thinks I'm dead. There won't be one lick left in the beer bucket, once I get home. She and the rest of her hoity-toity crowd, they can all croak, for the little I care."

The Queen Mother met the King, crossing the court. She stopped to palaver with him. "And how's our little darling Anne this morning?" she inquired.

"I'm glad you've come to your senses," said the King, "about that ring business. You know there would be snow in July before I'd ever chop off your finger. I always told you you'd be better off keeping the ring in the vault. People see it and they get ideas. So, yes, I was only humoring Anne, which pretty I have not seen since daylight, when I left her eating crumpets and grapes."

The Queen Mother beamed, for this was good news.

"And where are you off to now, my liege?"

"I am off to the foxes," said the King. "A man has got to get some little sport around here."

"Good," smiled the Queen Mother, "the hunt will relax you, I am sure." Yes, she thought, and leave the Prince free to pursue his chore.

They kissed and parted, and the King passed on down to his stables. Yet he was not entirely deceived by the Queen Mother's smiles and gay banter. She's up to something, he thought. Conniving old hen. But he couldn't decipher her maneuverings, and contentedly straddled his horse and galloped away.

"Rape!" Anne called. "Rape!"

The Prince was indeed upon her. He was thrashing and squirming and attempting to stroke her bosom.

"Hush," he told her, "and it will go easier."

Anne studied this bounder, with beseeching eyes. If only, she thought, my Mummy had told me.

The tattoo man began singing over the stereo. *Dearth, dearth,* he sang. *Dearth of admiration . . . chance bray . . . applause falling . . . rather fortifying . . . dearth, dearth, oh dearth, away.* The Prince was distracted. The sound grated upon his ears. Bile chugged up to his throat, where it stayed, sliding back and forth. His stomach heaved. He wondered whether this was post-binge deliriums or whether the tattoo man's rhythms were so sickening. "A pot," he wheezed. "Bring me a pot."

Anne slid from beneath him. She cracked a shoe across his head, then pitched, all at once, with both hands, six eggs into his face. "Call yourself a Prince!" she thundered. "Why you're no better than the commonest sort!"

The Prince cocooned himself. He began to cry.

Anne's heart was not softened. She would have no mix with, no sympathy for, a base rapist.

"People will hear of this!" she shouted. "I'll tell the whole world! Your goose is cooked, Prince! The people will have you for supper!"

And she kicked him out of her bed, onto the floor, and kicked him to the door—then she sat at her writing table and wrote out a proclamation, affixed with the King's stamp, and therefore authentic, which would go out to all peoples. RAPISTS BEWARE, it said. HENCEFORTH ALL RAPISTS, BE HE PRINCE OR PAUPER, UPON FINDING OF GUILT WILL BE CONVEYED TO THE TOWER AND THERE, ON A PROPER DAY, SHALL HE BE BEHEADED AND HIS HEAD SPIKED ON LONDON BRIDGE FOR ALL TO SEE, INASMUCH AS THE KING HAS COMMANDED IT THAT WOMANHOOD IN THIS DAY AND AGE SHALL NO LONGER AGAINST THEIR WILLS BE PUT DOWN.

She meant it, every word, and when finished, she ran out into the halls in search of the Prince, wanting to kick him until her very toes ached and her shoes splintered into his arse.

After which, the Prince was not seen for many a moon. The likelihood, in fact, is that he shall hereafter be dropped from this story, as he has revealed himself genuinely unworthy. ("My Prince, my Prince," the Queen Mother will weep. "Where has he gone? Why has the dark world swallowed him up?" "He is with my little Sam," Heloise will say. "You'll get used to it in time. Who knows, maybe we're better off. You never can count on how the little urchins will turn out. He's saved you heartbreak, ma'm, is what I hear.")

Enfeebled once more, the Queen Mother takes to her bed.

Anne holds forth at court. She rants and rails. At night she has her ladies-in-waiting, and all ladies, sequestered. "Women, unite!" she tells them. "If the man is a beast, then throw the beast out!"

Aye! Aye! Aye!

All over the kingdom one can hear her message sweeping about.

The King returned, sorely baffled, from his foxing. Foxes, yes, more than he can count, but in a Cotswold village a thing strange and disturbing has transpired. Women, great frightful hordes of them, have surrounded his horse, have swayed in upon him. Am I menaced? he'd wondered. Will they tear me limb from limb? No. These women have ripped away chunks of his legging, made mincemeat of his red coat, but it is all it seems in fun, in *respect* of him. Adoration, it would seem. "Long live the King!" they've chanted. "Long live our noble liege!"

"First things first!" they've said. "Emancipation from the horror! Our King has spoken: Let rapist husbands and scoundrel lovers beware! Down with the raper! God save the King!"

On coach doors, on street lamps, on thatched barns, he'd seen the Proclamation. And, on the whole, he has no argument with it. A good idea, he thinks. About time. Throw the beast out, if he's a beast, by all means. But the King worries a bit. He worries that his peoples can be so easily swayed. Worries that they can so swiftly shift their love and loyalty. A good King indeed, he thinks. Why, this is all Anne's work. She's the architect of these tidings. Not me. I have only been out foxing. He worries that the womenfolk no longer rage at his unjust taxing, at his import regulations. Will they so easily give up French hats? Give up frog legs and Spanish wines? Something is wrong here, he thinks. Phenomenon is what it is. These, his people, they are as fickle as the very wind. Are there so many rapists creeping about the realm that his peoples, these drab womenfolk, will put mortal safety above hunger? Above his yoke and oppression? Put harmonious coupling before the infant squawling for bread?

So it would seem.

So it would seem.

The King wonders. He wonders if the swirl of life is not swirling right by him. If his monarch's hand has not gone stale, if life's flux, the ability to determine events, isn't beyond him. At sea in the world. He wonders if he's kingly after all.

What kind of King am I? he asks. Am I not but a spineless jellyfish, a petty despot, a nasty, self-seeking tyrant? He likes it, the King does, this rare adulation coming his way. Are my peoples telling me something? he asks himself. Get off the pot, King? Walk with virtue, kiss virtue's hand? Hark to, to true nobility?

So it would seem.

Touched with this taint of the lamb, he seeks out Anne in the King's chamber. Lo! What's this? No more the tattoo man's raucous synthesizer. No crooning oldies. Gone are the zanies of Bing. Gone the Crewcuts, the Gospel Rollers, the Jackhammer Blues Band. Gone is Donovan.

"I've outgrowed it, King," says Anne. "There is more to life than music and trying out new lipsticks. There's good deeds, for instance."

The King's eyes pop out. What has happened to Anne? She looks *mature*. Why, darn it, she looks like a lady. Sexy, yeah, cute as a button, but she's acquired *class* somehow. Poise. She looks darn near *regal*.

"Thank you, King," she says. "You're right, I been practicing.I hired that dressmaker Heloise, at good wages, to make me some duds. A new leaf is what I've turned over. You look pale, King. You look like you got something hatching."

"No," says the King. "Just thinking."

"I'm feeling romantic, King."

"You are?"

"I'm needing a shoulder to lean my head on. Some bolstering up for my good work to come."

"That's lovely, Anne."

"I thought tonight we might have a quiet evening out by the pool. Haul in the candles. Maybe hire a gypsy violinist. Set us up for some billing and cooing. We'll work together on this thing. Get our problems sorted out. Sort out what needs first to be done for our peoples."

"That's good, Anne. That's a hot idea."

"Rest when we're weary, toil when the sun is shining in its bright glory. Always remembering the lesson of Jack the dull boy. Kiss me, King. Let's get this thing in gear."

The King kisses her, Anne kisses back.

"By God," says the King, "that was different somehow. Let's do it again."

The kisses begin adding up.

"We've got it, King," says Anne. "I think what we've found is true love."

"Yes," he says, "with more than a smidgen of mutual respect."

The moment is a sober one, though sanity allows a tickle or two of mirth to rush in.

"That was a good one, King. You've got a sense of humor I never noticed before. You're quite a good-looking guy, too. Why, it's as if I'm noticing you for the first time."

"That goes in spades, Anne. You're a honey, you are: frail flower smashing up stones. We're a good and noble pair, going to shake this kingdom up."

Their eyes sparkle. They give each other a solid hug.

Indeed the King feels, and feels that Anne is having it as well, a divine presence moving in him. A divine magnitude. Something exquisite showering down, finer than gold. It's love, he thinks. Love. Why not? Why not love, honor, and good works? Why not a King whose name will live through these? "The King did it," the people will say. "The Queen did it. *They* did it. *They* accomplished these miracles. Expunged import decrees, reduced our taxes, put food on our tables, put flowers in fields, opened up our lives to joy and sport, to times without hardship, showed us the way to harmonious coupling. Kept this very roof over our heads."

Why not? Oh, why not? Life doesn't have to be the horror, the humdrum wretchedness, the pinch, the niggardly scratch, the all-suffering have-mercy-unto-me-father scrunch and roll. No and nay, must not. Power to the people! Long live the King and Queen! Long live England!

"Do you feel it, Anne? Do you feel what I'm feeling?"

"I feel it. Boy oh boy do I feel it! It's divine. It's flowing down from on high."

From somewhere certainly, each thinks, it is flowing.

The King tells Anne to hold on. "Hold on," he says. "I'll not say another word until I've made my conscience clear on this one personal item."

"Personal, King?"

From his wallet he produces the worn picture of one Emy Dealiath. "See this likeness," he says. "That's Emy Dealiath. I went to court her and came by you instead. Remember? 'Anne,' I said, 'how did you get here?' Years now I've been locking myself behind doors and kissing her eyes. Thinking: whatever became of Emy with the velvet eyes? Talking to a phantom. Saying, 'Phantom, why are you not here?' Get it? Real kid stuff. Like a miser hoarding up gold I was hoarding up memory of Emy Dealiath. Now it's over. I've come to my true self. Old Emy, she's reduced to ashes, a thing of the past."

"Oh fuddle-duddle," exclaims Anne. "I've never minded Emy, though I've always looked up to the woman in her. Kiss me, my fine darling, and don't brood, for now I'm sixteen and ripe pickings for you."

Thus England survived and the line lived on.

Hoorah for royalty, for the decency and purpose and honor of olden times. Hoorah for love. Hoorah for you and for me and for them. Hoorah for a thumping good time. Bring on the pig, the juicy suckling pig. Let's get down to it. Let's slice up the pig and drink up the wine. Bottoms up, let's say. Here's a toast to Anne and the King, a toast to all. Long may we live. Long may good fortune fall.

So do you see it, here writ down.